FIREMANE

BRIANNA J. STEPHENS

LILY & LORE

ISBN: 979-8-9953708-0-2 (Paperback)

ISBN: 979-8-9953708-2-6 (Hardcover)

ISBN: 979-8-9953708-1-9 (eBook)

Library of Congress Control Number: 2026907445

Cover design by Brianna J. Stephens

Published by Lily & Lore

www.briannajstephens.com

First edition 2026

For Danni, Jo, Peter, and Sam.
The ones who inspired it all.

ASTOENIA
LIN
QISI
RUTANE OCEAN
HAAPA

AEON SEA
DUNRITH
FONTALIS
ZUHUORIEL
DUCRIA
FROSTHORN MOUNTAINS
MILDERRE
CERVOS
ECLORIAN REDPASS
ECLOR
VIRONA
PHAGO
ATRAL
CATAROS
PRESTOS OCEAN

PROLOGUE

Lightning split the sky in jagged white veins, illuminating a lone figure on the highest peak of the mountain. They did not flinch.

Wind screamed through the pines, stripping branches bare as the sky emptied itself in an unrelenting deluge. The roar of thunder followed, a deafening boom that shook the peak itself.

The man's eyes were closed as he chanted in the language of the gods. His voice was hoarse and his throat was dry, for it had been nearly three days. Three days of chanting, weeks of treacherous passage, and years of unanswered prayers.

High above in the heavens, the Sea Goddess looked down on the mortal man with curiosity. She'd followed him across the sea, venturing to the heavens when he'd reached the holy mountain. There she and the other gods had tested his determination, sending creatures and quakes and storms. Still the man fought on, asking aloud for the gods to aid him in his quest.

"Larideia," the deep voice of the Sky God broke her musing. "Join us."

The Sea Goddess turned to her brothers and sisters, who sat upon their thrones, and settled on her own.

Mortals frequently asked for aid and received no godly intervention, but never before had the gods been so boldly sought out. They exchanged looks, reaching an unspoken understanding.

They would grant this mortal an audience.

The Sky God nodded once, and the raging of the storm ceased. Standing, the Goddess of Light waved her hand in a graceful arc over her head, flooding the space with blinding light. Wrapped in her sister's power, Larideia was transported from her throne, and when the light faded, all seven gods stood atop the mountain.

The mountain was not her domain, the feel and smell of damp earth different from that of her oceans churning far below.

The mortal still chanted, voice barely a whisper. His clothes were dripping, his face and limbs scraped. The Sea Goddess hummed a faint tune, sending it deep into the man's being, and, finally, he fell silent.

He opened his bloodshot eyes, which widened in awe at the gods. Though he was worn and weary, the man bowed his head, falling to his knees.

It was Aspos who spoke. "I am the God of the Sky," he said. "And we have heard your prayers. What is it you seek?"

The mortal answered, eyes still trained on the ground. "I seek a way to even the balance between men."

"Is the balance not even?"

"The world favors men of wealth and power. Why should one man live a life of luxury from inheritance while another only lives by the will of the man who owns him?"

"We do not concern ourselves with the affairs of mortals," Aspos replied, even as the Sea Goddess tilted her head. Was the wealth of man truly so disproportionate?

Lifting his head, the mortal dared to look upon Aspos. "How can you consider yourselves gods if you do not care for those you rule over?" His words were filled with desperation. "The people of this world praise you with every breath. You are revered in every aspect of their lives, whether it be in thanks for their food or in pleas for the rain! Do they not deserve an ounce of compassion?"

The Sky God's voice cracked like thunder. "Is not the rain an *ounce* of compassion? We tend the forces of the world. Why can man not tend himself?"

The man shrank back, cowering, shame coloring his face. He looked as if he wished to say more but was unable to find the words.

"You have said your piece. We will not alter the power of man. Let us be done."

Let us be done.

Though Larideia wished to speak—to change the outcome of the Sky God's ultimate decision—she dared not go against him. Among her brothers and sisters, it was Aspos who reigned supreme.

The Goddess of Light once again waved her arm in that same graceful arc, her light encompassing the others. The mortal reached out an arm as if to touch the gods.

Whispering, he said, "I just want to end the suffering..."

Larideia raised a hand, shielding herself from the brilliance. Her heart thundered in her chest. Her siblings did not wish to understand mankind the way she did—and she could not bring herself to abandon this mortal's desperate plight. Larideia lowered her hand as the rest of the gods disappeared, save for one. Upon seeing that Orrazoth, too, had remained, she shrank back into the cover of trees. The God of Darkness had not seen her, his black eyes intent on the mortal man. Where there had been godly brilliance, now the only light came from the stars high above. Orrazoth spoke with a voice that was meant to be savored and feared. "I, too, wish to change the fate of mankind."

The mortal raised his eyes to the God of Darkness, uncertainty flashing across his face. "I will do whatever is it you ask of me, so long as you grant me the power to do it."

The god smiled a menacing smile. "Then it is done. You will become my creation. A bringer of darkness to those who are not worthy of the light."

Larideia tensed. Orrazoth was her brother, and a god, but they were not the same. Where she wished to help and heal, Orrazoth wished to hurt and destroy. The gods had always kept him in check, but with another at his command, there would be no telling how far his darkness would spread. This mortal was seeking balance—there would be *no* balance. Only misery and darkness.

The mortal rose to his feet. Lifting his chin, he said, "I will be your Darkbringer."

It was too late to warn the others. The God of Darkness began his ritual, raising his hands into the air as black tendrils gathered, swirling around his open palms. He thrust his arms forward, slamming the blackness into the man's chest. The mortal screamed in agony, his limbs shaking violently as Orrazoth's dark power tore through him—*changed* him.

Larideia, without another option, plucked a single white pearl from her headdress. She held it to her mouth, breathing into it the power of attraction—used to lure men and creatures alike—now to be used on something much more significant: the Dark God's power itself.

She cast the pearl outward, toward the bridge of darkness between the god and the man. Her aim was true, and, upon contact with the pearl, the bridge severed. The mortal fell back with a groan, lying motionless on the damp soil, but the darkness continued to flow, sucked directly from the Dark God into the small pearl. Nothing, not even godly power itself, could resist the pull of Larideia's magic.

She could stop it... but she wouldn't.

Orrazoth's face contorted from triumph to absolute rage as his strength was leached from his very being. The God of Darkness sank to his knees as the last of his godly power left his body.

Cautiously, Larideia glided from the cover of the trees. Upon seeing her, Orrazoth attempted to rise, accusation on his tongue. But without his power, the great god was weak.

Larideia plucked up the pearl, examining it between her fingers. Though once white, the pearl had blackened to obsidian, darkness swirling just beneath the surface. She gripped it tight, and, in a handful of strides, looked over the sheer cliffs of the mountainside.

Orrazoth growled, panic flashing across his harsh features. "What are you doing?"

Larideia focused on the surface of the ocean far below and hummed softly. At her call, her creature emerged from the depths, its serpentine body coiling upward—a vicarus, the mortals called it. She stretched out her arm, dangling the black pearl over the edge.

"Larideia..." The warning was full of malice, sending a chill through her.

She let go of the pearl. As it dropped down the cliffside, a terrible scream filled the air. Orrazoth clawed the ground in a desperate attempt to reach the power that had been taken from him.

The vicarus caught the pearl in its mouth and disappeared beneath the water's surface without so much as a ripple. She would call upon the beast later. For now, she would return with Orrazoth to the heavens.

Larideia strode to where her brother knelt.

"You will regret this," he seethed.

She did not meet his eye as she placed a hand upon his shoulder. They ascended to the heavens together, leaving the mortal alone and unmoving on the highest cliffs of the mountain.

ONE

Sam strode through the congestion of Market Square, her fingers brushing against passersby. Every street teemed with life, lined in makeshift stands boasting a variety of smells, colors, and sounds from across the world. Children roamed freely, their giggles mixing with the dull roar of chatter while patrons shopped shoulder to shoulder for their daily goods, backs hunched against the seasonal cold.

Sam hadn't come to shop. She was in the busiest part of the city because the tightly packed market and ever-changing occupants created the perfect opportunity for thieves.

Passing a woman in a brightly colored gown, Sam guided her hand discreetly into and back out of the lady's dress pocket. It took less than a second.

Sam continued walking, hood up and head down as she pocketed the woman's purse.

Until she crashed into a husky man.

"Oi!" The man whirled on her. Fisting her cloak, he hauled Sam onto her tiptoes, spraying her face with spittle. "Watch it, scum!"

He tossed her aside like rubbish. The cobblestones scraped her palms raw as she tried to catch herself.

Clenching her teeth, she glared at the man laughing above her. Day-old stubble darkened his jaw, and though he wore the uniform of Ducria's Royal Navy, the blue coat bore creases and stains. His brass buttons implied an unimpressive rank. Lieutenant, perhaps.

Still snickering, the lieutenant flicked his gaze between her and something to her right. He crouched to snatch the purse she'd just pilfered. It must have fallen from her pocket.

"That's mine," she said coolly.

The lieutenant straightened and hefted the purse, testing its weight. It rattled with coins. *Her* coins.

Sam swiped at his legs, but she wasn't fast enough. With one hand, the lieutenant thrust her away, having the advantage in size, strength, and age. As a slim sixteen-year-old, Sam counted on being *unseen* to do her work.

She landed hard on her back, her hood falling. Silently cursing, Sam sat up, yanking the hood back over her head. Too late—those nearby began to murmur about her vibrant red hair.

With a wicked, yellow-toothed grin, the lieutenant pocketed her purse. "Mine now."

He turned, disappearing into the throng of people that filled the busy streets of Milderre. Sam scrambled to her feet and, ignoring the intrusive gazes still fixed on her hood, squeezed her way through the crowd.

Sunshine peeked through the lingering haze of midmorning, casting the square and its occupants in a yellowish hue. She could just see the lieutenant's head bobbing among the mass of bodies and followed at a distance, revenge on her mind.

A lulling tune cut through the sounds of the market, drawing Sam's attention—as if the song called to *her* specifically. She glanced around, searching for the source. *There!*

Standing in front of a tent dripping in brightly colored fabrics, a white-haired young woman sang swirling tales of the Sea Goddess Larideia and the magnificent creatures roaming her oceans.

Sam approached the tent, staring, and when the woman's ice-blue eyes captured hers through the gathered crowd, they pinned her to the spot. Those eyes, knowing and wise, seemed to see right through to Sam's soul. When she finally looked away, Sam swallowed hard.

She blinked, shaking her head before remembering—the lieutenant! How long had she been distracted?

Standing on tip-toes, she thankfully spotted the lieutenant moving amongst the stalls not far off. When she finally caught up, he appeared to be arguing with a vendor over the quality of their goods. Sam groaned, counting several other Navy friends now by his side. Even so, she plunged her hand into the lieutenant's blue coat pocket, grasping at not one but two purses.

She knew the move was clumsy and braced herself for what surely would come next.

As expected, the lieutenant turned, his face blotchy with anger. "You again!"

Sam snagged the strings of both purses, sliding them free as she darted into the congestion of the square. Adrenaline coursed through her body, and her senses sharpened.

Here in the throng, *she* held the advantage—smaller, lighter, faster, plus something else.

No one knew these streets like she did.

Equally full of panic and delight, she bobbed through the mass of colorful skirts and gaudy vests, dancing around people while the lieutenant and his friends barreled through them. Marketgoers gasped and cursed as they were shoved aside. Sam darted over a large blanket covered in spices. She felt slightly guilty as she tripped over jars, their contents sprawling in a colorful puff, the smells of ginger, nutmeg, and something sweetly aromatic filling her nose. Next, she hurled herself around a vegetable stand, pausing briefly to dump a barrel of potatoes behind her. The red-faced vendor shouted curses, but Sam raced on, already at the eastern edge of Market Square and flying toward an alley.

Smiling brazenly, she turned and spotted the lieutenant and his comrades, who were only just reaching the barrel of fallen potatoes. She gave a flourishing bow, sweeping her arms wide.

"Pleasure doing business with you, lieutenant!" she called, holding the purses high and jingling their contents. Then Sam disappeared into the complex maze of buildings that was Milderre.

As she traveled, Sam took several steadying breaths to calm her pounding heart. If there was one thing she could count on to rescue her, it was Milderre's haphazard building placement. With some reaching four or five levels high, scattered without distinct streets, the mismatched buildings created a puzzle that few knew how to navigate. It was a chaotic beauty that Sam had learned to appreciate in the three years she'd been on her own.

Though no longer running, Sam kept her steps brisk. She'd hoped to gather more than two purses today, but with the show she and the lieutenant had put on, it would have to do. She'd been too eager to exact revenge, and it had cost her an entire day's profit.

Sam blew out a breath. For a moment, she'd almost let the lieutenant go. That mesmerizing lullaby flashed in her mind. The woman singing had been mesmerizing, too—icy blue eyes, white hair, dark skin. . . . She must have been from Haapa. Although Milderre was an incredibly diverse trade town, she rarely saw Haapari people anywhere but at the docks where they loaded and unloaded their highly sought-after textiles.

Humming the Haapari woman's tune, Sam pushed her hood back. In Market Square, people always gawked at her uniquely red hair—as a thief, it was a rather inconvenient tell. She'd tried to color it, rubbing the locks with powdered coal and dirt, even going so far as to use the same dyes her mother had used on fabrics. But it never lasted.

Satisfied with her distance from Market Square, Sam stopped at a fountain to rest. A breeze blew across the street, ruffling the loose red curls cascading down her back. Sam lifted her face to the sky. As always, it was a sickly shade of brown. Too many people crammed in too small a place made for an ever-present smog.

Sam checked the lady's purse first. It contained a handful of coins—mainly coppers, a few silver. It also held a steel thimble and a silver ring she could pawn to Mistress Nunley. The Bronze Barrel's tavern lady paid poorly, reselling everything for at least three times what she paid Sam, but she also didn't ask questions.

Sam set the coins aside, inspecting the purse itself and finding it to be high-quality silk. Perhaps today hadn't been a total loss after all. The money she would make from Mistress Nunley would provide food for at least a few days, maybe a week if she was careful with it.

Three years ago, she never could have imagined she'd become any sort of thief—let alone a talented one. But it was either this or the workhouses, and Sam could never be happy slaving away in a place where she couldn't even see the sky.

The lieutenant's purse came next, and Sam smirked. Perhaps next time he'd think twice before messing with "scum."

The purse was made of simple brown leather with matching cords that Sam tugged open. She tried not to allow disappointment at its meager contents. Remembering the state of the man, she shouldn't have been surprised.

Dumping the contents into her hand, she counted four coppers, a rolled scrap of parchment, and a small cloth pouch concealing something solid. Sam added the coppers to her pile of coins, scooping them all into the leather purse. She nearly tossed the parchment away but thought better of it. Information could be valuable, too, and Mistress Nunley paid well for secrets.

Before checking the parchment, Sam undid the cloth pouch, upending it. A silver coin, larger than any Ducrian currency she'd ever seen, fell into her palm. On the face of it was stamped a delicate flower—a lily.

Sam's blood ran cold. She fumbled the coin, trying unsuccessfully to stuff it back into the purse.

The Lily Company—Lily Co.—was a vicious gang. They had footholds everywhere, likely extending outside of Milderre, perhaps even across all of Ducria. Even the High Council turned a blind eye to their crimes. Nobody knew who the leader was, but the gang was gradually taking over the city piece by piece. Lilies could be found throughout Milderre in various forms: stamped on barrels, mingled in vases of fresh flowers, carved into the doorframes of homes and businesses. The gang kidnapped orphans off the streets daily—what to be used for, Sam didn't know. None had ever been found.

Sam had never personally interacted with the Lily Co., but less than a year prior, she'd seen a young boy snatched right off the dock. She'd never returned to that dock.

A pair of arms wrapped around her waist, hoisting her off the ground and sending her stolen goods sprawling to the cobblestones. Sam shrieked. Coins scattered beneath her.

The lieutenant!

She let her body go limp, using her weight to tear free from her assailant. Fumbling for the small knife in her pocket, she finally realized the figure towering over her wasn't a soldier at all.

Rhett took one look at Sam's face and bent over, hands on knees, bursting with laughter.

Sam fisted her hands on her hips. "Everett Avery, I could wallop you!"

Grinning wide and wiping tears from his golden-brown eyes, her tall, slightly gangly friend straightened. "I didn't know you'd react that way. Though the look on your face was worth it."

Sam shook her head, giving in to a smile as she smacked him on the arm. Rhett ducked his head and raised both hands in surrender, still chuckling. Sam crouched to gather the fallen contents of the purse, and Rhett stooped to help, his long arms reaching the coins she couldn't.

"What are you doing here?" Sam asked, accepting the coins from his outstretched hand. She scanned the ground for the lily-stamped coin and found it had rolled several feet away. She quickly snatched it up, stuffing it back into the purse while sending a furtive glance up and down the street.

Rhett gave his most dashing smile. "I thought I'd pay my favorite lady a visit."

Sam rolled her eyes, but her stomach filled with flutters. She raised an eyebrow. "You couldn't have known I'd be here. I didn't even know it myself. Besides, aren't you supposed to be working? Your half-day isn't until tomorrow."

Rhett's smile faltered, his shoulders slumping. "The workhouse closed."

"Closed for today?"

"For good."

Sam sucked in a breath. Rhett continued, "Master Balthier sold the property. The new owners won't be keeping on any of the current workers. I was on my way to Market Square to see if I could find new work when I spotted you."

He gave a half-hearted smile, averting his gaze. The world around them seemed to grow a bit paler.

"Oh, Rhett. I'm so sorry."

Even if work there was hard, the workhouse was Rhett's only source of income, food, and lodging. Sam reached out gently to lay a hand on his shoulder and felt the flex of his lean muscles as he shrugged.

He'd taken the position two years prior. Before then, they'd survived the streets together. He'd never liked the thieving, though, and while Sam became a master at it, Rhett had searched for another option.

A pang struck her chest as she remembered how he'd tried to convince her to come with him. "This is honest work, Sam," he'd said. "Thieving...is not."

But she couldn't bring herself to give it up, even for him.

Despite that point of difference, she was closer to Rhett than to anyone else. The way her stomach flipped at the sight of him, there was no denying she felt...something. Something *strong*. The only person she'd ever cared for as much was her mother, and her mother had died. If anything happened to Rhett...

Sam peered up into his saddened eyes.

"You could stay with me," she suggested, fighting the blush that threatened to rise. "I'm sure Billy and Perry wouldn't mind sharing their space. It'd be like old times."

But would it? Sam thought of the small abandoned haberdashery that she shared with two other orphans like herself. Besides Rhett, Billy and Perry were her closest companions. They'd all spent many nights sleeping next to each other, huddled for warmth in the cold winters. But that had been a time of survival, when they'd been little more than children. What would it be like now, to have him sleeping so close?

There was no fighting the blush that came this time.

Rhett smiled his crooked smile, though Sam could tell it was forced. "Tell them thank you, but I'll figure it out. I always do."

Sam believed him. No one worked harder than Rhett.

She squared her shoulders. "Right, then. Shall I accompany you?"

"I appreciate the offer, but not today."

Sam let out a breath and dropped her head, disappointed and yet slightly relieved. As much as she wanted to spend every waking moment with Rhett, she shouldn't return to Market Square just yet, and if she told him about the lieutenant, he'd only worry.

The scent of spicy-sweet cloves wafted through the air as Rhett stepped closer. Sam looked up into his handsome face as he tucked a loose strand of her hair behind her ear. His touch made her shiver. Her gaze roved over his familiar features, taking in everything from his unruly, curly brown hair to the first signs of stubble on his clean-shaven jaw.

Sam wondered if she stood on tiptoes if she could close the gap between them. Wondered what his lips would feel like on hers. But she contented herself with enjoying the golden-brown depths of his eyes.

"Meet me tomorrow?" Rhett murmured.

Sam smiled. "By the old fountain in Market Square? Perhaps we can have supper . . ." she added hopefully.

"Done."

With a squeeze of her hand, Rhett was off. She watched sorrowfully as his form disappeared around the corner.

Once he'd gone, Sam's attention returned to the coin purse. She discreetly pulled out the lieutenant's parchment. The edges were slightly worn, as if it had been rolled and unrolled several times.

It contained only a few words, under which a lily was stamped:

Brockers Warehouse

0200

Sam crumpled the parchment and threw it in the fountain, lingering briefly to watch it drift to the bottom before hurrying to the Bronze Barrel to sell her meager goods.

TWO

Upon entering the tavern, Sam spotted Mistress Nunley near the counter, boasting loudly to a rather gruff-looking bunch of patrons about the valuable items she had for sale. The plump woman had permanently flushed cheeks and a nasty temper to accompany them. Sam's relationship with her was simple: Sam brought goods, and Mistress Nunley purchased them—too often for next to nothing.

Sam slunk to the back corner table to wait for the woman, her mind still reeling.

Everyone suspected the Lily Co. had infiltrated the military, and the contents of the navy lieutenant's purse confirmed it.

It wasn't long before Nunley bustled over, a scowl plastered on her face. Sam could tell immediately that the pudgy woman was in a foul mood. If she wasn't so desperate for coin, she'd have left and come back another day.

"What you got better be worth my while." Nunley's eyes were hungry and bulging.

Sam stretched out her hand, the lady's coin purse dangling from it. "See for yourself."

Nunley snatched the purse, held it up to examine it, then dumped the contents into her meaty palm.

"Hmph. Nothin' else?"

Sam's thoughts flashed to the lily-stamped coin currently tucked in her bodice. "What do you mean 'nothing else?' The purse alone is worth at least two silvers."

"Ten coppers. For the lot."

"A silver."

"Fifteen coppers or no offer."

Sam gritted her teeth but nodded. "Fifteen."

Mistress Nunley pulled out her own purse and laid fifteen coppers on the table before her. Sam scooped them up quickly and left.

As she walked the few blocks back to the abandoned haberdashery, Sam pondered the words that had been scribbled on the stolen parchment. Between the lily-stamped coin and the vague note, there was no doubt the lieutenant was involved with the Lily Co. But what exactly did that entail?

Perhaps the note was the place and time for a meeting? Brockers Warehouse would be the location, though she'd never heard of it before. 0200 could be the time—two o'clock in the morning? No good thing ever happened at that time of night.

If she was correct in her assumptions, there was one key piece of information missing from the note—the day. Could it be possible that this secret gathering—if that's what it was—was scheduled for *tonight*?

Sam came to a halt, possibilities teasing her mind. Her thieving in the marketplace had been cut short, and Nunley's payout had been dismal, but information paid handsomely, so long as it came with some proof. She had the lily-stamped coin for proof. Surely Nunley would double what she typically paid Sam to learn of the Lily Co.'s plans.

She would have to find Brockers Warehouse first. Most of the warehouses were near the harbor, so she could search the harbor blindly, or...perhaps she could find the lieutenant and follow him. Milderre was a large city, but simply by the lieutenant's smell, Sam could rule out at least three quarters of it.

And what better place to start than at the loudest, most disreputable tavern there was?

Sam returned to the Bronze Barrel several hours later. She dawdled outside the tavern, watching as people came and went, until her rumbling stomach drove her inside.

The tavern buzzed with chatter, its patrons in various states of drunkenness. It reeked of sweat and tobacco, the pipe smoke lingering in the air, and the low ceilings made the place feel cramped. Large, dusty oil lamps hung from rounded wooden columns, and several long oakwood tables spanned the center of the room. Smaller tables were set around the perimeter, perfect for private conversation. A handful of stools lined the bar, and another was placed by the entrance. Mistress Nunley's muscled doorman sat atop it.

Sam settled herself at one of the small tables. When Mistress Nunley bustled in from the kitchen, she headed straight for Sam.

"What've you got for me now, girl?" Nunley demanded, hands on hips.

"No goods. Just here for some food." Sam pulled out a handful of copper coins, convincing herself that spending them was an investment in her future.

Nunley's eyes narrowed, but she snatched the coins, depositing them into her apron as she shuffled away. Minutes later, she plopped a plate in front of Sam, along with a half-empty mug of ale.

Sam prodded at the plate's contents. The Bronze Barrel wasn't known for its food, and this evening's meal consisted of bland, day-old fish, a hunk of hard cheese, and bread. A small sip confirmed that even the ale was stale. She ate slowly, listening in on conversations while watching for the lieutenant. A nearby couple squabbled—the husband guzzled his ale, ignoring his wife as she berated him for calling her a pig. Another man sat by himself, rocking forward and back, mumbling unintelligibly. At one point, somebody let out a high-pitched cackle that earned a round of hearty laughter in response.

It was well past dark by the time a uniformed naval soldier strode through the door in a rush of cold air. Excitement swelled within Sam.

Keeping her head down, she did her best to remain subtle as she observed the soldier, who settled down close by.

It was not the lieutenant.

Sam deflated. She'd been here too long, all for nothing. Mistress Nunley's doorman had been eyeing her for the last half hour, arms folded and muscles flexed, as if he knew she was up to no good. She glanced his way only to find his eyes already boring into her.

If she had any hope of finding the lieutenant before it was too late, she'd best head toward the docks, anyway. She grabbed her cloak but paused when she noticed the soldier flag Mistress Nunley over.

The few remaining crumbs on Sam's plate suddenly became quite fascinating.

After a quick word with the soldier, Nunley disappeared into the kitchens, reappearing shortly with a bulge in her front apron. Heads close, she and the soldier conversed in hushed tones before Nunley placed a purse onto the counter. The soldier examined the contents and, satisfied, pocketed the purse. He set a much larger purse down in exchange. Sam's eyes widened at the bulging sack, and she wondered what could be in the small purse that was worth so much.

She imagined the amount of money she could make pawning off Lily Co. secrets, and the thought further strengthened her resolve to find the lieutenant and the secret meeting.

"Come again, love," Nunley said as the soldier took his leave.

How hard would it be to pick just one more pocket today?

Standing, she slid her cloak around her shoulders and pursued him into the frigid night.

She followed the soldier from a distance, slowly gaining ground while running scenarios through her mind of the best way to get her hands on his purse.

"Ay, Reynolds!" A boisterous laugh followed the outburst, drawing Sam's attention to the two soldiers drunkenly approaching from the other side of the street. Outnumbered now, Sam fell back, slipping into the shadows and silently cursing that she hadn't already gotten her hands on the purse.

"Layman, Lieutenant," Reynolds addressed the two.

Sam perked up. *Lieutenant!*

There he was, in all his wretched glory, a blundering stroke of luck.

Reynolds joined the others, and Sam followed as the trio paraded around the unfavorable parts of town, laughing loudly, indulging themselves in copious amounts of ale from every tavern they came across while Sam waited impatiently outside. They stopped drinking only when Layman started vomiting in the streets.

The hour was late, the chimes of midnight come and gone, and they had not made it any closer to the harbor. In fact, they'd gone the opposite direction and were now nearing the outskirts of the Nobleman's District. Sam ground her teeth. She'd made a mistake in following the lieutenant. Was it possible he wasn't aware of the meeting? Or perhaps it wasn't tonight as she'd anticipated. She'd found the note in his purse... or was it even *his* purse?

She'd nearly given up hope, fuming at the thought of so many wasted hours, when the men turned into an alley she didn't recognize. It was darker than the surrounding streets, with only one lantern hanging at the other end of the way.

She crept closer, worried they'd disappear into the darkness, and watched as they approached one of the unlit doorways. Reynolds thunked a fist on the sturdy wooden door, prompting Sam to flatten herself against a nearby wall. The cold of the brick seeped through her cloak, sending a chill up her spine.

The scraping of a latch heralded a spill of yellow light as the door slid open.

"Blimey!" a harsh whisper rang out. "You're very nearly late, lieutenant. And look at the state of you three!"

"We're not late, so move aside," the lieutenant growled.

"I ain't seen your token yet."

Token? Sam thought of the lily-stamped coin and groaned inwardly. She'd already stored it with her other belongings.

The lieutenant slammed a palm against the door, pressing it inward.

"You know the rules, lieutenant," the man said, voice strained as he tried to push the door shut. "I can't let you in without that token."

"And I'm telling you to shove off." The lieutenant shouldered his way forward, the other two following close behind. Once the group had passed through, the doorman peeked out to scan the alley, and the door then hastily closed.

Sam considered her next move. From her spot against the wall, she couldn't make out any windows, but there appeared to be a gap between this building and the next. A worker's entrance, perhaps? Pulling her cloak tighter, she glanced over her shoulder before stepping into the alley.

The buildings were so close together that she could touch both sides at once. Keeping one hand against the chilly brick wall, she felt her way farther in. The shuffling of her footsteps echoed in the small space. A tickle in her nose could not have been timed more poorly. Sam scrunched her nose, pinching the bridge, willing the sneeze away.

Though she tried to muffle the sound, when the sneeze came, she may as well have been banging pots and pans. Silently cursing the gods, she stood frozen in the dark, heart pumping wildly. When nothing happened, she continued her shuffle forward, relieved when she came to a door. The door was locked, but that hadn't ever stopped her before. Slipping two hairpins from her hair, Sam felt blindly for the keyhole and inserted the pins at an angle. She jostled them until she was rewarded with a satisfying click. Quietly pushing the door open, she slid inside, grinning.

She appeared to be in a back room, the walls lined with partly filled shelves and stacks of crates—several of which were stamped with a black lily. Light seeped from under a closed door at the opposite end of the room, and Sam crept toward it on tiptoes.

Upon reaching it, she placed both hands on the door and took a steadying breath. She was about to eavesdrop on the most infamous gang in town. If she was caught, she doubted she would live to see another day. It wasn't too late to back out... but even as she thought it, she knew she wouldn't. Sam had plenty of experience sneaking around. The value of the information she would learn tonight outweighed any rational fear she may have otherwise had. She thought of Rhett, now jobless, and of her comrades who lived each day unsure of where their next meal would come from. This was an opportunity to help them all.

Peeking through the slats proved to be ineffective. Sam could hear the rumble of voices but couldn't make out what was being said. Cautiously inching the door open, she noted a stack of crates only a handful of steps away and shimmied out of the stock room to duck behind them.

She appeared to be on the ground floor of a large, circular room that rose at least three stories high. Between the lanterns and an oversize, rusted chandelier hanging from the rafters high above, the center of the room was bathed in a warm glow. Thankfully, wooden balconies lined the perimeter of the room above Sam, jutting outward over the open space and shrouding her hiding spot in shadow.

A cluster of twenty-or-so men and women gathered at the center of the room. It didn't appear as if there was anyone dallying around the edges, but she couldn't be certain and would have to keep her guard up in case someone wandered too close.

It came as no surprise to see several attendees in the red-and-blue coats of the Royal Navy. She was, however, startled to find that a number of the group appeared to be nobles, dressed in obvious finery. They stood in groups, the nobles distancing themselves from the military and common folk, noses turned up haughtily.

A booming voice rose above the rest, calling for order, and the room silenced. The enormous voice came from a rather frail-looking man who stood atop a platform in the center of the room. He wore his white hair smoothed back from his wrinkled face, and he billowed like a sail in a black cloak embroidered with golden lilies.

"Lilies of the Night! You have been gathered as the most valuable accessories of the Lily Company, individually selected for your *connections*, your *talents*, your *devotion*"—he drew out each word in emphasis—"and for you, I have news. The high council has received word that the king will be attending the upcoming Festival of the Gods here in Milderre. It will be our task to ensure that he sees the way of the Lily while here.

"We will utilize the connections of our high-ranking members to separate him from his guards," he said with a nod toward a noblewoman. "While employing the unique specialties of others to... persuade him to our cause." He gestured this time at a man who twirled a dagger menacingly between his fingers.

The group murmured while Sam slapped a hand to her gaping mouth.

"We're going to kidnap the king?" someone called out.

"You sound doubtful, my friend." The leader paced slowly across the platform, eyes lingering on each individual before landing on the one who had spoken. An eerie silence settled over the room. "Our master believes we can accomplish this task, and I have no doubt that we can. We are the prized Lilies of the Lily Company! A task such as this is but one step in achieving a much larger goal, and with the king in our midst, we will have power not only over Milderre but all of Ducria!"

Cheers of agreement rang out while Sam's mind reeled. What would happen if they succeeded? The thought of her payout seemed meaningless next to their world-altering plot.

Hot, sticky breath assaulted her ear as a beefy hand grasped her upper arm. "Now what do we have here?"

She'd been so invested in the speaker on the platform, she hadn't realized a man had neared her. His wretched breath caused her to gag as she struggled to pull free of his firm grip. Panic bubbled within her as she was dragged from the shadows and directed toward the crowd at the center of the room.

Sam dug her heels into the dirt floor, straining against the man as he bellowed, "Intruder! I found an intruder!"

As the man hauled Sam forward, everyone turned to look, their faces pressing in, mouths moving in accusation. Sweat beaded on her brow. She wanted to shrink back into the shadows.

One of the faces belonged to Mistress Nunley's burly doorman. His crooked eyes widened in recognition, and a smile split his lips, revealing rotted teeth. *Oh no.*

"This here's the little thief who frequents the Bronze Barrel!" he shouted, his finger pointed inches from her nose.

The lieutenant shoved forward. "She's the one who stole my purse this morning! There's not another soul in town with hair that color. Where's my token, you little waif?"

The room burst into a chorus of chaos. Some—particularly the nobles—panicked, calling for the meeting to be dispersed at once. Others loudly proclaimed that she was a High Council spy. The most terrifying voices declared that she knew too much and must be disposed of. Hands reached for her, tugging her this way and that as the men and women argued.

The leader's booming voice called for silence, quieting the room at once. His beady eyes landed on Sam as he beckoned her toward the platform. She swallowed thickly, her legs frozen in place, knowing the farther she made it from the entrance, the less her chance of escape.

"What is a pretty thing like you doing so far from home?" he crooned. Though his tone was smooth, there was no denying the menace in his eyes, the hardness of his features.

"I-I..." She couldn't speak. The man who had been twirling the dagger previously moved closer to her, ready to strike at a moment's notice.

From the platform, the cloaked man tsked. "Unfortunately, methinks you know too much. We can't have little birdies flitting off with prized secrets, now, can we?"

Sam's throat sank to her stomach as her eyes scanned the room, searching for an escape. The weight of her choices pressed down on her, suffocating her with regret, and Rhett's face flashed in her mind, his warm smile a stark contrast to the cold reality she faced now. Would she ever see him again?

The frail man stared down at Sam with a victorious smile.

"Please." Sam's voice came out as a whisper. "Let me go."

In her peripherals, she could see the lieutenant with teeth bared and Mistress Nunley's gloating doorman.

A rush of nausea flooded her. They weren't going to let her out alive.

THREE

S am startled at a loud clang from above. All attention turned to the chandelier as it came crashing down. Screams filled the room as people fled in every direction. The heavy frame caught the frail man, slamming him into the platform. The many candles atop the chandelier extinguished in an instant.

Sam's captors released her, hurrying forward to unpin their leader. Sam looked toward the rafters where the chandelier had once been, thanking the gods. She caught the flutter of something white high above, and then a thick oak barrel was falling toward her, followed by another. Gasping, she twisted out of the way.

Taking advantage of the attack, she darted toward the back room, chased into the alley by the sound of more screams. Slamming the exterior door behind her, she ran straight through the darkness. As she reached the main street, she could see the frantic meeting attendees spilling out of the warehouse's main doors. Sam ran in the opposite direction.

She didn't dare go back home. They knew who she was—had associated her with the Bronze Barrel, which was only blocks from where she slept. Even if they didn't know where she lived, surely they would go looking.

Lungs screaming and legs aching, she ran as fast and as far as her body would allow, weaving through alleys with no particular pattern or destination.

Tiredness eventually slowed her pace. She wished for her mother, for her comforting touch as she tucked Sam into bed, and the warmth of her body as they snuggled up together. With that thought in mind, Sam reached the building where her mother had passed away.

Sam stared up at the small window that used to be her own. She hadn't been back since that fateful day three years prior. To the left of the window was a small alley. Stepping around the corner, she observed a pile of ragged cloth that lay abandoned next to a splintered wooden tub. The sight of it had her chewing the inside of her cheek as she attempted to hold back the emotions that swarmed her—this was the very tub she and her mother had knelt around as they spent countless hours scrubbing stains. She was surprised it was still here after all this time. Sam approached the tub, lightly resting her fingers on its rim.

Exhaustion clawed at her, and she sat down hard on the dirty cloth. The cold quickly worked its way in, chilling the sweat on her skin. She wrapped her cloak tighter around her body, curled up on the dirty rags, and took several deep breaths. *Sleep.*

Despite her weariness, sleep was slow to come. She tossed and turned, her mind alive with the Lily Co.'s meeting. The information she had obtained was undeniably valuable—they were planning on kidnapping the single most powerful person in Ducria! But would anyone believe her, let alone *pay* her, if she told them?

Though Sam was keenly aware that she may cross paths with someone from the Lily Co., she'd promised to spend the afternoon with Rhett while he searched for work, and she kept her promise. She waited anxiously by their usual fountain in Market Square, and upon seeing him, rushed into his arms.

"Whoa!" he said, startling before returning her embrace. "Is everything all right, Sam?"

She squeezed him tighter, taking in his familiar scent. A long breath calmed her racing heart enough to step back. Rhett wore a simple, clean shirt under a brown vest and trousers. He'd combed back his damp, curly hair and shaved his face. Handsome as ever.

"Everything is fine now that I'm with you," she said, pasting a smile on her face.

Rhett didn't appear convinced but held out an arm for her anyway. "Shall we?"

Sam checked that her hood covered her hair before tucking her arm through his. Together, they journeyed into the busy square, enjoying a comfortable silence as they walked. Sam glanced at Rhett, taking in his familiar profile, the way his hair caught the sunlight, the easy confidence in his stride.

"How do you do it?" she asked.

Rhett raised an eyebrow. "Do what?"

"Walk around so confidently. Like you own the place."

He chuckled. "I've got a natural swagger."

Sam grinned and nudged his shoulder with hers. "It's more of a strut, really."

"Oh? And what would you call the way you walk?" Rhett leaned in slightly to study her.

Sam tilted her head, pretending to think it over. "Graceful, with just a hint of mystery."

"Mystery? Is that what you're going for?"

"Absolutely. Keeps people guessing."

He chuckled again, this time softer, and Sam's chest fluttered at the sound. The way he looked at her—like she was the only thing in the world worth his attention—made her heart race in a way both thrilling and terrifying.

As they wove through the square, vendors called out eagerly, shaking wares in hopes of making a sale. The moment it became clear that neither Rhett nor Sam intended to buy, they were swiftly dismissed, shooed away before Rhett could so much as get a word in to ask about work.

With each failed attempt, his shoulders tensed, frustration building. She searched for a distraction, something to break the weight pressing down on him.

"Look at all those spices," she said, nodding toward a stall where neat rows of colorful jars lined the wooden shelves. "I wonder what they use in Eclor."

"Saffron," Rhett answered without hesitation.

"Saffron?"

"It was a staple in all of my father's favorite meals."

Sam had nearly forgotten—Rhett's parents had emigrated from Eclor to Ducria only a few years before they fell ill. He rarely spoke of them.

She opened her mouth, unsure what to say, but before she could fumble through a response, Rhett offered a small, lopsided smile. "I'll have to remember to make you some saffron rice one of these days."

The tension in Sam's chest loosened. Whatever memories had surfaced for him, they hadn't dragged him down further.

"I'll hold you to that," she said, then perked as a familiar, captivating voice reached her ears. Gently tugging on his arm, she led Rhett to where the Haapari woman was once again singing in front of the textile tent. A crowd had already gathered.

Sam watched the woman openly this time—young woman, she should say, who couldn't be more than four or five years Sam's senior. The young woman sang about the Goddess of Light, her ice-blue eyes finding Sam and lingering.

> *"...With eyes as the sun and hair like spun gold,*
> *From the void she rose—a radiant, fiery core..."*

The woman's voice faded, and she took a step toward Sam. Startled, Sam squeezed Rhett's hand, abruptly pulling him back into the crowd and toward the opposite side of the market, leaving the Haapari tent behind.

"I've never heard a voice like that," Rhett said minutes later. "It was…"

"Entrancing." Sam nodded. Her mind whirled with questions. Why had the woman looked only at Sam? What did she intend when she took a step closer?

Nothing good, Sam was sure.

"Entrancing," Rhett agreed.

It was a shame they hadn't been able to examine the Haapari textiles. The island nation was known for them. Brightly colored and intricately woven—Sam knew because, as a girl, she had helped her mother care for many. She had dreamed of wearing the beautiful bright dresses, and on more than one occasion, her mother had scolded her for twirling with a noble lady's laundry instead of scrubbing it. That didn't stop her from imagining herself a foreign princess draped in the lovely colors.

Function over fashion, her mother always said.

Swallowing thickly, Sam tugged at the neckline of her own simple, dull, *functional* brown dress as her thoughts landed on the memory of her mother. She grasped Rhett's arm a little more tightly than before.

As they walked past a stall selling detailed wooden carvings, Rhett paused to admire a small figurine. "This reminds me of you," he said, holding it up for Sam to see. It was a carving of the Sky God, Aspos.

"I remind you of a . . . man?" she teased.

"No. It's because it's small but full of details," he replied, his tone sincere. "It's delicate yet strong, just like you, and Aspos represents the sky, which you're oddly obsessed with, though all there is to see is chimney smoke and smog."

Sam hadn't realized her fascination with the sky was so obvious. It wasn't that she was intrigued by what she could see—he was right about the smoke and smog. It was more the knowledge of what lay *beyond.* An endless depth containing untold mysteries. And the hope that she *would* see it one day.

As she reached out to gently take the carving from his hands, their fingers brushed, sending a tingle up her arm. "You're quite observant, Rhett. And full of poetic compliments, it seems."

"Only when I'm with you," he said softly, his gaze holding hers.

Sam ducked her head in a smile, a flush heating her cheeks. Though she wished she could keep it, she reluctantly returned the carving of Aspos to its shelf.

They stopped several booths over only to encounter a particularly grouchy vegetable vendor.

"Filth," the vendor spat at Rhett, who, to his credit, remained calm. "I'd sooner fertilize my carrot patch with you than let you take a share of my profits just for moving a wheelbarrow."

Sam had no hesitations about lifting the vendor's coin purse. While he berated Rhett, she lithely slipped it from his person. It was only fair—if he wouldn't offer Rhett a job, the least he could do was pay for their evening meal.

While Rhett was speaking with a cobbler, Sam explored the adjacent shop. It lured her in with soaps in a multitude of scents, and she was once again overwhelmed with memories of her mother. She was halfway out of the tent when a familiar scent caught her attention: cloves. Rhett's favorite. She searched through the bars until finding the right one and, after a brief debate, purchased a small bar of clove-and-cinnamon soap. After the vendor wrapped the bar and tied it with a small piece of twine, Sam slipped it into her pocket. It would be a gift for Rhett after he secured a new place of work.

Sam couldn't help but constantly check over her shoulder throughout the afternoon and into the evening. She worried what the Lily Co. might be planning and if it involved finding her.

"Sam, are you sure everything is all right? You've been... distracted."

Sam snapped her head back to Rhett. He'd stopped walking, his attention solely focused on her.

She wanted to tell him—she *should* tell him. There was no one she trusted more in the entire world. Yet, she could imagine the disapproving look he would give her, and then he would surely become involved regardless of her protests. What could he do against the Lily Co.?

"I didn't sleep well last night," she said—which was true, regardless of the reason.

Rhett frowned.

"Truly, I'm fine." Sam forced a smile. He shouldn't be worrying about her—the entire reason they were in the market together was for *him*. "Let's try another stall."

Rhett didn't push, and she was grateful. Instead, he tucked her arm back securely into the crook of his, his hand lingering over hers. She savored its warmth.

The next tent belonged to a lampmaker. Lanterns hung across the entrance, cluttered makeshift displays, and even lined the ground around the tent itself. Candles and candlesticks took up any meager space left between the lanterns. As they drew closer, Sam could see that each lantern had a different, unique design carved into the glass panes.

The vendor, a short woman with tanned skin and curly hair similar to Rhett's, sat outside on a colorful rug. Oddly, her tent flaps were closed. Upon seeing their interest, the woman rose swiftly to her feet, beckoning them closer.

"Lovely lantern for a lovely lady?" The woman picked up one of the lanterns, its glass panes rattling as she lifted it for Sam to see. "Yes. Come, come! I show you how they shine."

She lifted a tent flap, revealing even more lanterns inside, their beautiful designs dancing along the interior walls.

"Actually—" Rhett started. Before he could say more, the vendor disappeared inside, eagerly motioning for them to follow. They were about to enter when Sam spotted a smaller lantern off to the side of one display, on which was carved a lily.

She stopped in her tracks.

"Rhett." She tugged on his arm, the panic rising in her voice even as she did her best to remain calm. "I'm actually famished. Let's go get something to eat."

"Weren't you the one who said to try one more stall?"

She swallowed her dread, eyeing the symbol of the Lily Company.

"I changed my mind," she said, her words coming out harsher than intended. "If I don't eat something now, I might faint."

She made a show of wiping her brow with the back of her hand. Rhett seemed torn but ultimately relented with a short nod. Sam held back her sigh of relief, looking over her shoulder more than once as they walked away from the lanterns. Thankfully, the vendor didn't chase them down.

They stopped at a nearby tavern to eat. Even though Rhett had little to no money, it still took some convincing before he agreed to let her pay for his meal. Maybe he'd seen her swipe the vegetable vendor's purse. If so, he at least didn't bring it up. He waited outside while Sam ordered two bowls of stew, bread, and some ale.

Rhett found them a small table just outside the tavern's entrance. Lanterns glowed to life throughout the square as sunset faded into night, though the dark did nothing to deter people from the market.

Sam took a moment to lift her face to the sky, letting her hood fall from her head now that darkness better concealed her flaming hair. Stars rarely shone through the smog. Tonight was no different.

"There she is."

Sam tore her eyes from the sky to find Rhett watching her.

"What do you mean?" she asked, picking absently at her stew.

"You've been hiding beneath that cloak all day. I'd much rather see you like this all the time."

Sam fiddled with a lock of her hair. "I don't like the attention it draws."

"Your hair is beautiful, Sam. *You* are beautiful."

Any retort Sam had died on her tongue. Her insides fluttered instead. With a quiet, "Thanks," she turned her attention downward and finished her meal. Rhett had only taken a few bites.

"You should eat, Rhett."

He turned hollow, golden-brown eyes on her, and it wasn't until then that Sam could truly see the full weight of the situation wearing on him. In the three years she had known Rhett, even after long days in the workhouse, this was the most drawn she'd ever seen him.

Even though she knew he wouldn't like it, Sam said, "You could always take up pickpocketing."

Rhett gave her a look.

"What?" she retorted. "It pays well."

"Until you get caught."

Sam sighed, her nostrils flaring at the judgment in his tone. Just as quickly, her irritation deflated.

She *had* gotten caught. And she was lucky to have escaped with her life. She thought of the lily-stamped coin stashed with her belongings at the haberdashery. She'd thought it would lead her to a big payout. Instead, it had almost led to her death.

Sam realized Rhett was waiting for her to say something, so she directed the conversation to something less controversial: their friends.

"Billy keeps asking after you. Perry, too."

Rhett leaned back in his seat, crossing his arms. "Oh really?"

"You haven't been by in months. They miss you."

"I don't get many days off."

"But you see me."

"I *want* to see you."

Sam felt another blush creeping through her cheeks. "You don't want to see them?" she teased.

"Of course I do, but I have my priorities."

"Well, now that you aren't slaving away in that workhouse, perhaps they deserve a visit."

Rhett looked at her for a second. "Then let's go," he said abruptly, rising to his feet.

Startled, Sam rose, too, bumping into the table as she did so.

A genuine smile cracked Rhett's face. "Easy there."

Sam scoffed and snatched up the bread Rhett hadn't touched. Stepping around the table, she placed it in his hands. "Eat."

Rhett did as he was told, biting off a chunk and chewing. Satisfied, Sam turned to walk home and froze.

Not twenty paces away, the lieutenant was striding through the market.

FOUR

The lieutenant saw her at almost the same moment she saw him. Recognition lit his features while Sam watched, mouth ajar, unable to convince herself to move.

A light touch at her shoulder made her flinch.

"Sam, what's wrong? Who is that?"

"The lieutenant…" she breathed, then looked up into Rhett's warm brown eyes. She'd never forgive herself if Rhett got hurt because of her actions.

She had to lead the lieutenant away.

With that thought in mind, she turned to elbow her way through the townspeople gathered in the square. She heard Rhett call out her name, but she refused to slow. She raced for the nearest alley and, with it, the cover of darkness.

"Not this time, you filthy rat!" the lieutenant bellowed behind her. He let out a shrill whistle.

As Sam pushed her way through the crowd, she spotted a man to her left and another to her right hurrying in a direct path to intercept her. With a last jolt of speed, she hurtled into the alley before they could grab her.

But the lieutenant still gave chase.

Sam pressed onward, straining her legs for speed they wouldn't give. If she could just get deeper into Milderre, she'd be safe.

The lieutenant caught her cloak and yanked, slamming her backward to the ground. Her head met stone with an agonizing crack. She fumbled for the ties at her neck, pulling them loose. Rolling to her side, she attempted to sit up, her vision spinning, but the lieutenant grabbed a handful of hair and hauled her against a stone wall. She whimpered. Two more men entered the alley.

With the tip of his knife pressed against her throat, the lieutenant purred, "You were never going to get away."

Before she could speak, he pricked her neck. Sam strained to pull away from the dagger, standing on tiptoes. Holding her in place, the lieutenant pulled the knife away to examine the red that now coated it. "Where's my token?"

If she told him the truth, she'd have no leverage—nothing to stop the lieutenant from slitting her throat right there in the wretched alleyway.

"I sold it," she lied, gritting her teeth against the pain.

Anger flashed in the lieutenant's eyes before he seemed to cool. "No matter. We'll take care of you the same way we do all the others."

"All the others?" she whispered hoarsely.

"Orphan *scum*. Should've kept your nose clean." He seized her wrist and twisted it painfully behind her back.

"I didn't tell anyone, I swear," she protested.

The lieutenant chuckled darkly. "That was a handsome young friend you had back there at the market."

Sam couldn't help her gasp. "Don't you touch him!"

The lieutenant smirked before he whistled again. In response, the other two men snapped to attention.

"Tell the master I found her and that I'm taking her to the Slaver."

Slaves were illegal. Surely there wasn't a slave trader here in Milderre.

"You saw the boy with her. Bring him, too."

The two men grunted in acknowledgment, exiting the alley and heading in separate directions.

"No—" Sam's cry cut off as the lieutenant pressed against her twisted arm.

"Not a word out of you," he growled.

Sam was forced to take one step. Two. Desperately, she flung her already tender head backward, colliding with the lieutenant's jaw. He howled angrily but, rather than let go, squeezed even harder. Sam yelped. This time, she did as she was told, walking where the lieutenant directed. She felt a hint of satisfaction to see a trickle of blood seeping from the corner of his mouth.

Unfortunately for her, every alley they turned into was completely void of life. Few lanterns were lit, and they traveled in near darkness. Sam knew they were headed toward the harbor. It would only be a fifteen-minute walk, at most. She spent her time searching for an escape and praying to the gods that Rhett got away.

As they walked, the lieutenant rambled. "I should have killed you the moment I saw you. But I've got to get my money's worth out of you. It wouldn't be fair otherwise. You took my purse, after all, little crimson thief. I'm sure the master won't mind me taking my cut."

All the while, his grip remained tight.

The lieutenant steered Sam toward the part of the shipyard where ships were anchored to be repaired. It was quiet this time of night. Between two large naval ships was a smaller boat with a single light hanging near the bow.

A thick Haapari man stood at the front of the planked walkway that led to the ship. In the dark, the water beyond appeared black and ominous. The man eyed them as they approached. "It's a bit late for business, isn't it?"

"The best goods run loose at night." The lieutenant gave Sam a firm, meaningful shake.

"Help me!" Sam pleaded before the lieutenant silenced her with a wicked clap across her ear. Her head jerked at the force of the impact, and she gasped at the pain. A persistent ringing filled her ears.

The Haapari man flicked his gaze to Sam, then back to the lieutenant. He nodded once, moving aside. Sam didn't speak again but begged with her eyes. The man ignored her.

Stepping onto the wooden dock, the lieutenant ushered her forward, heading toward a gangplank that had been laid between the pier and the ship anchored there. When they reached the gangplank, they did not go aboard the ship; rather, the lieutenant tugged Sam against one of the posts as if to tie her there. Her heart beat erratically in her chest. This might be her last chance to escape.

Nervous energy built within her as she waited for the right moment. When he bent to grab a length of rope, his grip on her slackened.

Now.

Sam jerked her knee upward with as much force as her body would allow. It connected with his groin, and the lieutenant crumpled to the ground, holding himself and shouting curses. His knife clattered down beside him. Sam bared her teeth as she pushed away from the post.

She snatched up the knife and made to leap over the lieutenant's body, which was still curled on the dock, but he caught her ankle midair. With no leg to land on, she tumbled forward. Though she bruised her knees as they met the hard wooden planks, she refused to loosen her grip on the knife. Twisting onto her backside, she steadied herself by placing one hand on the dock behind her and held up the knife in warning.

She should have slashed at the hand still grasping her ankle.

The lieutenant lunged, knocking away the knife and pinning her by the wrists as he straddled her. She screamed, helpless under his weight. The lieutenant clamped a thick hand over her mouth and leaned down close to her ear.

"Try that again," he hissed. "And you'll wish you were dead."

Would it be better to die? What horrors would she be put through as a slave?

She did not want to die.

Sam stilled, feeling broken, and the lieutenant climbed off her. She noticed the Haapari man watching them, but he made no move to intervene, and a new hatred flared within her. After roughly tugging Sam to her feet, the lieutenant tied a length of rope around her upper body and the post.

"Not a peep out of you," he warned, then stalked up the gangplank and onto the boat.

Once he was out of sight, Sam tugged at the rope, testing the knots, but it held firm. Even if she could get away, would the Haapari man let her pass? Defeated, she leaned her throbbing head back against the post and listened to the soft lap of the water against the docks. She stared at the sky, searching for unseen stars. Maybe as a slave she would be sold somewhere she could see them.

But she would never see Rhett again.

Just as that thought nearly undid her, a snarl echoed across the water. Sam whipped her head around in time to see Rhett pummeling the Haapari man. Gone was the calm, collected Rhett she'd always known—he looked positively wild.

Sam nearly cried with relief at the sight of him. "Rhett!"

The Haapari man lay unmoving as Rhett rushed toward her. He began working at the knots with shaking hands, and though every instinct told her to do otherwise, Sam remained still, anxiously scanning their surroundings for any additional threats.

"Hurry," she stressed. "There's a knife just there."

Rhett grabbed the fallen knife and used it to hack at the ropes binding her.

"Neff, what's all the ruckus?" a gravelly voice called. Sam glanced at the unconscious Haapari man, knowing he wouldn't respond. "Neff!"

A moment later, the lieutenant appeared on the deck with another man who looked like he'd been stretched thin, all spindly limbs and pinched features. Sam could only assume it was the Slaver.

Rhett finally severed the rope. Sam shimmied out of the last few loops.

The lieutenant roared and rushed for the gangplank. Rhett placed himself protectively in front of Sam, shoving her toward the city as he urged her to get away. Before she had the chance to respond, the lieutenant barreled into Rhett with such force that they tumbled backwards right into her. The knife in Rhett's hand went skidding over the side of the wooden dock.

Rhett sprang to his feet, but the Slaver had caught up, brandishing a dagger. Rhett dodged the small blade, twisting and turning out of reach with skill Sam didn't realize he had.

The lieutenant made a grab for Sam, and she scrambled backward out of reach. They got to their feet in unison. The lieutenant glanced between her and Rhett before turning to fight alongside the Slaver. It was two against one now.

Sam scanned her surroundings frantically, searching for a knife, a brick, *anything*, knowing she would be useless against the two men without some sort of weapon. It was an awful feeling—being *useless*.

The horrid sound of a blade slicing through fabric filled her ears. Time slowed as she watched the red that blossomed across Rhett's chest. She wanted to scream, to fight, to do something.

Rhett didn't so much as glance at the wound, instead using the opportunity to wrap himself around the Slaver's outstretched arm. Hurling himself forward, Rhett flipped the Slaver, sending him sprawling, and, in the same movement, spun with a raised fist to cock the lieutenant squarely in the jaw.

The lieutenant stumbled backward, rubbing his face, then glared as he raised his fists in return. The Slaver, to Sam's relief, lay unmoving several paces away. If she could help Rhett overcome the lieutenant, they'd be free.

She spotted the motionless form of the Haapari man and noticed an open crate next to where he'd been standing. Scurrying to it, she found several full glass bottles of ale. Sam grabbed a bottle in each hand and raced back to the fight as the lieutenant landed a blow that doubled Rhett over.

She screamed as she sprinted forward, throwing one of the glass bottles at the lieutenant. It hit his shoulder and crashed to the ground, glass shattering around his feet. He grunted, turning, only to meet Sam with the other bottle. She slammed it into his head.

Glass shards sliced into Sam's hands as the bottle broke, but she didn't care. The lieutenant staggered toward Rhett, who took it as an opportunity to end the fight. Ducking under the lieutenant's outstretched arms and using his body weight, Rhett hurled the man over his shoulder and straight off the dock. The lieutenant hit the dark water with a slap, floundering and sputtering as he surfaced.

Rhett grabbed her hand, and, with one last peek at the water, Sam followed him off the docks and into the dark alleys. They listened to the lieutenant curse and bellow as he waded for shore, but by the time he reached solid ground, they would be long gone.

FIVE

Sam trudged up the haberdashery stairs with Rhett on her heels and entered the small bedroom she shared with Perry and Bill. There they both collapsed—Rhett on a rickety chair and Sam on her rumpled mattress. They spent several minutes in silence catching their breath.

It was Rhett who spoke first. "Who are those people, Sam, and why are they after you?"

Sam rolled to her side to look at him. One of his eyes was swollen, and his lip had split. She winced as she sat up. "Can we talk about it later? You're hurt."

"No. We can talk about it now."

She sighed heavily, too tired to argue. "All right. But I am going to check on your wounds first."

Rhett nodded, shifting to sit upright in the chair. Sam fetched a small basin of water and a clean cloth, then knelt before him.

"You'll need to remove your shirt," she said, eyeing the red line of dried blood across his torso.

The muscles on Rhett's arms and chest flexed as he tugged his shirt off, and Sam wondered what work he'd been doing to allow such a noticeable change to his physique so quickly.

She cleared her throat when she realized she'd been staring.

Rhett prodded at the gash. "Doesn't look like it's too deep," he said, and a new wave of guilt washed over Sam. She looked away, a frown creasing her face.

"This was all my fault," she admitted softly. "Those people... They're members of the Lily Company. And they want me dead."

"What?" Rhett's features turned severe.

Sam's hands fell into her lap as her head drooped, the full weight of her situation settling over her like a blanket of lead. "I'm so sorry you got dragged into it."

She told him how she'd robbed the lieutenant and about the events that followed. When she finished, Rhett opened his mouth to respond and then closed it again.

It was several minutes before he spoke. "I almost lost you, Sam. When you disappeared into that crowd, I never imagined I'd find you like I did."

"How *did* you find me?"

"You mentioned the lieutenant, and then I saw him give chase when you ran." He paused, grinding his teeth. "Why did you run, Sam? I could have helped."

Sam's lip began to tremble, but words escaped her.

Rhett continued, "You were swallowed up in the crowd, and two men nabbed me. I didn't know who they were or what was happening, but when we passed your cloak and fresh blood in the alley, I feared the worst." Rhett closed his eyes. "They didn't talk much, but after a while, it was obvious where we were headed. I slipped them a few blocks from the shipyard and followed my gut that you'd been caught, too."

Sam shuddered. She didn't want to imagine what would have happened had he not found her when he did.

"Thank you," she said, still staring down at her knees. "For finding me. For taking a knife for me. For saving my life."

Rhett leaned forward to cup her chin. Tilting her head up, he said, "I'd do it all again if it meant keeping you safe."

A lump formed in her throat as she searched his face. Her gaze drifted from the familiarly stubborn set of his jaw up to his eyes. Carefully, she reached out, brushing a loose strand of hair from his forehead. Her fingers lingered, tracing the outline of his temple. Rhett held perfectly still, his focus solely on her.

The silence stretched, and Sam inhaled slowly, her hand trembling as she brought it down his cheek. He winced, catching her hand and cupping it in his. Sam's breath hitched as his thumb stroked her skin, his callused palm was warm against it.

"Guess I'm bruised there too," he murmured, his voice husky.

Sam stared at their connected hands, a blush creeping up her neck. The room seemed to shrink, the world outside fading away.

Rhett's gaze held hers, his eyes dark and fathomless. She swallowed, her throat suddenly dry.

"Sorry," she whispered, drawing back.

But Rhett didn't let go. He leaned down, his movements achingly slow until there was hardly any space between them. When he spoke, his voice was rough with emotion. "Sam, I—"

The door to the room burst open, and they both jumped, pulling apart from one another as Billy entered the room with Perry on his heels.

Those two have impeccable timing. Sam's cheeks flushed, her lips pressing into a grimace as her body—her heart—was left wanting more.

"What's goin' on in—by the gods, Rhett, is that you? Somebody shake me! I don't believe my eyes. Step aside, lovebirds, and give me a proper greeting!"

Sam groaned. "Billy! I know we share this room, but can't you ever knock? What if I was changing?"

Her heart still pounded from moments before, but she moved to allow the boys to get reacquainted.

"Ain't nothin' I haven't seen before."

Sam's mouth dropped open. "You have not!"

Billy guffawed, his black hair falling forward into his eyes, and Sam glanced at the makeshift curtain she'd pinned to the ceiling in the corner, now questioning the fabric's opacity. She narrowed her eyes. Someday she would have a space of her own.

Billy nodded to the cut across Rhett's chest. "What's she been doin' to ya, Rhett?"

Peeking out from behind Billy, Perry paled. "You're bleeding."

Rhett chuckled, rising from the chair to ruffle Perry's scraggly mop of brown hair. "It's only a scratch, Pare. Sam's patching me up."

Right. *That's* what she was doing.

Sam looked at the cloth she still held, then re-wet it and directed Rhett to sit back down on the chair.

"Good to see you, Billy," Rhett said as Sam began blotting the wound.

"It's about time you show your face around here," Billy said with a grin, and though he jested, Sam knew there was some truth to it.

"I know. I'll be better." Rhett sounded sincere. "Perry, you've grown!"

Perry straightened to his full height, beaming at Rhett's attention. Even stretched tall, he was still half a head shorter than Sam.

"All done," Sam said as she finished wrapping Rhett's chest, tucking in the excess bandage. "You can put your shirt back on now."

"Gotta cover up the goods." Billy smirked.

Sam rolled her eyes, even though she couldn't help appreciating those "goods."

When Rhett held his shirt up, Sam bit her lip. Besides the bloodstains, the thing was practically shredded.

"Take one of mine," Billy offered, rummaging through the belongings he kept in a small rucksack at the head of his bedroll.

With a word of thanks, Rhett dressed.

To avoid staring at him, Sam washed her hands—only just noticing the small slices across them—then wetted a cloth and patted at her neck. The skin was tender where the lieutenant had cut her, but it didn't appear to still be bleeding. It *had* dripped onto her dress though. She frowned at the stain, blotting it with the cloth.

Then she touched the back of her head. Though there was a rather large, painful lump, it wasn't bleeding either.

"Are you all right?" Rhett asked quietly as he came up behind her.

"A little sore," she admitted, "but otherwise unscathed."

Rhett nodded. "I should be going, then."

Before Sam could reply, Billy cut in. "You're stayin' here tonight." The way he said it left no room for discussion. "You can even have me own blessed pillow, if you like. I've got me best mates together for the first time in a good long while, and I'm gonna enjoy it while I can."

Rhett eyed Sam questioningly, and while she shrugged nonchalantly, her stomach twisted in a hundred knots. A hundred more when Rhett smiled that handsome, crooked smile of his. "Sounds like I'm staying."

Sam lay wide awake on her mattress, listening to the sound of Rhett's steady breaths from several feet away. Billy snored lightly from the ground at her feet, and Perry slept silently to her right.

In her mind, she replayed the events of the last few days again and again. She thought of the Lily Co. The Haapari woman who stared. The Lieutenant and his stupid purse. The ropes that had bound her.

And Rhett.

The soap she'd failed to give him that now sat like a brick in her pocket.

The blood across his chest.

The feel of her hand in his.

The way he'd leaned in close...

Sam shivered, her blanket a useless heap atop her. She should have closed the gap. Should have pressed her lips to his.

A muffled crash sounded from downstairs, breaking her mind free of itself. Sam's entire body stilled, her chest suddenly so heavy she could hardly suck in a breath.

This was her safe place—she was *safe* here.

With trembling hands, she managed to shake Rhett by the shoulder. He rolled to face her, eyes fluttering open.

"I think someone's downstairs," Sam breathed.

A thud echoed from below, and Rhett sat up, alert. He gestured toward Perry. Sam woke him as Rhett nudged Billy awake. "What in the—"

"Intruder," Rhett whispered.

Sam could barely see their silhouettes in the dark. The sounds from below had ceased. She pressed her ear to the floorboards, where she heard not a crash or a thud but whispers. Not the wind, not the creaks of the aged building. A different whisper. Hissing. Faint and rhythmic, emanating from somewhere on the floor below.

And then her nose picked up the scent of something new. The air turned acrid with the cloying bite of smoke. Panic clutched her chest and twisted her gut.

Fire.

Billy rushed for the door. As it opened, smoke billowed up, a thick black curtain obscuring the doorway. Coughing, tears stinging her eyes, Sam threw open the shuttered window. She leaned out over the side, gulping in clean air, and saw orange flames licking up the exterior of the stone wall.

She clenched the windowsill, knuckles turning white. In the distance, she could see a uniformed man striding away. She wanted to scream, yet, as the lieutenant disappeared into the darkness, all she could do was stare.

Sturdy hands clasped around Sam's waist, hauling her back into the room.

"Come on! We have to get out of here," Rhett said urgently, his forehead already shining with perspiration.

Sam let him lead her across the room and into the hall. Flames were already peeking up the stairs. Perry was halfway down, swatting at the flames with a blanket as he and Billy attempted to reach the lower level.

The floorboards creaked under Sam's weight. Heat radiated from the walls. She wondered if it was even possible to make it out. Rhett ushered her forward. Two steps down, she halted, gasping as she remembered her mother's brooch still hidden away in her bedroom. The fire would destroy it, and it was the one thing she had left of her mother.

"What are you doing?" Rhett demanded, blocking the way as she attempted to squirm past him.

"My mother's brooch," she said as she pushed through and ducked back into the bedroom. Rhett followed her closely, hovering as she pried up a loose floorboard near the wall. The board slid free, and, from the space beneath, she removed the small wooden box in which she kept her most valued treasures. She opened it hastily, wanting to ensure the brooch was accounted for, before clasping the box shut and shoving it in her pocket.

Rhett coughed, ducking low to avoid the smoke spilling into the room. "Let's go," he insisted, grabbing her by the wrist and tugging her toward the doorway.

She glanced at the room one last time as the rest of her meager possessions were left to the unforgiving flames.

They rushed back to the staircase only to find it completely aflame. Waves of heat crashed into them, the fire raging from walls and ceilings. Rhett swore and pulled her in the opposite direction. Sam stumbled at the abrupt turn and tripped directly into Rhett.

They both toppled to the ground, limbs tangled. A long groan sounded from the floor beneath them. They locked eyes only moments before it collapsed, sending them plummeting down amid flaming debris.

SIX

Dazedly, Sam heard her name and opened her eyes to see Rhett kneeling above her, caked in grime. Blood trickled from his hairline, catching at his brow. She realized he was shaking her shoulders.

"Sam! Samantha, can you hear me?"

"Yes," she managed as the ringing in her ears slowly dissipated. She moved to sit up but yelped at a sudden pain through her upper body.

"Rhett," she gasped. "My arm. I don't think I can move."

Rhett stiffened. Sam followed his gaze to the large wooden beam resting atop her right arm, pinning her down.

Rhett threw his shoulder against the beam, grunting as he strained to lift it. Sweat shone on his brow from heat and exertion. Sam tried to help, pushing with her free hand and a surge of adrenaline, but the thick wooden beam barely moved. She cried out as the full weight of it settled back onto her.

"I can't move it, Sam. I've got to get help," Rhett said quietly.

Tears streamed from Sam's eyes, leaving wet trails down her dirty cheeks as she nodded her understanding.

"Then take this." She reached into her pocket with her good arm and fumbled with the small wooden box, accidentally dumping the contents. Coins splayed across the ground. With a shaking hand, Sam grabbed the brooch and held it out for Rhett.

"Sam—"

"Please take it. And..." Sam eyed the flames that were already too close. "If I don't make it, keep it safe. It's my most prized possession."

Rhett's reassuring smile faltered. He reached out to cradle Sam's face in both of his hands. "Samantha Atherton, you listen to me. Everything will be fine. I'll grab Billy and come right back, I promise."

He pressed a kiss to Sam's sweaty forehead and took the brooch from her outstretched hand. Pocketing it, he picked his way through the smoldering rubble.

"I love you..." Sam whispered.

It was the first time she'd said those words aloud. Her heart pounded, but if Rhett had heard her, he didn't acknowledge it before sprinting away.

Sam watched until he disappeared from view, then leaned the back of her head against the ground, squeezing her stinging eyes shut. The thought of never seeing him again made her nauseous. Or maybe that was the throbbing in her arm.

Her fingers brushed the scattered coins and closed around the largest of them. She knew if she held it up, she would see a lily stamped into its silver surface. Sam clenched her teeth as a flare of anger—or was it regret?—rushed through her.

Perhaps she deserved it—this consequence she was now enduring. She'd been a fool to tangle with the Lily Company.

Though Sam tried to remain calm, every creak and crackle spiked her panic. Each time she shifted, she whimpered at the pain.

Where was Rhett? Sam wondered how long it had been. A few minutes? Surely there were others just outside. The entire block must have known of the fire by now.

Smoke filled the air, dense and suffocating. Sam placed her good arm over her mouth, breathing through her sleeve. The heat licked at her skin as the flames closed in on her.

The panic grew overwhelming. She yanked her right arm, which was now numb, but couldn't free it. With all the breath she could muster, she screamed for help. Her yelling turned to coughing as she breathed in tendrils of smoke.

This is it, she thought. *I am going to die.* But she had so much more to live for than her measly sixteen years!

As if she'd willed them into existence, muffled voices sounded from not far off. Hope sent a burst of energy through her weakening body, and she called out with everything she had.

The voices became clearer. She heard her own name and then Rhett's.

"Here!" she cried. "I'm here, please help!"

Billy and Perry rushed to her aid. Rhett was nowhere to be seen. They both held their shirts to their mouths and noses, attempting to filter out the smoke. Sam stowed the lily coin she'd held as they reached her.

The two boys hefted the beam, muscles straining. Sam felt the pressure lessen on her body and wasted no time wrenching herself free. The pain worsened, throbbing now that her blood flowed freely again. Sam felt herself getting dizzy.

"Let's get you out of here, Sam." Billy pulled her up from the ground, slinging her good arm over his shoulder. Perry was there an instant later, holding gingerly to her other side.

"Where's Rhett?" Perry asked. He nearly had to yell just to be heard.

"Out," Sam coughed, all she could manage. Hadn't Rhett sent them?

The three of them trudged out of the ruined building, soot-covered, coughing, and drenched with sweat. As they broke free from the rubble, Sam gobbled up the fresh, crisp air. Her lungs burned, and her body ached, but Billy refused to stop moving. Sam swung her head wildly as she searched the streets for any sign of Rhett. People from neighboring houses and shops brought water buckets and shouted for help, rushing up and down the street.

"Rhett," she croaked, throat stinging from the smoke.

"You said he got out, right? We'll find him once I know you're all right," Billy responded with more seriousness than Sam had ever heard from him before.

Sam glanced back at what remained of her home and came to a halt.

There, spanning the entirety of the brick wall, someone had used the ash to paint a lily.

"Do you think it's broken?" Sam asked through gritted teeth.

Billy had dragged her to a small nearby alley where he made her sit before peeling off what remained of her sleeve.

Billy's brows furrowed as he examined Sam's right forearm. It was swollen, scraped, and covered in ugly red blisters. It burned as if it was still on fire.

"We'll need to set the bone before wrapping it, I reckon… but it won't be pretty with those burns," Billy replied.

Sam swallowed hard. "Do what you have to."

"I'll get something for the burns," Perry mumbled, already backing squeamishly away.

"Grab a light, too," Billy added as he tugged his shirt over his head. He began tearing it into strips.

Perry returned a short while later with a lantern, a water bucket, and a bowl of dark paste. Sam didn't know where he'd gotten it all, but she was grateful for his resourcefulness. He set the lantern nearby and brought the bucket close, then slowly poured the contents over Sam's arm, his face wan in the lantern's glow.

Sam hissed as the water made contact, but the burning immediately lessened, and she sighed as she watched the water dribble over her skin. It didn't look like her skin. The shadows enhanced the ugly bumps. She had no doubt it would scar.

Crouching next to her, Billy said, "This is gonna hurt."

"Have you ever set a bone before?" Sam asked nervously.

"Nope."

Sam's insides squirmed, but she nodded and lifted her face to the sky, wishing for just one star to focus her attention on.

Then came the agony. With each twist of the bandage, each knot drawn tight, the scream that clawed its way out of Sam's throat was drowned out by the roar in her ears. Sweat mingled with tears, painting her face in a mask of grime and desperation.

Finally, her arm was wrapped tight and immobilized in a sling. Sam leaned back against the wall. Her body ached, and her mind was a whirlwind of exhaustion and relief.

Looking at the boys beside her, she felt suddenly overwhelmed with gratitude. "Thank you for helping me." Tears stung her eyes, and she reached up to clasp each of their hands in turn. "I would have died if you hadn't come along."

"Naw," Perry said shyly. "Nothin' can kill our Sam."

Billy clapped Perry on the back and grinned his goofy smile. "You got that right, Pare. Hear, hear!"

These boys always knew how to make the best of any situation. "Now I can call you both my heroes," she teased.

Billy puffed up his chest, and Perry ducked his head, blushing.

But there was still one hero missing.

"We need to look for Rhett," Sam said.

With help, she stood and hobbled out of the alley. No matter who they asked, everyone shook their heads at Rhett's description, and the knot of worry in Sam's stomach grew tighter. Then a young boy came barreling right at Billy, shouting his name.

"Billy, they've got someone!" he spluttered breathlessly. "I was out there doin' my civic duty, you know? Dousin' the fire. And then I saw them draggin' a boy down an alley. I came straight for help!"

"Who's got someone?" Billy asked.

"Them ruffians who's always kidnappin' kids and takin' them away. The lilies. One of 'em was even wearin' a cloak with big ol' lilies all over it."

Sam looked at Billy, wide-eyed. "It's Rhett. They have Rhett."

"We don't know that. What would they want Rhett for?"

There was no time to explain it all. Clenching her fist, she fought through the fatigue setting in. "We've got to go, *now*."

She took a step forward, but Billy grabbed her shoulder, holding her back.

"*You* aren't going anywhere," he said, eyeballing her crudely wrapped arm.

"Yes, I am! I know where they're taking him." Sam tugged her shoulder free. "You can't stop me."

She didn't check to see if they followed before racing down the street, headed for the docks. Her breaths came in ragged gasps as she ran, but desperation fueled her speed.

As she neared the docks, the salty tang of the sea filled the air, pungent and nauseating. Her pulse quickened as she broke free of the alleys.

She passed ship after ship. With each step, her bones chilled from more than just the cold, like a premonition.

Her heart sank as she came upon the spot the Slaver's ship had occupied. As she stepped onto the empty dock, her feet crunched on broken glass, and she realized it was shards from the bottle she'd hit the lieutenant with.

But the water beside her held no ship.

"Where is it?" she said aloud, her voice tinged with rising hysteria. "It's supposed to be here!"

"What's supposed to be here, Sam?" Billy asked, panting heavily as he and Perry finally caught up.

"The Slaver's ship. It was here just hours ago." Sam sucked in large breaths, willing herself to remain calm even as the world felt like it was caving in.

"The what?"

"The Slaver! He was here. Right *here*."

"We're lookin' for... a Slaver?" Perry asked, face clouded with confusion. "I thought Rhett was taken by the Lily Co."

"That's what they do with the children they kidnap, Perry. They sell them."

Perry shrank back. Billy placed a comforting hand on his small shoulder. "That's not gonna happen, all right Pare?" He shot a look at Sam. "And how do you know that?"

"I know it because I was here only hours ago!" Sam wrapped her good arm around herself as guilt gnawed at her. "If it wasn't for Rhett, I'd have been sold too."

"That's how Rhett got hurt," Billy said, piecing it together. "You could have told me," he added softly.

Sam barely heard it. Turning her back to the boys, she scanned the dark water for any sign of Rhett or the Slaver's ship. Maybe the ship was still here, and it had simply been moved.

Billy caught her around the arm as she brushed past. "What else aren't you telling me?"

Sam's breathing hitched as she swept her gaze over the boys. Billy's black hair hung limply, just brushing his jawline. She could see the way his bony shoulders jutted from his threadbare clothes. His usually goofy grin was absent. Perry stood at his side, looking so small. He had so much life ahead of him.

She couldn't jeopardize that. Yet she knew they deserved the truth as much as Rhett did.

Trembling, she pulled out the silver coin that had miraculously ended up back in her pocket and placed it in Billy's hand. His eyes widened at the lily.

"Where did you get this?" he asked.

Sam explained that she had overheard the Lily Co.'s plans and escaped, only to fall prey to the lieutenant and the Slaver.

"The Lily Co. is responsible for the fire," she said, recalling the lily painted on the haberdashery wall. Angry tears burned in her eyes. "Now they have Rhett, and it's all because of me. If I hadn't—if I had been more careful..." Her words died on her tongue.

Billy met her gaze, his expression fierce. "I'm not sayin' you made all the right decisions, but let's get one thing straight—the Lily Co. kidnapping Rhett ain't your fault. If it wasn't Rhett, it would've been some other kid."

"That doesn't change the fact that they have him now," Sam said, swiping at her nose. "We need to keep looking."

"Maybe someone else saw him," Perry offered.

Sam nodded. "Go see what you can find out. Billy, you should go with him."

"You sure?" Billy said, hesitating.

"Yes. We'll meet back here."

As the two boys scurried away, Sam headed the opposite direction, following the curve of the harbor. She searched until her weary legs dropped her on the dock. Moving to the edge, she sat, letting her legs dangle. The water lapped softly against the wooden piers, the sound mocking in its tranquility.

She toyed with the lily-stamped coin, turning it over in her hands. It was a painful reminder of her bad decisions, yet she couldn't bring herself to let it go. The endless "what ifs" tore at her very being.

What if she hadn't gone to that meeting.

What if she hadn't gone to the market with Rhett.

What if she hadn't gone back for her mother's brooch.

"Was it worth it?" she whispered. Those precious seconds she'd wasted going back for it. Now Rhett and the brooch were both missing.

The coin in her hands glinted, catching the moonlight, and a thought occurred to her. This wasn't just a coin. When she'd gone to the meeting, the man had asked to see a *token*. And if Sam had the token, she could infiltrate the Lily Co. She could find the Slaver.

Shooting to her feet, she clutched the coin tightly, a new hope bubbling in her chest.

SEVEN

Muddy cobblestones gleamed under the greasy glow of lamplight, each flickering flame a reminder of that horrid night Rhett had been taken away. Rain fell in icy needles, soaking through Sam's clothes. But the chill that gnawed at her bones couldn't compare to the raw feeling always inside.

"Sam."

Billy appeared in front of her, blocking her path. His threadbare coat was thoroughly soaked. He had to be freezing.

"What are you doing here?" Sam grumbled, shouldering past him. Her splinted arm protested the movement, her skin burning as it rubbed against the bandage. It would be weeks yet before she could use it properly again, but she didn't have that kind of time to waste.

Billy turned, keeping pace with her. He shoved his hands into his pockets as they walked. "I just don't want to see you get hurt. You've been goin' like this for almost two weeks now, searching for Rhett. Your eyes are sunken, you ain't eating much, and your arm ain't even healed." He eyed the sling over her shoulder. "You need rest or you're gonna collapse and never get back up."

Some days Sam felt like doing just that. She whirled to face him. "Help me, then, because I'm not going to stop until I find Rhett."

Billy was quiet for a moment. "All right," he said, sounding defeated. "What's the lead this time?"

Her search for Rhett had led her through the labyrinthine streets, past overflowing ale houses and thieves shrouded in shadows. She'd bartered her few remaining coins for bits of information, each rumor a flicker of hope that had eventually led her here.

Motioning for Billy to stay put, Sam ducked beneath a dripping awning. The stench of rotting vegetables assaulted her nose. A broad wooden door lay before her.

She clutched a scrap of soaked parchment, the ink barely legible. It hinted at a Lily Co. rendezvous in the easternmost part of the city, where the alleyways shadowed the darkest crimes and the cobblestones held the echoes of screams. Sam rarely ventured here and Billy shouldn't have followed. No one in their right mind ventured here. Her gut screamed at her to turn back, but she lifted her fist and pounded on the sturdy wooden door.

It swung inward, revealing a dimly lit interior and the silhouette of a scraggly man.

"Looking for something, love?" His voice rasped like nails scraping against stone.

Though her insides squirmed, Sam held up the lily-stamped token.

"The Slaver," she said, her voice surprisingly steady. "Where can I find him?"

The man let out a guttural laugh, sending echoes dancing in the alleys. "Put the token away, love. No need to shove it in my face. Now, why would such a pretty little thing be looking for a man like that?"

Sam's heart drummed against her ribs. "That business is my own. "

The man's eyes glinted with amusement. "The Slaver's a difficult man to find."

"But you know where he is."

A cruel smile formed on the man's face. "Come inside and we can... discuss his whereabouts. For a price, of course."

"How much?"

"I wasn't speaking of coin, love." His smile showed his teeth now.

Nausea rolled in Sam's stomach, but she wouldn't be taken advantage of by this man. She could take care of herself—but it was still comforting to know that Billy was only a shout away.

"Then we have no deal." Sam turned away.

"All right, all right. Ten silvers."

Sam's eyes narrowed as she faced the still-grinning man. "One silver."

It was all she had left.

The man stared at her, considering. They were at a standstill, but Sam called his bluff. As she began to turn away once more, he said, "Agreed."

He motioned Sam closer, holding out his hand expectantly. Sam reached in her pocket, feeling the cold surface of her last silver coin. Her hand shook only slightly as she placed the silver in the man's palm. If this information was not legitimate or did not bring her to the Slaver—to Rhett—her efforts would die here.

"The Slaver comes to town once every fortnight," the man said. "He's due back at the docks the day after tomorrow. Ship blends right in with the rest of 'em. Search carefully, or you might miss him altogether."

"Sam! It's here," Perry exclaimed, thrusting aside the curtain. The fabric pulled away from where Billy had pinned it up as a makeshift doorway to their temporary home. The crates they'd squeezed between could hardly be called a home. They had no furniture, no mattress, just a few ragged blankets. Sam sat up swiftly, the hard ground pressing against her joints as she did so. Though she'd been attempting to sleep, there was no sleep in her now.

"The Slaver?" she asked.

"Can't be sure, but I think so. Got in just now, lanterns all doused and whatnot. Fits the description you told me."

"Stay here, Per," she instructed, then nudged Billy awake. "Time to go."

With a soft groan, Billy pushed himself up but didn't complain.

Nervousness mixed with anticipation as she and Billy exited the shelter and headed toward the docks. They'd discussed a plan, but now that it was time to act, Sam's nerves jolted in a thousand directions.

She'd been to the docks dozens of times in the last two weeks, always hoping, always coming up empty.

Tonight would be different.

Shivering, Sam clutched her cloak tighter around herself. It did little to fend off the cold.

As they approached the docks, fog rolled in like a tide of tattered shrouds, obscuring the hulking silhouettes of ships moored along the docks. Jagged masts clawed at the inky sky. A single lantern bobbed in front of them, casting an eerie orange glow. Every whisper of the wind sent jolts of unease through Sam's chest.

They stuck to the shadows, their backs to the walls of the nearest buildings. Her fingers traced the dagger she'd placed in her dress pocket. The cold metal provided little comfort.

Finally, Sam spotted what she was looking for.

The ship *was* unremarkable, and though it was docked in a spot different from before, standing at the front of the pier was the same thick Haapari watchman.

With a nod, Billy split away and walked toward the watchman. Sam remained in the shadows. This was no different than a typical day's work in Market Square, Sam convinced herself, and yet her heart still raced.

The Haapari man's face was unreadable, though his body language suggested he was at ease. He stood with legs spread and weight unbalanced, like he'd been standing for some time, and he held his arms loosely crossed beneath a sheathed dagger across his chest.

Billy stopped directly in front of him. "I'm here to see the Slaver."

"For what business?" the man rumbled.

"Lily Co. business," Billy replied loudly, raising the lily-stamped token Sam had given him.

Sam cringed, shooting a glance in either direction. Billy had never been one to be subtle in any circumstance.

The Haapari man seemed unconvinced, and Billy shot a nervous glance back at where Sam was hidden. She wanted to scream at him when the Haapari man's gaze followed, turning suspicious.

"Let me see that token again," he said, his tone taking on a threatening note.

Sam frantically shook her head, clamping her mouth so she would stay silent. That token was the only leverage she had to get information about Rhett. If the man were to take it from Billy—

"You saw it already, mate. Gonna let me pass or no?"

"No."

Billy shrugged, then, quick as lightning, snatched the man's knife right out of its sheath and ran. With a roar, the Haapari man gave chase. They didn't run toward Sam, thank the Goddess of Good Fortune.

This was not the plan, but it would work.

She sprang from her hiding spot, racing for the pier. She didn't slow until she was halfway down it and safely crouched behind a barrel. The gangplank sat only a handful of paces away.

Sam's chest rose and fell as she caught her breath, and she peered through the fog, searching to see if the Haapari man had returned. She hoped Billy had led him far, far away.

All was clear; all was silent.

Sam eased the dagger from her pocket and cautiously climbed the gangplank onto the ship, her confidence building with each step. If there was one thing she was good at, it was sneaking.

She peered onto the deck and found it empty. Toward the rear, a faint orange light glowed from under a closed cabin door. Sam crept toward it. Reaching the wall, she flattened herself against the shadows, clutching the dagger tightly in her fist.

Find Rhett, strike quickly, she reminded herself.

She blew out a breath and cracked the door, waiting only a moment before slipping inside.

The door creaked loudly, and Sam's breath caught in her throat. The Slaver looked up from where he was reading in a stuffed armchair. For a split second, their gazes locked.

Then the Slaver lurched to his feet. "Well, well. A stowaway."

Ignoring his leer, Sam pulled off her hood and raised her dagger. "I know you remember me. Tell me where the boy is."

A cruel smile lit the Slaver's face. "A lot of boys come through here, crimson one."

Sam fought to remain calm. "This boy is different."

"How so?"

"He's mine."

Sam lunged at the Slaver, swinging the dagger in front of her. She wasn't sure what she was doing—successful thieving meant avoiding confrontation altogether. She swung again, her splinted arm tucked uselessly to her side. The Slaver cackled as he swatted her away like a fly.

A moment later, Sam froze mid-swing, knife still high as she stared into the black barrel of a pistol. She hadn't even seen him pull out the gun.

"I like you," the Slaver said. "So full of spirit. Perhaps I'll keep you for myself."

For a split second, all Sam could hear was the roaring in her ears, and then her body moved on its own. She slammed the wrist of her broken arm up into the gun, the pain nearly incapacitating. An ear-splitting bang rang out as the Slaver pulled the trigger. The bullet whizzed past Sam's head, lodging into the wood-paneled wall.

Sam slashed with her other hand, catching the Slaver across the arm. He dropped the gun, and Sam kicked it away, but instead of going for the gun, the Slaver lunged to wrap a spindly hand around Sam's neck. With his other hand, he caught her around the wrist, squeezing until she let the blade drop to the ground.

"No more games," he ground out as he backed Sam against the wall.

Sam couldn't breathe. The Slaver's fingers dug into her throat, merciless and tight. She pried at the hand that refused to budge.

Icy tendrils of fear slithered down her spine.

But somewhere within the panicked fog, a spark ignited. Not desperation—primal, cold fury. This wasn't the end. Not for Rhett. Not for her.

Sam stopped prying at the hand around her neck, instead grasping at the wall around her. Her hand closed on something cold and hard, and, with the last of her energy, she swung. The item collided with the Slaver's head. His grip fell away as he collapsed to the floor, and Sam doubled over as she sucked in gulping breaths.

She dropped the item, which appeared to be an iron statue of some god or goddess, and stepped shakily over the Slaver's crumpled form. Using the cord from one of the curtains, Sam managed to sit the Slaver upright and tie him to the base of the chair. Satisfied with her work, she picked up her knife and rummaged about the cabin, scanning shelves and opening drawers, not completely sure what she was looking for.

A shelf full of log books caught her eye. She pulled a stack of books down and plopped them on the desk, several spilling to the floor. Opening the first book, she flipped through the pages. It took her a moment to realize the book didn't list typical goods—the "goods" were *people*.

She scanned each page, but the entries were dated years ago. She opened another log book, then another. Finally, she found one with dates from the current year. She frantically flipped to the end of the entries.

There! Dated two weeks ago, the second-to-last entry read:

12 Oct., P.C., Male, 17, Surname: Avery

This was her confirmation—Rhett had been sold.

Sam's fingers were numb as she ran them across the entry that represented Rhett. She was one step closer to finding him, yet still so, so far away.

She picked up the book and then used it to slap the Slaver across his face. He woke with a jolt. His features pinched as his focus landed on Sam.

Holding up the log book, Sam crouched in front of him. "Tell me about this book. *Now*. Where were they sent?"

The corner of the Slaver's mouth tilted upward in a smirk, his lips pressed shut as he savored what little power he held over her. Sam pressed her knife against his neck. Each word was accentuated through her clenched teeth as she repeated, "Where were they sent?"

His eyes met hers, but they were not filled with fear as she expected. They were filled with... laughter.

Sam yelled in frustration but lowered her knife, unable to bring herself to kill or even maim the man. She turned back to the log book, searching for something—*anything* that would lead her to Rhett.

"You're never going to find him," the Slaver taunted.

She'd had enough of this man. Sam breathed through her nose, fighting to remain calm as she tucked the log book under her arm and exited the cabin. Still tied to his chair, the Slaver cackled.

Sam stalked down the gangplank. Noticing the thick ropes that kept the Slaver's boat moored, she undid them and then gave the boat her best shove. She wasn't strong or large enough to have moved the boat, but she liked to think the Sea Goddess was on her side as the vessel slowly began to drift.

She shouldn't have lingered—the guard could show back up at any minute. Still, she watched the ship until the gangplank tumbled into the water with a satisfying splash. Then, clutching the log book tightly, Sam walked away. The Slaver's words still rang in her ears.

You're never going to find him.

It only made her resolve stronger.

Her voice, when it came, was a ragged whisper. "I'm coming, Rhett. Even if I have to search through every continent of the world."

EIGHT

Sam breathed in the salty sea air. She'd spent almost every spare moment of the last week at the harbor. When she'd first started visiting the docks, she'd worried about running into the lieutenant, but the local fishermen said the Naval ships had set out for another port. She'd also checked the entirety of the harbor for the Slaver's ship and, thank the Goddess of Good Fortune, it was nowhere to be seen.

Sighing, Sam gazed across the bay, folding her arms loosely. The blue water churned faintly brown with dirt and other things Sam didn't want to think about. The pungent smell of fish hung heavy in the air.

Men and women bustled through daily work while greedy seagulls circled above in hopes of an easy meal. Even though she knew it unlikely, she found herself always watching for Rhett's familiar face, his reassuring smile...

He was never there.

Perry currently guarded the log book she'd stolen from the Slaver. She'd shown it to him and Billy—after Billy dodged the Haapari man and returned with a proud grin, brandishing the man's shiny dagger—and she'd also told them her decision. That she intended to leave Milderre for good.

Sam's fingers slid along her bandaged arm. Though it was healing well, the scar would be a permanent reminder of Rhett and the events that had upended her life.

After a week of silently observing sailors, sea boys, and the ships themselves, tonight was the night she would finally make it happen. She would take her search to the seas.

With no coin for passage, she'd chosen a ship to stow away on—the *Queen Mary*, a merchant vessel that traveled from port to port, nation to nation. Wherever Rhett was, this ship could get her there.

A booming voice dragged her from her musing.

"Out of the way!" the man barked, nearly barreling into her with a large crate in his arms.

She'd drifted too close to the *Queen Mary*—this man was its first mate. He stalked past with a slight limp, then paused to sweep his gaze up and down Sam's petit body. "You lost, wee lass?"

Sam dropped her eyes to the ground, her hands quickly becoming sweaty under his scrutinizing stare. The last thing she needed was to draw attention to herself.

"No, sir, not lost," Sam answered, glancing his way but avoiding eye contact. She resisted the urge to touch the shawl over her hair.

Deep wrinkles lined the man's tanned, leathery face, concentrated around his forehead and eyes. She guessed he was in his mid-forties, his black hair speckled gray around his temples. He wore a dark green vest over a white, puffy-sleeved linen shirt. Tan breeches, white stockings, and a black pair of well-crafted leather shoes completed his expensive look.

He scrutinized her a moment longer, and part of the uncanniness of his stare came from his mismatched eyes, one a piercing dark brown and the other a glazed milky white. "This ain't the place for youngins like yerself. Git now, lassie," he said, nodding toward town.

Sam did as she was told but only scurried off far enough to get him to resume his business. She still wanted to study the ship.

A tall, commanding woman wearing a scandalous pair of fitted men's trousers stopped the first mate for a conversation. The woman's deep golden-brown skin contrasted her striking white hair, tied half-up in hundreds of braids. The woman turned, giving Sam a better view of her face and icy blue eyes.

Recognition dawned on her. This was the woman she'd seen weeks ago in Market Square! The one with the enchanting voice.

Sam nearly tripped over her feet as she scrambled to get a closer look. She ducked behind a crate, catching the last words of the woman's sentence. "...still haven't found what I've been looking for, Bixby."

Her thick accent made her *t* sound more like a *d*. It reaffirmed to Sam that the woman truly was from Haapa.

Sam peeked over the crate, flicking her eyes to the first mate. Bixby.

Bixby sighed. "Princess—"

Sam's mouth dropped open. This woman was a princess?

Rolling her eyes, the woman cut him off. "I've told you a thousand times to stop calling me that."

"And you'll have to tell me a thousand more. It's proper respect, it is," Bixby grumbled. "But, Princess, I've already spoken with the captain. We've dallied here too long—winter is nearly upon us."

The woman's nostrils flared. "I think I will speak to him myself," she said and stalked up the *Queen Mary*'s gangplank.

Bixby's gaze followed her, a half-frown appearing on his face.

Sam frowned too. She was counting on the *Queen Mary* setting sail first thing in the morning. The next merchant ship wasn't set to depart for at least another week.

After a silent debate, she blew out a long breath. She would sneak aboard tomorrow as planned.

"You're really leaving, then?" Billy asked, though it wasn't so much of a question as it was a statement. His dark eyes bored into Sam, pleading without words.

A cold, wet breeze blew in through the gaps around their makeshift door. Sam shivered. She accepted the Slaver's log book from Perry and tucked it under her arm with a quick word of thanks, then checked to make sure the bar of clove soap was securely in her pocket before replying, "You know I have to, Billy."

"I'm not always the voice of reason here, Sam, but you—you're only sixteen. These men, the Lily Company—they're trained mercenaries."

"Then come with me."

Billy took a half-step back, guilt crossing his features. "I can't."

Sam sighed. "And I can't stay. Rhett was the last piece of me that wasn't swallowed up in that fire. Without him, I have nothing left."

Hurt flashed across Billy's face, but Sam couldn't retract the harsh words.

"And you're going to travel across the entire ocean lookin' for him? Sam, you ain't never even been on a boat."

Embarrassment crept up Sam's cheeks. She didn't like this *reasonable* side of Billy. Where was the reckless abandon she was used to?

"It's better than hanging around here, acting like none of it ever happened," she sniped, then clamped her mouth shut. This wasn't his fault.

Silence filled the space.

"That day changed you," Billy finally said.

Sam didn't know why, but anger flared within her. "Changed me? It *destroyed* me!"

As she said the words, a sharp pain tore through her chest. It felt as if her heart was being ripped apart piece by piece.

This was not how their final conversation was supposed to go. She fisted Billy's shirt while trying to contain her overflowing emotions. She wanted to shove, to push, to do something violent. Instead, she dropped her head and cried.

"Oh, Sam." Billy quickly swept her into his arms. Perry was there an instant later, his hug wrapping both of them.

Sam clung to them and whispered, "Please forgive me for leaving."

"The things people do for love," Billy teased.

Between large sniffles, Sam chuckled. Eventually, she collected herself enough to peel away. Straightening and smoothing the skirt of her dress, she remembered the Lily Co. token. She removed it from her pocket. "I want you to have this. It won't do me any good out on the water, but perhaps it can get you two out of a pinch someday."

"What is it?" Perry asked.

Billy plucked it from her outstretched hand. "Dangerous is what it is. We'd prolly be better off if I tossed it in the river. Don't want to be messin' with that sort."

"Do with it what you will," Sam said, then proceeded to kiss both boys on the cheek. "I'll miss you both."

"I hope you find him," Perry said softly.

"Goodbye, Sam." Billy wrapped her up in one more suffocating embrace. "Tell Rhett he owes me a drink for all the trouble he's put me through."

With one last smile, Sam was off into the night.

She'd made it halfway down the alley when Billy called after her, "Get yourself a pair of trousers, my friend. I'm bettin' a dress ain't no good on a ship."

NINE

As Billy suggested, Sam pilfered a pair of trousers and a shirt from a clothesline on her way to the docks. She tugged them on, discarding her dress in an alley. Her plan was simple: sneak aboard the *Queen Mary* amid the hustle and bustle of morning. Although sunrise barely peeked over the horizon, already the docks were alive with movement. Fishermen returned with that morning's catch, sailors loaded their masters' wares, and townspeople chatted, eager to haggle for that day's goods.

Sam weaved through the throng, keeping her head down, her fiery red hair hidden beneath her cloak. As she neared the *Queen Mary*, she opened the Slaver's log book, pretending to inspect the lists even as she kept an eye out for trouble.

She heard Bixby's gruff barks and paused. There was a chance he'd recognize her if she got too close, and he was stationed near the gangplank.

It was too late to sneak aboard another way, so Sam waited, the log book becoming very fascinating until Bixby's back was turned. The moment it was, she snatched up a bolt of exotic fabric—holding it intentionally so it was between herself and Bixby—and, though her heart pounded in her ears, strolled aboard the *Queen Mary* as if she were always meant to be there.

She walked straight to the shadowy embrace of the cargo hold. Clambering down the stairs, she set the bolt atop another that had been placed prior. With a quick glance to ensure she was alone, she ducked between two stacks, wedging her way in until her back met the wood of the ship's hull. Then she sank to the ground, knees pulled in tight, and waited.

Sam licked her parched lips. Every squeak of timber and gurgle of sea-water was a drumbeat on her nerves.

Stacks of fabric lined the walls, barrels and ropes placed strategically to keep the cloth in place. Sam had nestled herself between them and hadn't moved in the entire day since. Her joints ached, her stomach rumbled, and she was certain she'd turned some sickly shade of green. The ship's unsteady sway had already caused her to lose the contents of her stomach. She'd mopped up the bile with—and surely ruined—some of the fine fabric that surrounded her.

Doubt warred with hope in her gut. She only had to stay hidden until they reached the next port, where she could slip away and search for Rhett. But how long would that take?

Sam swallowed, the action grating against her dry throat. She needed to find water. And food. Cautiously, she shifted to her knees and crawled forward. Peering around the side of a stack, she searched for the water barrels but froze when a pair of sleek black boots stepped directly in front of her. Sam's gaze followed the boots up long legs clad in tight black trousers, past the billowy white shirt, and then she was staring into a pair of ice-blue eyes.

Sam shot up, standing with her back against a stack of fabric. She swayed, throwing out her good arm to keep her balance.

"I thought I smelled something suspicious," the Haapari princess said in her heavily accented Ducrian. She eyed Sam up and down before flicking her eyes to the pile of soiled cloth. "What are you doing here?"

Sam didn't miss the subtle shift of the woman's hand toward her belt dagger. She considered drawing her own dagger but feared if she let go of the stack, she'd lose her balance entirely.

"I need passage," Sam breathed. "Just to the next port. Please."

"This is not a passenger ship."

"I know."

The princess was quiet for some time. Suddenly, she closed the gap between them and ripped the cloak from Sam's head, spilling her thick red locks across her shoulders.

"I knew it."

Sam instinctively raised a hand to her hair, the strands like silk against her fingers.

"Princess," Bixby called out, entering the hold. Though he favored one leg, it didn't appear to slow him down.

Upon seeing Sam, Bixby's brows furrowed. "What is this?"

Sam glanced between the princess and Bixby, preparing to spew a torrent of excuses, but wasn't given the chance to speak.

"She's the newest member of our crew," the princess said casually.

Sam barely masked her shock. Why would the princess vouch for her?

Whatever the reason, she wasn't going to squander the opportunity. Recovering quickly, she said, "I'm a good worker, sir—better than any other sea boy you'll come across. And when it comes to laundering, there isn't a stain I can't get out."

Begrudgingly, Bixby leaned against a crate, folding his broad arms across his chest as he scrutinized Sam. He lingered on her arm. "I'm expected to believe we intentionally brought on an invalid?"

"It's nearly healed," Sam said quickly.

The princess leaned over, whispering something in Bixby's ear.

The man sighed, fisting his hands on his hips. "What's your name, lass?"

"Sam, sir. Samantha Atherton."

"Atherton, eh? You're not afraid of the open sea, are ye?"

"No, sir."

"And heights?"

"Of course not!" She'd climbed the tallest buildings in Milderre just on the chance that she might be able to touch the sky.

"Aye, good thing, too. We've got a lot o' sails that need trimming. Follow me, lass." He stalked toward the stairs.

As he ascended them, Sam heard him grumble, "Captain's not going to like this."

After a brief introduction to Captain Marlowe and a subsequent argument between him, his first mate, and the Haapari princess, a contract was laid out before Sam. Much to her relief, she would *not* be thrown overboard. The caveat: she would have to officially join the crew.

Sam hesitated, the quill in her hand hovering just above the parchment. She'd read the contract. The term of service was two years.

If she served aboard the *Queen Mary*, would it help or harm her chances at finding Rhett?

Sam wouldn't have any control over her destinations or the duration of her stay in each port. But then again, she would be guaranteed passage to new ports and places and would even earn a little coin along the way.

She pressed the quill to the parchment and scribbled her name.

"Welcome to the crew, lass." Bixby clapped her firmly on the shoulder. "Best be gettin' some rest—I expect you to be up bright and early to make the mornin' meal for the rest of us."

"Aye, sir," Sam said and ducked out of the captain's quarters.

The princess was right behind her, catching her arm before she could slink away.

"I vouched for you back there, Atherton, because I have questions and an insatiable hunger for knowledge. Do not mistake it for compassion." The woman then thrust out her hand in introduction. "I'm Sefina. If you wish to keep your tongue, do not ever call me 'Princess.'"

Sam nodded and hesitantly put her hand into the woman's. Sefina's grip was strong, her hand marked by the hard calluses earned by long hours of work.

"Sam," she replied, even though Sefina knew her name.

"Come, I'll show you to an empty hammock." Sefina turned, her long white braids bouncing, but paused to add over her shoulder, "And then you can clean up that vile mess you left below."

TEN

Grinning ear-to-ear, Sam watched the *Queen Mary*'s large, cream-colored sails fill with wind. The skies were no longer a murky brown but had shifted to a stunning blue. The air was fresh and salty and chilly.

And then she leaned over the railing, her stomach ridding itself of its contents.

Five days at sea. She wondered if she would ever keep a meal down again. At least her arm was no longer in a sling.

Gripping the railing, Sam hung her head and looked at her white-knuckled fingers. Her skin was pale, her veins standing out starkly. She took several long breaths, spat one last time, and wiped her mouth.

"The sea still has its hold over you."

Sefina strode toward her. The sun glinted off the many metal clasps dangling in her braided hair, and Sam marveled again at the woman's beauty.

Sefina leaned casually back against the railing. "Perhaps you are not suited for life on the water."

"I can handle it," Sam stated firmly but paused. She *had* been struggling. "I just need some time to adjust."

"How much time, Atherton? We've been five days on the water now. And while you've been draped over the side of the ship, everyone else has been completing their own work in addition to your unfinished tasks. 'Better than any other sea boy,' you said. I have yet to see you accomplish anything that would even remotely compare to what a ship's boy could do."

Sam's face flushed at being so openly criticized. Her performance aboard the ship thus far had been lacking, but being as sick as she was, could they not be a little understanding?

Sefina paused briefly before continuing. "It is my reputation that is being tarnished at your incompetence. Get your sea legs before I toss you over myself."

Sam opened and closed her mouth like a fish out of water. Sefina was beautiful, full of attitude, and straightforward. Someone Sam aspired to be like. To have that person so boldly imply that she was worthless... She didn't know what to think of it.

Before Sam could come up with a response, Sefina left.

The words stung.

She still wasn't sure why Sefina had vouched for her. She'd said she had questions, but this was their longest interaction so far.

Face still hot, Sam looked up at the bright sky.

I am not incompetent.

With new resolve, she stepped away from the railing and returned belowdecks, where she aggressively peeled potatoes for their evening meal.

After serving the rest of the crew that evening, Sam scooped her own portion of the meal and plopped it onto her tin plate. The tables were full, so the extra men took seats on barrels or leaned against walls. Sefina's white hair stood out amidst heads of blonde and brown. When one of the men started pounding his table, the rest of them followed. They thumped in unison, getting louder until Sefina stood. She climbed atop the table while men hastily moved their plates out of the way. Then she sang.

> *"I'll tell you a tale of depths far below,*
> *Of creatures that glow like the stars.*

With beauty and music—songs that kill,
Of sirens that hunt for your souls.
Way, ho, on the briny blue,
Where the waves are high, the wind strong and true
Way, ho—"

As Sefina continued through another verse, Sam watched the spectacle longingly. Sefina was confident, bold...

Back in Milderre, Sam was that person. Look at her now.

Of the roughly thirty crew members, Sefina was the only other female aboard the *Queen Mary*. It was apparent she'd been sailing for some time, and no one called her "princess" save for Mr. Bixby. Sam wondered if she truly *was* a princess, and, if she was, what exactly a princess would be doing aboard a merchant ship.

Sailing better than you, Sam thought guiltily.

It was obvious Sam had never been on a ship before. No one was struggling the way she was. She felt their judgmental stares daily.

A wave of cheers erupted as the song finished. Sefina hopped down and settled back on the bench, returning to her meal along with everyone else.

Sam looked around once more, hopeful someone might invite her to sit with them. When no one so much as glanced in her direction, she bit her cheek and headed above deck to eat by herself. Sitting against the rail of the main deck, she picked at her meal of fish and boiled potatoes. Her stomach tightened at the thought of throwing it all back up again, so she set the plate aside, no longer hungry.

She looked up at the sky, blazing from a lowering sun, and thought of the smog back in Milderre. As bad as it had been, she missed some things buried in that smog—the thrill of stealing a purse, the challenge of bargaining with Mistress Nunley. She missed Billy and all his obnoxious jokes. Sweet Perry and the way he blushed anytime Billy spoke of girls.

But most of all, she missed Rhett, and he couldn't be found by looking back.

The clove soap Sam had intended to give him had found a permanent home in her pocket. Every so often, she would pull it out and inhale the familiar scent, hoping it would fill the void left in her heart.

It never did.

The excitement she'd felt at taking the next step in her journey to find Rhett had dissipated quickly. When she wasn't belowdecks prepping meals—which greatly contributed to her nausea—she was cleaning the chicken coops or mending stockings. Alone. Always alone.

She leaned back, closing her eyes.. For once, the slow rocking of the ship felt soothing.

She didn't know how much time she spent there, but when a sturdy hand landed on her shoulder, she opened her eyes to find Mr. Bixby standing above her. Sighing, she grabbed her uneaten plate of food and stood to leave. "I'll get right to washing the dishes, sir."

He held up a hand to stop her.

"Stand with me for a moment," he said, turning to rest both forearms on the rail. Sam eyed him uncertainly, then followed suit, looking out at the endless blue of the water. The sun hung low in the sky, the first rays of sunset turning the clouds a soft pink. It was beautiful.

"What's on your mind, Atherton?" Mr. Bixby asked, cocking his head to look at her with his good eye.

At that moment, a round of laughter rose up from the galley be-low—where everyone was gathered except *her*. She angled her head so Mr. Bixby couldn't see the emotions strewn across her face. "Nothing, sir. Just taking my evening meal."

"Alone again?"

He was more perceptive than she'd realized.

"I prefer the fresh air," she lied.

"Do ye, now?"

Sam looked anywhere but at the middle-aged man, her facade slowly falling apart. She dropped her head. "No. I don't."

Mr. Bixby waited for the truth.

"Life at sea is harder than I anticipated," she admitted. "I can't seem to shake the seasickness, and the crew despises me for it." She huffed a breath. "I didn't think I could be any lonelier than I was back in Milderre, but I just—I don't belong here..." Her shoulders slumped. Realizing just how tightly she'd been gripping the rail, she released it and flexed her fingers. She stared at her hand, watching it regain color as the blood slowly returned. "I don't belong anywhere," she muttered, more to herself than anything.

"Ah, sweet lass. Everyone belongs somewhere." Mr. Bixby hefted a large hand to pat her shoulder and then said with a twinkle in his eye, "Sometimes the challenge is simply finding where that somewhere is."

"Where that *someone* is," Sam mumbled.

Mr. Bixby pushed off the rail, straightening. Before leaving, he added, "Keep your chin up. I think you'll be surprised at how well you will adapt. I can tell you have a strong spirit."

Sam felt a spark of warmth deep within. Mr. Bixby believed in her—maybe she could believe in herself too.

But first she needed to keep down at least one meal for an entire day.

With perseverance, Sam's ability to keep food down improved rapidly. Nearly a week after her conversation with Mr. Bixby, she was finally able to find joy in her surroundings, and, more importantly to the crew, she was able to carry her weight on the ship. Sam finished her tasks in half the time it had taken when she first received them and had even learned to tie a variety of knots. She volunteered for tasks the others did not want, and, in response, the crew began to warm. Most evenings, she watched Sefina sing lullabies or merry jigs, but she sometimes slipped away to scour the words of the Slaver's log book.

Sam's nerves warred with excitement as the *Queen Mary* neared its first destination. The ship charted a course south, skirting west to avoid the infamous Eclorian Redpass, aimed to stop in Cervos, the main town on Eclor's only island. From there, they would continue along the Eclorian mainland, hugging the coast and docking at each major port along the way before reaching the southern nation of Phago.

Sam had never left Milderre before, let alone Ducria. And now she was about to set foot in an entirely new country.

They would stay two weeks in Cervos, and, while she was expected to assist with selling wares during the day, she would be given leave to do as she wished in the evenings. That would be her window to search for Rhett. But when she tried to begin early by asking Mr. Bixby what he knew of slaves, she received a stern look and a warning not to mess where she shouldn't. The few others she approached were equally tight-lipped.

With a handful of hours before they made port in Cervos, Sam settled herself against a barrel up on the deck, pulling her knees tight as she propped open the log book across them.

Flipping to the page where Rhett's name was inscribed, she gently traced her fingers over the ink.

"What is that you have been reading?"

Sam jumped. Sefina, who had appeared seemingly out of nowhere, cocked her head expectantly.

"Oh—this?" Sam bit her lip, considering. What harm could it do to tell the truth? "It's a log book. It has information on what I'm searching for."

"What are you searching for?"

After a split second of hesitation, Sam admitted, "A boy."

Sefina's features hardened. "That is why you came aboard our ship. Because you are chasing a *boy*? Foolish girl."

Indignation lit within Sam's chest, and she stood. Even raised to her full height, she still had to tilt her face upward to address the woman. "He was *sold*, Sefina. Taken from his home and shipped off by the owner of this log book the way you ship fabric." She clenched her fists. "I don't need to justify my actions. He may mean nothing to you, but he is *everything* to me, and you have no idea what I've gone through to get to this point—what I'm willing to go through still, so long as it takes me to him."

Sefina stilled, a flicker of surprise crossing her beautiful face. Sam swiped at the angry tears welling in her eyes. Her attention caught past Sefina, on the rise and swell of the waves. The endless expanse. And the world suddenly seemed so much larger.

When Sam spoke again, it was barely a whisper. "This book is the only clue I have."

Silence stretched between them for several minutes.

"It is still foolish," Sefina said softly, "but I would have done the same. May I see the book?"

Sam considered saying no but raised her hand anyway, depositing the book into Sefina's. Sefina took it almost reverently, opening to the first page. As she scanned through it, she said, "These are names. People."

"Yes. I took it from a man they call the Slaver. In Milderre, orphans disappear all the time, but people don't care. I believe the Slaver works with, or perhaps for, the... Lily Company." Sam whispered those last words. A part of her was afraid, even now, that they would find her simply by her speaking the name.

Sefina nodded, her brows drawing together. "I know of this 'Lily Company,' but I have not heard of the Slaver."

"I fear not many have."

"Your boy is listed in these logs?"

Moving to Sefina's side, Sam turned to the final entries. Pointing, she said, "His name is Rhett." Saying his name aloud made her stomach clench. "He's been gone nearly five weeks."

"You do not know where he is being taken?"

"No. I can make sense of everything but this one column. See these initials? 'P.C.'" Sam flipped to another page. "I originally thought they were the Slaver's initials, but then if you look at these entries, the initials are different. 'W.R.' here. 'S.F.' here."

Sefina pursed her lips as she studied the logs, flipping pages back and forth in comparison.

"I do not believe these are a person's initials," she said. "If I am not mistaken, these are ship names, the way the *Queen Mary* is abbreviated to 'Q.M.' in docking logs."

Sam shot to attention. "Ship names?"

Sefina gave a quick nod and then met Sam's wide-eyed stare. "So all we must do to find your Rhett is discover what ship 'P.C.' stands for."

ELEVEN

Sam barely waited for the gangplank to be lowered before she skittered onto the docks of Cervos. She marveled at the colorful houses painted ochre, sienna, and cobalt blue. Wrought-iron balconies jutted from them, adorned with red clay pots brimming with lush flowers. Laundry lines danced in the breeze. The scent of wood smoke mingled with the aromas of garlic and basil wafting from open windows, promising culinary delights.

But first—Rhett.

She'd not made it a dozen paces when she heard her name.

"Atherton!"

Sam froze. Slowly, she turned to meet Mr. Bixby's stern gaze as he shuffled down the gangplank, holding one end of a large crate.

"Get back on the ship and grab a load. Save your exploring for tomorrow," he said.

With a longing glance at the town, Sam returned to the ship. *Just one more day*, she told herself.

After setting up a tent in the town center, Sam and Sefina manned it, selling Haapari fabric while the rest of the crew tended to the ship or acquired new wares.

As soon as she was allowed to roam, Sam wandered back to the docks and inquired after a ship with the initials "P.C." In return, the dockmaster gave her a spiel in Eclorian. The only thing she understood was when he shooed her away.

Slinking back to the *Queen Mary*'s textile tent, she began asking nearly every patron about the mystery ship initials instead. When people began avoiding their tent, Sefina insisted Sam sit back for a while.

"We are supposed to be bringing in business," Sefina said, "not driving it away."

"Shall I take off my headscarf?" Sam asked sarcastically. *That* would bring attention to their booth. As had been the case in Milderre, not a single person had hair the color of Sam's. But was it so bad to have red hair? To draw attention to herself? She wasn't a thief here.

"No better sales technique than drawing in the attention of the people." Sefina tilted her head. "The color of your hair intrigues me as well. I am curious what you know about it."

Sam hesitated. She'd grown used to the comments, the lingering stares, but she had never considered why it was this color. It was just... hers.

"Very little," Sam admitted. "My mother had dark hair, and I know nothing of my father. Nobody else ever looked like me."

Sefina hummed thoughtfully. "It is rare. More than rare—remarkable."

She pulled out the small instrument she kept in a leather case on her belt—a kalimba, she called it, made of wood with small metal prongs that she plucked with her thumbs—and started weaving a tale through song.

> *"A great land of might, disappears into night,*
> *This tale of the old land Astoenia.*
> *A kingdom of power, knowledge, and sway,*
> *Now in ruins, forgotten, its people all slain..."*

Sam's brow furrowed. The name rang a distant bell, but only as something heard in passing. "Astoenia?" she echoed.

Sefina nodded. "A nation lost to time. Two hundred years ago, it was a kingdom of great power. Mortals and children of the gods resided side by side." She paused, plucking another few notes. "Then, one night, it was gone. Destroyed. Some believe it was a natural disaster—a great flood or a fire that swept across the land. Others think the gods struck them down, afraid they had become too powerful."

Sam leaned in slightly, intrigued despite herself. "And what does that have to do with me?"

"The people of Astoenia were known for one thing above all else." Sefina reached out, gently lifting a strand of Sam's hair from beneath the scarf. "Hair red as an ember."

A chill ran down Sam's spine, though she wasn't sure why. "But that was centuries ago. If they were wiped out, then—"

"Then there shouldn't be any left," Sefina finished for her. She studied Sam for a moment longer before releasing the strand of hair and sitting back.

Sam frowned, staring down at her hands. A people wiped from the world. And yet... here she was. A strange weight settled in her chest. She had never put much thought into her hair beyond the occasional frustration of it tangling in the wind, but now... now she wondered.

"If that's true—if I *am* connected to them somehow—why has no one ever mentioned Astoenia when they see my hair?"

Sefina stowed her instrument. "Because history is shaped by those who survive it. And those who write it."

Sam swallowed, feeling unsettled. "Well," she said, "I suppose drawing extra attention is the best chance I have at getting answers about Rhett."

"You are not going to find your answers with the common people. You must know where to look."

"And I suppose you know where that is?"

Sefina shrugged and turned away to adjust the layers of fabric around the tent. Slumping onto the edge of a crate, Sam blew out a long breath, knowing Sefina was probably right.

As business began to flow again, Sam let Sefina take the lead, watching with awe. The Haapari woman had mastered the art of haggling, speaking in the people's native language. Sam wondered how many other languages Sefina spoke.

Well, Sefina could haggle, but Sam could do something much more exhilarating. As Sefina conversed with a patron, Sam took the opportunity to slip behind them. A sly grin played on her lips as her fingers darted, deftly navigating the layers of fabric the patron wore, relieving them of their purse.

Sefina's eyes widened ever so slightly as she flicked them between Sam and the customer, but they hadn't noticed. Sam knew they wouldn't.

In full view of Sefina, she made a show of examining the purse and its contents—coins—and then, as easily as she had removed it, she slid the purse back into place.

As soon as the patron left the tent, Sefina rounded on Sam. "What do you think you are doing?"

"I put it back."

"You put our business in jeopardy!"

"I could pick every pocket in this market and not a single person would know," Sam shot back.

Sefina still glowered.

Folding her arms, Sam said, "You don't believe me?"

"I believe that we have goods to sell."

"Oh, come on, Sefina. Try me. Any person. We can make it a challenge."

If there was one thing Sam knew, it was that Sefina wasn't just curious but competitive.

Sefina crossed her arms, mirroring Sam's challenging position. Sam could see the battle raging within the Haapari woman. Eventually, she asked, "What are the terms?"

Sam held back her smile. "Three patrons. Your choice. I'll do what I do best and—"

"You will return whatever you find without their notice," Sefina finished.

"If I succeed, you help me find Rhett."

Sefina held her gaze, considering, before giving a curt nod. "I must admit that I am curious about your abilities. But know this, Atherton: Bixby will flay us both if you fail."

"Good thing I won't fail, then," Sam said with a grin.

"Convince me with your actions," Sefina said.

Several hours later, Sam greeted a scraggly looking local who had come to the tent for what had to have been the tenth time that day. The man again gawked at the beautiful Haapari woman who was trying not to engage with him. He approached Sefina anyway, asking something in Eclorian.

With the way he practically drooled, Sam almost wondered if he was going to propose.

While Sefina showed him a bolt of bright yellow cloth, she looked over her shoulder at Sam and mouthed, "This one."

Sam smirked. Consumed as his attention was, this would be all too easy. Sam glided forward, and as her nimble fingers brushed against the man's pocket, she felt a brief sense of normalcy in her otherwise upside-down world.

She plunged her hand into his pocket, wrapping her fist around something soft. It felt almost like... feathers?

Removing her hand, item in tow, Sam's eyes bulged at the palm-sized bird blinking up at her.

With a shiver, the bird fluffed its feathers and then spread its wings. Sam clamped her other hand over the little bird before it could make its escape.

This was *not* what she'd expected. Coins, a purse—even a fruit? Sure. But an actual, living *bird?*

Sefina tried and failed to stifle a laugh, keeping the man's attention as Sam stuffed the bird back into his loose pocket, praying it wouldn't suffocate in the fabric. Only moments later, the man patted the pocket softly, and Sam could hear faint chirping from within.

"G'day, sir." Sam waved to the man as he left.

As soon as she looked at Sefina, they both burst out laughing.

Eyes bright with amusement, Sefina said, "After that, I don't need any more proof. You win this one, Atherton."

After they finished selling at the tent for the day, Sefina handed Sam a handful of copper coins. Sam's first real earnings. Her insides swelled. Rhett would be proud she was finally making an honest living.

As they walked to the inn, Sefina bought two fresh sweet rolls slathered in honey and red fruit jelly. She gave one to Sam, who gobbled hers up greedily. Along their way, Sam paused at a booth to purchase a new pair of trousers.

The inn was cozy. Warm lantern light spilled across the main room, illuminating a dozen long tables across the middle. After they seated themselves at one of the communal tables, Sam watched, mouth watering, as Sefina finally took a bite of her own roll. Sam regretted eating hers so quickly.

"Stop drooling—you had your own," Sefina said, a smirk forming on her lips.

Sam shifted guiltily and cleared her throat. "So you're from Haapa, right? What brought you to the *Queen Mary*?"

Between bites, Sefina answered, "It is my father's ship."

"Your *father's* ship?"

"Yes. He used to have many, but the *Queen Mary* is one of his last."

"What happened?"

"Some were lost to storms, others to pirates. Merchants used to seek out our island, desperate to trade for Haapari fabrics, and my father realized his opportunity. He began exporting it directly from Haapa.

"While my father is content to remain at home, I have always wished to increase my knowledge, to explore. Eventually, I realized that my small island was not enough to satiate my hunger for the unknown. I wanted to see the world. To be known not as a princess but as a person. Bixby came and went from my island for many years, bringing stories of distant lands. One day, I decided to join him."

"So you really are a princess?" Sam asked timidly.

Sefina chuckled. "My father is the chief of Haapa."

Shivers worked themselves down Sam's spine. She was traveling with *royalty*.

"Now tell me about this 'Rhett,'" Sefina said, the topic of princess no longer up for discussion.

"We met on the streets years ago." Sam exhaled, the memory as vivid as if it had happened yesterday. "I was in Market Square, trying to work up the courage to steal an apple." A wry smile tugged at her lips. "I kept hesitating, running through all the ways I might do it—slip it in my pocket, grab it and run—but, before I could decide, this boy darted right in front of me and did it first.

"He was fast, but the vendor was after him in an instant, shouting and calling for the guards. I don't know why, but I followed—after swiping an apple myself, of course. Figured no one was watching after all the commotion. Eventually, I trailed him to an alley where I found him crouched behind a crate."

Sam grinned as she remembered the look he'd given her. The look of someone who'd absolutely been caught red-handed. "I told him he was too close to the square, that the guards would catch him if he stayed. He almost bolted again, but I pulled out my own apple and told him I'd taken one too." Her voice grew soft. "That's when I got a real look at him—his clothes hanging off his frame, his face sharp from hunger. But his eyes..." She hesitated, searching for the words. "There was this *fire* in them. Like no matter how rough things got, he wasn't going to quit."

Sam paused, then smiled again. "I liked him immediately. Told him my name. He said his was Rhett. And we were off.

"We were near inseparable after that. We learned to navigate the streets together." Sam chuckled. "He was a terrible thief—there was this one time he somehow managed to collapse an entire tent on himself. We didn't eat that night, but I'll always remember the look on his face as he popped out from beneath the tent."

She sobered. "He hated being a thief. Hated that I was one too. Not long after that, he got a job at the workhouse." She paused, toying with a gouge in the wooden table. "They treated him like rubbish, and he stayed anyway. Rhett is the hardest working person you'll ever meet. Charismatic and sweet and loyal to a fault. He always saw the best in people—even me."

Sefina hummed, the sound low and comforting. "Sounds like a rare treasure."

"He was—is." Sam's voice dipped. "That's why I have to find him."

"He is lucky to have one as devoted as you."

Sam spotted Mr. Bixby as he entered the inn, flanked by several of the *Queen Mary*'s crew. He plopped down beside Sam.

"There ye are, Atherton," Mr. Bixby said.

A moment of panic shot through her—had she done something wrong?

"You've done well this week."

Sam released the breath she'd been holding. "Thank you, sir."

"Aye. And I think it's time you be recognized as one of the crew." He pulled out a small piece of folded cloth. Handing it to Sam, he then called for several mugs of ale.

Sam unfolded the cloth. Laying within was a simple gold hoop. She stared at it, grateful but confused.

"To the newest member of the *Queen Mary*!" Mr. Bixby hollered, raising his mug. "May her skills be sharp, her spirit strong, and her presence bring us good fortune!"

The room filled with a round of "ayes."

Sam smiled wide, lifting her own mug.

The inn remained festive throughout the evening. Mr. Bixby led them all in a very out-of-tune jig, after which Sefina favored them with tales of the gods. Sam indulged in more ale than she'd ever had in her life, and though the desire to find Rhett still pressed at her, in this moment, she was happy.

It was well into the night before she returned to her room with Sefina. Sam gently pulled the gold hoop from her pocket and set it on the desk. It was a generous gift, probably worth a lot, but it was too small to fit on any of her fingers. She frowned over it.

"Sefina, did you see my gift from Mr. Bixby?"

"The earring?"

So that's what it was. Sam bit her cheek. "I've never worn an earring before."

Sefina raised her head from where she had been lying across the bed. "No?" Sam shook her head, and Sefina sat up to rummage through her drawer. "Come, I'll put it in for you."

It wasn't until Sefina stood over her, holding a sewing needle, that Sam began to second guess what she was about to do.

TWELVE

S am gritted her teeth as she climbed the rope ladder to the topmost point of the ship. Her muscles strained with each step upward. Her hands were tender where they grasped the rough ropes, and she knew it would be some time before she would build up calluses like the rest of the crew, but she could not be content staying on the decks below.

The *Queen Mary* was moments from departing Cervos, and Sefina had not returned.

Hauling herself into the crow's nest, Sam gripped the rail, her eyes scanning the bustling docks below. She squinted against the sunlight, searching for the familiar flash of Sefina's white braids among the throngs of people.

Bixby shouted from the deck below, demanding the gangplank remain down. Captain Marlowe stood near him, arms crossed, his face tight with tension. They would lose the tide soon.

Sam's stomach churned. After hearing about Rhett, Sefina had honored her word to aid in the search, and Sam had found comfort in her strength and confidence. They'd convinced the dockmaster to allow them to scour his records. When that proved fruitless, Sam sought out other ways to gather information. She hunted through taverns, interrogated sailors, and even questioned several locals. Few spoke her language, and of those who did, none seemed to have noticed anything out of the ordinary.

The futility of it all weighed heavily on her, and she rubbed tiredly at her eyes. It was all so disheartening, but sharing the burden with a friend had helped. If she lost Sefina too…

She did a double take as she caught a flash of white moving swiftly through the crowd. Her heart leapt as she spotted Sefina striding with purpose toward the *Queen Mary*.

"Sefina's been spotted, sir!" Sam called down to Mr. Bixby, pointing in the direction Sefina was coming from.

"Princess," Mr. Bixby said sternly as Sefina stepped aboard. Almost as soon as her feet met the deck, the gangplank was lifted.

"I know," Sefina replied calmly. "I had business to take care of."

"Take care of it sooner next time," Mr. Bixby grumbled.

The corner of Sefina's mouth twitched upward as she gave a short nod. Satisfied, Bixby turned and began shouting orders. To their credit, the crew had been waiting, and, within minutes, the *Queen Mary* lurched away from the dock, its sails unfurling as they headed for the open sea.

Later that day, as the ship rocked gently on the waves, Sam found herself alone with Sefina, a pile of mending between them.

"Captain Marlowe nearly left without you this morning," Sam remarked, trying to keep her voice light but unable to hide the lingering worry. She speared her needle through a stocking, pulling the thread taut.

Sefina shook her head. "He would sooner have stayed in port another day than left without me. Would you have been sorely disappointed if I was left behind?"

Sam thought she could almost sense a smile in that question. "Only because I like your stories."

And the goddess-like voice that comes along with them.

Sefina laughed, and even that was musical. "Do you not wish to know what kept me?"

Of course Sam did. "I didn't want to pry…"

"I have news of your Rhett. That is, of the ship he may be aboard."

The stocking slipped from Sam's hands as her heart skipped a beat, her breath catching in her throat. "And?"

"The *Port Clipper* docked in Cervos three weeks ago."

P.C.—*Port Clipper*. Could it truly be the ship she was searching for? Doubt quickly followed. She shook her head, her brows furrowing. "Sefina, we looked at the dockmaster's logs. There was no *Port Clipper*. No ship at all with the initials P.C."

Sefina's expression darkened, her lips pressing into a thin line. "A ship like this would not have appeared in the dockmaster's records."

"So you looked somewhere else," Sam surmised. Hope bubbled within her. "What news do you have of it?"

"The *Port Clipper* departed from Cervos only a day before we arrived. It was last seen heading south, toward Phago. From what I gathered, it left rather urgently."

Sam's stomach dropped. She had been so close, without knowing, and now Rhett could be halfway across the world. It felt as if she would never catch up. Her hands trembled as she clutched the edge of the railing for support.

"What do we do now?" she asked hoarsely.

Sefina's steady gaze found Sam's. "Phago is our next destination," she said. "Let us hope they've docked for a time and that we hold the favor of the winds."

The next ten days were near torture. The tips of Eclor's west coast mountains were visible as the *Queen Mary* sailed south to Phago, teasing Sam with the illusion of progress. The salt air, once invigorating, now seemed to choke her; the usual calming sway of the ship only aggravated her impatience. Every creak of the wooden beams and every snap of the sails made her stomach churn—not from seasickness but from the growing uncertainty that had taken root inside her.

Rhett was close. He had to be. The thought was a mantra she repeated to herself every night as she lay in her hammock, staring at the dark expanse above. She could picture him, shackled and bruised but alive. He was strong. He could endure. He would survive until she reached him.

Still, doubt gnawed. What if she was too late? What if the *Port Clipper* had passed Phago and sailed to a different land? What if, despite everything, Rhett was already beyond her reach?

She couldn't afford to think that way.

Mr. Bixby kept her busy with ship duties. Sam went through the motions—mopping decks, checking riggings, keeping the sails tight—but her thoughts remained on Rhett.

By the time they reached the bustling harbor of Phago's capital, Atral, Sam had become a coiled spring, every muscle tense with urgency. The *Queen Mary* docked under the midday sun, met by the scent of grilled meats and exotic spices carried by the wind. Merchants and sailors called out from the docks, eager to barter with the new arrivals.

The port was loud, chaotic, alive with energy, but Sam had no time for any of it. The moment the gangplank lowered, she was off the ship, her feet barely touching the wood as she made her way through the crowds with Sefina on her heels. They weaved through the bustling dock of Atral, passing seaside stalls with fresh fish and jewel-toned fruits while the occasional voice yelled out a deal or greeting. Sam ignored it all. She had one destination in mind: the nearest tavern. A place where the dockhands, sailors, and mercenaries gathered after a long voyage—a place where she might find answers.

Sefina kept pace beside her, her presence a silent support.

The tavern she found was a low, squat building, its wooden door slightly ajar, allowing the sounds of laughter, clinking mugs, and off-key sea shanties to spill out into the street. After stepping inside, the dim lighting and sharp smell of ale hit her senses. Sailors, locals, and merchants all jostled for space at the bar or crowded around tables with tankards in hand.

Sam scanned the room quickly, her attention catching on a tanned woman speaking loudly in a language she actually understood. Ducrian. Sam rushed up to the table, Sefina close behind her, and wasted no time addressing the woman.

"Excuse me, ma'am."

The woman took a swig of ale, then looked up, her eyes narrowing slightly as she examined Sam. "Ducrian, eh?"

"I'm looking for a ship. The *Port Clipper*—have you heard of it?"

The woman leaned back in her chair, pondering a moment before turning her head toward the bar. "Oi, Loren," she called out, her voice booming. "The *Port Clipper*. Was that the one what them naval Duc's tried to commandeer a few weeks ago?"

Sam's heart leapt into her throat, her breath catching as she waited for the man's response.

A man behind the bar, Loren, paused in his task of wiping down a mug. His face lit up with recognition. "*Sí*, the slave ship!" he exclaimed, voice thickly accented. "*Escandaloso*. Can you believe the slave trade was operating right out of our own port? Ah, but no longer. You did not hear of this?"

Sam shook her head.

Loren continued animatedly. "The Ducrian Royal Navy chased them all the way here! The slavers fought to the very end. Took the entire ship with them—" He paused and made an arc with his hand. "Sunk right to the bottom."

THIRTEEN

Sam's world seemed to tilt. The excitement she had felt moments before soured in her stomach. She swallowed hard, trying to keep her voice steady as she asked the question she feared most. "And what of the slaves aboard?"

Loren shrugged, completely oblivious to the storm raging inside of her.

"Went down with the ship, I reckon," the Ducrian woman answered.

"Were there any survivors?" Sam rasped. "Anyone who made it out alive?"

"Sure, a bunch of Ducrian soldiers, but those slaves never stood a chance. I heard the slavers bolted the grates, locking everyone below." The woman shook her head. She raised her mug to her lips and said, "Poor souls, may they find solace with the Sea Goddess," before taking another swig.

The words hung in the air, pressing down on Sam's chest like the weight of the ocean itself. For a moment, she couldn't breathe, couldn't think.

No survivors.

Her mind rejected the reality before her, clinging desperately to the hope that had carried her here. Rhett couldn't simply be *gone*—not after everything. Not after she had come this far.

Before she realized what she was doing, her voice tore through the tavern, raw with anguish. "No!"

The room fell silent, all eyes turning to her, but she didn't care.

Rhett wasn't gone. After all Sam had endured, after all she had fought for—he couldn't be gone. The gods wouldn't be so cruel.

"Thank you," Sefina said, addressing Loren and the woman with a small nod, then turned to Sam. "Come."

The words felt distant to Sam, muffled as though spoken through water. The world had become a blur—shadows of movement, muted voices, everything distant and disconnected. The numbness that swept over her was complete. It was as though her body forgot how to function; even breathing seemed like an impossible task.

A gentle hand at her back guided her out of the tavern and onto the bustling street. The noise of the town, so full of life and energy, washed over her, but she couldn't process it. Sefina walked quietly beside her, saying nothing, offering only the silent comfort of her presence. Sam was grateful for the silence, grateful that she didn't have to explain the crushing weight of sorrow that threatened to swallow her whole.

The din of the harbor faded with each step as they left the noisy town behind, the landscape opening up into a copse of trees that lined the cliffside. The world here was quieter. The only sounds were the rustle of the wind through the trees and the distant crash of waves against the jagged rocks far below. Sam's legs gave way beneath her, and she fell to her knees, her fingers curling into the dirt.

"I need some time alone," Sam managed, her voice barely more than a whisper. The dam holding back the torrent of emotions had cracked but not fully broken. She needed space to let it fall apart.

Sefina hesitated for only a moment before retreating. "I'll be close by."

Her footsteps faded as she left Sam to the sanctuary of the cliff.

Sam stared out over the cliff's edge, where the endless expanse of ocean stretched to meet the horizon. The water's surface churned restlessly beneath the biting wind. The scent of salt and seaweed filled her nostrils, along with the softer scent of rosemary bushes that clung to the rocky ground. The wind whipped around her, tugging at her hair and clothes, pulling her into its fury. She let it. It felt right somehow, as if nature itself mimicked the storm raging within her heart.

And then the wall burst, a lifetime of emotions crashing over her in relentless waves. Denial, grief, anger, despair—each more overwhelming than the last. It was as though her heart had shattered, leaving only sharp fragments of pain in her chest.

Rhett was gone.

Her vision blurred with tears, her chest tight and heaving with sobs that she barely had the strength to suppress.

No. Rhett couldn't be gone. How could someone who meant so much, someone who had been a part of her for so long, just vanish? It was impossible. It was unbearable. It was cruel.

Sam lifted her face to the sky, the wind chilling her tear-streaked cheeks, her hair whipping violently around her. The grief swelled inside until she could hold it in no longer.

She screamed.

It was a raw, primal sound that tore from her throat, echoing across the cliffs and out over the ocean. The sound reverberated through her body, leaving her trembling, breathless, her chest heaving.

And still, the sea rolled on below her, indifferent to her suffering. It did not care about her pain, her loss. It simply existed, vast and impassive, just as it always had.

But Sam felt changed. Irrevocably. Something inside her had broken, something that could never be fixed again.

The remaining days in Atral passed in a blur. Sam stared at the mass of land that grew smaller and smaller as the ship once again headed out to sea. Around her, the crew went about their daily tasks as if the world hadn't been totally and completely shattered.

Rhett was gone. The ship that had carried him, and all her hopes, now lay at the bottom of the sea.

She could feel the fury building inside her, grief feeding it like kindling on a fire until her blood boiled. She couldn't sit here, idle and powerless, while the Lily Company continued to thrive. They had taken everything from her, and she couldn't—*wouldn't*—let them go unpunished. The Ducrian Royal Navy was no better. Surely they could have freed the innocents aboard.

Sam stormed across the deck, her fists clenched at her sides. She reached the rowboat that hung suspended from the side of the ship and began fiddling with the ropes. The Lily Co. was out there, somewhere, and she was going to find them. She had no plan, no clear idea of what she would do when she found them, but she didn't care. She just needed to act, to do something, *anything*, to dull the pain threatening to consume her.

"Atherton," Sefina's voice cut through her haze of fury, but Sam ignored her.

She would go back to Milderre, get the lily token from Billy, then find the Lily Co.'s next gathering. They were a slippery bunch, always on the move, but if there was any chance of finding them, she had to take it.

"Atherton, stop!" Sefina's hand caught her arm. The woman's eyes were hard, her features tinged with concern. "What are you doing?"

"I'm going after the Lily Company. They're the reason Rhett is dead, and I'm going to make them pay."

Sefina's expression darkened. "You're not thinking straight. Going after them alone is reckless—you'll get yourself killed."

"I don't care!" Sam shouted, her voice raw. In her peripherals, she could see several of the crew members staring uncomfortably, and she fought the urge to bare her teeth at them. "Rhett's gone, and the people responsible are still out there."

Sefina's grip tightened. "Revenge isn't going to bring him back. It's not going to change what happened."

Sam wrenched her arm free and returned her attention to the ropes holding the small boat. "What's left for me now, anyway? I won't stand by, and if I have to take them down alone, so be it."

"You think you're going to sail back to Ducria in a skiff and then what? Kill a few men? The Lily Co. is not some small band of criminals you can take down in a single night. They have infiltrated an entire city—entire country, perhaps. I may not have known your Rhett, but I do know he wouldn't want you to throw your life away."

Sam froze, her heart twisting painfully. She squeezed her eyes shut, trying to block out the image of Rhett's face—the way he used to smile at her, the warmth in his eyes.

He was gone. Nothing could bring him back. But revenge—revenge was something she could still have.

"I can't just do nothing," Sam whispered, her voice cracking. "I can't let them win."

"Then don't. But we are not in Ducria now. There is no Lily Co. here. What you are trying to do is reckless."

Sam *wanted* to be reckless, but Sefina was right. If she wanted to hurt the Lily Co.—truly hurt them—this was not the way. Letting the rope fall slack, she took a step away from the skiff.

"I'm going to bed," she said, turning on her heel and stalking away.

She wasn't sure yet how she would make it happen, but she knew one thing for certain: The Lily Co. would feel her wrath.

Sam's fingers tightened on the edge of her worn hammock, the fabric twisting beneath her grip. On her lap lay the Slaver's log book, the scrawling text within now imprinted on her mind, the remaining initials a puzzle to be solved.

W.R., S.F., O.P.

Just as *P.C.* had stood for *Port Clipper*, Sam was sure these initials represented vessels that ferried captives like Rhett to their fates. Already, a fortnight had passed. She had used that time to craft a plan. It was too late for Rhett, but Sam was determined to save as many others from that same awful fate as she could.

She wasn't sure where the Slaver's vessels were now, but the *Queen Mary* was back in Eclorian territory and would be docking in the capital city within the hour. Cataros was a bustling port—someone there would know.

"Furl the mainsail!" came the call from above.

They were entering the harbor.

Sam stood abruptly and stuffed the log book into her hammock. The weight of the knife she'd stowed at her hip reminded her that she wasn't powerless. Throwing on her cloak, she climbed the steps up to the deck. The sky glowed dusky orange, the sun nearly set, and the lights of the large city came to life before her eyes.

Sneaking off the *Queen Mary* unseen was surprisingly easy. In the bustle of docking preparations, Sam slipped quickly down the gang-plank and melded into the crowd.

Sam's pulse raced as she weaved among the crowded streets, her hood pulled low to obscure her face and hair. She searched for the nearest portside tavern. Coming upon one quickly, she pushed open the heavy wooden door, assaulted by the reek of stale ale and pipe smoke. It re-minded her immediately of the Bronze Barrel. Dim light flickered from hanging lanterns, casting a glow over rough-looking men and women seated around weathered tables, some playing cards, others drinking deeply.

Seating herself in the farthest, darkest corner, Sam scanned the room. She spotted the taverner minutes later, a stocky man with deep frown lines, emerging from a back room with a handful of mugs, which he deposited on tables as he moved through the room. His expression was as worn as the floor beneath his boots.

Sam leaned forward in her chair, her heartbeat pounding as she waited for the taverner to approach. He weaved through the tables, drawing nearer with each step. When he finally drew close, Sam caught his attention with a subtle wave.

"Cosa nala voi?" he barked in Eclorian, his scowl deepening as he looked her up and down.

Sam bit the inside of her cheek, cursing inwardly. Her plan hadn't accounted for the language barrier.

"I—" she started, her words slipping clumsily from her tongue. "Do you speak Ducrian?"

The taverner's brows furrowed, and he grunted. "Many people speak Ducrian," he muttered, his accent thick. "Cataros is trade town. I am man of business." His tone made it clear he wasn't interested in whatever Sam had to say. "I bring you ale."

He turned to leave.

"Wait!" Sam raised her hand to halt him, her pulse quickening with urgency.

He turned back, his scowl etched even deeper.

Sam leaned in, lowering her voice. "I'm looking for information about a ship. Well, several ships—that carry a very specific set of... goods."

The taverner raised a skeptical brow. "Goods?"

She glanced around the room. No one seemed to be paying her much attention, but she couldn't be sure. She leaned even closer, her voice barely a whisper now. "Children," she breathed. "Slaves."

The man's reaction was immediate. His face went pale and his scowl vanished, replaced by something darker. Fear.

"Out," he hissed, his eyes darting to the other patrons as though someone might overhear. "Sar usicar."

Sam blinked, caught off guard. "Wait—"

"I said *out*!" His voice rose a little louder, drawing the attention of the nearest patrons. He took a menacing step toward her, waving his arm toward the door. "Shop your business elsewhere. Non vindo. I no want trouble."

The entire tavern seemed to still for a moment as all eyes turned toward Sam. A wave of heat flooded her skin, and she stood quickly, pulling her cloak tighter as she hurried toward the exit.

As soon as she stepped outside, the cool night air hit her like a slap. What had she expected? That a tavern in Cataros would openly deal in information about something so dangerous?

She was about to slip away into the shadows when a voice stopped her.

"You're either very brave or very stupid." The words came in perfect Ducrian.

Sam's head snapped toward the speaker, her heart jumping into her throat. A short, wiry man leaned casually against the wall just outside the tavern. His dark, messy hair fell over sharp eyes. Despite his relaxed stance, something about him—perhaps the sly tilt of his smile—set Sam's nerves on edge.

Her fingers instinctively brushed the hilt of her dagger beneath her cloak. "What do you want?"

The man held up his hands in mock surrender, though the predatory gleam in his eyes never wavered. "Easy now. I overheard you inside. You're asking the wrong sort of folk for that kind of information."

Sam's eyes narrowed. "And you know who the right ones are?"

The man's smirk widened, his sharp eyes glinting with mischief. "At your service," he said, inclining his head. "But nothing comes for free, especially not in Cataros."

"What's your price?" she asked, keeping her voice steady despite her coiling tension.

For a moment, his expression became serious, calculating. He stepped away from the wall and came closer. "Coin, naturally. But that's not all." He tilted his head, studying her. "A favor. Something tells me you're the sort who gets into interesting trouble. Perhaps with an interesting talent to accompany it."

Sam stiffened. "I don't make blind deals."

His grin returned, but there was a sharp edge to it. "No? But you're willing to chase rumors in open taverns without a second thought?" He let the words hang. "I can tell you what you want to know. What's that worth to you?"

Sam crossed her arms. Her instincts screamed at her to be careful, to turn around and return to the safety of the *Queen Mary*, but Rhett's name echoed in her mind, and her anger at the Lily Co. urged her onward. She needed answers, and this man, shady as he was, seemed like her only option.

"How do I know the information is good?" she asked, eyes narrowing.

The man chuckled, shaking his head. "If you're as desperate as I think you are, I doubt you care. You want information, and I'm the only one offering."

Sam hated that he was right. She bit her lip, weighing her options. Deal with this man or abandon her search.

Finally, she reached into her cloak, pulling out a few silver coins. She held them up between her fingers. "This is my offer. Nothing more."

The man glanced at the coins, then back at her, amusement flickering in his gaze. "And my favor?"

"No favor."

He gave her a small pout but plucked the coins from her hand, tucking them away before leaning in. "It just so happens you're in luck. Shipment arrived early this morning. Quiet little cove on the east end of the harbor, just beyond the shipyard." His lips curled into something far too pleased. "They're being held there until the next tide."

Sam's stomach soured. *Shipment*, he'd called it. These were lives.

Her grip on her dagger tightened beneath her cloak. She exhaled slowly, forcing her expression to remain neutral. "And the ship?"

He tapped his temple. "That'll cost you more."

Sam's jaw clenched, but she forced herself to nod. She needed every bit of information she could get. Reaching into her cloak, her fingers brushed against the small pile of silver and copper coins. With a steadying breath, she pulled out another silver and held it up.

The man grinned, taking the coin with an infuriating slowness, as if savoring the moment. "Pleasure doing business," he murmured before slipping it into his pocket. "Ship's called the *Ocean's Pride*. Look for a figurehead of a weeping siren."

Sam froze. *Ocean's Pride*. O.P.

Her chest tightened with a mix of exhilaration and dread. This was it. A real lead.

She turned sharply, ready to leave, but before she could take a step, the man's hand clamped around her arm.

"Careful now," he said, voice low. "Few who go aboard ever come off again. And trust me, you don't want to be caught among the likes of them."

Sam jerked her arm out of his grasp, leveling him with a glare. "Noted," she said, forcing steel into her voice. Then, without another word, she hurried into the night.

Sam rushed for the *Queen Mary*, eager to tell Sefina and Mr. Bixby of the *Ocean's Pride*. By the time she reached it, her breaths came fast, her pulse hammering with adrenaline. She barely had time to register the familiar creak of the wood as her boots hit the deck before—

"Where in the depths have ye been?"

Mr. Bixby stormed toward her, his face red. Sefina followed just behind him, her expression unreadable.

"I—"

"You've been gone for hours!" Bixby cut her off, voice rising. "You're part of a crew, lass. That means pulling your weight, not vanishing into the city without a word. You think Cataros is a place for a leisurely stroll? You could've gotten yourself killed—or worse!"

Sam flinched at his tone. She'd never seen Mr. Bixby be truly angry with her. Guilt twisted her stomach, and her fingers tightened at her sides.

"I'm sorry," she said quickly. "I didn't mean to worry you."

Bixby exhaled sharply, shaking his head. "Meant to or not, ye did." His tone was gruff, but beneath it, there was something else—concern. A kind of fatherly worry that made Sam's stomach twist even tighter.

She dropped her gaze for half a second before forcing herself to straighten. "I found something," she said, locking eyes with Sefina. "A name. *Ocean's Pride.*"

Sefina's brows furrowed. "One from the logbook?"

Sam nodded, trying to shift focus away from the weight in her chest. "It's here. Docked in the east cove." She looked between Sefina and Mr. Bixby, hoping they would understand. "We have to get aboard."

"No." Sefina's response was immediate. Firm.

Sam's stomach dropped. "Sefina, this is it. A real lead. If we can just—"

"You have no idea what you are walking into," Sefina interrupted. "Do you know who runs that ship? How heavily it is guarded?"

Sam clenched her fists. "I can handle it."

Mr. Bixby scoffed. "Real convincing, lass. After sneaking off like a reckless child."

Sam knew Mr. Bixby only scolded her like this because he cared. She swallowed hard, trying to push down the guilt, trying to make him understand. "Please. I couldn't free Rhett, but what if I can free the others?"

Stepping forward, Sefina shook her head. "We don't have a plan. We don't have the numbers. You are not going aboard that ship."

Sam's jaw tightened. She heard the warning, but she couldn't bring herself to accept it. Not when she was this close.

If they wouldn't help, then she was on her own.

"Fine," she said sharply. "I'd best get back to my duties—don't want to be accused of not 'pulling my weight.'"

She stalked off, but she wasn't going to attend to her duties, and she wasn't going to sit by and wait. She would get onto that ship—one way or another.

FOURTEEN

The east cove reeked of salt and rot, the tide rolling in sluggish waves against the docks. Lanterns flickered in the misty air, their glow barely cutting the murky dark. It was quieter here—the kind of quiet that made the hairs on the back of Sam's neck stand on end.

She crouched behind a stack of crates, her pulse thrumming in her ears as she scanned the handful of ships. Then she saw it—carved onto one ship's bow was a woman with two flowing fish tails where legs should have been. Her hair swept up and away as if floating in water, and her hands covered her face. A weeping siren. The *Ocean's Pride.*

There was no time for second-guessing. Sticking to the shadows, she crept forward, her boots silent against the damp wood. The flickering lanterns cast just enough light to see a handful of crewmen milling about near the gangplank.

She needed another way in.

Her gaze drifted to the mooring ropes. They stretched, thick and sturdy, from the dock to the ship's hull. A reckless idea formed in her mind.

As soon as the moment presented itself, she raced forward, only slowing when the ship's mooring ropes were within her grasp. Gripping the rough fibers, she climbed, muscles burning as she pulled herself upward. The ship swayed slightly, and the ropes dipped, Sam along with them. She bit her lip to keep from gasping. After what felt like an eternity, she reached the gunwale and swung one leg over, slipping onto the deck.

Her breath came fast as she pressed herself into the shadows of the quarterdeck. Voices carried across the deck—then, movement. A group of sailors stumbled past her and down the gangplank, laughing as they headed into the city. How easy it seemed for them, drinking and joking while knowing what sort of cargo they carried.

Sam waited until they were gone before scanning the deck again. She hadn't anticipated the half dozen men who still lingered. She forced herself to breathe slowly, then crept toward the nearest hatch.

The steps leading down creaked under her weight, and she winced. Her skin prickled as she descended, the air becoming thick with sweat and something fecal.

Her stomach twisted.

At the bottom, she pressed herself against the wall, listening. Voices drifted from further in, low murmurs, but no heavy footsteps.

It was now or never.

She slipped forward, heart hammering.

And then she saw them.

Rows of iron bars. Boys and girls—some her age, some even younger—crammed too tightly together. Eyes, hollow and exhausted, staring at nothing. The dim lantern light showed bruised skin and too-thin limbs.

Rage and helplessness crashed into her at once.

She clenched her fists. She wouldn't leave them here.

With a glance over her shoulder to ensure no one was coming down the stairs, Sam dropped to one knee, fumbling with the pin she always kept on her person. Her fingers trembled, slick with sweat, as she jammed it into the lock.

She sent a prayer to Perixia, asking the goddess for her blessing of good luck. Then came a sharp click as the lock sprang free.

"Go," she whispered urgently, shoving the door open.

The figures inside hesitated for only a heartbeat before pushing past her, their eyes wide, their movements uncertain. Their nervous murmurs and stifled sobs tore at her heart, but she forced herself to move on to the next cell.

Another click. Another door thrown open. More young captives spilling into the narrow corridor, their bodies pressed close, their hushed whispers rising.

Click.

The final door swung open, and hope surged in her chest—

"What in Eflos is goin' on?" The words echoed loudly through the dim hold.

Sam whirled, her stomach plummeting. A crewman stood at the base of the stairs, lantern raised high. His eyes darted between the open cells and the cluster of freed captives, understanding dawning on his features.

"Run!" Sam shouted.

The captives surged toward the stairwell, shoving past the crewman. He barely had time to curse before he was swallowed by the rush of bodies.

Sam bolted after them, her ears ringing.

Up on deck, it was chaos.

The ship's bell clanged in alarm as crewmen appeared from every direction, shouting, swarming. They converged on the group, rough hands grabbing the runaways. One of the girls shrieked as a sailor caught her by the wrist. A boy tried to dodge, only to be thrown hard against the mast.

Sam's heart sank. There were too many men. She couldn't fight them. She couldn't save the others.

She tore away from the crowd, desperate for an escape.

The mooring rope—her way out. She sprinted toward it even as tears streaked down her face.

She glanced behind. No one had followed her. In the next move, she swung her legs over the railing, her boots scraping against the hull as she lowered herself to grip the thick rope, starting her descent.

Above, the gunfire started.

No.

Her heart slammed against her ribs.

Some of them must have gotten away. Some of them must've—

Her fingers slipped.

A sharp gasp ripped from her as she fell.

The last thing she saw was the curve of the hull above before cold, black water swallowed her whole. The ocean crushed the air from her lungs, salt filling her mouth and nose. Her limbs flailed in every direction, pressing against the heavy blanket of water surrounding her, yet making no progress. Her lungs started to burn. She was fully aware—of her life, of how quickly it could be taken away, of how fragile it all was.

Though she kicked harder, the surface loomed farther and farther above, until her limbs slowed. Her vision darkened as her body was pulled down.

I'm sorry, Rhett.

Sam awoke to the scrape of wooden planks beneath her cheek. She sucked in a heaving breath—then choked, coughing up seawater that burned her throat as she rolled onto her side. Above her, a shadow moved.

"Sefina," Sam rasped, her voice raw.

"Quiet." Sefina's voice came in a sharp whisper. Moonlight slanted across her, catching the water still dripping from her long white braids. She was crouched low, every muscle tense, her gaze darting toward the distant docks. Sam could hear it now—the faint shouts, the clang of metal, the lingering chaos she had left behind.

Sam tried to push herself up, arms trembling with effort. "The others—"

"Their fate is in their own hands now."

The words sent a fresh wave of guilt crashing over Sam. Her jaw clenched. Had any of them made it? Or had she just led them to their deaths? She wanted to ask, but Sefina was already pulling her to her feet.

"We need to move."

Sam's boots left wet footprints in her wake, her clothes clinging to her skin as Sefina half dragged her away from the cove. Only when they reached the main docks did the Haapari woman slow her pace. Sam bent forward, resting her hands on her knees as she tried to catch her breath.

Sefina spoke, her tone sharp. "What were you thinking?"

A flush of shame rose in Sam's chest, but she pushed it down. "I had to try. For Rhett."

Sefina grabbed her by the shoulders. The intensity in her eyes made Sam's breath catch.

"This isn't about Rhett anymore," Sefina whispered fiercely. "This is about *you*. You are on a path that's going to destroy you."

The words hit like a slap.

A lump formed in her throat as she looked away. "I just wanted to save them."

"There's a difference between fighting for something and getting yourself killed for *nothing*."

Sam clenched her jaw, her hands balling into fists. She refused to meet Sefina's gaze, afraid of what she might see there—pity, disappointment, truth.

But Sefina wasn't finished. "And what of the Lily Company?" she pressed. "You still think you can take them down?"

Sam's nails dug into her palms. "I can try."

"You'll fail," Sefina snapped. "And then what? More bodies? More names to haunt you?"

Sam sucked in a sharp breath. The sounds of gunfire and screams echoed freshly in her mind. She hadn't known any of their names. And she had failed them all.

Sefina seized her arm and marched her back to the *Queen Mary*. As they stepped onto the deck, Sam's gaze lifted—and landed on Mr. Bixby.

Her heart sank. He stood waiting, arms crossed, his face unreadable at first. But then she saw it. His look wasn't just anger or disappointment. It was deeper than that. A quiet sort of hurt. She had risked everything, thrown herself into danger without a second thought, and for what?

Sefina delivered her to the sleeping quarters. After releasing her arm, she said, "Learn to swim, Atherton. You live on the water now, and if you do not tame it, it will swallow you."

"Thank you," Sam whispered. "For pulling me from the water. You saved my life."

Sefina's lips pulled down at the corners. "Then do not waste it."

She left.

Sighing, Sam found her hammock and collapsed onto it, her body aching in ways that went beyond exhaustion. She had been reckless—stupid, even.

She'd nearly died.

The tiredness in her bones became unbearable. A weariness that sank into her very soul. As her eyes grew heavy, she wondered, fleetingly, what it would be like to stop. To stop searching, stop fighting, stop running toward a revenge that might never bring her peace.

Could she ever forgive herself if she did?

FIFTEEN

Confined to the *Queen Mary*, Sam's anger soured and then numbed. Her drive to move forward, to do anything, became nonexistent until she barely functioned. Barely spoke. Barely did more than sleep.

She was aware of the rhythm of the ship, how it rocked gently with the movement of the sea, and she echoed its unsteadiness. Inside, she was adrift.

She often stared at her scarred arm, the permanent reminder of her loss. Her fingers curled unconsciously into fists every now and then as her mind conjured memories of Rhett. If she concentrated hard enough, she could almost hear his laugh, almost picture his face—but every time the image sharpened, it dissolved, dripping like water through her fingers.

What if he's still out there?

The words looped through her mind like a chant, a prayer to some unseen force she hoped would change the truth. After all, there had been no body. No real proof. Ships sank, yes, but sailors survived, didn't they? Maybe Rhett had made it to shore. Maybe he was stranded on an island somewhere, waiting for her to find him. Maybe...

She thought of her own brush with death, of plunging into the water, unable to swim. Of sinking.

Sefina and Mr. Bixby often hovered nearby, as if they were afraid to leave Sam alone for too long. Sam had never asked them to do that, but she also hadn't asked them to stop.

"Atherton," Sefina said softly as she came down the stairs.

She waited expectantly, so Sam finally forced herself to sit up in her hammock.

For a long moment, neither of them spoke. Sam could see the worry creasing the corners of Sefina's eyes, the way she was trying to find something to say that would pull Sam out of this suffocating fog. But Sam wasn't sure she wanted to be pulled out.

Maybe she wanted to sink.

"You're to report to the galley. Captain's orders," Sefina finally stated, her voice gentle but firm. "Bixby's threatened to toss you overboard if you don't eat."

Sam managed a small smile, but it didn't reach her eyes. She didn't feel a sharp hunger anymore—just an empty hollowness that gnawed at her insides and never went away.

"I'll eat later," she whispered. "I'm fine."

"You're not fine," Sefina countered. "And no one expects you to be. But you can't stay down here forever." There was a small hesitation before she added, "The crew needs you."

Sam flinched. She knew Sefina was trying to remind her that she still had a place here, still had a purpose, but the words only made her feel more trapped.

Rhett had needed her. The other slaves had needed her.

"I need some time," Sam said quietly.

Sefina sighed, glancing over her shoulder. Sam followed her gaze to where Mr. Bixby stood by the stairs. She hadn't even seen him come in. He watched from a distance, his arms crossed and his usual stern expression softened by concern. When Sefina shook her head at him, he gave a small nod and turned away, leaving Sam and Sefina alone once more.

After a long pause, Sefina finally spoke again. "I know you are in pain. This pain can wrap itself around you like a storm, and for a while, it feels like there is no hope of ever finding the shore.

"Pain is a part of us. We can't run from it or bury it deep inside, hoping it will simply disappear. It won't. Like the ship sailing through a storm, the only way out of it is through it. We must face it, acknowledge it, and let it hurt."

An icy fire sparked behind Sefina's impossibly blue eyes. Sam couldn't tear her gaze away. "We *cannot* let it consume us. We do not abandon our helm and leave our rudder to the whims of the waves. Pain is powerful, but so are we. We have the strength to endure, to rise above it. You don't have to forget what you've lost or pretend it doesn't hurt. But you do have to keep moving forward, wave by wave, no matter how hard the sailing may be. Do not let it define you. And know this... You are not alone."

Sam squeezed her eyes shut, trying to block everything out, but Sefina's words wriggled through. For the first time in days, something shifted inside. It wasn't acceptance, not yet. It wasn't healing. It was just a crack in the armor encasing her grief.

Late that night, Sam found herself on deck for the first time in days, her eyes drawn to the stars above. They glittered in a vast blanket across the sky, and at times during her voyage, they'd seemed close enough to touch. But tonight, they felt distant, as if even the heavens had withdrawn.

"Stargazing, are we?"

Sam turned to see Mr. Bixby approaching. They hadn't spoken in so long, she found her tongue frozen.

He grunted, then leaned against the railing beside her and turned his gaze skyward. "You know, the stars have guided many a lost soul through dark times. They're a constant, even when everything else seems to be falling apart."

Sam absorbed his words. What she needed right now was something constant.

The smallest bubble of curiosity formed within her.

"Could you teach me more about them?" she asked tentatively.

Mr. Bixby raised an approving eyebrow. "You read, don't you, lass? Come with me."

He led her to the ship's navigation room and allowed her to pore over charts and maps by lantern light. They spoke of constellations, and he provided names, though he said he'd leave the stories behind their naming to Sefina. Each star became a beacon of light in the darkness that had settled over Sam's heart.

"I want to understand how it all works," she said. "The stars, the maps. How they all work together to guide travelers from one destination to another."

She ran her hand over a star chart that centered around the constellation Aspos, named for the leader of the gods. There was a notation at the bottom, and Sam murmured it aloud, "Aspos always leads true."

Mr. Bixby nodded. "The stars don't lie; that's true. They've guided sailors for centuries, long before you or I ever set foot on a ship. Perhaps now they will guide *you*."

SIXTEEN

The sun was setting on the horizon, painting the sky in hues of orange and pink, as the crew of the *Queen Mary* gathered on deck. Though there would still be snow in Ducria, this far south, the air carried warmth. The smell of the ocean mixed with the savory aroma of supper cooking in the galley. Tonight, the crew celebrated their own little Festival of the Gods—a Ducrian festival that had gained in popularity across the nations. It took place every year just before spring and gave people an extra boost of morale to survive the last month or two of winter.

Sam hung back, feeling almost like a stranger after so much time alone. As she leaned against the ship's railing, her gaze drifted toward the crew, laughing and joking amongst themselves. Captain Marlowe pulled out his fiddle, the familiar sound of a lively jig filling the air. At first, Sam hesitated, unsure if she was ready to join in their merriment. But as the crew's laughter grew louder and the music became more infectious, she found herself drawn toward them.

With a knowing smile, Sefina waved her over. "Come, Atherton. You can't stand there brooding forever."

Sam hesitated for only a moment longer before she pushed herself off the railing and stepped closer.

Mr. Bixby appeared at her side, clapping her on the back with a grin. "Aye, ye've been standing there long enough. Time to dance, lass!"

Before she could protest, Mr. Bixby took her hand and spun her into the center of the group. Sam's heart raced as she stumbled, her feet unsteady, but Bixby stomped and clapped with no sense of rhythm at all, encouraging her to just let loose. His energy was contagious, and Sam couldn't help but allow herself to be swept up in the music.

Then she laughed—a sound almost foreign to her after so long. As the dance continued, her steps grew lighter and her smile wider. She wasn't dwelling on Rhett, or the Lily Company, or the pain that had haunted her for weeks. She was simply here, in this moment, surrounded by the people who had become her unlikely family.

When the song finally ended, the crew erupted into applause, and Sam found herself breathless but exhilarated. She glanced around at the smiling faces, feeling the warmth of their camaraderie seep into her bones.

"You've got a pair of legs on you, Atherton!" One of the crew called out with a wink. "We'll make a true sailor of you yet."

Sam grinned, wiping a stray lock of hair from her face. "I'll hold you to that."

The crew laughed, and Sam felt the festival doing its work, giving her the strength to make it through winter.

Sweat gathered on Sam's brow, the weather already hot though it was still early spring. She wore her trousers along with a lightweight cotton shirt and a headscarf she'd adopted after her first brutal sunburn.

With one last dunk of the mop, she swabbed the final corner of the forecastle deck. Her arms ached from hours of labor, but the monotony of work was welcome, a much-needed distraction from the storm of dark thoughts still hovering beneath the surface.

After stowing the mop and bucket, she paused at the railing, gazing out at the endless horizon of sparkling sea. The gentle breeze caressed her face, and, for the first time in a long while, she felt... lighter. She took her meals with the crew again, no longer hiding below decks. And she'd thrown herself into the daily tasks aboard the *Queen Mary*, finding comfort in the ebb and flow of life on the ship.

The growl of her stomach pulled her from her thoughts, reminding her that she hadn't eaten since before dawn.

In the galley, Sam found Mr. Bixby sitting at one of the long wooden tables, a plate of biscuits and dried pork before him. Sam scanned the room, seeing no other readily available food, and, in response, another loud rumble rolled through her stomach.

Mr. Bixby glanced up, chuckling. "Care for a biscuit, lass?"

Sam sat across from him, gratefully accepting the offered biscuit.

"You've been busy up top, I hear," Mr. Bixby said.

Sam shrugged. "Helps to keep my hands busy."

"Well, you'll want to finish up soon. We'll be docking in a few hours."

"Already?" They'd left the last port less than a week prior.

Mr. Bixby nodded, then slid his plate in front of Sam and stood, brushing the crumbs from his trousers. "It's about time you got off the ship again. Take a day or two to explore. It'll do ye some good."

Sam hesitated, her biscuit hovering near her mouth. "You think I need it?"

He gave her a pointed look. "Don't you?"

She opened her mouth to deny it but found she had no retort. Instead, she nodded slowly. "Perhaps I do."

Though Symethra sat hidden in a tiny southern cove of Eclor, its market exploded before Sam in a blur of color and movement. The sights, the smells, the *life* overwhelmed her senses. Vendors called out from their stalls, offering ground spices, fresh seafood, and even live animals.

Sam wandered the lively market with Sefina and a handful of the *Queen Mary*'s crew, wide-eyed as she took it in. The energy of the place filled her with something she hadn't expected to feel again.

Excitement.

"Here." Sefina held out a small, roasted piece of fruit. The fruit's deep purple skin gleamed in the midday sun. "Try this."

When Sam bit into it, the flavor burst on her tongue—sweet and tangy, with a hint of smoke—and she couldn't help but smile. "That's incredible!"

Sefina grinned. "I knew you would like it."

She made it her mission to try every food that caught her eye—crispy fried fish drizzled with honey, warm bread stuffed with spiced meat, flaky pastries slathered with sweet fruit jellies. Each bite brought a new sensation, a small joy she hadn't expected to find in a small town off the rugged coast.

As Sefina handed her another strange, delicious morsel, Sam caught herself smiling again. And standing in the sun-washed market with salt on her tongue and laughter in her ears, she realized she had a choice.

She could chase vengeance. The Lily Company still thrived. The part of her heart that had belonged to Rhett still whispered for justice.

But that wasn't her only choice.

She could choose the people who stood beside her now. She could choose the sea and the stars, choose experience, choose to bide her time and live long enough to one day face the Lily Company on her own terms.

"You coming, Atherton?"

Sefina's voice drew Sam away from her thoughts. She blinked, then smiled. "Yeah, I'm coming."

Sam returned to the *Queen Mary* that evening not out of obligation but because she wanted to. Belowdeck, she pulled out the bar of clove soap that had claimed a permanent spot in her pocket. Turning it in her hands, she let the scent wash over her, warm and familiar. A small tribute. A reminder—not of loss, but of what Rhett had meant to her.

With one last inhale, she wrapped it carefully in a spare handkerchief and set it in the bottom of her small chest. It would always be there, just like the memory of Rhett. But it didn't need to be at the forefront of every thought. And when she lay down to sleep, she felt at peace.

Life aboard the *Queen Mary* settled into a steady rhythm after that. Days slipped into weeks while the sea carried them from one bustling port to the next. Sam traveled unfamiliar streets, tasted foods she couldn't pronounce, bartered with merchants over trinkets she didn't need, and let herself be present in a way she hadn't been for a long time.

Her seventeenth birthday came and went, passing in a blur of warm spring air and daily tasks. She had nearly forgotten the date entirely until Mr. Bixby set a mug of spiced cider in front of her and Sefina presented her with a silk scarf in a deep, oceanic blue—"so you'll always carry a bit of the sea with you."

There had been no grand celebration, but it was more than she'd expected.

Occasionally, as they visited different towns, Sam caught sight of something that made her stomach twist—a painted crest on a crate, a carving on a storefront sign, or even a decorative motif woven into fabric. A lily.

Her first instinct was always suspicion. A tightening in her chest, a lingering question at the back of her mind. *Could it be connected?*

But the crew kept her busy, and the sea called her forward, and the thoughts of the Lily Company—of revenge—slowly drifted to a small corner of her mind. Still there, still constant, but no longer all-consuming.

Summer passed in a golden haze, and though the seasons changed, the nights remained warm. The crew took their meals out on the open deck, and evenings quickly became Sam's favorite time of day. She let herself laugh with the others. Let herself sway to music or jump up and dance. Let herself *belong*.

Occasionally, she thought of her previous life—of Billy and Perry. They had once been a family, of sorts. Had they found somewhere that they, too, belonged?

She would see them again, she decided. The next time the *Queen Mary* docked in Milderre, she would seek them out. She would bring them something. A food they'd never tasted or a trinket from a place they had never heard of. She would tell them about her adventures, the late nights on deck with the wind in her hair and the stars overhead.

And she would tell them about Rhett.

The pain she still carried.

She still missed him. Always would. But she understood that moving forward didn't mean forgetting.

She wasn't just surviving anymore—she was *living*. The way Rhett would have wanted her to.

And with life came stories.

Many nights, as the *Queen Mary* drifted beneath a sky full of stars, Sefina favored them with myths and legends of the gods, woven with the plucked melodies of her kalimba. Sefina was a firm believer in the gods, worshipping them as Sam's mother once had. Sam had never been certain whether she truly believed in their influence, but there were moments when she found herself whispering prayers to them anyway. Maybe it was habit. Maybe it was hope.

Regardless, she never tired of the stories. Especially when Sefina spun them into song. Her voice had a way of making the world around them blur, of making Sam's skin prickle as if the gods themselves were listening and looking down on a single merchant ship in the wide open sea.

SEVENTEEN

The *Queen Mary* sliced through the waves, her sails taut with the steady ocean breeze. Sam sat in the crow's nest, tying and untying knots as she gazed out at the endless blue. It had been a quiet day, the kind where the wind favored them and the sea was merciful, rolling gently beneath the hull. The crew worked with an easy efficiency, tending to their duties with the occasional shouted command.

Sefina sat cross-legged near the bow, her kalimba resting in her lap as her fingers idly plucked. Sam watched her for a moment before making her way down the rigging to settle beside her.

"You always seem so at home on the water," Sam remarked, pulling her knees up to her chest. "I know you weren't born on a ship, but you make it seem like you were."

Sefina gave her a knowing smile, her fingers pausing on the metal prongs. "The sea and I have an understanding. I was born on an island, after all."

"Do you miss Haapa?"

She didn't know much about Sefina's homeland, only that it was a place of warm waters, dense jungle, and the origin of the *Queen Mary's* textile trade. They were due to return and restock in a few months' time. Already much of the colorful fabric supply had been sold.

Sefina shrugged. "At times, yes. My path should have been simple—marry well, serve my people, raise the next generation. But I wanted more than that. And now here I am. A storyteller on the sea, gathering tales from every port, every people, every sailor who has something worth remembering." She paused, looking at Sam with a thoughtful expression. "But you—what stories will you tell when you have seen the world?"

Sam shrugged. "I don't know yet."

"Then we must start somewhere. Here—I will teach you." Sefina reached over, placing her instrument in Sam's lap.

Sam blinked down at the kalimba. "I can't play."

"You couldn't climb the rigging when you first came aboard either," Sefina pointed out. "And now you are as surefooted as any sailor."

Biting her lip, Sam smiled, warmth spreading through her at the compliment. She lifted the instrument and allowed Sefina to adjust her fingers.

"Start with this," Sefina said, guiding her through the first notes of an old tune. "The song of Aspos. I know how you enjoy that one."

Sam smiled wider this time.

Later that night, after the crew had settled and the ship gently swayed beneath a moonless sky, Sam found herself on deck once more, humming the song of Aspos. She lay on her back, hands folded behind her head, transfixed by the stars' quiet beauty, by their stillness in contrast to the churning sea.

The stars had always been there, constant and unchanging, distant and eternal. She never tired of them. As she gazed up at the endless expanse, a humbling realization settled over her of just how small she was, how small *everything* was, in the vastness of the universe. And yet, that smallness did not make life insignificant. If anything, it made it precious.

Sam let her gaze trace the familiar constellations, even lifting her fingers to draw their patterns in the air. There was something about the way the stars burned so far away, untouched by the world's mess, that filled her with longing. She wondered what it must be like for Aspos, God of the Sky, to command the wind and weather, to have control over every shifting cloud and burning point of light. Did his power reach the smallest pinprick in the heavens? Or perhaps even that and beyond?

According to the small book on astronomy Sam had acquired at a port, many of the constellations represented the different gods or their famed creatures of myth, though not all were visible at once. The change of seasons reflected a change in the sky. There were only a handful of stars visible throughout the entire year, and they shone brightly high above. The more she studied it, the more the sky fascinated her.

A gentle breeze blew past, heavy with the scent of brine, and Sam blinked slowly, her eyelids heavy. She knew she should get to bed. Mr. Bixby would expect her to be up first thing to help with the morning meal.

She was about to sit up when a figure came clomping up the steps. Sam smiled and tore her eyes from the stars to greet her companion. "Good evening, Mr. Bixby."

"Evening, lass. Mind if I join you?"

Sam motioned him forward. "Of course. You're always welcome."

Mr. Bixby sat down with a slight grunt. His pipe hung from the corner of his mouth, a strand of smoke trailing from it. He puffed several times.

"I hear you've taken a liking to music," he said.

"Hmm? Oh, yes. Sefina is teaching me how to play her kalimba." Sam folded her arms behind her head again, the tune she'd learned still fresh in her mind. "I fear my fingers will never recover."

Mr. Bixby chuckled. "I'll stick to listening, then."

He took a long draw of his pipe, and they sat quietly next to one another for a short while.

"Your love of the stars could get you far in the seafaring world," he remarked. "Good navigators are hard to come by."

Sam sat up. "But I'm not a navigator.."

"No, but you could be, with a bit more training." Mr. Bixby puffed his pipe again. White smoke drifted in the air around them, slowly dissipating into nothing.

"You've got a knack for reading the stars," he continued. "I'm willing to bet you've got those maps memorized, too. Don't think I haven't noticed you studying them in your spare time. Refine that skill, and you make yourself an asset."

"Am I not already an asset?" Sam teased, feigning offense.

"In so many ways, little lass."

His words warmed something inside her she hadn't even realized was cold.

How had so much changed in a single year at sea?

She had spent so much of her life fighting—fighting to survive, fighting to be seen, fighting to hold on to the people she loved. But here, aboard the *Queen Mary*, she hadn't needed to fight for her place. She had simply found it. A family. A home. Everything she had never dared to hope for.

Mr. Bixby reached into his vest, retrieving something small and round from the front pocket. He regarded the golden piece with a half smile, rubbing his thumb fondly over the face of it, then turned the piece so that Sam could see it fully. A pocket watch?

"This was my first compass," he said, clicking it open to reveal the inside.

"May I see it?" she asked, and he handed it to her.

Sam admired the simple instrument. The inside featured a star-like design with letters at each of the tips and numbers circling the perimeter. A thin, needle-like arrow hung raised above it. As she twisted the compass back and forth, she was enthralled with how the arrow remained pointing in the same direction no matter which way she turned.

"What does it do?" she wondered.

"It helps you find your way. The needle always points north. And these," he said, referencing the numbers, "are degrees to help determine which way you want to travel."

She nodded, still unsure of how to actually use the compass, but with a general understanding of its purpose.

"How did you come to be on the sea, Mr. Bixby?"

"Well, lass, I became a seafaring man when I was not much older than you. I grew up in a rather dull town in the far north of Ducria, where nothing of importance ever happened. So when the navy recruiters came, I eagerly volunteered for the war and was assigned to a small naval ship called the *Dawncaster*."

The war between Ducria and Eclor had been before Sam's birth—she hadn't realized that it was so recent. Or that Mr. Bixby had been part of the Royal Navy. Considering Sam's experience with Ducria's military, she was surprised that someone as good as Mr. Bixby ever could have served.

He continued, "And rather like you, I didn't take to the sea easily. That's when I met my best mate, Jonathan. That dippy do-gooder, always making up excuses for my incompetence. He came from a merchant family, see, and had already spent years on the water. He taught me everything I know about navigating. If it weren't for him, I'd probably still be cleaning privies." He shook his head, smiling fondly. "Two years we spent on the *Dawncaster*. Thick as thieves."

Mr. Bixby's demeanor sombered, and the wind seemed to still in response. The smoke from his pipe hung like a ghost in the air. Eventually, he continued, "Then our ship was sent to the front of the armada, sorely underprepared. During the battle, a cannonball blew through our ship like it was nothing. The blast shattered my knee and sprayed the right side of my face with splinters.

"The *Dawncaster* went down quickly, but we got the dinghy untied before she was gone. Only Jonathan, myself, and two others made it off the ship alive. It was chaos—the waters rough and full of bodies and debris. We lost the oars and were helplessly adrift as the battle waged on.

"I wasn't the only one hurt." Mr. Bixby slowly tapped his chest. "One of the railing posts had gone straight through Jonathan's chest. I think we all knew there was little hope for him, but that didn't stop us from trying. He gave me this compass as his parting gift, and I held him as he died."

Sam breathed through a familiar pain, remembering her own losses. The stars held a silent vigil above.

"Eventually, everything went quiet," Mr. Bixby said. "We were stranded in what had become a ships' graveyard. We went days without food or water, paddling with driftwood, but with the compass and knowledge Jonathan had taught me, we made it to dry land. Ducrian territory, no less. Without him, we would never have survived."

Mr. Bixby turned his head to the sky. Sam copied the gesture, staring into the vast openness.

"Read the stars right, and you'll always find your way," he declared softly. After a moment's pause, he cleared his throat. "I was discharged soon after that. My leg was permanently damaged, see, and I'd gone blind in one eye. No use for an invalid during war."

Sam now understood how he'd received the limp and milky eye. It had felt too intrusive of her to ask about them before.

"I spent a few years learning to be a bookkeeper, but nothing could replace my love of the sea, so I found my way back. With the help of Jonathan's last gift."

Sam closed the compass and attempted to hand it back, but Mr. Bixby gently folded her fingers over it.

"A gift I now pass on to you," he said. She tried to protest, but he was adamant. "My navigating days are close to an end. It's your turn, little lass."

Sam thanked him, and he groaned as he got to his feet. He hobbled down the steps to the main deck, puffing on his pipe and muttering, "I'm getting too old for this."

Sam held the compass above her head, studying it in the moonlight. Part of her felt like a thief had no business trying to be a navigator, but another part rose to say she'd just be stealing direction from the stars. With a faint smile, Sam clicked the compass closed again and cradled it to her chest.

In the following weeks, Sam threw herself into studying navigation with a feverish intensity. She spent her nights memorizing the stars like a giant map. If the world below ever descended into chaos, she wanted to be certain she could find her way by the silver light above.

Under Mr. Bixby's patient eye, she mastered the compass. She learned to trust the trembling needle, understanding that as long as the arrow pointed north, she held the power to dictate her own path. As long as she read it right, she could determine any direction.

Sefina taught her of the ocean. Of the different temperatures and the pull of currents in the water. Most importantly, her swimming lessons taught Sam how not to drown.

As she improved, Captain Marlowe encouraged her to assist in setting the course for each day. Her first attempt at setting a course nearly ended in disaster when she misjudged the depths. If the captain hadn't intervened, they would have been broken on the beach by midday. But as the weeks bled into a month, the charts began to make sense.

One night, as she traced her finger over the ink-stained trade routes, a quiet thought formed in her mind. The Lily Company ferried slaves to ports around the world. Their slaver ships traveled routes that they knew better than their prey.

But if Sam learned those same secrets, could she find a way to intercept them?

The thought only invigorated her further. She *would* master navigation, and she would use that skill for good.

Bolting upright in her hammock, Sam's eyes sprang open as she gasped. She was drenched in sweat, her heart racing, but as she whipped her head around, there was no water, no flames, no screams... no lieutenant or Mother... no Rhett.

Sefina appeared at her side, concern flashing across her face. "Atherton, are you unwell?"

Sam swallowed hard but felt her body slowly relaxing. "I'm all right," she said weakly. "Only a nightmare."

But she'd never had a nightmare so vivid before. This one left her feeling uneasy.

Now awake, Sam rolled out of her hammock. She rubbed the sleep from her eyes and pulled on her shirt and trousers, noticing how they fit a bit more snugly than they had only months prior. Then she smoothed her curls back to tie on her headscarf. Finally, Sam pulled on her boots and trudged up the stairs.

It was still dark when she stepped onto the deck, but the stars had already faded, the first signs of light trailing across the sky.

She reached the ship's rail. Firmly gripping the rope ladder that led up the mainmast, she swung her leg over the edge and climbed, breathing in the salty air as it whipped past her. She reached the crow's nest and settled in just in time to watch the sun crest the horizon. The rising sun bathed both sea and sky in shades of pink and red and orange, bright and vivid, while the waves sparkled and danced in its light. The sight was breathtaking, and it banished the lingering gloom of her nightmare.

They were finally returning to the west after months on their trade route, stopping a final time in Phago's most southern cities to sell the majority of their remaining wares. Winter had already come and gone, the mild weather gradually becoming hot and muggy as the seasons progressed. Her contract would be up in only six more months.

Had so much time passed already?

She would sign on for another two years—another four, even—so long as Captain Marlowe allowed it.

But for now, it was time for the *Queen Mary* to return to Haapa to replenish their supply. Sam could only imagine the tropical haven that was Sefina's home.

But when she took her place back down on the deck, the usual cheerful greetings from the crew never came, a heaviness hanging in the air.

Seeking out Mr. Bixby, she asked, "What's going on?"

"We're entering dangerous waters, lass, so we're taking extra precautions."

"Dangerous waters?"

Mr. Bixby's jaw clenched. "The stretch between Phago and Haapa. Pirates have been known to lurk here, preying on merchant and passenger ships alike."

Sam shifted her gaze to the water, her imagination running wild. Every splash, every creak of the wood beneath her feet seemed louder and more ominous.

"Do you think they'll come for us?" Sam asked quietly, not looking at Bixby but hoping he'd have an answer that would ease the growing knot in her stomach.

Bixby sighed, rubbing a hand over his beard. "They could. They're hungry for ships like ours. Cargo. Crew. Blood."

"But we will be prepared," Captain Marlowe said as he approached them. "Bixby, post the watchmen. We'll outrun them if we must. You know what to look for."

The day stretched out before them like an uncharted expanse of tension. Everywhere Sam looked, the crew was on edge, their movements deliberate and measured, the usual banter replaced by whispered conversations and stolen glances toward the water as everyone's eyes scanned the horizon for the infamous pirate ship called the *Golden Krina.*

For hours, Sam busied herself with small tasks, her mind playing out every possible scenario. She could almost hear the phantom sound of cannons, imagine the full sails of pirate ships appearing on the horizon. But no such sight came.

Even Sefina, normally so calm and composed, seemed unsettled, her mouth pressed into a thin line. There were no songs on the *Queen Mary's* deck that day.

The hours dragged by, the weight of anticipation almost unbearable, until, finally, night descended.

Down in the galley, Sam settled herself beside Sefina.

"Any new stories tonight?" she asked. Anything to get her mind off the possibility of what lurked in the open sea.

She almost thought Sefina would decline, but then the Haapari princess spoke. "I think tonight I will tell you about Delmada, Goddess of Light."

She sang softly, without her kalimba. No matter how often Sam heard Sefina's voice, she still felt its mesmerizing pull as intensely as that first time in Market Square.

Sefina sang of how the Goddess of Light cared so much for the men of the world that she tore free a piece of her soul so that it could become the sun, ending the world's perpetual darkness. Orrazoth, God of Darkness, felt cheated and demanded that dark reign supreme once again.

Before a battle could ensue, the seven gods held a trial, where it was determined that both light and darkness would rule equally throughout the world.

And thus the day and night were created.

But the first time Delmada's light was shrouded in Orrazoth's darkness, she was so distraught for her precious world that she shed a tear, a tear so pure that it shone brightly in the sky even through the dark of night.

> *"To this day, Delmada's tear remains.*
> *And each night, though the sun sleeps,*
> *the moon still guides men home."*

Sefina stopped singing but continued the story, her face darkening. "What the song does not say is that Orrazoth was furious with the goddess, and he was cunning. He journeyed to a place beyond this world, where he bargained with an unknown being who granted him immense power—power greater than even that of the great god, Aspos—which he planned to unleash upon the gods who sided against him in favor of Delmada and her light. Power that was torn from him one fateful night when he made a bargain with a mortal man."

Sefina ended abruptly, slapping both hands onto her knees as she stood.

Sam spluttered, "Is that it? How did Orrazoth lose his power? What bargain did he make with the man?"

Sefina smiled mischievously. "Another story for another night."

Long after Sefina bid her goodnight, Sam remained sitting, thoughts churning of gods and pirates and mysterious powers. Unable to sleep, she returned to the deck and volunteered for a shift on the night watch. While scouting the dark, she imagined she was swathed in a blanket of stars that watched over and protected her and her crew.

As dawn began to awaken, a low murmur spread through the ship. Sam hurried to the bow, following the crew's gaze toward the horizon. From the crow's nest, the watchman signaled the first signs of land. Not long after, Captain Marlowe gave the all clear.

The knot in Sam's stomach loosened as the warm light of the sun rose above the horizon. The heavy silence that had weighed on them lifted, replaced by chatter and the occasional song drifting up from belowdecks.

Sam leaned against the rail, her eyes on the clear blue sky. They'd made it through the night unscathed, and for that, she thanked the gods. A thanks for Aspos, for the stars that led their way. A thanks for Perixia, for their good fortune. And a thanks for Larideia, for the calm seas and strong currents that led them out of harm's way.

Mr. Bixby approached, a slight smile playing on his face. "Seems the sea was kind to us today."

Sam nodded, then stifled a yawn.

With a quirk of his head, Mr. Bixby gestured to the doors that led into the belly of the ship. "Get a few hours rest, lass. We still have several days before we reach the mainland."

Sam didn't argue. With one last glance at the horizon, she turned and made her way belowdecks for some much-needed sleep.

With one hand tightly wrapped around a length of rope, Sam closed her eyes and let the cool breeze caress her cheeks as she leaned over the salty waters below. Her other hand stretched outward as if she could touch the skies. She loved being in the rigging where few others went freely. Her connection to the sky was one of the reasons that navigating had come so easily to her. By now, the stars were as familiar to her as her own reflection, and she knew each of the constellations by heart.

A ruckus below caught her attention—the chickens were loose again. A handful of men scrambled to catch the feathery things before they made their way overboard, and Sam rushed down to help. Sefina was there, too, sleeves rolled to her shoulders against the recent heat.

Sam noted the thin black lines wrapped around the golden-brown skin of Sefina's upper left arm. She'd seen the tattoo a handful of times but never asked if it held any meaning. Unlike the crude lines that some of the men carried, Sefina's tattoo was intricately detailed and delicate.

Sam only caught a glimpse of the design before a fat, feathered chicken leapt up to flap its wings in her face. Startled, she almost let it get away, managing to clap her hands around its belly in the nick of time. It flapped haphazardly for a second longer, then calmed as Sam tucked it beneath her arm, gently stroking the back of its neck.

Sefina wrangled another of the chickens as Sam was placing hers back in the coop, and Sam couldn't help but stare again at the tattoo peeking from beneath Sefina's rolled sleeve.

Sefina noticed. "It is a tattoo."

"I know it's a tattoo," Sam said. "I just haven't seen one like it before."

"You wouldn't. They are a custom of my people. Each has a unique meaning specific to the individual." Sefina shooed the chicken back into its coop, latching the hatch behind it. "For example..." She pointed to what looked like an interpretation of a flower. "This means 'daughter,' and the waves here—"

A loud squawk drew their attention as a rogue hen made fools of the crew members. While trying to grab it, one man tripped over ropes and another spilled the contents of the mop bucket. Sam hid her mouth behind her hand as she giggled. Together, she and Sefina helped round up the remaining chickens.

Sam didn't have the chance to ask more about the tattoo because, just as they finished, a call came from the lookout: storm approaching.

EIGHTEEN

Sam watched, mesmerized, as the darkening sky grew close. In her year and a half as a sailor, she'd never seen anything like it. Lightning flashed, brightening the sky, before the rumble of thunder rattled her bones. In that flash, Sam could have sworn she saw something in the midst of the black, swirling storm.

Borrowing a spyglass from one of the grumbling sailors, she peered through it, searching.

Yes, there it was.

In the center of the whirlwind, a ship sailed, clouded by thick layers of black fog.

Before she knew what to make of it, the storm was upon them. She joined the rest of the crew hauling in and securing the ropes, sails, and any other loose items. She spotted Sefina tying down one of the loose barrels atop the main deck and hurried to her. Already, the wind whipped violently, the rain torrential. The waves had grown significantly in the last several minutes, and the ship rocked, throwing nearly everyone off balance.

"There's a ship in there," she told Sefina, nodding her head toward the tempest while she held the barrel in place. "Do you think they're in need of aid?"

"*We* will be in need of aid if we are unable to get out of here soon," Sefina quipped, water dripping from her nose. Her white braids writhed like deadly snakes in the wind. "Pray that the Sea Goddess gives us safe passage this day."

Sam nodded and pulled taught on the rope to ensure the barrel was secure. She muttered a quick prayer to the Sea Goddess Larideia, just in case, but felt her gaze drawn back to the black mass and the ship she knew sailed inside. It was almost as if she could feel raw power radiating from it...

She shook her head and wiped the rain from her eyes.

"We should go below before it gets worse," Sam shouted over the wind.

As if in answer, the ship lurched violently. The deck dropped out from beneath her feet, and for a breathless moment, Sam hung weightless before slamming back down as the ship pitched in the opposite direction.

A wall of water surged over the rail. Sam gasped as the ocean swallowed her, salt burning her throat as it dragged her across the deck. Panic swelled within her as she clawed for purchase, fingers scraping uselessly against the slick wood. She struck something solid with a bone-jarring impact, pain screaming up her spine as the wave finally receded.

Coughing, she forced herself upright. She had been hauled more than half the length of the deck and now found herself pressed against the wall of the captain's cabin, legs trembling beneath her.

Sefina was there a heartbeat later, her long fingers closing tightly around Sam's arm. "There's no getting below!" she shouted. She yanked a length of rope from where it was looped over her shoulder and cinched it around her waist, tying the opposite end to a heavy wooden cleat. Then she hauled Sam close and secured her beside her.

The wall offered little shelter from the onslaught, but, together, they huddled against the storm, clinging to one another and to the ropes that bound them as the sea raged. Sam whispered hurried prayers to any god who might listen.

A handful of men still struggled across the deck, but the majority of the crew simply held on for their lives. Sam could just see Captain Marlowe at the helm, wheel in hand, with Mr. Bixby braced dutifully at his side.

It felt like hours as the cyclone pounded against them. Every inch of Sam's body was soaked through, her hair and clothing heavy. Her body ached from the effort of remaining upright, the rope around her waist biting painfully into her stomach with each jolt of the ship.

Until, finally, the storm broke.

As suddenly as it had started, the rain stopped, the waves settling almost unnaturally to a gentle lull. The *Queen Mary*'s foremast lay across the deck in cloth and splinters, proof of just how violent the storm had been. They were fortunate it hadn't slid off the ship and into the sea.

But the sky was still dark with clouds when an eerie dark fog swirled in atop the waves, encompassing the *Queen Mary* wholly and blocking the light. The effect was disorienting, and it felt as if the world was holding its breath. Even the crew was silent, the only sound the lap of waves against the hull and the occasional creak of the wooden masts.

"Is everyone accounted for?" Bixby's voice pierced the silence.

A chorus of "ayes" echoed throughout the ship, Sam and Sefina's included, though there was no real way to tell if someone was missing without doing a full checklist. Now that the silence was broken, Captain Marlowe called all hands to work, and the crew shuffled away, though their usual chatter remained muted.

Sam untied the rope around her waist and handed the end to Sefina, who wrapped it skillfully as she went to stow it away. Up above, the topsail hung limp and shredded.

Sam could see little of the deck and what needed to be done. She knew she'd be no help repairing the damage and headed to climb the surviving mainmast into the crow's nest. Given the amount of mist rolling in, she wasn't sure she could figure out their bearing, but she would try.

Captain Marlowe, Mr. Bixby, and the ship's carpenter were surveying the damage to the foremast, and she caught part of their conversation as she passed.

"Lucky we've got the tools."

"Aye, we'll get her to Haapa."

Thank the gods. What would it be like to be stranded in the middle of the Rutane Ocean?

She reached the rail and gripped the rope netting, swinging herself around and up. She smiled as her calluses scraped the rough, sturdy weave. Those calluses had been hard earned these months. With her foot on the lowest rung, she used her weight to test its strength. The last thing she wanted was to come tumbling down if the ropes had come loose.

The fog around her didn't just drift; it pulsed, wet and ubiquitous, pooling ever closer until it swallowed up everything outside of arm's reach. Somewhere in that gray soup, a vicarus could be uncoiling its length, its many-fanged maw ready to devour her, and she'd only know it once the slime of its tentacled mane brushed her cheek.

Sam lifted onto the next rung up but hesitated.

Thump. Thump. Thump.

The low, steady beat of a drum cut through the fog. Sam's knuckles whitened as she gripped the ropes harder, twisting her head as she searched for the source. From the silence around her, the others heard it too. A few of the men below her whispered, but Sam felt as if her mouth had been clamped shut.

The drumming vanished like a snuffed candle. The silence that followed was worse than the noise. Even the waves seemed to stop splashing.

Hair prickled on the back of Sam's neck. Rather than continuing her climb, she lowered herself slowly to the sturdy planks of the deck. Blinded by the fog's veil, she pressed a shaking hand to the rail and began shuffling forward, praying the next shape to emerge from the mist would have a human face.

A hand clamped onto Sam's shoulder, and a jagged inhale hitched in her throat. She spun, finding Mr. Bixby looming over her with Sefina close behind. Any flicker of relief Sam felt died the moment she saw the first mate's face. It wasn't just stern; it was a mask of tension, his eyes tight, lips set in a grim line.

"Belowdecks *now*," he breathed. "Both of you."

Sam didn't move fast enough. Mr. Bixby's urgent shove sent her scrambling toward the hatch. Sefina's blue eyes flashed with a silent protest, but she didn't utter a word as they were ushered down the steep stairs. As the heavy wooden door closed above them, they plunged into near darkness. The lanterns had been doused to prevent fire from catching during the storm, and with the canvas still lashed tight over the deck grates, the only light that reached them was through the cracks in the door.

Sam paced at the foot of the stairs, pulse hammering, unsure of what she should be doing with herself or how long she would be kept below in the dark. Somewhere nearby, she could feel Sefina.

They had been submerged for barely a minute when a howl broke the silence.

Pure, frantic instinct took over. Sam lunged for the stairs but cracked her shin against the bottom riser. She stumbled, a cry catching in her throat, and Sefina caught her before she could fall.

Sefina didn't speak, but the silhouette of her head moved in a forceful *no*.

Scowling, Sam wrenched her arm free. Something was terribly wrong up top, she could feel it. That howl hadn't been a sound of the sea.

Ignoring Sefina's silent reprimand, Sam inched her way up the stairs. She pressed her eye to a jagged crack in the wood. Sefina was there a moment later, her own curiosity peeking through.

Through the fog on deck, Sam could just make out the forms of Mr. Bixby and a handful of men who stood in a ragged circle, clutching belaying pins and cutlasses.

More howls broke out, along with high-pitched whoops and war cries, the noise deafening after the silence of before. Figures dropped to the deck as if from nowhere.

Pirates?

They swarmed, slithering down the mast and vaulting over the rails like a pack of starving wolves. A heavy thud rattled the door hinges inches from Sam's nose as a thick, barrel-chested man landed with his back to the door. Sam flinched but couldn't tear her eyes away as he prowled toward her crew.

The rigging crawled with silhouettes that perched like vultures among the ropes. Not a single human face was visible. Bone, wood, cloth... every pirate wore a mask. Some wore hollow-eyed skulls while others boasted intricate designs. Still others had strips of fabric over their mouths or eyes. To Sam, these were not men. They were a faceless army of monsters.

She watched, speechless, as her crew was surrounded. One by one, her shipmates raised their hands in surrender, sinking to their knees. They were outnumbered at least two to one.

She noticed almost too late that a group of the masked figures had detached from the fray, marching straight toward the door where she and Sefina stood. A sharp tug on her shirt snapped her into motion. Sefina was already at the bottom of the stairs, racing for cover. Sam dove after her, boots skidding on the floorboards as they scrambled behind the nearest stack of crates.

The door crashed open, slamming against the interior wall with a bang. A bulky figure filled the entirety of the doorframe. As the man clomped down the stairs, a smaller but no less intimidating figure took his place, pistols glinting in each hand. Two more men followed behind.

The pirates made no effort to move quietly, kicking over barrels and snarling behind hideous masks. As they moved closer, Sam whipped her head toward Sefina, but she had already melted into the darkness, dislodging a blade from her belt. Sam crept back in a crouch, easing her own small dagger from her waistband.

Sam held her breath as the men moved only paces in front of her. She flinched as the crate next to her was kicked over, rolls of fabric sent sprawling. Silent as the grave, she inched underneath a length of the fabric, praying to Perixia that the shadows and heaps of cloth hid her form. As she lay, dagger tightly against her chest, a tremble escaped her.

She didn't know where Sefina was, what was happening above deck, or how any of it would end.

The heavy clomp of boots echoed against the wood as the pirates finally retreated.

"All clear!" a man barked, his footsteps fading as he ascended the steps.

She waited a minute longer and then sprang from her hiding place, her head whipping left and right as she searched for Sefina.

She took one step. Thick, callused hands clamped around her waist, dragging her back against a chest that felt like a wall of stone. A low, gravelly chuckle vibrated through her spine. "Well, look what I found hiding in the dark."

Panicking, Sam twisted in the brute's grip, driving her dagger into the man's upper arm. He roared a curse, his iron grasp slackening just enough for Sam to wrench herself free. She bolted. The stairs were her only escape. A desperate thought of the black water outside crossed her mind. A leap into the sea was certain death, but in this moment, the ocean felt kinder than the hold.

She threw a glance over her shoulder at the mountain of a man who growled at her, teeth bared. Then she turned back to the stairs only to slam into a second pirate. He grasped her wrist, twisting until her dagger clattered to the floor. In one seamless, humiliating motion, he hoisted her over his shoulder like a sack of grain.

Shrieking, Sam kicked and pounded on his back to no avail as the man returned above deck and bellowed, "Looky here, lads! Perhaps we will have a missus after all!"

His outburst was greeted by hoots and hollers, but it was the vessel floating alongside them that stunned Sam into silence. Was this the ship that had been within the storm?

The pirate ship was an enormous three-masted galleon. Its cream-colored sails rose dizzyingly high. The sleek hull was painted a green so dark it was nearly black, with golden railings and accents from stem to stern. A fearsome arsenal of cannons and swivel guns peeked from their perches, and from the tops of the masts high above, three large golden flags swayed. Long wooden planks had been secured between the vessels, where the *Queen Mary*'s meager goods were already being loaded onto the assailing ship.

Sam turned her attention back to the *Queen Mary*, which paled in comparison to the other magnificent ship. At the center of the main deck, tools and weapons lay in a pile, while her crewmates stood surrounded by pirates.

As the man carrying her paraded past them, bouncing Sam on his shoulder with another crude remark, she locked panic-stricken eyes with Mr. Bixby.

Resolution settled on his face a moment before he threw a fist at the nearest pirate, then lithely pulled the pistol from the pirate's hip. He faced Sam, firing a single shot toward her. The man beneath her cried out as the bullet ripped through his gut, and he collapsed. Sam fell with him, landing hard on her stomach.

Arm still raised, gun barrel smoking, Mr. Bixby held her gaze. His face reflected all the joy, pride, and love he'd ever shown toward her.

He didn't get to shoot again, because a glinting cutlass pierced the soft skin of his chest. In that instant, the world seemed to still. Mr. Bixby still looked at her, his lip quivering slightly, and then his body crumpled to the ground.

It took Sam a moment to realize the screaming that filled her ears was her own. She clawed her way forward on hands and knees, trying to reach the only father she'd ever known. Firm hands gripped her arms, and two pirates hauled her away from Mr. Bixby's lifeless body while her screams turned to sobs.

Captain Marlowe exchanged grim glances with the rest of his crew as an understanding passed between them. The captain of the *Queen Mary* clenched his jaw, and, with a single nod, the crew jumped into action, tackling pirates and seizing weapons.

There was nothing Sam could do as she was dragged toward the massive pirate ship. Kicking, biting, and scratching, she watched in horror as her entire crew, her *family*, was sliced or shot down one by one in defense of their ship.

Nineteen

The pirates dragged Sam to one of the cabins aboard their ship, dumped her ungraciously to the ground, then shut the door, closing her in.

The final moments of Mr. Bixby's life were seared into her memory. She took heaving breaths, feeling as if she may be sick.

Several minutes later, the door banged open as someone else was shoved inside, cursing and kicking. Sam slowly lifted her head. It took a moment for her to register. *Sefina*. Alive.

The realization landed dully, without the rush of relief it should have brought. It registered the way everything else did now—muted, distant, as if her body had decided there was only so much it could feel at once.

The door slammed shut. Sefina hurled herself at it, shouting what Sam could only guess were obscenities in her native tongue.

Turning from the door, Sefina locked eyes with Sam. Neither of them spoke. Sefina's shirt sleeve had been torn free, exposing her tattooed arm. Blood soaked the ends of her long white braids, dripping on the polished wood planks, and Sam wondered distantly if it had come from fighting pirates or from holding dying friends.

Slowly, she raised puffy eyes to glance around the rest of the room. A polished desk adorned with gems and baubles sat before an impressive glass window. Weapons and maps decorated the walls. Drapes along the right side of the room framed a plush bed.

This was the captain's cabin.

With it came the scent of aged wood and a faint trace of ink. It was silent but for the occasional sniffle that Sam cursed herself for not being able to control. The cabin was dim, the only light source a faint foggy glow that seeped through the glass panes of the window. The lanterns sat cold on the walls.

Click.

Sam stiffened and cautiously raised herself to her feet as Sefina moved to stand beside her. The door to the cabin opened, revealing the hulking figure of a man.

He strolled into the room, face darkened by shadows. A well-tailored burgundy frock hung to his knees, the gold-embroidered edges glinting ever so slightly as he shifted. The cream-colored shirt he wore beneath was low cut and lay open. He wore no cravat, instead exposing the thick muscles of his bronze chest and the edges of a black tattoo peeking out from over his heart. An old brass key dangled from a plain leather cord around his neck—unlike the multiple jeweled rings on each hand.

The man's voice was as smooth as the velvet frock he wore. "I am Salik Kharzul, Captain of the *Golden Krina*. Welcome aboard." He spread his arms wide. "It is not often that we are gifted with a woman's presence while at sea. I fear my men are not well-versed in the treatment of a lady."

While Sefina stuck out her chin defiantly, Sam's mouth parted slightly. *This* was the pirate ship everyone feared. Did this captain think that after his crew *murdered* her family, he could suddenly play nice, and she would play along?

"You mean to keep us here?" Sam rasped.

"Of course," Kharzul purred. "I am a generous man and will ensure that your fate is not the same as that of your shipmates."

Sam's eyes widened. "You're going to kill them all..." she whispered.

Kharzul stepped close to Sam, his large frame filling the space in front of her. She froze as he reached out to cup her chin. His touch was icy cold, his fingers callused but gentle. He reeked of rum, sweat, and the tang of the sea. It was a potent, almost nauseating combination.

With a finger, Kharzul tilted her head upward. His eyes glinted like molten gold, holding the cunning of a predator. He looked to be in his mid-thirties, with dark stubble and a jagged scar dividing one eyebrow. His black hair was swept away from his face, strands falling over his brow, and though it was long enough to be tied back, he let it hang loose around his shoulders.

This was the sort of man she'd avoided in the streets. One dripping with power and cruelty.

"I only save what is useful," he stated coolly. He dropped Sam's chin to turn to Sefina. "I'm sure your skill sets will prove to be quite valuable." His hand trailed the tattoo along Sefina's arm, then dropped to the wooden kalimba box at her hip. "Won't you favor us with a song, Princess?"

Sefina snarled, launching spittle in his direction. Captain Kharzul avoided it gracefully, tsking. Sam's eyes darted between the two.

How did he know Sefina was a princess?

Kharzul walked steadily to the door, opened it, and gestured for them to exit. "We will speak again soon," he said, pinning Sam with his stare.

Flanked by two men on each side, she and Sefina were escorted from the captain's cabin. As they crossed the deck of the *Golden Krina*, she saw flames consuming the *Queen Mary*. She stopped abruptly, a whimper escaping her lips, unable to tear her eyes away from the wreckage.

One of the men shoved her forward. She caught her step, but barely, staggering to the stairs that led below.

Belowdecks, she and Sefina were deposited into a small room. The door locked behind them.

Sam fell to her knees with heaving sobs, grasping her face with both hands as her mind burned in the flames of two fires—the one that had stolen Rhett and the one that now consumed Mr. Bixby and the crew. Sefina knelt beside her, wrapping lean arms around her shoulders in comfort. They sat there until Sam's tears dried up, her strength sapped.

She pulled out the golden compass gifted to her by Mr. Bixby and gripped it tight, her fingers pressing into the smooth, familiar surface. Bringing it to her lips, she kissed it softly before clutching it to her chest. She rocked in Sefina's arms, but no amount of comfort could stop the grief.

"We navigate the pain," Sefina whispered, and the words didn't seem to be solely for Sam's benefit. "We navigate the pain."

Sam felt a hardness overcome her. Spilling tears wouldn't bring them back, and she had spilled enough already. For her mother. For Rhett.

Ripping a thin strip of fabric from the hem of her shirt, she used it to secure the compass around her neck. A symbol of a promise. A reminder.

She had failed once before—failed Rhett. This time she wouldn't.

This time, she would have vengeance.

"He called you *princess*."

Sam sat in the cramped room they'd been locked in, staring at the low ceiling as the ship creaked and swayed around them. She did her best not to blink, because every time she closed her eyes, her mind replayed death and flame.

Sefina didn't pretend not to know what she meant. "He did."

"How does he know?" Sam asked.

"I told you tattoos have meanings in my culture. It appears this Salik Kharzul can decipher them as well."

The door groaned as it opened, a wiry pirate standing just outside. "Cap'n wants an audience."

Sam and Sefina both moved, but the man held up a hand. "Red only."

Panic flooded Sam. She locked eyes with Sefina just before stepping out of the room. A moment later, her last remaining friend was out of sight, locked behind the door.

Sam squinted as she stepped onto the deck and into the light of the sun. A chorus of jeers and catcalls greeted her. Steeling herself against the roguish men, she stared out at the vast sea beyond. The storm clouds from before had dissipated, leaving clear blue skies as far as the eye could see.

And as much as she hated to admit it, the *Golden Krina* was truly a sight to behold. It was at least twice the size of the *Queen Mary* and, from the way the water rushed past, twice as fast. The oak planks beneath her feet glowed deep brown in the sunlight, polished to a shine, and she walked past glistening golden rails, waiting as her escort rapped on the heavy oak door to the captain's cabin. Each knock tied another knot in her stomach.

"Enter," the captain's voice called.

Sam's escort opened the door and glowered at her until she moved forward into the cabin. Her heart pounded anxiously, and she wished Sefina had been allowed to come with her. The door thudded shut.

As her eyes adjusted to the dimmer lighting, Captain Kharzul greeted her. His jeweled fingers sparkled as he gestured for her to sit in a lavish, velvet-covered chair facing the desk. She sat tensely.

Rather than taking his place behind the desk, Kharzul stood in front of it, leaning against the polished wood.

"What is your name, poppet?" His voice was rich and seductive, the way she imagined a sea snake would talk.

Sam stared at her hands in her lap, refusing to meet his eyes. He didn't deserve to know her name when so many others had died nameless at his command.

A moment ticked by.

Then a wave of darkness filled the space. Sam gasped at the smoky black tendrils billowing around her ankles.

"I will not ask again." Any warmth in Kharzul's tone had died.

Sam's eyes shot upwards, meeting his, and she felt the blood drain from her face. Rage flickered in his golden eyes, and darkness radiated from his very being. Sam froze, petrified, her firm facade shattered. For a heartbeat, she wasn't a grown woman before a pirate lord—she was a child huddled beneath her blanket, paralyzed by the Darkbringer of Mother's bedtime stories.

"Sam," she rasped. "Atherton."

Kharzul's face remained severe, but the darkness seemed to lift ever so slightly. "And your age, Miss Atherton?"

"Eighteen," she whispered. Her crew had celebrated with her not a week prior.

"A young beauty," he murmured. "Miss Atherton, I can be quite generous, but that will quickly change should you not show the respect I demand."

Sam nodded. Kharzul lifted his eyebrows, expectant.

"Yes, Captain," she answered.

It seemed to be the response he was looking for. "You are not our prisoner, my poppet," he reassured her, "but it should be known that I cannot let you leave. You are part of my crew now, and you will be assigned duties just like the rest of them." He shifted forward, reaching for her.

Sam stood abruptly and would have stepped back had the chair not stopped her. Kharzul moved even closer, invading her space and sending icy shivers down her spine.

"This hair is quite lovely," he said, toying with one of her tresses. "So vibrantly red."

Sam swallowed at his sultry tone, unable to find her voice as his hand trailed near her collarbone. With a finger, he lifted the ragged fabric hanging around her neck. Her compass dangled in the air between them. "What is this trinket?"

"A compass." She wrapped her hand defensively around the piece.

At her reaction, a small smile lifted the corners of his mouth. "What would a young woman such as yourself be doing with such a thing?"

"It was a gift." She pushed away the image of Mr. Bixby's smile in her mind before it could undo her.

Captain Kharzul was thoughtful for a moment. "A rather unique gift. Useless for one who does not understand its purpose. Can you use it?"

Sam nodded slowly. "I can." A part of her was afraid to say just how well.

Kharzul pinned her with sharp, predatory eyes. "Show me."

He strode past her and was nearly out of the cabin before Sam realized she was meant to follow. She hurried after him. They reached one of the portside railings, where Captain Kharzul stopped. "Set a course for Atral."

"I... What?" Sam's brows drew together.

"A course. For Atral."

Eyeing the shadows that had gathered at the captain's feet, Sam fumbled with her compass. She tilted her head to examine the position of the sun in the sky and the way the sails caught the wind.

She didn't know exactly where they were on the water, but she did know that Phago's capital, Atral, was northeast of where the *Queen Mary* had been raided. With the way the winds were blowing, the *Golden Krina* couldn't have traveled far from there, and she could determine the overall direction they would need to take.

Gesturing to the starboard side of the ship, near the bow, she said, "I... I believe we would need to sail in this direction to reach Atral." Then she added quickly, "I would need to study stars and maps to know more accurately."

She couldn't read the captain. His gaze rested on her like a heavy weight before he turned to survey the deck.

"Cavenaugh!" he shouted.

The pirate who answered was tall, with a broad, muscular frame that hinted at years of hard work at sea, though he couldn't have been more than twenty-five—perhaps even younger. His shirt hung open at the chest, the loose ties at his collar left undone and the sleeves rolled up past his powerful biceps. He'd tied back his sun-streaked blonde hair, though a few strands still fell across his tanned face. A thin scar cut through the short beard on his jaw. His eyes—sharp and blue-gray, like the sky before a storm—examined Sam with wary appraisal.

"Yes, Captain," he replied, his voice steady and surprisingly deep. He stood straight, hands loosely clasped behind his back as he awaited the captain's next instruction.

"She is your charge now." Kharzul gave a clipped nod toward Sam. "As is the Haapari princess. Show them to the women's quarters."

Sam's heart raced as the pirate—Cavenaugh—slid a hand around her arm. His fingers were rough and callused, but his grip remained loose, showing control rather than malice.

As they stepped away, Kharzul's voice called out once more, making them pause. "Oh, and Cavenaugh... I would not see this one harmed. She has untapped potential—see what she can do."

"Yes, Captain," Cavenaugh said without hesitation.

They moved belowdecks, the lantern light casting shadows that danced along the narrow passageways. The deeper they went, the more the weight of the ship's silence closed in around them.

As Cavenaugh walked beside her, Sam stole a glance at his profile. Many of the pirates left their beards ragged and unkempt, but his short beard was neatly trimmed, framing a strong jawline. A small silver ring adorned his ear, catching the light with each step.

Cavenaugh halted and turned without warning, stepping in close—so close that the space between them disappeared, and she found herself nearly chest-to-chest with him. He was massive up close, his broad shoulders filling the narrow space of the passageway, and the sheer size of him made her feel cornered, though she fought to hide any intimidation.

She had to tilt her head up to meet his gaze, her breath catching as his stormy eyes flicked over her. She kept her expression defiant.

His lips curved into a slow smirk as he leaned down, one arm braced against the wall beside her, caging her in. "You've been staring," he murmured, his voice low and slightly amused.

Sam met his gaze, forbidding herself from stepping away even as his proximity sent a twinge of unease through her. "Just figuring out what kind of man Kharzul trusts to play guard dog."

A quiet laugh escaped him, rough around the edges. "Guard dog? I do a bit more than that, Red. But call me what you like. Just know it's my job to keep you in line... and I'm very, very good at it."

"I won't be a prisoner. And don't think I'll simply 'play along' with whatever is going on here," she replied, her voice edged with challenge.

Cavenaugh's smirk deepened. "You're not a prisoner. You're crew."

"I'm not part of your crew. I didn't ask to be here."

He leaned back just a little. "No one *asks* to be here. But you'll do your part just the same as the rest of us." He traced a finger lightly along the wall, his eyes drifting back to hers, full of that same unreadable intensity. "Otherwise, you'll find life aboard this ship quite... difficult."

For a moment, they stood in tense silence. There was something about this man that unsettled her. Not the way the other pirates did with their leering stares and crude remarks or the way Captain Kharzul did with his darkness. Cavenaugh's unsettling presence came from the way his calm control made her feel as if he could see right through her defenses.

"Listen." His gaze dropped to her, lingering a moment too long before he straightened, finally putting an inch of distance between them. "Do as you're told, and you'll be fine."

"And why should I trust you?" she asked, her voice defiant.

"You shouldn't. I am a pirate, after all." The words came out playful but with an edge to them that made Sam's chest tighten. She couldn't read him. "Stay close, and I'll keep you alive. That's the deal."

She clenched her jaw. "I'll keep myself alive."

Cavenaugh's smirk softened, and he cocked his head, studying her.

With a nod toward the passageway, he gestured her forward, though he didn't move, forcing her to brush past him if she wanted to continue. As she did, his voice followed her, a dark and knowing whisper that sent a chill through her. "The fire in you might be what saves you... or burns you alive. Let's see which it is."

TWENTY

S am swung her legs over the side of the bed, heart beginning to pound. "We should escape," she whispered. "Right now."

The women's quarters were only marginally bigger than the room they'd initially been deposited in. They hadn't seen a soul in hours. No guards. No footsteps. And now it would be fully dark. If there was ever a moment, now was it.

Sefina lay sprawled across her own narrow cot, one arm tucked behind her head. She lifted an eyebrow as she turned her face toward Sam, ice-blue eyes catching the lanternlight. "We are in the open sea."

Sam ignored her, pulling on her boots. "I have to try. I'm not staying here. I won't."

Sefina settled deeper into the thin mattress, eyes sliding shut as she released a slow breath. "They're watching us, Atherton."

Sam didn't answer. Her hairpin was already in the lock.

"I can handle myself," she muttered.

"If you say so," Sefina replied, her voice flat. "I'll be here when you return."

Click.

Fingers grasping the handle, Sam hesitated.

Just a peek, she told herself. To see how far they could make it. She could never leave Sefina behind.

The door eased open with barely a sound, just wide enough for Sam to slip through. Lanterns cast long shadows across the walls of the hallway beyond. The ship creaked around her as it swayed on the waves. Sam moved cautiously, her boots padding across the worn wooden planks.

She reached the end of the hall and paused at the sound of footsteps approaching. She ducked behind a crate, holding her breath as two crewmen passed by, their conversation low and unintelligible. When they disappeared down another passageway, she exhaled slowly, her pulse still racing.

With the corridor clear, Sam pressed on, inching her way up toward the main deck where she hoped she could untie a skiff. She'd get Sefina and row.

She thought of the open sea, of finding a way to Haapa, but just as she rounded a corner, she came face to face with Cavenaugh.

His broad frame blocked the passage, and Sam stopped dead in her tracks, her heart sinking. His eyes narrowed slightly as he took in the sight of her sneaking about the ship.

"Trying to escape, are we?" His tone sounded more amused than angry.

Sam clenched her jaw, trying to muster up confidence despite the sinking feeling in her gut. "I'm just... getting some air."

He stepped closer, his voice dropping lower. "If the captain were to hear that you were sneaking about, things could go badly for you and your Haapari friend. *Very* badly."

Sam swallowed, a chill creeping down her spine. "I'm not scared of him," she lied.

"You should be," Cavenaugh said, his eyes darkening. "Kharzul doesn't take kindly to deserters."

Sam's bravado faltered, and she cast a quick glance toward the stairwell that led to the deck, calculating her chances of making it past the man standing before her.

"Go back to your quarters," Cavenaugh said. "Before you do something stupid that gets you killed."

After a long pause, Sam reluctantly turned and made her way back down the hallway. Cavenaugh followed her closely, his heavy boots thudding quietly on the wood behind her.

When she re-entered her quarters, Sefina was sitting up in bed, her arms crossed as if she'd been anticipating Sam's return. "I told you."

Sam glared at her but said nothing as she sat heavily on the edge of her cot. Cavenaugh lingered in the doorway for a moment.

"Next time, I might not be the one to find you," he warned. "The others wouldn't be so forgiving. Remember that."

With that, he turned and left, the door creaking shut behind him.

Sam sank onto the edge of her mattress, dropping her head into her hands.

Sefina's voice cut through the silence. "We'll find a way off this ship. It may take some time, but I promise you this is not the end for us."

Sam clenched her fists. Deep down, she'd known there was no chance at escape, but she'd been unable to see another path forward. The all-consuming despair that had gripped her after Rhett's death hovered at the edge of her senses, waiting to make its claim again. She held it back by opening her compass and staring down at the quivering needle, steady in its direction.

She knew her direction.

She would just have to bide her time to reach it.

Sam slouched against the wall, arms crossed as she watched Cavenaugh attach yet another dagger to his belt. As instructed, she had stayed close to him the entire week she'd been aboard the *Golden Krina*.

Grief still clung to her—inescapable, drowning her in quiet waves. She hadn't been much use on the ship, nor had she cared to be. Her body moved when commanded; her hands performed simple tasks when ordered. But her mind was lost in the memories of the *Queen Mary*, of Mr. Bixby's booming laugh, of the crew's songs echoing over the waves.

She hadn't let herself cry since that first night. Not when she and Sefina received different work orders, separating them during the day on the ship. Not when she lay awake at night, staring at the ceiling and listening to the distant laughter of men who had murdered her friends. She'd spent her tears.

The cabin she sat in now was dimly lit, the flickering lantern casting shifting shadows against the walls. The scent of oil mixed with the ever-present salt, but it didn't smell right. It didn't smell like the *Queen Mary*. She was out of place here, and she was still trying to figure out why Kharzul had let her live. Was it amusement? Pity? Or did he truly think she could be useful?

She scoffed under her breath, watching as Cavenaugh adjusted the belt across his chest.

"How many knives does one pirate need?" Sam asked, forcing dry humor into her tone as she eyed the assortment strapped to him—the blades, the twin pistols, the heavy iron of a small axe. But her gaze kept slipping.

It was impossible to ignore the way his linen shirt cut low to reveal the powerful swell of his chest, or how the leather harness emphasized the broad set of his shoulders. The man was dangerously easy to look at. His rugged, sculpted symmetry felt like a personal insult to her.

Without looking up, Cavenaugh checked the edge of a dagger. "Depends how many fools I expect to encounter in a day."

Sam blinked, heat rising to her cheeks at the realization that she'd been staring. She quickly snapped her gaze back to his face, her lips pressing into a frown.

Cavenaugh's expression turned thoughtful as he finally glanced her way. "I assume that since the captain assigned you to me, you've got some talent when it comes to direction."

Sam couldn't think of navigation without thinking of Mr. Bixby—the way he had traced her fingers over maps, had pointed to the sky and taught her which stars to follow.

She bit her lip, the grief clawing at her, fresh and raw. Was this why Kharzul had spared her? To make use of what little skill she had? It was cruel.

"I might," she said slowly. "Why?"

Cavenaugh fastened the last of his weapons, rolling his shoulders before answering. "I need another set of eyes when we hit rough waters. Can't be everywhere at once." He gave her a calculated look. "The captain said you might be useful. I plan to find out if that's true."

Sam's grip tightened around her arms. Was this her fate now? To be useful to the people who had taken everything from her?

"So I'm just another tool for you to use?"

Cavenaugh's gaze met hers, his expression unreadable. "Everyone pulls their weight here."

"And what if I don't pull my weight?"

His lips curved into a slow, dangerous smirk. "Then I'll throw you overboard myself." His tone was teasing, but the glint in his eye made it clear he'd seen too much to make idle threats.

Before she could snap back, the ship pitched suddenly as a wave crashed against the hull, sending a violent shudder through the deck. Sam stumbled forward and fell to a knee.

Cavenaugh was unfazed by the movement. He motioned for Sam to follow him out onto the deck. "I'll show you how to handle navigation during this kind of weather. The seas here can turn against you quickly, and I'd prefer not to lose the ship—or anyone on it."

Sam hesitated. The idea of becoming something they wanted her to be grated against her. And yet...

The sea called to her almost as much as the sky. Navigation wasn't just something she had been taught—it was something she had grown to love. A skill that had made her feel powerful and in control, even when the world around her turned to a storm. If she let them take that from her, if she refused to use what she knew just to spite them... what did that leave her with?

Nothing.

She clenched her jaw as she followed Cavenaugh up onto the deck. The wind hit her first, a sharp gust that sent her hair whipping around her face. The ship lurched beneath her feet, but she steadied herself this time, letting the familiar ebb and flow of the waves guide her movements.

She had spent enough time aboard a ship to know how to balance with the sway, but Cavenaugh made it look effortless. Natural. As if he was part of the ship itself. Sam watched the way he moved—calm and steady. He adjusted the sails, his hands moving deftly over the ropes as he checked their course.

A quiet frustration stirred in her chest. She didn't want to assist, but the idea that the pirates might look at her and see someone incapable—someone who didn't belong on a ship at all—felt even worse.

She wasn't some lost girl plucked from the sea. She knew how to navigate. She knew the stars, the currents, the feel of the wind before a storm. And she'd be hard-pressed to let them think otherwise.

Grabbing onto the rigging, she hoisted herself up into the lower ratlines, each movement fluid and confident. She had climbed the mainmast of the *Queen Mary* more times than she could count. The heights had always belonged to her.

"Watch yourself, Red," Cavenaugh called with a sideways glance at Sam.

She ignored him, gripping the ropes tighter as she climbed higher. "I don't need your coddling."

But just as the words left her lips, the ship lurched over an unexpected swell, and the force sent a jolt through the rigging, dislodging her boot from the worn ropes. Her grip faltered as her foot caught awkwardly in the ratlines, twisting her balance at the worst possible angle. She gasped as she tipped backward, her body pitching out toward the open sea below.

Before she could plummet into the waves, a strong arm hooked around her waist, yanking her out of the air.

Cavenaugh.

He held her pressed against him, one of his hands gripping the small of her back, the other holding the ropes where she had lost her footing. Sam clung to him for a breathless moment, her fingers clutching his shirt, her pulse hammering against her ribs.

Cavenaugh exhaled a low chuckle. "If you wanted to escape, you might've picked a less dramatic way."

Sam scowled. "I wasn't trying to escape."

"Uh-huh."

She realized Cavenaugh still had his hand around her waist. She pushed against his chest, ignoring the warmth of his skin beneath his open collar. "You can let me go now, Cavenaugh."

His grip loosened, but he didn't step away just yet. "Kensley," he corrected.

Sam hesitated, pulse still unsteady. "Sam."

For a beat, neither of them moved. Then, with a slow nod, Kensley finally stepped back. His eyes lingered a moment before he returned to his work. Sam watched the easy way he moved, as though the moment had cost him nothing at all. The warmth of his touch still clung to Sam's skin, lasting far longer than it should have.

TWENTY-ONE

"Oi, Cavenaugh!" a voice jeered as Sam followed Kensley across the main deck. She'd been shadowing him for three weeks now, a period of time that felt both like a lifetime and a heartbeat.

Sam cut a glance to where the voice had come from. A small group of men sat in a circle while mending a shredded sail. One man, a grizzled pirate with lips so thin they were nearly invisible, spoke again. "That Red's too pretty for just one man, ain't she? You ought to share the bounty."

Sam clenched her jaw and kept walking, eyes fixed on the back of Kensley's head. She was no stranger to men like these. She'd endured all manner of taunts growing up on the streets. Words were just that—words.

Let them think she was weak. Let them believe they could shake her. Her fingers brushed lightly against her belt as she passed, feeling the added weight there. The quiet proof of her own small victories. A coin pouch here, a ring there. Things they hadn't even realized were missing yet.

Kensley didn't slow down, but his voice carried back, sharp and deceptively cool. "If you put as much effort into that stitch as you did your mouth, O'Toole, we might actually catch the wind by sunset."

A few of the other men snickered as O'Toole's smug grin faltered, his gaze dropping back to the canvas in his lap. As Sam watched the men shrink back into their work, a realization clicked into place.

She and Sefina hadn't been touched since boarding, and Sam knew it wasn't because the pirates had grown a conscience. It was because of Kensley. He held sway over this ship in a way that had nothing to do with rank. It wasn't the captain or even the quartermaster keeping the brutes in check. It was the man walking in front of her.

That thought followed her as they reached the hatch. Kensley dismissed her with a brief nod, his attention shifting to the rigging as he left Sam to descend into the belly of the ship.

Stepping into the galley was like stepping into a different world, one that replaced biting salt-spray and howling wind with a humid, steamy embrace. The pungent scents of fish stew, salt pork, and bread filled the air, and the clatter of pots and knives muffled out most of the noise from above deck.

The cook, skin permanently glazed in grease, grunted an instruction. In response, Sam pried open the barrel of salt pork, rolling up her sleeves before pulling out pieces of meat for soaking. Sefina worked at the opposite end of the galley, a pile of small silver fish in front of her.

Whether it was scrubbing laundry until her knuckles bled or prepping meals in this sweltering box, the work was a relief compared to facing the crew. An hour passed in a blur. Sam swiped hair from her eyes with the back of her wrist, hands covered in a thick layer of pork fat and salt. Though she'd braided her hair tightly that morning, several curls had worked themselves free and now hung irritatingly across her face.

She was just getting to boiling the meat for the midday meal when scrapes and thuds sounded above her, quickly followed by a stream of men bursting down the stairs. She hastily pressed herself against the wall as they rushed past and on to the hold below.

Sam investigated the commotion. Peeking down the stairs to the hold, she gaped as the men pulled out massive wooden oars, slid them through slots in the ship's hull, and took their rowing positions. The steady pounding of drums vibrated through the ship. The men rowed in time to the beat, pressing and pulling with long strokes.

Turning, Sam ran up the stairs to the main deck. The crew was a blur of motion, tying ropes and scaling the rigging. The quartermaster's voice cut through the air with a command to prime the cannons. Pacing the gun deck, Kensley barked orders. At his command, the sails were hauled tight to catch maximum speed. He was nearly unrecognizable with his jaw and nose hidden behind a bloodred scarf that left only his eyes visible. Others, too, had donned masks. Just as they had when raiding the *Queen Mary*.

Sam rushed to the railing and leaned over it, craning to see what lay ahead. Not far off, a lone ship fled. Too slow.

The *Golden Krina* sliced through the water, but its speed wasn't what left Sam breathless with fear. It was the way it sailed with an inexplicable darkness at its heels, shadows writhing across the water.

Magic? There was no other explanation, though she'd only ever heard of such in bedtime stories and legends of the gods.

Sam withdrew from the railing, but the sight on deck was hardly better. She watched in horror as the crew prepared for plunder, masked and snarling like animals.

Captain Kharzul stepped up beside her, presenting her with a black lace mask. Sam stared at it, unable to make herself take it from his hand. At her pause, he wordlessly moved behind her, raising the mask to her face and securing the ribbon at the back of her head. She touched it, feeling like an imposter. There was no protection in wearing the mask. No purpose other than to strike fear into the hearts of others.

She turned to face Kharzul. "Why?" she asked. "Why the... theatrics?" Theatrics was the only word she could come up with that accurately described her image of Kharzul and his crew.

Kharzul cocked his head as he admired her, then stepped much too close. His chest was only inches from her face—that same musky scent enveloping her and sending a chill through to her bones. Before she could step back, he reached around her neck, pulling the length of her braid forward so that it dangled over her shoulder. Sam stood frozen in place as he loosened the leather binding. Her plait unraveled, and her red curls blew softly under her chin.

Kharzul stepped back, satisfied, and when he responded, his voice was smooth. "Why not, poppet? We have an image to uphold. After all, we *are* the infamous Pirates of the Rutane."

Ruthless, dreaded, merciless beings. And now they were her shipmates.

"But plundering *every* ship you come across?" she pressed.

Kharzul looked at her with a mixture of sympathy and amusement. "A fish that chooses to swim alone in a sea of sharks is begging to be eaten. These sailors are no different. Some attempt to flee, which only serves to make the hunt all the more *exhilarating*."

Sam gaped at him. At her display of shock, Kharzul reached out, stroking her jaw with the back of his hand. Cold slithered through her at the touch, and it took every ounce of willpower not to flinch.

"You will soon become accustomed to our way of life," he remarked before turning to take a position behind the helmsman, hands laced behind his back.

Then, with a casual flick of his fingers, he gestured to his left. "By my side, poppet. You will watch."

A lump formed in Sam's throat, but she obeyed, forcing her feet to move forward.

A moment later, Kharzul called, "Langley!"

The quartermaster approached swiftly. "Yes, Captain?"

"I require the Haapari princess."

"Aye, aye, sir."

The *Golden Krina* closed the distance, her massive hull cutting through the waves with unmatched speed. The merchant ship ahead was running, but it was a futile effort. Sam had seen it before—she knew how this story ended. She could almost hear the terrified shouts carrying across the water, see the desperate hands yanking at ropes, pushing the sails to their limit. It wouldn't matter. The *Golden Krina* was faster. Stronger. Unstoppable.

Her stomach twisted as she stole a glance at Kharzul, standing tall at the helm, his posture relaxed, his expression anticipatory. For him, this was routine. Expected.

For Sam, it was a nightmare replaying itself.

She gritted her teeth, her breaths turning shallow. How many times had they done this? How many innocents had they already drowned, butchered, stolen away?

Langley reappeared, Sefina in tow. The sight of her friend—face masked, back straight, a quiet storm in her eyes—should have steadied her, but it only made the weight in Sam's chest heavier. Because they both knew exactly what came next.

And they could do nothing to stop it.

Her hands curled into fists as she forced herself to stand still, to swallow down the bile rising in her throat. The sails of the merchant ship billowed desperately, straining for freedom.

But the *Golden Krina* was already upon it.

The air reeked of blood and smoke.

Though Kharzul had disappeared into the chaos below, Sam obeyed his order to stay by the helm. She shifted closer to the rail for a better vantage point, Sefina silent beside her. Her knuckles whitened as she gripped the wood. The black lace of the mask itched on her cheeks.

Across the narrow gap of churning sea, the *Golden Krina*'s crew had swarmed the merchant ship, a violent tide of masked figures moving in ruthless synchrony.

Screams split the air.

Sam watched, eyes wide, as a merchant sailor lunged with a cutlass only to be struck down where he stood—his body lifeless before it even hit the blood-slicked planks. Another tried to flee up the rigging, but a pistol shot rang out, and he tumbled, landing with a sickening crunch. Sam flinched.

From the corner of her eye, she saw Sefina shift. When Sam turned, she found her staring at the carnage, her mouth set in a grim line. Then Sefina murmured, "Do not let them see your fear."

Sam wasn't sure she could speak. She watched as pirates tore through the ship's cargo, kicking open crates and barrels. A barrel of salted fish spilled its contents across the bloodstained planks. Valuable commodities were piled up to be taken back to the *Golden Krina*—rolls of fabric, sacks of grain, and tightly wrapped bundles of fine goods.

Sam gritted her teeth, feeling helpless.

And then she saw him.

Kensley.

He fought skillfully, a cutlass in one hand, an axe in the other. A man charged him—a desperate swing of a rusted saber—only to be met with a swift parry, a sharp pivot, and an axe driven deep into his gut. Kensley barely spared a glance as he tugged the weapon free.

The flames came next, spreading like a living thing, licking up the mast, consuming the sails. Smoke billowed into the sky. The merchant ship groaned. More bodies fell, some beneath blades, others swallowed by fire.

Sam squeezed her eyes shut, but shutting them didn't stop the sounds—the clash of steel, the final screams, the crackling flames. She was back on the *Queen Mary*. Watching, again, as Mr. Bixby tried to save her.

The weight of that day crushed her chest, squeezing the breath from her lungs.

A hand seized her arm and yanked her out of the way as a bullet whizzed past.

Sam gasped, opening her eyes to find Sefina staring back at her.

Turning, heart thundering, Sam locked eyes with the man who'd shot at her from across the gap. The barrel of his pistol was still smoking. He looked… terrified.

Then he was struck down from behind.

Sam swallowed, bile burning her throat, eyes on the now-lifeless man.

"Always be aware of your surroundings," Sefina scolded, gripping Sam's face to draw her gaze. Sam could only nod, still breathless, still shaking. "Come," Sefina said, leading her away from the rail and behind the relative safety of the helm.

With a last glance at the merchant ship, Sam again spotted Kensley moving amid the carnage, his face hidden by his bloodred mask. She had thought him different, had convinced herself he was not like the others. But now, watching him participate so effortlessly in the slaughter, she wasn't sure anymore.

Maybe she had been wrong about him.

Maybe Kensley Cavenaugh was just as ruthless as the rest of them.

Maybe he had been from the start.

TWENTY-TWO

S am knelt beside a wooden tub filled with murky water, her sleeves rolled to her elbows, hands raw from scrubbing. The makeshift washroom at the stern of the ship was little more than a space between barrels, with a few buckets of seawater and lye soap. Sunlight flickered off the red-tinged water, which was rapidly darkening to crimson.

Her stomach clenched, threatening a rise.

She willed herself to focus on the motion—dip, scrub, wring, repeat. Laundering was something she could do. She'd done it countless times before.

But never with the weight of death soaked into every thread.

Beside her, Sefina scrubbed in silence, moving as if she didn't see the blood at all.

Sam dipped a new tunic into the water. A fresh wave of red bloomed from the fabric, swirling like ink. Her throat tightened, and she had to squeeze her eyes shut for a moment to keep the bile back.

"If they see you flinch, they'll know it bothers you," Sefina murmured, her voice like stone. "And if they know it bothers you, they will use it against you."

Clenching her jaw, Sam returned to her work. She wanted to argue, wanted to say something about how none of this was normal, but what good would it do? Sefina was right. During her few weeks on the ship, the pirates had already made it clear they saw her as an outsider, an inconvenience at best. Showing weakness would only make things worse.

The sound of boots scuffing the deck made Sam's hands still. A shadow loomed over her.

"Well, now," a voice drawled. "Ain't it somethin' how quickly one gets used to the sight of blood?"

Sam didn't look up, but she recognized the voice—Joss, one of the crewmen who took particular enjoyment in sneering at her and Sefina.

A shirt sailed through the air and landed with a wet slap against Sam's arm, sending droplets of red spattering across her hands.

She stiffened, flicking her eyes up at the man. Two others stood just behind him.

Joss chuckled, crossing his arms as he looked down at her. "First time cleanin' up after a kill, Red?" He grinned widely. "Won't be your last."

Sam removed Joss's shirt from her arm, her nails digging into the wet fabric.

"Give it time. You'll be scrubbin' out your own stains soon enough," Joss mused. "If you live that long."

Something inside Sam snapped.

She stood and hurled the bloodied shirt back at him. It landed against his bare chest with a sickening squelch.

Joss's grin faltered. Slow as a predator savoring the moment before a kill, he peeled the tunic away. "Red's got some fire after all," he said with a step forward.

Sam's heart pounded against her ribs, but she held her ground, her hands curling into fists.

"Enough," Sefina said. She hadn't moved, but Sam could feel the tension radiating off her.

Sam ignored the warning.

"You act like you're proud of this," she spat, her voice low and shaking. "Like you're big and tough for cutting down innocent men. You're nothing more than a sickly dog, waiting for scraps."

"You gonna let her talk to you like that, Joss?" one of the pirates asked.

Joss's expression darkened. "You little—"

Sam grabbed another soaking shirt and hurled it straight at his face. It hit with a wet slap. The red-tinged water dripped down his cheek while the others erupted into laughter.

Joss roared in fury and lunged, arms sweeping wide, but Sam ducked under him, twisting out of reach.

Sefina leapt up, striking Joss across the back of the knees with a well-placed kick. Before he could recover, she yanked a sodden tunic from the wash bin and looped it around his thick neck, pulling it tight.

Sam darted forward, grasping his arms to pull them away from where he clawed at his neck. More crew gathered, shouting and jeering, some cheering for Joss, others simply entertained by the spectacle. Joss let out a strangled growl, veins bulging against his temple, his strength wavering.

Then a voice cut through the chaos.

"Now, now, poppet. Time to let go."

The laughter died instantly. Kharzul's voice was smooth, dangerous, and perhaps a bit amused. It sent a shiver down Sam's spine.

The crew parted, clearing a path for the captain. He stood on the steps leading to the helm, his coat open, the silver clasps glinting. He looked relaxed, like he'd been watching the fight unfold as if they were nothing more than animals entertaining him.

"You as well, Princess."

Sam let her grip go slack. Hesitantly, Sefina did the same. Joss staggered back, coughing as he ripped the tunic from his throat, his eyes burning with anger and humiliation.

Kharzul's gaze swept over Sefina and settled on Sam. "I believe you both have duties to attend to in the galley."

It wasn't a suggestion.

Sam swallowed hard. "Yes, Captain."

As she turned to go, Joss rasped behind her, "You'll regret that."

She glanced at him over her shoulder, meeting his furious gaze with steel in her own.

No, she thought. *I won't.*

The soft clang of metal against metal filled the galley as Sam scrubbed at the last of the evening's pots. The warm scent of stew still lingered in the air, though the crew had long since cleared out. Even the cook had retired, leaving piles of dirty dishes in his wake.

Sefina worked behind her, gathering food scraps before heading upstairs to dispose of them.

Then, for what felt like the first time since Sam had boarded the *Golden Krina*, she was alone, just her and the dishes.

She chewed on her cheek as she scrubbed and rinsed, scrubbed and rinsed, reeling as images from earlier that day flashed through her mind with ruthless clarity.

Crimson-streaked planks, screams that pierced the air, flames licking at sails.

It was like living out her nightmares.

Sam's hands stilled for a moment as another image invaded her thoughts—Kensley. He'd been there, too, fighting without hesitation and without mercy. She'd thought him softer, more respectful than the others.

Sam's jaw clenched. She couldn't afford to forget what kind of men these pirates truly were, no matter how civil one of them might appear. They were killers, every one.

A slow clap sounded behind her.

"Didn't think you were the violent type, Red."

Sam stilled.

Joss.

He leaned lazily against the doorway, his smirk curling in the lantern's glow. The bruise forming across his neck was stark in the firelight.

Sam picked up another pot and scrubbed harder, refusing to acknowledge him.

Joss chuckled. "What? No words for me now?" He stepped closer, his voice lowering. "You and that Haapari shrew made quite the spectacle of me earlier. I don't appreciate that."

Though she tried to remain calm, Sam's pulse raced. "Nothing you didn't deserve."

"Speaking of deservin'... I ain't been with a woman for quite some time."

Sam stopped her washing. Gripping the handle of a pot tightly, she turned to find Joss swaggering toward her, a malicious smile on his suntanned face.

"And it'll be some time yet," she said with feigned confidence. "Shove off."

Rather than be persuaded, he kept up his approach. "I like when they put up a fight."

She could either stay and fight or run for help. With little experience fighting, she took her chances with the latter, bolting for the stairs to the main deck.

She was halfway up when Joss caught hold of her ankle. The pot clanged loudly against the stairs as she slid down several.

Sprawled on her stomach, Sam swung the pot awkwardly. Joss caught it easily, wrenching it free. She opened her mouth to scream, the sound cutting off as his hand clamped over her mouth. He leaned over her, pressing his nose into her hair, and inhaled deeply.

She'd been determined not to cry anymore but couldn't hold back the tears that sprang to her eyes as she fought helplessly against the man. The stairs dug into her chest and stomach as she squirmed underneath his weight. She felt blindly for the small dagger on her belt, but the sheath was empty. She glanced at the table, eyes wide with panic, remembering she'd left it there after slicing vegetables for pickling.

If she made it out of this, she would never be caught without a weapon again.

A faint tune reached her ears, too beautiful for the moment. It wasn't any song from the pirate crew. This was... enchanting.

Joss's weight lessened, then disappeared entirely as he climbed to his feet.

The song grew louder, and Sam craned her neck to watch as Joss slowly ascended the stairs, his eyes unfocused as if in a trance. She crept up the stairs behind him, curious as to the source of the sound, and peeked her head out onto the main deck.

Dense fog encompassed the ship, but she could hear the voice coming from her left. Whoever—or *whatever*—it was sang in a language Sam had never heard, the song alluring and dangerous. Irresistible.

Joss continued walking in the direction of the voice through the mist. Sam found herself wanting to join him, to follow the voice to whatever end.

Without meaning to, she took a step forward, then another. Joss walked ten or so paces in front of her.

Until he climbed the railing and stepped right off the side of the *Golden Krina* without a sound.

At that, Sam's trance was broken. She tripped backward over her feet and landed hard on her backside. There was no music to be heard, nothing beyond the splash of waves against the ship. What had come over her?

Sefina rushed to her side as if she'd never left. "Atherton! Are you all right?"

Sam shook her head, trying to rid herself of the haunting tune still lingering in her ears. "Joss... jumped overboard. I don't understand."

Sefina's face hardened. "Do not concern yourself over him."

"Did you hear the voice?" Sam took several steadying breaths. "It was like a dream. I've never heard anything like it."

She wondered if it had been a siren, known for luring men to their deaths. Although she shivered, she also thanked Perixia for the timing.

Sefina scrunched her eyebrows. "Voices can have great power. But they can be dangerous—especially out on the water. You should not seek it out again." She stood, holding out a hand for Sam. "Come, we will finish in the galley."

"I didn't seek it out... It found me," Sam mumbled as she grasped Sefina's outstretched hand and was pulled to her feet.

Back in the galley, Sam stooped to pick up the discarded pot. She stared down at the half-clean pot, her posture rigid. With a little coaxing, she told Sefina about Joss's visit leading up to the strange voice. She didn't like imagining what would have happened had Joss succeeded in what he set out to do.

"I didn't have my knife tonight..." she said softly. "And even if I did, I don't know that I could have protected myself against him. I—"

"Evening, ladies."

Sam whirled at the voice, blood draining from her face before she spotted Kensley thudding down the stairs.

His smile faltered as his gaze landed on Sam. "Is everything all right? You look..."

"Everything's fine," Sam mumbled, turning back to her pot, her hands shaking as she resumed scraping.

"No, everything is *not* fine," Sefina interceded, shooting Kensley a glare. "One of your men decided he would take advantage of a woman while she was alone." She dropped the rag she'd been using to scrub and crossed her arms, her eyes blazing with accusation. "Where were you?"

Kensley's expression hardened, his jaw tightening as a dangerous glint sparked in his eyes. His voice dropped low. "Who was it?"

Sam swallowed, keeping her gaze on the pot. "Joss. But he's not an issue anymore." She wasn't sure how to explain the voice that had come out of the mist, that haunting, strange melody that had saved her.

But Sefina wasn't backing down. "He nearly got what he was after, Cavenaugh."

Kensley took a step toward Sam, his voice softer. "Are you all right?"

She paused, feeling the weight of his gaze on her back. "I'm fine." She forced the words out, but they emerged shaky, unconvincing even to her. She turned to face Kensley, her voice firmer now. "But I shouldn't have to rely on voices in the mist to save me."

Kensley's brow furrowed. "Voices?"

"I need to learn how to fight. To defend myself. I'm tired of being helpless."

Sefina nodded. "If you can't guarantee her safety, then at least teach her how to defend herself."

Kensley let out a slow breath, rubbing the back of his neck as he looked between the two women. There was a storm brewing behind his eyes, but he didn't argue.

"You want me to teach you how to fight?" he asked, his tone a mystery.

"Yes." Sam gestured to Sefina. "The both of us. We need to be able to hold our own if we're going to survive on this ship."

Kensley's gaze lingered on Sam, as if searching for something. Then, slowly, he nodded. "I'd wager the captain would allow it."

Sam exhaled, overcome with a sense of relief.

"But you should know," Kensley added, "it won't be easy. If you're serious about learning to defend yourself, you'll have to work for it."

Sam met his gaze evenly. "I'm ready."

A small, approving smirk tugged at Kensley's lips, though his eyes still held that fierce, dangerous edge. "Then we start at dawn. Don't be late."

TWENTY-THREE

In the ship's belly, where barrels were stored and rats scurried freely, the air smelled of aged rum and old iron—an appropriate place, Sam supposed, to learn the art of the blade.

Besides, it was the only place on the ship she and Sefina could train without prying eyes. Kensley had led them there, depositing two curved cutlasses at their feet before disappearing back up top.

"Try not to make me regret trusting you with a blade," he had remarked before vanishing. That had been hours ago.

Sam had snatched up one of the swords the moment he was gone only to find it heavier and more unwieldy than expected. The steel bit into her palms. Still, she swung. Again and again, she hacked at an old barrel, her strikes clumsy, her wrists jolting with each impact. Blisters were already forming on her hands, and her muscles burned from the effort, but she refused to stop.

The ship's creaking timbers added to the eerie atmosphere, and, in her mind, the shadows dancing around her became her enemies. She gritted her teeth and swung, determined to be rid of her helplessness.

By contrast, Sefina moved gracefully a few feet away, her own cutlass spinning with precision and ease as she sliced through the air. Sam stole a glance at her friend, watching as Sefina parried invisible blows with perfect poise. It was infuriating how naturally the movements seemed to come to her, as if she had been born with a blade in hand. Sefina's footwork, her balance—it was all impeccable.

Meanwhile, Sam's arms ached, her feet stumbled, and her frustration mounted.

"You are struggling," Sefina pointed out, her voice light as she deftly blocked Sam's feeble attempt at a strike. "You've taken to other skills far quicker."

Sam huffed, planting her feet as she prepared to take another swing at the barrel. "Maybe it's because I don't exactly come from a long line of swordsmen."

Sefina lowered her sword. "My father is a chief. I have handled many weapons, including swords, in at least some capacity. You must stop fighting against your weapon. *Flow* with it. Like this."

Sefina demonstrated with bent legs as she sliced her sword across a barrel.

Sam grunted, trying to mimic how Sefina had stood, then slicing at her own barrel with less accuracy than she'd hoped for. She swung again, startled when her blade met steel, jarring her wrist.

She yelped, dropping her weapon as Kensley stepped out of the shadows, his cutlass poised from blocking her strike.

"You're holding it wrong," he said, his voice gruff and slightly amused.

Sam shook out her aching wrist and muttered a curse under her breath. "I'm sure it would help if someone were around to, you know, *teach* me. You've been gone for hours."

"I agreed to train you, but I still have duties to attend to," he said, sheathing his cutlass. "I don't get to drop everything just because you're impatient."

Sam bit back a retort, recognizing the sharp edge in his voice. He was frustrated. There was tension in his shoulders, tightness in his jaw. She wondered if she was the cause of it. After all, she'd been assigned to help him, but, so far, her contribution to navigation had been nominal at best.

Kensley sighed and smoothed a hand over his hair. "Look, if you want to learn, then stop swinging wildly and listen." He stepped closer, his tone shifting from irritation to something more measured. "Otherwise, you're going to hurt yourself."

Sam glared, tempted to tell him off. Instead, she wiped the sweat from her brow and bent to pick up her weapon.

"Fine," she said. "Teach."

Kensley nodded, his blue-gray eyes watching her with that ever-present sternness. He adjusted her grip, pulling her hands to the proper positions on the hilt. His touch was firm, the calluses on his hands rough against her skin. A sharp, traitorous jolt of heat shot up Sam's arms at the contact, making the fine hairs on her nape prickle.

Stepping back, Kensley watched her swing the blade once, twice, three times.

"Your footwork is a mess," he said bluntly. "If your feet aren't steady, nothing else will be either."

He stepped behind her, hovering just inches away. Sam's breath hitched as he nudged her lead foot wider with his own, his hand coming to rest briefly on her waist to square her hips. The heat of his palm burned through her clothes, sending a frantic thudding against her ribs that she prayed he couldn't hear.

Sefina paused her own practice, watching with curiosity as Kensley corrected Sam's form. She flashed Sam a look, eyes narrowing with a hint of knowing, before returning to her own effortless routine.

Kensley modeled the footwork, surprisingly light on his feet as he demonstrated the proper way to balance. Sam did her best to follow, though each step felt awkward, like her feet were on separate paths. Her growing frustration made it harder to focus. She tripped over her own feet for the third time, stumbling into a barrel.

She was never this clumsy while thieving. What was so different now?

With a growl of frustration, Sam threw her hands up in the air and stalked away to the far wall. Her chest heaved with labored breaths.

Kensley watched her calmly. "You're fighting yourself more than you're fighting the sword. It takes time. Tomorrow, we'll focus more on the basics. Until then, let it rest."

Sam stared at him, her back stiff with frustration. But she knew Kensley was right—there was no rushing this, no quick way to master a skill entirely foreign. With a reluctant sigh, she nodded. "All right. We'll try again tomorrow."

Kensley's gaze softened just a little, a small hint of approval behind his eyes. "Good. You're not doing as badly as you think."

"Could've fooled me," Sam muttered under her breath, earning a chuckle from Sefina.

She stepped forward and held out the cutlass hilt first.

Kensley didn't take it.

Instead, he reached beneath the stairs and produced two leather scabbards, worn but well cared for. He held them out, one to Sam and one to Sefina.

"They're yours now," he said.

Sam blinked. *Yours.*

For so long she'd had nothing. The few pieces of herself she'd managed to reclaim aboard the *Queen Mary* were resting at the bottom of the ocean now. Her hand-drawn charts, her beloved books of the stars, even the clove soap—all of it had been swallowed by the waves.

She bit her lip, accepting the scabbard and buckling it around her waist, then awkwardly tried to guide the blade home. It caught, scraping softly against the leather.

Kensley stepped closer and steadied her hand, angling the cutlass until it slid into place. "Careful," he said, grinning. "Wouldn't want you stabbing yourself before you've had a proper chance to stab anyone else."

Sam glanced toward Sefina, whose cutlass already rested at her hip. Maybe Sefina was right—maybe Sam was thinking too much, trying too hard to control what was meant to be instinctual. One thing was certain:

she wouldn't stop until she mastered it, no matter how many hours or days it took.

Knock knock. Sam paused her braiding, a length of dark ribbon threaded through her fingers as she pulled her red locks tight.

"Yes?" she called.

"It's Kensley."

"Come in."

The door opened and Kensley stepped just inside. "I have a few minutes and thought you might like to continue training," he said, leaning back against the doorframe.

"Yes," Sam replied, resuming her braid, "I'll just be a moment."

Kensley pushed off the frame and moved further into the room. "That looks familiar."

Sam's hands slowed. Her gaze snapped up, following his to the small table beside her mattress. A folded sash sat there—deep green, edged in gold. Not hers. Too fine for anything she owned.

Sam forced her fingers to keep moving, tying off the braid with a little more care than necessary. "Does it?" she asked lightly.

"An exact match to one I've seen Williams wearing."

Her shoulders tensed. "And?" she said, aiming for casual but not quite achieving it.

Kensley looked at her properly then. An almost amused expression settled onto his face. "You're getting bold, Sam."

Sam's stomach tightened. What would happen if he took this to Kharzul? "I can put it back."

"Did I say you should?" he asked, mouth quirking.

Sam hesitated. That wasn't anger.

Kensley stepped closer to the table, lifting the sash between two fingers. "Williams has been out of line lately," he said mildly. "Along with a few others."

Sam remained silent.

Then, as he set the sash back down, he added almost idly, "Corrigan's on watch duty tonight."

She studied him, trying to decide if this was some sort of test. "That is specific."

"Helpful," he corrected.

So he wasn't going to report her. Was choosing not to.

Sam pushed herself to her feet and reached for her cutlass. "Let's go. I think I can take you today."

Kensley's mouth curved as he stepped aside to let her pass. "Careful, Red. Confidence like that tends to get people into trouble."

"Only if they get caught."

Sam swiped her sweat-dampened hair from her eyes, her arms trembling from the relentless sword training. Beside her, Sefina moved with her usual grace while Sam still clomped around.

"You are improving," Sefina remarked, lowering her sword to observe Sam's stance. "But you are still too tense. Relax your shoulders."

Sam grunted, her frustration palpable. She'd spent every spare hour training—multiple days of waking before the sun and staying up to the wee parts of the night—and while Sefina seemed to improve with every practice, Sam felt like she was barely keeping up. But she couldn't surrender.

Kensley appeared at the base of the stairs. His broad silhouette filled the entryway. "Practice is over."

Sam exchanged a wary glance with Sefina. "What do you mean?"

"Captain's orders." Kensley stepped closer and held up a familiar black lace mask. "We're nearing a merchant vessel. Kharzul expects all hands for the raid."

He tossed a separate mask to Sefina, who made no move to grab it, instead letting it fall to the planks at her feet. Kensley's lips pressed into a frown.

Sam's stomach dropped. "Raid? You mean he expects us to…" She trailed off, her mouth dry.

Kensley nodded stiffly. "Aye. Do you think he approved your sword training with no intention to put it to use?"

Sam's mind reeled. Images from the last raid flashed in her mind—blood on the deck, the terrified faces of the captured sailors, and the cold efficiency with which Kharzul's crew dispatched their victims. She couldn't be expected to participate in that!

"I'm not doing it," she said, the words slipping out before she could stop them.

Kensley's eyes hardened, his voice dropping low. "You don't have a choice, Sam. No one refuses the captain's orders."

Sam shook her head, stepping back. Her heart pounded in her chest. She wasn't like them. She wasn't a pirate. "I won't kill innocent people. I can't."

Sefina placed a hand on Sam's arm. "Neither will I," she said with a defiant look at Kensley.

His jaw tightened. "Then you'll answer to Kharzul himself."

He turned and beckoned them to follow. With a hesitant look at Sefina, Sam stowed her weapon. Following Kensley up the stairs, she heard him mutter, "Not everyone on those ships are as innocent as you think."

Sam worried her lip the entire way up to the main deck. The faint morning light outside felt blinding after hours in the shadows of the lower deck, though fog had already begun gathering around the ship. The chaotic hum of the crew preparing for the raid surrounded them, but Sam fixated on the commanding figure of Kharzul standing near the helm, his dark coat flaring in the wind.

Kensley led them straight to the captain, his usual confidence replaced with something more reserved, almost hesitant. Kharzul's golden eyes turned to them, his attention making Sam's skin crawl.

"Cavenaugh," Kharzul drawled, his voice as dark as the clouds above. "What is this?"

Kensley cleared his throat. "The women... they're feeling unwell, Captain."

Sam's stomach flipped. Kensley was trying to protect them.

Kharzul didn't appear fooled. His eyes glinted with a sadistic spark as he stepped closer. "Surely the excitement will be... rejuvenating."

Sam's stomach soured. "No," she whispered.

Kharzul's attention snapped to her, his stare piercing. "What was that, poppet?"

Though her legs trembled, Sam lifted her head defiantly. Her voice was louder when she said, "I won't take part in this."

"That is not your choice to make."

"I think it is," Sefina said from beside her, voice laced with venom.

Kharzul stilled. "You may go finish your preparations, Cavenaugh," he instructed.

Sam thought she saw Kensley hesitate for just a moment before he said, "Yes, Captain," and turned away. Without his solid presence, Sam suddenly felt cold, and though she wished to look for him, she forced herself to keep her eyes on the captain.

Kharzul stepped toward Sefina, each footfall a slow, deliberate threat. With a twist of his hand, thick tendrils of darkness took form, slithering up and around Sefina's neck. Her eyes widened, choking as the tendrils tightened. No matter how she clawed at the darkness swirling around her neck, her hands passed right through it.

Sam watched in horror as her friend gasped for air.

Kharzul watched, cold and unflinching.

The darkness... Kharzul was controlling it.

"Stop this!" Sam yelled.

"I do not tolerate disobedience," Kharzul stated.

"*Please.*"

"You think me so forgiving?"

Sefina stumbled and collapsed, her face pale. Sam fell to her knees beside the other woman, grasping at her shoulders, searching for a way to make it stop. There was nothing she could do.

Except give Kharzul what he wanted.

"I'll do it!" she screamed desperately, pushing to a stand so that she could face the captain directly. "I'll fight—kill—do whatever you ask! Just let her go."

Kharzul smiled, though it didn't reach his eyes. He held her stare for a moment longer—long enough Sefina went limp and Sam feared he would kill her out of spite—before finally relaxing his hand. The dark tendrils around Sefina's neck dissipated. Free of the magical chokehold, Sefina sucked in a large breath but didn't wake.

With a snap of his fingers, two men appeared at Kharzul's side. "Lock her in the brig," he commanded. "Perhaps a few days there will remind her of my generosity."

They grabbed Sefina's arms, dragging her toward the door that led belowdecks. Nausea rolled through Sam as she watched Sefina's limp silhouette disappear down the hatch.

Kharzul leaned close, his voice a soft caress in her ear, though the words chilled her to the bone. "Next time, she dies."

TWENTY-FOUR

Sam's fingers tightened around the hilt of her sword, slick with sweat and trembling despite her best efforts. This time, Sefina wasn't there. Sam had never felt more alone. The clash of steel rang in her ears, the roar of battle pressing in from every direction.

Kharzul fought with precision several paces away. His dark power rippled through the air like a living thing, coiling and snapping as he carved his way through the chaos. Blood arced from his blades, staining the deck in sweeping strokes. He was unrelenting, calculated, with a wild hunger alight in his golden eyes. And she was expected to fight alongside him.

Her breathing came in short gasps as she parried an incoming strike. The enemy's eyes showed her she wasn't the only one terrified. They were just men, desperate to defend their ship and their lives.

A shot rang out close by, making her flinch. She turned in time to see Kensley a few paces away, a pistol still smoking in his hand. He moved with the same precision as Kharzul but none of the hunger.

Then, suddenly—a sharp pain sliced across her shoulder. She twisted violently, instinct taking over as she drove her sword deep into her attacker's stomach. The man gasped, eyes wide in shock, dropping his cutlass as he crumpled to the deck.

Sam stumbled back, staring down at his lifeless body, her heart hammering.

The screams and clashing of weapons dulled around her, as if she'd plunged underwater. The reality of what she had done pressed in from every side, suffocating.

But there was no time to think. A shadow loomed before her—another opponent, another threat. A sailor with a rusted pike leveled it at her chest, his face twisted in a snarl as he lunged for her exposed side while she was still reeling.

Before the steel could reach her, a flash of blonde moved through her peripheral vision. Kensley was there, a blur of motion that slammed into the sailor with the force of a tidal wave. He parried the pike, his free arm shoving Sam firmly behind the safety of his back. With a single, brutal strike of his hilt, he sent the man sprawling into the fog.

He didn't turn around, eyes scanning the scene before them. "Stay behind me, Sam," he said. "Eyes up. Don't look down."

He stepped forward to meet the next opponent, a human shield between her and the carnage. Sam swallowed the bile in her throat, her fingers tightening around the hilt of her cutlass.

Survive. That was all she could do.

The aftermath was as brutal as the fight itself. The *Golden Krina* drifted alongside the wreckage that Sam currently stood upon. Bodies lay where they had fallen, and the stench of death mingled with the lingering scent of gunpowder. Even now, as the adrenaline faded, the echoes of battle still rang in her ears.

She stood stiffly near the rail, fighting the nausea roiling in her stomach. She'd killed a man today. She could still feel the resistance of her blade meeting flesh, still see the dread in his eyes as his life drained.

She tore her gaze from the bodies and fixed it on Kharzul instead. Did his features seem more gaunt than usual?

Kharzul stood before the merchant captain—a wiry man with graying hair, his fine coat torn and bloodied. His desperate eyes darted wildly, searching for an escape.

"Not me," the merchant captain gasped, blood dripping from his lip. "You want a man? Take him."

He yanked a crewman forward. A sailor with olive skin, who couldn't have been much older than Kensley, staggered as he was shoved. Although dazed and bleeding from a wound on his temple, he did not fall. He did not beg.

Sam's brows furrowed. The merchant captain was trading another man's life. Selling him to save himself. Distant memories of the Lily Company stirred.

The sailor, to his credit, stood tall.

Kharzul studied the injured sailor, then looked back at the merchant with cold amusement. "You believe this to be a fair trade? Your life for his?"

The merchant nodded frantically. "He'll be good use to you, sir. More valuable than any of my cargo."

Kharzul turned to Langley. "Take the lad."

The merchant sagged in relief.

Sam exhaled. *Was Kharzul showing mercy?*

Then he spoke again. "And sink the ship."

The merchant's expression crumpled, but there was no time for pleading. Sam's stomach soured. Within minutes, the crew of the *Golden Krina* were back aboard their own ship while the merchant vessel was being swallowed by the waves.

Kharzul approached her then, his golden eyes crinkling at the edges. "You fought well today."

Sam's jaw tensed. She didn't want his approval.

He stepped closer, his gaze drifting to where the sailor was being led belowdecks. "A shame the boy had such a master," Kharzul murmured. "He'll have a better life here."

Better.

Sam's throat tightened. He spoke as though he had done the man a favor. As though he hadn't just sentenced the rest of the merchant's crew to drown.

She didn't trust herself to respond.

Kharzul exhaled, surveying the wreckage, his voice almost thoughtful. "Every step we take brings us closer to establishing the balance the world so desperately needs." His gaze slid to hers. "You'll see that in time."

Sam's hands curled into fists at her sides as the captain returned to his cabin. Balance. What did any of this have to do with *balance*?

The young sailor had been spared, but not out of kindness. The image of the merchant captain's fear-filled eyes seared itself into her mind. Sam wasn't sure if Kharzul's decision had been a show of power or a lesson in cruelty—either way, it left her cold.

Kensley came to stand quietly at her side. His gaze settled on the last remnants of the wreckage.

"I killed a man today," Sam whispered.

He didn't look at her. "One life for another."

"Who's to say mine was worth more than his?"

At that, Kensley met her gaze. "You don't value your own life?"

"I do," Sam said with a sigh, "but where do I draw the line on taking another's?"

"That's for you to decide."

His words brought her no comfort. She let out a slow breath, her thoughts still heavy. For a while, they were silent, watching the waves lap against the ruined driftwood of what had once been a ship.

Then Kensley spoke again. "Come with me."

Sam hesitated but followed.

Kensley gave orders to the men stationed near the rigging, directing them to loosen or tighten the sails so the ship could catch the wind once more. Sam moved with him, noting how the crew responded without hesitation. Under Kensley's command, the *Golden Krina* stirred back to life.

She expected him to lead her back to the upper decks to chart a new course as they'd done over the last several weeks. Instead, she found herself being led below, to where the new recruit had been taken.

The man sat slumped against a barrel, his wound hastily bandaged, the cloth spotted red. His expression was distant, as though he hadn't yet processed what had happened and what he had lost.

Sam knew that feeling all too well. That numb, suspended state between shock and acceptance. She wasn't ready to face it again—not in him, not in herself. So she hung back as Kensley crouched beside the man and pulled out a flask.

"Welcome aboard, mate," he said. "You're alive, which is more than most can say."

The sailor hesitated, murmuring something in a language Sam did not understand, before accepting the outstretched flask, fingers trembling as he lifted it to his lips.

They lingered only a minute longer before Kensley stood and moved through the lower deck. He checked wounds, handed out water, and offered reassurances to the injured. Sam followed in silence, watching as men who had moments ago been groaning in pain managed tired smirks and quiet words of thanks. She'd never given much thought to how injuries were handled on a ship like this; she'd assumed it was every man for himself. But now as she watched, she noticed something.

The crew respected Kharzul. They feared him. But Kensley? They *liked* him.

Later that night, Sam sat cross-legged beside Kensley at the small table, poring over the sea charts he'd spread out. She chewed on her cheek, unable to focus. She hadn't seen Sefina since she had been taken to the brig that morning, and concern gnawed at her gut. For what had to be the fifth time, her fingers trailed over a line indicating the coast of a distant land. The nearby lantern cast warm light over the parchment, highlighting lines and marks more complex than anything Sam had studied aboard the *Queen Mary*.

"Sefina will be fine."

Kensley's rumbling voice broke her from her thoughts, and she glanced up to find him looking at her.

"Will she though?" she asked quietly.

Nodding, Kensley said, "I've made sure she gets food and water, but the rest is up to her."

Sam's chest tightened at his words. Sefina was proud, resistant to Kharzul's rule, and he clearly saw that as a threat.

Kensley seemed to sense her unease. "She's been defiant from the start. Kharzul sees her as an animal that needs to be broken." He paused. "The sooner she plays along with that, the sooner he'll let her out."

Play along. That was what it always came down to on this ship—survival by bending to Kharzul's will. Sam couldn't imagine her friend submitting to *anyone's* rule. But if it was the only way to stay alive...

Sefina wasn't only tough; she was smart, too. Sam had to believe that Kensley was right—that Sefina would be fine.

"I've never seen power like Kharzul's," she said softly a minute later. "That's why everyone is so compliant, isn't it? They're all afraid of him. Of the power he wields."

Kensley was quiet as he collected his thoughts. "Power such as his is unheard of, that's true. But there are those who follow him for reasons that go beyond their fear."

Sam shook her head, confused at how anyone could be loyal to a man who ruled the way Kharzul did. Blowing out a breath, she turned back to the map, tracing that same coastline once more.

Kensley leaned over, pointing to a small symbol she hadn't noticed. "That's a seamount. Dangerous waters, especially for a ship like this. You'll want to chart a course well around it."

Sam frowned, studying the mark. "I've never seen charts like this before. I didn't realize how much detail went into them."

Kensley gave a slight nod. "Navigation isn't just about knowing direction—it's about avoiding hazards, reading currents, knowing how the wind can change. It's why we plot courses instead of sailing blind."

She looked up at him, genuinely intrigued. "How did you learn all of this?"

Kensley's expression shifted, his gaze softer. He leaned back against the wall, resting his arms across his knees, the moment suddenly more personal. "My father taught me. I grew up on a merchant ship. Spent more time at sea than on land." He glanced down at the map, a half-smile forming on his face. "He was the navigator, and he started teaching me when I was just a boy."

"A merchant ship? So when did Kharzul..."

"It was a long time ago."

Sam waited quietly while Kensley collected his thoughts.

"My father was a good man," Kensley began, his voice steady. "We worked hard, kept the ship running, sold our goods reliably. But the man who owned the ship was vile. Greedy. No matter how hard we worked, it was never enough for him."

He paused, any hint of a smile now gone. "One day, my father got injured on deck. It wasn't his fault, but do you think the merchant cared? No. He said my father couldn't complete his duties and sent him off at the very next port." Kensley's jaw tightened, his gaze hardening. "But not me. He told me it was now my responsibility to fulfill not only my contract but my father's as well. With interest."

Sam felt a pang of sympathy in her chest. "That's terrible," she whispered.

Kensley nodded, his expression grim. "I was sixteen. And the work became impossible. I was practically a slave. Then one night, Kharzul's ship attacked."

Sam's breath caught in her throat. "Just like the *Queen Mary*."

"We didn't stand a chance. Kharzul's men boarded us, and… well, I made a choice. Instead of defending that merchant and his vile ship, I asked to join the crew that had overpowered us. I figured I'd rather take my chances as a pirate than spend the rest of my life working off a debt that would never be paid."

Sam's eyes widened. "And Kharzul just accepted you?"

"He did," Kensley said, a touch of surprise in his own voice. "Turns out good navigators are few and far between."

Sam was reminded of when Mr. Bixby had said something similar.

Kensley continued, "That was eight years ago. It's not a pretty life, but I've been treated more fairly here than I ever was under that merchant." He met her gaze, his blue-gray eyes steady. "Kharzul may be ruthless, but he understands the importance of a loyal crew."

Sam looked down at the map, her thoughts racing. She couldn't imagine being trapped in that kind of life—forced to serve, stripped of all choice. A part of her understood why Kensley had made the decision he had, even if she couldn't accept it for herself.

"And what of your life?" Kensley asked.

"What about it?"

"Have you always been at sea?"

"Oh." Sam wrapped one hand around the compass at her neck. "No," she said. "I grew up in Milderre."

Picking at a notch in the table, she dredged up memories of her past. "I got into some trouble there. And someone else died because of it." She paused, her gaze falling to her lap as she continued, "His name was Rhett."

Kensley was quiet. Eventually, he concluded, "You loved him."

"I did," Sam whispered. She lifted her eyes to meet Kensley's.

"I'm sorry," he said.

"So am I."

They stared at one another for a long moment. Finally, Sam cleared her throat. Looking down at the map, she pointed to another unfamiliar symbol.

"What's this one?"

Sam gave her cutlass a swing, stifling a yawn from being awake much too early. Seven days. That was how long Sefina had been in the brig thus far. She had spent that time honing her skills, repeating movements until they became familiar. Each stroke and parry became sharper, more precise. She hoped that, one day, the heavy sword would become an extension of her arm.

She intended to show Kensley just how much she had improved.

They faced each other on the lower deck, the dim light of the swaying lanterns casting shadows that danced along the wooden planks. Kensley stood in his usual relaxed stance, sword in hand, his face a mask of calm. He had a habit of letting her come to him—testing her, pushing her, but never making the first move.

"Ready?" Kensley asked, raising his sword, the steel glinting in the low light.

"More than," Sam replied, gripping her weapon tighter. Her heartbeat quickened with anticipation, her muscles humming. As they began circling one another, the weight of his gaze settled on her, studying her every move.

She lunged forward, attacking with a series of practiced strikes. Kensley blocked her easily at first, his blade meeting hers with smooth precision, but Sam had learned to anticipate his movements. She parried his next blow, then riposted with swift, calculated steps, moving in a flawless combination that sent Kensley stumbling.

His eyes flickered with surprise, but Sam wasn't finished. Seeing the opening, she kicked out, aiming to send him to the ground. Kensley was quicker than she expected, catching her by the ankle and halting her mid-motion.

"Not bad," he said, a slow smirk tugging at his lips.

Sam gasped, her heart hammering against her ribs as she hopped to keep her balance. With a sharp tug, Kensley pulled her leg forward. In one fluid motion, his hand slid up to catch her thigh, his fingers biting into her skin as his sword arm wrapped around her waist. He hauled her flush against him, pinning her own sword arm down in the space between their chests.

"Your move." Amusement danced in his stormy eyes, his face so close she could feel the warm brush of his breath.

Sam's breath came fast, her pulse thrumming in the heat of his gaze, but she wasn't about to give up. A grin split her lips, and with a quick flick of her free wrist, she poked Kensley's ribcage with the dagger she'd slipped from her hip sheath.

His eyes widened in shock before he released her, stepping back with a laugh. "Well done, Sam. Though if I recall, we were supposed to be practicing with our swords."

Sam shrugged, twirling the dagger in her hand before sliding it back into its sheath. "And if *I* recall, I've been learning from a pirate who doesn't play by the rules."

Kensley's features lit in a way Sam wasn't used to seeing. It wasn't just a smirk or a flash of amusement—this time, he smiled wide, revealing a set of surprisingly white teeth. "Touché. I suppose you've learned more than just the basics."

A strange warmth unfurled in Sam's chest. She hadn't expected to enjoy this—enjoy *him*. But there was something about sparring with Kensley, the banter, the unspoken challenge between them, that made her feel more alive. It wasn't just about training anymore; it was about proving herself, about earning a kind of respect she hadn't even realized she wanted.

"You've gotten better," Kensley added, his expression more serious now. "Much better."

Her heart skipped a beat at the compliment. "Thanks," she said, wiping the sweat from her brow. "Guess I'm finally starting to keep up."

"Let's see how you fare against Sefina before you make that claim."

"Hey!"

Kensley only laughed in response.

As Sam flopped onto her bed that night, she groaned. Her body ached in places she didn't know could ache.

The door to her quarters gave a long creak as it slowly opened. Sam raised her eyes. Sefina stood in the door's frame, looking chaotically beautiful.

"Sefina!" Sam exclaimed, aches momentarily forgotten as she leapt off the bed to embrace her friend. "You smell awful."

With a *hmph*, Sefina said, "You would, too, if you'd spent the last week in that noxious, unkempt, dismal excuse for a space."

Sam laughed weakly. "Isn't that what a brig is meant to be?"

Sefina didn't respond. She pushed past Sam, falling face first onto her mattress and letting out a muffled sigh.

"Tell me everything," Sam said, climbing onto the mattress beside Sefina. "Are you hurt? Did they feed you?"

"Yes, yes." Sefina waved a tired hand. "I was fed. I am alive."

Her neck still bore the faded marks. The yellowing of a bruise that was nearly healed. Kharzul's magic had left that.

"Sefina, why did he let you out?"

Sefina's fingers curled into the bedding. For a long moment, she said nothing. Then she rolled onto her side, propping her head on one arm and fixing Sam with her familiar, glacial stare.

"He wanted something," she said flatly.

Sensing the seriousness in the words, Sam quickly went to the door, peering out at either side of the hallway before shutting it.

She settled herself on the mattress across from Sefina. "What kind of something?"

"Control." Sefina's jaw tightened. She exhaled slowly. "I agreed to sing."

Sefina hadn't so much as unclasped her kalimba since they'd boarded the *Golden Krina*. She hadn't hummed under her breath, shared stories, or sung Sam to sleep. It had been two months of silence. Sam had assumed it was grief, or anger.

Now she understood—it had been defiance.

"You *agreed*?" Sam asked.

Sefina's gaze flicked away, just for a heartbeat. "He does not want my voice because he enjoys it. He wants it because it is mine."

Sam felt something twist in her chest.

Sefina went on. "He believes that once I sing for him, I will have crossed a line. That obedience will be easier the next time. And the time after that. He is wrong."

"That was enough for him?"

"For now." Then, as if deliberately changing the subject, Sefina tilted her head. "And you? Unharmed from the raid, I see."

Sam swallowed. Physically unharmed, yes. But inside...

"I killed someone," she admitted. "It was his life or mine. I know that." Her fingers toyed with the hem of her shirt. "But a part of me wonders if it would have been better if I'd have let him kill me instead."

Sefina was quiet.

"I've been sparring with Kensley," Sam went on, grasping for something solid. "He's different than I thought. The crew listens when he speaks. They laugh around him. He fights hard, but he looks after them, too. They like him, and I think I'm starting to see why."

Sefina sat up, going rigid as she studied Sam. "*You* like him."

It wasn't an accusation, but Sam felt guilt bloom in her gut.

"He is dangerous, Atherton. A charming face does not change the fact that he kills without hesitation."

"I know that," Sam said quickly. "I've seen it. But there's more than that. He's not like—"

"Like Kharzul," Sefina finished. "*No one* is like Kharzul. He wields a dark magic unlike anything I've ever seen."

Sam nodded, the image of that magic still fresh in her mind—the way the air had thickened, the unnatural chill that had crept over the ship, and the shadowy noose that had coiled around Sefina's neck like a serpent. It was a sight Sam wouldn't easily forget.

"But he has used it only a handful of times since we've been aboard," Sefina continued. "Why?"

"I... don't know."

"That is what I wish to find out." Sefina's expression darkened. "Why this man, if he truly controls the power of darkness, keeps that power in check. Why he lords over a single pirate ship rather than taking over entire kingdoms."

A shiver worked its way to Sam's core. She had never considered that before. Kharzul's power had seemed terrifyingly vast, something she dared not question or think too deeply about. She had witnessed the destruction it could bring, but she hadn't stopped to wonder why he wasn't using it more ambitiously.

The truth was, Sam hadn't thought past the fact that Kharzul possessed some kind of magic. Magic that frightened her—*deeply*.

Sefina had nearly died because of that magic.

Sefina continued, her voice low, as if afraid to speak too loudly lest Kharzul overhear, even though they were alone. "I cannot believe he holds back out of mercy or restraint."

Sam frowned as she turned over the possibilities. "Maybe he's limited by something," she mused aloud. "Or maybe he's saving it for something bigger."

"Maybe," Sefina echoed. "Power always has a cost."

The silence that followed was thick. Knowing there was more to the cruel pirate lord was unsettling, and Sam didn't want to dwell on it when she had no way of avoiding him, to find answers that could bring her closer to something she wasn't ready to face.

"We'll be docking in Virona soon," Sefina finally said.

Sam blinked. "Virona?"

"I overheard one of the crew mention it while I was in the brig."

Sam didn't recognize the name. She had never seen it listed on the *Queen Mary's* maps—and she'd practically memorized them. "Where is it?"

"Somewhere along the innermost portion of Phago's peninsula. The town has never been recognized by Phago itself and serves as a haven for outcasts and thieves. I would venture to guess that Kharzul will restock supplies and trade there. That's when we'll leave."

Hope stirred in Sam's chest for the first time in days.

"They'll be watching us," she said cautiously, her voice barely above a whisper. "How do we get off the ship without being seen?"

"Leave that to me," Sefina said, her ice-blue eyes glinting.

"You're serious?"

"When am I not?"

Sam bit her lip, her mind racing with possibilities. Could they do it? Could they escape Kharzul and his crew for good? It was dangerous, and if they were caught, Kharzul wouldn't just lock her or Sefina away next time.

And then there was Kensley.

She thought of the heat of his hand on her waist during training and the way he'd stepped in front of that pike to save her life during the raid.

He'd become a steady presence in her world, the only person who made her feel like something other than a prisoner.

No.

She pushed the hesitation aside, hardening her heart. As drawn to him as she was, staying meant more pirating, more bloodshed.

Sam exhaled slowly, nodding. "All right."

"We'll make it, Atherton."

Sam returned Sefina's smile with one of her own. Virona. Freedom. They just had to make it off the ship.

TWENTY-FIVE

Nearly the entire crew had gathered—some leaning against coils of rope, others perched on crates or the low rail itself. A few called out as Sefina was ushered forward, crude whistles and half-drunken encouragement rippling through the deck. One man laughed. Another blew her a kiss.

Sam hung back, unease flooding her while she searched for Kensley. He wasn't up top.

Kharzul stood near the helm, hands clasped behind his back, his attention fixed on Sefina. The noise ebbed as Sefina drew close to him. After being out of the brig a full day, Sefina had been summoned to fulfil her agreement.

Kharzul said, "Let us hear your song, Princess."

Sefina's nostrils flared. For a moment, Sam thought she might still refuse. Then she unclasped her kalimba.

"Over here," Kharzul added, gesturing toward the rail. It was the most visible place on the deck.

As Sefina moved to the spot, lanternlight caught her pale hair, turning her into a beacon against the darkening sea.

Her first notes were soft, the melody deceptively gentle.

The deck stilled. Even the men who had clearly planned to watch only out of obligation leaned forward. Sefina's voice, lovely as ever, carried across the planks.

But as the tale unfolded, Sam's pulse quickened.

Sefina never spoke Kharzul's name. She didn't need to. The imagery sharpened with every verse—of power undeserving, of voices silenced, of a ruler who mistook obedience for devotion and wondered, in the end, why he stood alone.

Sam's gaze flitted over the crew. A few faces had changed, brows furrowing, expressions tightening with worry or recognition. Others shifted uneasily. She glanced at Kharzul. His expression remained smooth and unreadable, but his eyes gleamed with interest rather than anger. That frightened her more than fury.

Stop, Sam willed, gaze snapping back to Sefina. *Please.*

If Kharzul decided this went too far—if he chose to make an example of her now—Virona would vanish from reach. There would be no escape. Only punishment. Or worse.

The song ended on a single, lingering note that faded into the night. For a long moment, no one breathed.

Then Kharzul clapped. Slowly.

"Beautiful," he said, his smile thin. "So much passion. I do admire a woman who can dress her resentment as art."

Sefina didn't look at Sam as she stepped away from the rail. Her jaw was set, her shoulders rigid, kalimba clutched too tightly in her hands.

Palms sweaty, Sam followed her belowdecks.

"That was reckless," she hissed once the door was shut.

"It was honest," Sefina replied.

Neither one of them slept easily that night.

Sam woke to the soft creak of the door. She was upright in an instant, fingers closing around the cutlass she now kept within reach of her bed. She swung the blade up, and a hand latched around her wrist, firmly but carefully pressing it down.

"Woah there, Red," a familiar voice murmured. "Easy."

She exhaled. She could just make out the broad silhouette and the pale color of sandy-blonde hair.

"Kensley," she whispered.

He released her, raising his palms in surrender. "Just me. Stars, you're quick."

Sefina stirred, rolling onto her side. "Why," she asked sleepily, "are you in our quarters, Cavenaugh?"

Kensley glanced at her, then back to Sam, a crooked smile tugging at his mouth. "I wanted to show Sam something."

"At this hour?" Sefina accused.

"It's about navigating," he added, as if that explained everything.

Sam narrowed her eyes.

"You'll want to see it," he said. "I promise."

She hesitated, curious yet also exhausted.

"We won't be long," he reassured her.

Sefina snorted. "If you drown her, I will haunt you."

"Fair."

Against her better judgment, Sam sighed and swung her legs out of bed. "Fine. Five minutes."

It was quiet up top save for the creaking of the hull and the sound of the waves far below. The moon was only a sliver in the sky, the night exceptionally dark beyond the scattered glow of lanterns. A lone watchman nodded at Kensley as they passed, clearly unconcerned about their presence.

As they neared the bow, Kensley snuffed out the nearest lantern.

"Kensley," Sam whispered sharply.

He moved to the next one. "Trust me."

Sam caught the hint of a smirk just before the flame vanished beneath his fingers.

Darkness closed in around them.

Carefully, Kensley guided her to the rail, one hand hovering near her elbow. "Look out over the water."

At first, Sam saw only black. Then, slowly, her vision adjusted.

Blue glimmered just beneath the surface. It spilled away from the bow in luminous trails, glowing like submerged stars. Each movement of the ship stirred more of it awake, until the sea itself seemed alive.

Sam's breath left her in a quiet gasp.

"What is it?" She leaned forward precariously.

Kensley's sturdy hands caught her waist, keeping her from toppling over the edge.

"Lume," he said near her ear. "It only gathers like this in shallow, warm currents. There's a reef not far off—you can't see it, but the Lume knows it's there."

She nodded absently, barely hearing him. She was suddenly aware of his presence. The warmth of his hands through her thin shirt, the way his breath brushed her hair, his solid form at her back.

"A navigator who only looks at the stars is half blind," he continued, still speaking close. "You have to read the blood of the ocean, too."

Her heart was beating too fast. She swallowed.

For a moment, neither of them moved.

Then the sharp ring of a bell cut through the night.

Kensley stiffened. His hands lingered at her waist for half a heartbeat before he stepped back.

"That's my cue," he said, a touch rougher than before. He turned away quickly, smoothing a hand over his hair before looking back at her. "Get some more rest. We'll be docking in Virona soon."

TWENTY-SIX

As the *Golden Krina* entered the shallows of Phago's peninsula, Sam leaned over the railing to observe the approaching land. It had been so long since she'd stepped off a ship.

Kensley stood near the helmsman, the breeze catching strands of his hair as he looked out over the prow. His voice carried across the deck, guiding the crew as they maneuvered the beastly ship through the treacherous shallow waters. He looked so entirely in his element—a man who belonged to the sea.

Sunlight caught the rugged line of his jaw, the curve of his strong brow.

It was a strange irony to think that the same man who had spent weeks teaching her how to hold her ground was now steering her toward the very place she intended to flee.

She was still watching him, tracing the familiar, broad line of his shoulders when a shadow fell across her.

"Below," Langley growled. Kharzul's quartermaster loomed beside her, frowning. "Captain isn't ready to lose his investments by letting them wander off in Virona."

Men moved in at once, hands firm as they herded Sam toward the hatch. Across the deck, Sefina received the same treatment.

Panic bubbled up inside Sam. This hadn't been part of the escape plan. They were meant to blend in, to disappear into the outpost with the rest of the crew. They couldn't do that if they never set foot on land.

"Wait," Sam protested, twisting against their grip. No one listened.

She and Sefina were shoved down the stairs, the hatch slamming shut above them. Moments later came the clanking of a heavy lock.

Sam shouted a string of curses that echoed uselessly through the hold. Laughter drifted down in response. With a growl, she spun toward the nearest porthole, pressing close as frustration burned in her chest. Through the small, round window, she could see sandy beaches stretching into the distance, lined by dense clusters of tropical palms swaying in the breeze. The *Golden Krina* had slowed to a near crawl, gliding through the turquoise shallows, the ocean's once-rough waves now calm and sparkling under the sun.

Sam craned her neck, watching as the ship turned to follow a narrow river. The waterway twisted through the jungle, overhung with vibrant greenery. It felt like they were being swallowed by the dense landscape.

As they approached a bend in the river, Sam saw it—tucked between the thick trees and rocky outcrops was a small dock. The thieves' outpost. Virona. The dock wasn't bustling, but she could make out figures moving in the distance, silhouetted by the trees.

"They're docking," Sam muttered, glancing over her shoulder.

Sefina sat with her back against the wall, legs crossed, expression maddeningly calm.

The ship creaked as it eased into place. The vibrations of the crew at work rumbled from above, the scrape of crates and barrels echoing as they were heaved off the boat. Through the porthole, Sam caught glimpses of the crew. Men sweating in the tropical heat as they unloaded goods, their voices low, their movements deliberate.

This should have been their moment. Instead, they were trapped below, listening.

It wasn't long before the ship became quiet. Only a handful of men were left on board to keep watch, rotating shifts. Gruff, silent guards who barely spared her a glance. Frustrated, she hurled insults at them through the grate when they passed.

Finally, defeated, Sam plopped down beside Sefina.

"What do we do now?" she asked quietly.

"We escape," Sefina responded. "When night falls."

"How? The grate is locked."

"I have an idea, but you must promise me you will do exactly as I say without question."

Sam didn't hesitate. "I promise," she said.

With a nod, Sefina stood. "I have a few items to gather. See if you can find us food and coin."

Sam didn't waste a second. She moved through the shadows of the crew's quarters, starting with the hammocks, her fingers flying through rough blankets and unattended rucksacks. In the first few, she found only dirty stockings and a half-eaten biscuit, but her luck turned when she reached the back of the hold.

Kneeling before a heavy sea chest she pulled two pins from her hair. The lock gave way seconds later.

Nestled among linen clothing, she found a small velvet roll. Unfurling it revealed a small dagger. She slipped it in her boot before rummaging through the chest once more.

She found two more chests, earning herself a handful of copper and silver coins, and a silk pouch of loose jewels. Stuffing them into a pouch of her own, Sam pulled the drawstring tight and headed for the galley where she gathered dried meats and biscuits.

Sam waited by the porthole, a sack of food by the stairs, her cutlass at her hip, and a knife tucked into her boot, watching the sun dip lower on the horizon. The world changed beyond the hull as Virona came alive. Lanterns blazed to life, casting a golden glow over the streets, which pulsed with activity. The sounds of the outpost drifted through the air—distant laughter; the clinking of glasses; the wild, erratic notes of a fiddle playing a melody full of freedom and danger. Sam could imagine dancers twirling through the streets, boots scuffing the dusty ground in wild abandon. It reminded her of warm evenings aboard the *Queen Mary*, of stories shared, of Sefina's elaborate tales.

For a minute, she said nothing. Asking felt... wrong. Kharzul had already taken enough from Sefina—her freedom, her defiance, her voice. Sam didn't want to be another person who demanded something of her, even something as small as comfort.

But as the silence carried on, her thoughts became louder.

"Sefina," she said at last, her voice quiet. "Will you tell me of the Sky God again?"

"You've heard those tales many times over," Sefina replied.

Sam nodded. She had. And still she waited. Hoping.

Sefina exhaled softly. "I will tell you of the Goddess Perixia instead."

The tension left Sam in a rush. She settled beside Sefina, expecting her to unclasp her kalimba, but she began speaking instead.

"Born from the land itself, a maiden did come.
The embodiment of kindness and beauty.
Guardian of the land, she protected it from harm.
The God of the Sky, in a fit of rage, did throw down his thunder and lightning.
The ground shook so hard that mountains sprang up, and fire o'ertook the land.
Finally, the thunder did cease and the Sky God let down his rain,
But, by then, the world was nothing but barren wasteland,
Jagged spikes and blackened hills.
The maiden could not hold her cries.
So powerful they were, her tears became rivers.
Where her fingertips brushed, entire forests grew.
She called to the land, and the land did respond, creating new life.
The hills filled with flowers, the mountains with trees, and, with it, the bees and the deer.
Creatures once lost appeared again.
And thus did Perixia become goddess."

Sefina's voice faded, leaving behind the familiar comfort Sam had sought.

"Did all of the gods start off as humans?" she asked.

"Perixia was not human; she was born of the land. I would imagine something closer to a dryad."

"Dryad?"

"A tree spirit."

"Oh... Are all trees dryads?"

Sefina laughed. "I believe each tree has their own spirit, but not all of them are hiding willowy maidens within. And those that remain are bound to the forests in which they reside."

Sam chuckled uncertainly. Creatures like dryads and sirens were only myths...

A moment later, Sefina rose and strode to the base of the stairs. The sun had finally set and moonlight filtered through the grates above, casting silver shadows across her perfect skin. She looked ethereal in the glow. And dangerous.

"It is nearly time," she said.

The mood shifted like the tide, comfort washing out and replaced by anxiety.

"Sefina? If one of us gets caught..." Sam didn't want to finish her thought.

Sefina returned to her side, her eyes shadowed and intense, betraying none of the fear Sam felt coursing through her own veins. "The other still goes if they have the chance," she said, putting into words what Sam had not.

Sam nodded, a lump in her throat. "Yes."

"Let us pray to Perixia that it does not come to that." Sefina pressed a wad of fluffy cotton into Sam's palm. "Put this in your ears," she instructed.

Sam stared at the cotton for a moment, curiosity on the tip of her tongue. Was Sefina planning to blast their way out? But she'd promised to follow without question. With a determined nod, Sam pressed the cotton into her ears until the sounds of the ship became muted and distant.

Sefina positioned herself as close to the grate as possible, her gaze fixed upward. Then she began to sing.

Even muffled through the cotton, the sound was captivating. Sam couldn't make out the melody, but she felt it more than heard it—a vibration in her chest, an irresistible pull that made the air around her pulse with something otherworldly. Sam's mind raced, flashing back to the moment she'd been protected from Joss and seen him walk overboard. Could it have been Sefina? Was it her voice that had drawn him into the sea?

There wasn't time to dwell on the thought.

The watchman approached as if in a trance. His eyes were glazed, fixed on the spot where Sefina stood singing. He came closer until he was directly above her, his body swaying slightly. Sam's breath caught in her throat as she watched him, mesmerized by the power Sefina seemed to wield.

Swiftly, Sefina's hand shot out through the grate and wrapped around the man's legs. He fell, landing with a heavy thud. A moment later, she knocked him unconscious, fished out his keys, and unlocked the bolt.

With a wave, Sefina beckoned Sam forward, and, together, they heaved the grate open.

Sam was greeted by the warm night air, carrying the scent of saltwater and distant trees.

"Come," Sefina mouthed.

Sefina moved first, crouching low and reaching for the unconscious man's belt. She claimed his knife sheath while Sam grabbed his pistol.

Once armed, they locked eyes. Sefina's expression was hard. Sam removed the cotton from her ears.

"If we do not succeed," Sefina said in a low voice, "there will be no more freedoms. One or both of us will surely be killed—at the very least, severely punished."

Sam felt the weight of those words settle over her like a shroud, but she didn't waver. She knew the risks. There was no turning back now.

She let out a slow breath before responding. "Let's go."

TWENTY-SEVEN

It was as if Kharzul had known they'd try to escape. He'd posted men at multiple locations. They didn't make it ten steps off of the ship before being spotted.

Then they ran.

Shouts reverberated off the buildings at Sam's back, a group of the *Golden Krina's* crew in close pursuit. She sprinted along the cobblestone alleyway with renewed vigor, Sefina pulling several paces ahead. They should have been headed toward the city center where they could be lost in the crowds... only, somehow, they must have run in the opposite direction. These streets were empty of life beyond lanterns, and as they ran, their shadows chased them along the walls like dark creatures of the night.

They leaped a barrel, Sam doing so with slightly less grace than her long-legged friend. As she landed, she stumbled. She threw out her arms to catch herself and landed hard, scraping all the way from her palms to her elbows. Clenching her teeth, she scrambled up, but the pirates were closer now.

Sefina slid to a stop, turning hastily to grasp Sam around the elbow. Together they ran, turning into yet another alleyway.

Only this one had no outlet.

Sam whipped around, pulling out her stolen pistol and raising it high. To her right, she heard the hiss of sword against leather as Sefina unsheathed her cutlass.

The crew members cornered them, and Langley stepped to the front of the pack. "Now be good girls and put those weapons down."

"We're not good girls," Sam quipped. "I thought you'd have figured as much out by now."

While some of the others ho-ho'd, Langley stepped closer, glowering. "You're comin' with us, and you'll put them weapons away."

"We will not."

At her bold response, a couple of the men looked uncertain. One of them spoke. "You can't go. We'd be deader than the pig in last night's stew. Cap'n made it clear: You don't return, we don't either."

"You're welcome to come with, or you're welcome to stand aside. Which is it?" Sam responded, cocking her pistol.

"Or you can die here," Sefina added coolly.

The group inched toward them, and Sam slowly backed up until she felt the scrape of the wall against her back. She swallowed but steeled her features, gripping the gun a little tighter.

Another man spoke, this time to her right. "Bet you'd come crawling back if Cavenaugh asked, eh, Red?"

She looked him dead in the eyes, aimed the pistol, and pulled the trigger.

She hadn't thought—had barely even aimed. Her hands had been shaking, her breathing shallow, her mind screaming at her to do something, anything. And yet, somehow, the bullet found its mark.

The man's scream tore through the night, sharp and ragged, and Sam's pulse thundered in her ears. She'd hit him. Not killed him, but she'd *hit* him.

He crumpled, his hands clutching his shoulder, blood seeping between his fingers. A moment stretched too long, Sam's body frozen in place, the weight of what she had just done pressing down on her.

It wasn't courage. It wasn't skill. It was sheer, blind luck.

Her grip on the pistol tightened, her fingers numb around the hilt. She had pulled the trigger without thinking, without questioning, without hesitating to consider the life she had just tried to take. Not under Kharzul's command but her own.

Fear settled over her—because if she could do this once, she could do it again.

Langley took advantage of her distraction, slamming her backward into the wall. He wrenched the gun from her grasp, but that didn't stop her from thrashing. Bringing her legs up, she kicked, using the wall as a support and sending Langley stumbling away.

Sam rolled, sliding out her dagger and slicing somebody's leg in one swift movement. She rose from her crouch, swinging at another opponent. Sefina fought several paces away, brilliantly dancing away from two men, but there were still more.

A foot shot out in front of her, and Sam tripped, landing hard on her elbows. Before she could even shimmy to her knees, a blade was at her back.

Obeying a barked command, she dropped her knife in defeat. It was quickly kicked away.

They tried to restrain Sefina, but she broke free. She'd maneuvered near the mouth of the alley. If she ran, she'd have a chance of escape.

"Go—get out of here!" Sam yelled.

Sefina's eyes met hers. Time seemed to slow in that brief moment as grief passed between them.

Then, with a tiny nod, Sefina spun, dodging out of the way of blades before disappearing with several men on her heels.

Sam gave up the fight, letting her forehead fall to the ground.

"Ye behave now," someone said above her. Gritting her teeth, she nodded. The pressure on her back lifted, and they yanked her to her feet.

She was forcefully escorted back to the *Golden Krina*, directly to the captain's cabin. Sam tried to appear unfazed, but there was no hiding her trembling. She prayed to Perixia that her punishment would be swift.

Once in the captain's quarters, Sam ripped her arm from the grip of the man who'd held her. He exited quickly, shutting the door behind him with a thud.

Sam held her arms at her sides and raised her chin. She glanced around, struck by the disorder of the usually tidy place. Maps and orbs littered the ground, and several bottles of brandy had been smashed, their contents soaked into the floor, leaving only shards of glass behind.

Captain Kharzul stood facing the large window, swathed in swirling shadows. As he turned, he raked his golden eyes down her, his face a mask of rage. The dagger he had been polishing glinted in his fingers.

Suddenly, he lunged. Sam froze as he ran the smooth side of the dagger's blade down her cheek.

Grabbing her, his body uncomfortably close, he leaned in and whispered with hot breath in her ear, "There is nowhere you could go that I would not find you."

Sam swallowed thickly, eyeing the hovering shadows.

"I told you that, next time, the princess would die." Kharzul released her and strode to his wall of weapons. "Alas, you are here alone, and that can only mean she has not returned with you."

Sam felt a flicker of relief at Sefina's escape. "You'll never find her."

"And yet someone must be punished." Kharzul plucked up one of the weapons—a brutal whip with knots tied among its multiple leather strands. "Cavenaugh has failed in his task, it seems."

Kharzul's intent dawned on her. *Kensley.*

"No!" Sam gasped. "Punish me; it was my doing."

"Ah, but this will get the point across much clearer, don't you think?" Kharzul toyed with the whip, twisting the wicked cords in his fingers.

Instantly, Sam paled. *He knows.*

The realization crashed into her, leaving her breathless. Kharzul had seen it before she had—had picked apart her defenses and was already exploiting something she hadn't even admitted to herself.

This would wound her in a way no whip ever could. Because it wasn't her own pain she feared. It was his.

She didn't know when it had happened. Kensley was a pirate, and she wasn't supposed to care. And yet a sharp, twisting panic settled in her chest.

As Kharzul took strides to leave the cabin, Sam moved in front of him, pleading. "Don't do this. Kensley is not to blame."

Kharzul stepped around her, glass shards crushing beneath his feet. "If it weren't for your insubordination, I wouldn't have to."

Sam's voice shook as she said, "You are cruel."

Kharzul paused, his body stiffening as he rose to his full height. He didn't face her as he responded, "Every choice has consequences."

Threat lurked beneath the surface of those words.

He continued out of the cabin, and Sam reluctantly followed. Upon reaching the open deck, her stomach dropped. Kensley was already tied with his stomach pressed against the mainmast, his arms stretched and bound around it. Sam rushed for him, but she couldn't get past the two men that blocked her way, and at Kharzul's nod, they hauled her back. Though she struggled, there was no breaking free of the grip on her arms. "No—let me go!"

Desperately, she cried out, "Kensley, I'm so sorry!"

Kensley turned his head and met Sam's gaze. His features were stoic, ready for whatever came next.

She tried to shout for him again, but one of the men holding her gagged her with a dirty strip of cloth. She grunted still, though the sounds were dulled.

Kharzul's powerful voice rose above the gathered crew. "Today we witness the punishment of one who has failed us." A wave of unease rolled throughout the crew. Kharzul gave the sentence. "Two dozen lashes for allowing his charges to escape and a dozen more for the one who did not return. Thirty-six lashes of the cat."

TWENTY-EIGHT

Thirty-six lashes.

Sam screamed her objection through the gag and struggled again to reach Kensley, then stilled as Kharzul began the lashings, shadows swirling at his feet. Over the noise of the crew, she could still hear each smack of the whip against Kensley's back.

At the first lash, Kensley flinched but made no noise.

At the third, his shirt ripped, exposing the tanned skin of his back.

Sam thought she might be sick. She wanted to apologize, to ask forgiveness, to take the punishment in his place. Instead, she was forced to watch.

Kharzul's voice carried easily over the deck. "Disobedience breeds weakness."

Another strike.

"Weakness breeds mutiny."

By ten lashes, hot tears fell from Sam's cheeks. She hadn't cried in a long time, but there was no stopping the flood that came as she watched Kensley's body sag. Crimson blood dripped onto the deck, yet the lashings continued.

Sam counted each lash, body shaking, and tried to think of a way that she could ever make things right.

Seventeen lashes.

Twenty-two.

Thirty-one.

She wanted to look away. To close her eyes and pretend this wasn't actually happening. But she forced herself to watch every strike.

The crew watched, too, and by the end, even they looked somber.

Finally, the count reached thirty-six. Though he had never made a sound, Kensley's body was held up only by the ropes that bound him.

Kharzul handed the cat to Langley, then walked to where Sam stood restrained.

"Next time, *he* dies," he whispered into her ear.

She shuddered. But there would not be a next time.

Kharzul gave the signal to let Sam free. The moment the hands on her arms loosened, she ripped the gag free and rushed to Kensley. She forced herself to remain calm, though her hands trembled as she pried free the bindings around Kensley's wrists.

No longer held up by the ropes, Kensley's thick body crumpled to the ground. Sam fell to her knees and listened for his shallow breaths.

Alive. Still alive.

"Get him off my deck," Kharzul commanded.

It took three men to move him. Sam hovered as they hauled him down the stairs, letting his limbs bang against each of the steps, before depositing him in a heap on the floor of a small room. It seemed to be a bedchamber, with a thin bed against one wall and a small desk bolted into another.

The crew members left, apparently eager to escape the wretched sight, so no one helped as Sam rolled Kensley from his side onto his stomach as gently as she could.

Quickly, she fetched water, rags, bandages, and a needle and thread. She didn't speak to anyone she passed, shooting her most vicious glares at any pirate who so much as looked in her direction.

Back in the room, she knelt by Kensley's side and carefully pulled off his tattered shirt. At the full sight of the damage, Sam fought back a wave of nausea that threatened to overcome her. His back was a mess of torn flesh, the jagged wounds left by the whip seeping blood down his sides.

Sam's hands shook as she worked, dipping a clean cloth into the basin of cool water and gently pressing it against his back. He hadn't made a sound during the whipping, stoically enduring each strike, but now, as the cloth touched his skin, a low groan escaped his lips.

Sam paused, watching his face. His eyes were still closed, his brow furrowed in pain. "Shh, I'll try to be quick," she whispered as she cleaned away the blood.

Kensley opened his eyes then, blinking slowly as he tried to lift his head. "Sam?"

His voice was hoarse, barely a croak, but the sound of her name on his lips caught her off guard. She swallowed hard, her hand freezing mid-motion.

"It's me," she confirmed, leaning over so he could see her face.

Kensley's gaze was unfocused, his usually sharp eyes clouded with exhaustion and pain. Yet there was something in the way he looked at her—a softness she hadn't expected.

"You don't... have to do this," he murmured, his words slurred as if they took too much effort.

"Yes I do." Sam shook her head, resuming her work. Guilt weighed on her. "You didn't deserve this."

He grunted in response, his eyes fluttering closed again. Sam dipped the cloth back into the basin, wringing it out before carefully stitching the worst of his wounds shut. Every time he flinched, her chest tightened. She began to sing quietly, sharing with Kensley her favorite of Sefina's tales: the story of the Sky God.

She watched his face finally relax as he fell into a deep sleep.

She'd tried to convince herself that Kensley was just another part of the crew, just another pirate. She wasn't supposed to care. Not for him. Not for any of them. But she *did* care. He'd been by her side all along, teaching her and protecting her. Kharzul had orchestrated it and then used it against them both.

A bitter taste filled Sam's mouth at the thought of Kharzul. How could he do this to one of his own crew? And how could Kensley be so loyal as to bear it silently?

She gritted her teeth. Salik Kharzul was no one's captain. He was a monster.

Sam awoke, pulled from a nightmare to the sound of a fist pounding on the door. She'd fallen asleep in Kensley's small room. Her eyes flicked to him, lying within arms reach. He was still asleep, his breathing steady. The bandages on his back would need to be changed soon.

"Oi, Red, I know you're in there! Captain demands an audience."

Sam raised herself to sitting and rubbed tiredly at her eyes. Her back ached from sleeping on the hard wooden planks.

"Hurry it up in there! Capt'n don't like to be kept waiting."

As quickly as she could, she slipped from the room, turning toward the stairs. When the man beckoned her farther belowdecks, she paused. "We're not going to the captain's cabin?"

The man grunted. "To the brig."

Sam's face paled. Had Kharzul changed his mind? Would he now punish her too?

She reached the stairs leading to the brig and nearly gagged at the smell. Sefina had spent a week in this.

A shriek echoed up the stairs, causing Sam's hair to stand on end. Kharzul was in one of the cells with a man she didn't recognize. A prisoner picked up in Virona?

The prisoner's hand was splayed on a wooden crate, held firmly in place by the captain.

"Who do you work for?" Kharzul asked.

"The—the Eclorian Throne," the prisoner whimpered.

Sam stiffened. What interest did Kharzul have in the Eclorian government?

Kharzul reached forward to snap one of the prisoner's fingers. Sam flinched at the sharp *crack*.

Kharzul's face was void of emotion as he asked again, "*Who* do you work for?"

"The throne!" the prisoner replied again, this time more frantically.

Kharzul snapped another finger. "Why don't you try just one more time?" He toyed with the next. "Who do you work for?"

"I work for... you."

A cruel smile lit the captain's face. "That's right."

He released the prisoner, who pulled his hand back gingerly, whimpering. Kharzul exited the cell, finally spotting Sam, or at least pretending to. He wouldn't have had her report to the brig if he hadn't intended her to witness more torture.

"Ah," he said. "Come with me, poppet."

Sam followed the captain up to the deck and across the ship. The sun was barely peeking above the horizon, the cool morning air crisp until they entered the dim of his cabin.

Kharzul moved to sit behind his desk and pulled out a roll of parchment, marking it in several places. "My Navigator has been temporarily incapacitated."

Sam's mouth fell open. *Temporarily incapacitated? By his own hand!*

"Fortunately," he continued, "we have another to take his place."

He stared at her expectantly.

She sucked in a breath, about to offer protests before clamping her jaw shut. Her words would never change his mind, and she'd witnessed enough of his anger.

But there were still problems. Sam had helped Kensley navigate for weeks, but she'd never directed the *Golden Krina* alone.

Carefully, she said, "I can find ports but not ships. If you want to plunder for sport—"

"We never plunder for sport, poppet." Kharzul cut her off.

Standing, he strode to his wall of weapons and fingered several of the weapons before picking up a brass spyglass. He traced the lines of detail carved into it. "We take from the wealthy what they should never have had in the first place and redistribute it." Kharzul glanced back at her, gold eyes gleaming. "The wealth of the world is so *unbalanced*, is it not?"

The streets of Milderre hovered in her memory; Sam knew all too well the imbalance between the wealthy and the poor.

She fidgeted with her fingers, contemplating her next words. Softly, she asked, "And what of the *Queen Mary*? We were not wealthy."

"But her master was."

Sam let the words sink in. Silence stretched between them until, finally, she spoke. "You would take hundreds of lives to bring down one man?"

Kharzul's eyes locked onto hers. "Over and over again, until every last one of the unworthy has known my wrath."

As she stared into his golden eyes, a blanket of understanding settled over her. Kharzul was not a simple monster looking for wealth. He was a man with a much greater plan, who was willing to do unspeakable things in the name of it.

Sam wanted no part of it, but her will to disobey had been lashed along with Kensley.

"Where to, Captain?" she asked quietly.

His lips turned upward. "You will report to me directly. Then you will relay all instruction to the helmsman. Should you fail to meet my expectations, you both will suffer for it. I wish to make port in Atral within a fortnight. I trust getting there will not be an issue."

Sam exhaled, willing the tension to leave with the breath, then inhaled through her nose. As her chest expanded, a sense of calm flowed through her. She would do this for Kensley. She could do this.

"I can get us there, Captain," she said, though her insides twisted. "But I will need access to all that Cavenaugh had."

Kharzul twirled the spyglass in his hands, then handed it to her and gestured to the rolls of maps and charts that filled several vases around the room. "Whatever you need, poppet."

TWENTY-NINE

Kensley's skin glistened with a light sheen of sweat. A full week of rest had closed most of his wounds, but one had begun to fester, the skin around the stitches angry and swollen.

Sam's brows knit as she soaked a cloth in alcohol, then pressed it carefully against the gash, trying to stem the fluid that seeped through.

Kensley hissed, his hands fisting the mattress he laid on.

"I'm sorry," she said quietly. "Not for trying to escape. But for what you're enduring because of me."

He didn't look at her. His gaze remained fixed on some point in the wall as his breathing slowly evened out.

"You think the world out there is better?" he asked at last. "It's a cage of gold and laws that favor a few while the rest starve. At least here..." He paused, searching for the word. "At least here, there's purpose. There's balance."

"Balance?" Sam asked, unable to keep the edge from her voice. "Is whipping your most loyal crewman to the brink of death part of that balance, too?"

Kensley's jaw tightened. "It was my mistake. You and Sefina were in my charge."

"It wasn't your decision," she pressed. "It was mine, and yet you're the one bleeding for it. How is that fair?"

"Kharzul is the captain," he said, voice firm. "He knows what he's doing."

Sam's grip tightened around the cloth. "Kharzul is *cruel*," she said. "And the only thing he cares about are his own ends."

For a moment, Kensley looked as though he might argue. He opened his mouth, then closed it again.

Sam exhaled and set the cloth aside. She reached for the bottle of ale instead, taking a swallow of the pungent liquid, then promptly coughing as it burned its way down her throat.

The door creaked open.

Connor, one of the gunners, leaned into the room. "Don't mean to interrupt."

"No," Kensley said quickly. "Come in."

Sam was already on her feet. "I was just leaving."

She slipped past Connor and into the corridor, the door closing softly behind her.

"Never should've punished you like that," she heard Connor say. "Wasn't right. Girl or no."

Sam couldn't have agreed more.

The charts were spread across the small desk, the corners weighted with Sam's compass and a half-eaten biscuit she had forgotten about. She'd been working at them for an hour, cross-referencing the coastal markings against the star tables, while behind her Kensley slept—or pretended to.

She heard the shift in his breathing before he spoke.

"You've marked the Phagaen current wrong."

Sam turned from the desk. He was watching her from the bed, his head propped against the wall. His face was pale, still drawn tight with pain, but his eyes were clear.

"I haven't." She frowned down at the chart, turning it more fully toward him. "It runs north by northeast from the cape. I checked it against your own notes."

"My notes were from the summer passage. It shifts in the colder months."

Sam paused. She looked at the chart, then back at him. "Show me."

He couldn't lean forward easily—the wounds on his back would pull with any movement—so she crossed the room instead and held the chart where he could reach it. Kensley's finger traced the line, a slow correction running two degrees from where she'd drawn it. His hand was steadier than she expected, given the fever of the last two days.

"Here," he said. "And here. The reef at the southern tip creates a back-pull. You'd feel it before you saw it, but by then you're already fighting it."

Sam studied the correction, then gave a short nod. If Kensley said it was wrong, it was wrong. He'd sailed these waters far longer than she had. "I'll fix it."

She was already straightening when his hand came off the chart. And instead caught hers.

"Sam."

She stopped. His fingers weren't tight, just steady against hers.

She became sharply aware of the contact, of how he was choosing to touch her at all after everything.

Kensley was looking at her with an expression she didn't know how to name. It wasn't pain—she'd learned that one too well over the past week. It wasn't frustration or patience or his usual edge of amusement. It was something more careful than that.

His thumb shifted once against her hand, barely there.

Then his jaw shifted, as if he caught himself. He looked down at the blanket. Let go.

"Nothing. Just...be careful with the reef. It creeps up on you."

Sam nodded slowly. "I will."

Only then did she step back. At the desk, she uncapped the ink, though her hand wasn't quite as steady as it should have been. The quill scratched across the chart in precise lines, correcting what needed correcting.

She focused on that. The scratch of the quill, the smell of wood, the faint iron tang of the bandages she'd changed that morning.

And she wondered what Kensley had actually meant to say.

Sam almost dared to believe they would reach Atral without incident until the storm came out of nowhere. Different from the ones that often followed the *Golden Krina*.

One moment the ship was cutting through calm seas, and the next, black clouds swallowed the horizon, rolling in like a hungry beast. The wind howled through the rigging, and the sea churned violently beneath them, waves swelling into towering walls of water that slammed against the hull.

Sam stood at the helm, her hands gripping the wheel so tightly her knuckles had turned white. The helmsman was gone. Thrown from the ship with the last violent crash of waves.

"Hold steady!" Kharzul's voice roared above the din of the storm, though even his powerful command seemed small against the fury of the elements. His shadowy figure loomed by the mast, his hands raised as if he were trying to manipulate the winds. But even his powers, foreboding as they were, couldn't tame this storm.

Sam's hair was plastered to her face, the rain coming down in sheets so thick they were sailing blind. She could barely make out the other crew members scrambling across the deck to secure loose sails, fighting to keep upright on the slick planks.

Sam fought to keep her balance, too, her body braced against the wheel as she sent prayers to the Sea Goddess. Every gust of wind and every crash of a wave threatened to wrench it from her grip.

"Come on, come on…" she muttered through gritted teeth, trying to keep the ship from turning broadside to the waves and capsizing. The ship groaned under the strain, and the cold bite of saltwater stung her skin, but if she gave up, they would *all* perish.

A sharp crack sounded overhead—a line had snapped, and the main sail unfurled wildly, flapping in the wind. The ship veered, and Sam lost her footing, slipping on the wet deck. She staggered back, catching herself against a railing as the wheel spun of its own accord.

Through the chaos, a figure emerged, limping across the deck—Kensley.

Sam's heart lurched as she saw him. Kensley looked pale, his face tight with pain, but his eyes were sharp and determined.

"What are you doing here?" she shouted over the roar of the storm, pushing herself away from the helm to reach him. "Your wounds haven't healed yet!"

A massive wave crashed against the ship, sending a rush of water across the deck. Sam lost her footing again, and the ship tilted dangerously.

Another loud snap echoed through the air. The foremast splintered above her as it broke in half.

Panic gripped her—she was going to be crushed.

But then strong arms circled her waist, pulling her back just as the mast crashed down, landing where she'd been moments before.

"I've got you," Kensley panted, his breaths ragged gasps.

Sam looked up at him, her heart pounding not just from the storm, but from the sudden closeness between them. His blue-gray eyes shone with intensity, framed by wet strands of hair that had slipped free from the knot at the back of his head.

Sam opened her mouth to thank him, but the deck lurched again, sending both of them sprawling against the railing. Kensley grunted as he took the brunt of the impact, shielding her.

"Kensley," she panted as she held onto him, their breaths mingling in the cold air. "You should've stayed below."

He let out a rough chuckle, though it was strained. "Couldn't let you get swept away. I'd never hear the end of it."

Despite the storm raging around them, Sam couldn't help but smile. Just for a moment, the chaos, the danger, and the cold all seemed to fade as she looked at Kensley, his face pale and soaked with rain yet still filled with that stubborn determination she had come to recognize.

"Come on," she said, grabbing his arm and pulling him toward the wheel. "I need you to help me steer this thing, or we're both going overboard."

Seaweed and splintered wood plopped into the ocean below as Sam swept debris from the ship's deck, each swipe of her broom punctuated by the creaking groans of the damaged *Golden Krina*. The broken foremast clung to the ship by a thread, its mighty sails dragging in the water, slowing the ship's progress to a crawl. The crew was drenched, their faces ashen from hours of battling the storm, and yet they moved swiftly, saws in hand, hacking away at the splintered remains of the mast. Kharzul's sharp gaze bore down on them, ensuring every hand was at work.

The damage to the *Golden Krina* was bad, but Sam knew it wouldn't be the end for the mighty ship. The foremast was the most urgent issue, followed closely by the sails that had been whipped to ribbons by the violent winds.

The storm had blown them wildly off course, but she wouldn't know just how far until nightfall when the stars emerged. She held out hope that if they could free the foremast and utilize what sails they had left, they could still reach Atral by tomorrow's end.

Langley was nowhere to be found—presumed lost at sea along with four others. It chilled Sam to think one of those could have been her or Kensley.

As Kharzul retreated to his cabin, he summoned Sam as well. The storm had taken a toll on the space. Sam picked her way over books and maps, baubles and gems, all scattered across the floor. It seemed most of the wall hangings—daggers, axes, relics from distant lands—remained secured.

Kharzul stood behind his desk, his hands braced against its edge, looking composed despite the wreckage around him. His eyes flicked up to Sam, showing a glint of familiar calculation.

"Cavenaugh has been appointed quartermaster in Langley's absence," Kharzul said without preamble.

Sam masked her surprise. Kensley was hardworking and loyal, yes, but after Kharzul's punishment of him, she would have assumed that Kensley was... well, not next in line to be quartermaster.

"You, Atherton," Kharzul continued, his gaze pinning her in place, "will fill the role of navigator permanently."

The words brought a rush of conflicting emotions. Sam had been handling navigation for only two weeks now. She'd done well in Kensley's absence, but to hear it made official—permanent—was something else. Pride mingled with anxiety, the enormity of the responsibility sinking in like the weight of the storm clouds still visible in the distance.

"Yes, Captain," she managed to say, keeping her voice steady.

Kharzul nodded once, his expression unreadable. "Get us back on course," he said, dismissing her as though she were just another cog in the ship's machine. "And do not fail."

As Sam left the cabin, stepping back into the sunlit aftermath of the storm, she glanced up at the torn sails flapping weakly in the breeze and let out a slow breath.

Navigator.

The word echoed in her mind. An official title. One that she'd dreamed of someday claiming—one that Mr. Bixby had encouraged her to go after. And now that dream had come true.

But at what cost?

She cast a glance toward the horizon, where the storm rolled away, searching for other ships to swallow. Her stomach churned—not with seasickness but with the bitter taste of her own choices. She was the navigator of the *Golden Krina*, a ship that left destruction in its wake.

Sam forced herself to confront the truth she had been avoiding for weeks. The next time they came across an unsuspecting merchant vessel or a poorly armed fishing boat, she couldn't claim innocence. Without Kensley's shadow to hide in, it would be her maps, her direction that led them to their prey.

Was she a pirate now?

She had resisted the idea that she could be anything like the rest of Kharzul's crew. But what choice did she have? If she were to try another escape, she would not only be risking her life but also Kensley's.

Her hands curled into fists at her sides. She hated Kharzul. Hated his power, his control, the way he saw everyone around him as pieces in his game. And yet, with a single word, he had handed her the very thing she once longed for—a position of authority, a role that defined her as more than just a prisoner or a stowaway.

The crew bustled around her, and Sam watched them work, her mind buzzing with conflict. If she embraced this role, did that mean she accepted the life of a pirate? That she condoned the violence and theft?

She closed her eyes, but there was no clarity in the chaos of her thoughts.

The helm creaked beneath Sam's grip as she steered the *Golden Krina* across the calm seas, the wind gentler than it had been in days. The sky was a soft gradient of oranges and purples as the sun began to sink toward the horizon, casting a warm glow over the ship's deck. But despite the calm, Sam felt a knot in her stomach.

Footsteps approached, and she glanced over to see Kensley climbing up to the helm, his broad figure backlit by sunset. He moved gingerly, a slight wince with each step, but had healed enough to be up and about.

He gave her a nod and settled beside her, leaning against the railing with his usual relaxed demeanor. "How's it going up here?"

Sam tightened her grip on the wheel. "Quiet. For now."

Kensley chuckled, folding his arms across his chest. "You've got something on your mind," he said. It wasn't a question.

She shot him a sidelong glance, hesitating before she said, "Do you truly think I can fill this role? I'm not sure I'm cut out for this."

Kensley raised an eyebrow. "You already proved you could get us through worse."

"Maybe. But this..." She looked down at her compass, its needle steady as the ship continued its course. "Being the navigator—it's not what I thought it would be. I mean, I've dreamed of this title, but not like this. Not here."

Kensley tilted his head slightly, studying her. "Because of Kharzul."

"Yes," she admitted, her voice quiet. "I can't trust him. One moment he's ruthless and cruel, and the next he's giving me the very thing I dreamed of."

After a moment of thought, Kensley sighed. "He's not all bad, Sam. I know it might seem that way, but there's more to him than just the violence, the power."

"You really believe that?"

"I do," Kensley said, his tone firm but not without hesitation.

Sam shook her head. "Kensley, he murdered my entire crew. And what of your back? The wounds aren't even healed yet and you're defending him!"

"He's... extreme, yes. And there are times when he's unnecessarily brutal. But he's kept this ship together, kept us alive. This crew—it's been pieced together by outcasts and the oppressed. There's a method to his madness, even if we don't always see it." Kensley looked away, his expression pensive. "Sometimes he reminds me of my old captain on the merchant ship. Harsh and quick to violence. But Kharzul, for all his darkness, has a purpose. He's just..."

"Willing to do whatever it takes to achieve it," Sam finished for him.

Kensley nodded. "And in this world, sometimes that's necessary. But you don't have to become him. You're the navigator, Sam. You chart the course. You make your own decisions."

Sam exhaled, a mixture of frustration and resolve swirling inside her. She wanted to believe him, wanted to think there was still a line she could walk between her own morality and the life she was now tied to. But every day on this ship made that line blur more and more.

Not ready to respond, Sam toyed with her compass, saved when a shout rang out from the crow's nest. "Land ho!"

She jerked her head up, eyes widening as the silhouette of land formed on the horizon. She had done it! It had taken two days longer than anticipated, but she had successfully navigated them back to land.

She glanced at Kensley, her breath catching in her throat as their eyes met.

"Well done, navigator," he said with a crooked smile, tipping his head slightly.

Sam managed a small smile in return. Handing the wheel to Kensley, she left the helm to scale the rigging, wanting to get a better view of the coastline. Reaching the crow's nest, she squeezed in beside the lanky watchman, pulled out her spyglass, and pressed it to her eye. She licked her lips, her mouth dry as she scanned the horizon, searching for the trails of smoke that accompanied cities and towns.

There. Relief washed over her.

Swinging a leg over the rail, she grabbed hold of the thick rope attached to it, then slid down. Air rushed past her ears before she landed safely back on the deck.

"Two degrees to the east," she called up to Kensley, who nodded in response and turned the wheel accordingly. Sam walked to the rail, checking her compass once more.

"You've done well, poppet."

She jumped at Kharzul's voice, turning to see him striding toward her, his hands laced casually behind his back.

Swallowing, Sam said, "Thank you, Captain."

"You should know that you will not be allowed to leave the vessel while we are berthed in Atral," he said, his tone devoid of warmth.

Sam expected as much. The last time they'd docked, Sefina had slipped through his grasp, and Sam had come close to following. She wondered where Sefina was now, if she was safe, or if, somehow, Kharzul's wrath had caught up with her.

"Understood," Sam murmured, her eyes fixed on the deck. She focused on the knots in the planks, tracing their patterns with her eyes to distract herself from the sinking feeling in her chest.

Kharzul stood there a moment longer, his presence oppressive, before he turned and strode away.

Kensley was watching her from his spot at the helm, but Sam didn't feel like talking with him. Instead, she climbed the ropes, heading back to the crow's nest.

From her vantage point high above the deck, Sam watched Atral grow larger on the horizon. The city reared against the sky, its spires and buildings perched at the tip of Phago's peninsula like an overlong, crooked tooth. It was a place that held some of her most painful memories. Tucking the spyglass into her belt, she leaned forward over the rail and rested her head in her hands.

The last time she'd been here, she'd learned of Rhett's death.

Back then, she had sworn revenge, sworn to honor Rhett by finding a way to destroy the system that had destroyed him. The crew of the *Queen Mary* had put that promise on hold while she honored another promise, the promise to live.

It seemed a cruel trick of the gods that she'd outlived them all.

She'd made promises to avenge them too. Was this really how she would honor their memory? By becoming the very thing that had stolen their lives? By serving under the likes of Kharzul, a man who wielded dark magic and commanded fear with every breath? The thought gnawed at her insides.

And Rhett... What would he think of this? No, this wasn't a slave ship, but it wasn't much better. The same evil persisted—the greed, the cruelty, the disregard for human life. She wasn't stopping it; she was helping to drive it. Every course she plotted for Kharzul's ship could lead to bloodshed, plunder, and ruin. Every decision she made now carried the weight of those consequences.

She stayed up in the crow's nest, thoughts storming, until the anchor had been dropped. Already, new goods were being loaded onto the ship. Then she swung down to the deck.

She noticed, too late, that two of Kharzul's men had been waiting. As they grabbed her from behind, she yelled a string of curses.

"Now, now, poppet. Your mouth is too pretty for such vile language," Kharzul said, descending the stairs to the main deck.

She stopped struggling but glared at the man on her left—Wilson? William? "Unhand me at once," she demanded.

The man did no such thing.

Kharzul chuckled. "Hush, it's only temporary. I warned you of this."

Sam wasn't given the chance to respond before being forcefully escorted down the two flights of stairs to her quarters. The scraping of the latch against the other side of the door told her she would not be leaving any time soon.

THIRTY

Sam breathed out slowly, clenching her teeth as she jammed her dagger harder into the thin crack between the door and its frame. She'd been locked in this cramped room for nearly a day, with no food or water and no place to relieve herself. The stuffiness of the air fueled her irritation with every breath.

She wiggled the blade, feeling the scrape of metal on metal as it nudged the lock. But the door refused to budge. With a growl of frustration, she slapped the door and left her dagger wedged there, protruding from the frame.

Eventually, she snatched it back, sheathing it in her boot with a huff.

The metallic scrape of a bolt sliding free sounded moments later. Sam didn't wait for it to fully open, grabbing the edge and throwing it wide to reveal Kensley standing on the other side, a satchel across his shoulder, a plate of food in his hands, and a smirk plastered on his ruggedly handsome face.

"I thought you were a master at picking locks," he said, amusement lacing his tone.

"This isn't a keyhole," she snapped, glaring at him. "There's a bloody bolt mounted on the outside."

He only chuckled as she pushed past him, not bothering to stop her.

First things first—she took care of her urgent needs. After that, she didn't head back to the stuffy cabin. She'd had enough of the small, windowless room. Instead, she climbed the steps toward the open air of the deck, craving a bit of sunlight and freedom.

Halfway up, her path was blocked by none other than Kensley again, arms folded as he leaned against the railing with an almost lazy air.

"Captain's orders," he said, his smirk back in place. "I can't let you go up there."

The thought briefly crossed her mind to make a break for it. All she wanted was some fresh air. Instead, she snatched the plate of food from his hands with a resigned "fine" and plopped onto a crate, shoving a biscuit into her mouth with an exaggerated chomp.

After she devoured her food and set the plate aside, Kensley said, "I brought something for you."

Sam stood, intrigued. "What is it?"

He cleared his throat, his movements oddly deliberate as he pulled a small box from his satchel. His usual smirk tempered into something more genuine. "I saw it at the market earlier and knew you had to have it."

He handed her the box. Sam eyed him curiously as she lifted the lid.

Then a small gasp escaped her. Nestled inside was a polished dagger, its handle wrapped in smooth leather and engraved with intricate flames.

It was beautiful, deadly, and undeniably hers.

"I've always known there's a fire in you." Kensley leaned in slightly as he studied her reaction. "Now you have something to match."

Sam ran her fingers over the blade, her heart swelling with something she couldn't quite name. "It's perfect," she murmured. "Thank you."

"Here." He stepped closer. "Let me. Just try not to stab me with it, all right?"

Kensley took the dagger from her hands and tucked it into her belt, his fingers brushing against her hip as he adjusted it. His touch lingered, warm and steady, and when he finally looked up, his eyes met hers with an intensity that stole her breath.

He was so close she could see his every detail—the way the blue and gray swirled together in his eyes, the way his expression softened just for her. His hand slid to her waist, and her body betrayed her, leaning ever so slightly into his warmth.

"Kensley..." she began, her voice trembling.

"Tell me to stop," he said, voice barely above a whisper. His free hand came up to brush a strand of hair from her face, his fingers lingering at her temple. "Tell me, and I will."

She didn't. Not immediately. The space between them shrank until his breath brushed her skin. Her heart thundered in her chest, her head spinning.

And then, just as his lips hovered above hers, she turned her face to the side, breaking the spell. "I can't."

Her voice cracked on the words, her own resolve betraying her. Kensley froze, his hand still at her waist, before he pulled back slightly, his gaze searching hers. For a moment, something flickered in his eyes—disappointment, understanding, perhaps even longing. But it was gone as quickly as it came.

"Not right now," she added, her voice barely audible.

Kensley released her slowly, as though reluctant to let go. He stepped back. "When you're ready," he said.

Sam nodded, her throat tight as she glanced away. Her fingers curled around the dagger in her belt, gripping it like a lifeline. Why hadn't she let him kiss her? She'd wanted to, hadn't she? The way her heart raced in his presence, the way his touch sent warmth radiating through her... She couldn't deny the pull she felt toward him. And yet, as his lips had hovered so close to hers, something inside her had resisted.

Rhett's memory flashed in her mind. Not just his face, but the promises she'd made, the ones she still hadn't fulfilled. The Lily Company had faded into the back of her mind, but she hadn't forgotten. And she had yet to make things right.

Kissing Kensley would mean letting go of a part of her promise. It would mean letting go—*really* letting go... of Rhett.

It wasn't Kensley. He was the one person on this ship who truly saw her. But she wasn't ready to be seen. Not like this. Not when there was still so much left undone.

She squeezed the dagger tighter.

"I'm going for a walk," she muttered, her voice taut. She turned quickly, but after a step, she hesitated. Her back was to him as she whispered, "Thank you for the gift."

Then she walked away.

As she wandered the dim corridors, the moment played over and over in her mind—the way he had looked at her, the warmth of his hand at her waist, the patience in his voice when he said, *When you're ready.*

Truthfully, she wasn't sure she ever would be. Not while the Lily Company still prowled. Not while Kharzul ruled. Not while she was still struggling to decide who she was and what she wanted.

And yet, a small part of her couldn't help but wonder—what would it feel like to let go, just for a moment? To let someone else share the weight she carried?

"Maybe someday," she whispered to the empty hall. But she didn't dare make another promise.

Sam eventually found her way to one of the portholes along the side of the ship. Through it, she could just make out the city in the distance. Atral sat under the sunlight, its narrow streets winding between wooden and stone buildings, perched against lush green hills. White blossoms speckled the trees beyond the bay, and Sam could almost imagine the scent of the flowers on the breeze. The sight tugged at her, the sense of freedom just out of reach.

Kensley found her again a short while later.

"Have a nice walk?" he asked.

Sam shrugged, eyes fixed on the dagger at her hip. She ran her thumb along the leather-wrapped handle, not really seeing it—just something to focus on that wasn't him. She hated how awkward she felt.

"You know you're going to have to learn how to handle that thing, don't you?" Kensley said.

Sam finally looked up, catching the slight smirk tugging at his lips. She couldn't avoid him forever, not on a ship like this. And honestly... she didn't want to.

"Pistols are more practical," she said, just to be stubborn.

Kensley raised an eyebrow. "You don't have a pistol, Sam."

"But *you* have two."

"I only *carry* two," he corrected.

"Exactly. So you have one to spare and can teach me."

Kensley chuckled. "I can't teach you to shoot down here. You'd blow holes through the hull."

Sam blew out a breath. He was right, and if she was being honest, she was itching to test the feel of the dagger in her hand. She rolled her shoulders, shaking off whatever tension still clung to her.

"I guess we can practice with this, then," she said, pulling the knife free.

Kensley grinned, loosening one of his own. "That we can do."

After a brief spar, Kensley had left her—back in her quarters—with a simple farewell. He hadn't stayed, and Sam hadn't asked him to, though she immediately missed him when he was gone.

The next day, however, he returned with unexpected news.

"You're free to move about the ship," Kensley told her, casually leaning against the doorframe. "Within reason, of course. You're still to remain aboard."

Sam stared at him, caught between suspicion and surprise. "That's... unexpected."

"I told Kharzul that you could be trusted."

She blinked. And Kharzul had allowed it just like that?

This could be an opportunity—a chance to find her way to freedom. The thought sparked in her mind, wild and desperate. If she could just find the right moment...

But even as she thought it, her chest tightened. If she ran, if she even *tried*, Kensley would pay the price.

She followed him up to the deck, her gaze lingering as he walked away. He had already moved on, attending to his own tasks. He wasn't hovering, wasn't waiting for her to make some reckless move. The choice was completely up to her.

And she was choosing *him*.

Sam settled herself cross-legged on the forecastle deck, spreading out several maps across the planks. Before leaning over them, she glanced out at the harbor, watching curiously as a ship that appeared to be nearing the port turned sharply and headed back the way it had come. She was sure the presence of the *Golden Krina* had something to do with it.

Trapped on deck was still a vast improvement over trapped in her quarters. Sam enjoyed the sea air and the sunlight, losing herself in navigational study.

At one point, she saw Kensley climbing deftly through the rigging of the mainmast, checking for any damage to the ropes and sails. Sam couldn't help but notice the way his muscles tensed and flexed with each pull. If his wounds still bothered him, he didn't show it. She forced herself to stop staring just as Kharzul's sharp voice sliced through the air.

Farther along the deck, Kharzul argued with the ship's carpenter. Impeccably dressed as always, the captain had added a large feathered hat to his ensemble, the vibrant plumage swaying in the breeze as he spoke. Sam leaned in, pretending to be engrossed in her maps as she strained to overhear.

"Three weeks?" Kharzul demanded.

The carpenter rushed to defend himself. "A new mast takes time to—"

"Perhaps I didn't make myself clear. I will allow you two weeks—at most."

Sam watched the carpenter's shoulders hunch under Kharzul's steely gaze. The carpenter stammered, nodding quickly. "I—Yes, sir. Two weeks, then. We'll find a way."

Satisfied but visibly tense, Kharzul stepped back. Sam wondered why he seemed so anxious to return to the open sea, though once she thought of it, she realized the *Golden Krina* hardly ever docked and never for long. The captain seemed constantly on the move, as though something lurked just beyond sight, driving him forward.

Kharzul's voice cut through her reverie. "Good morning, poppet."

Sam straightened, flushed to be caught eavesdropping.

"Captain," she greeted, a tinge of frustration seeping into her voice despite her effort to stay neutral. The confinement aboard the ship while the rest of the crew roamed Atral was beginning to wear on her patience.

Kharzul's eyes sparkled with amusement as he let out an exaggerated sigh. "I see you're upset with me. What a shame. Cavenaugh has informed me how well behaved you've been in my absence. I hoped you might accompany me about the town today. But if you're unhappy, perhaps we should—"

"I'd love to accompany you," Sam interrupted, the words slipping out before she could second-guess herself.

Kharzul smirked. "Good," he replied smoothly. "Your company will be welcome as I attend to some errands."

He extended his arm toward her, and Sam hesitated only a moment before slipping her hand into the crook of his arm. The velvet of his coat was unexpectedly soft beneath her fingers, and she had to resist the impulse to smooth her hand over it. The contrast of his cold demeanor and the warm fabric only made the moment feel stranger.

As Sam stepped off the gangplank, she couldn't help herself; she glanced back at Kensley. He stood by the railing, watching.

She wished it was his rough linen sleeve beneath her hand instead of Kharzul's expensive velvet. She wanted his steady, protective presence beside her, not the predatory grace of the man leading her way.

Sam turned away, swallowing the sudden lump in her throat, and breathed in the city. Though she'd been in Atral once before, the news about Rhett had prevented her from taking anything in, so it all felt new. The buildings came in shades of brown and soft greens—so different from the colorful clash of Milderre.

Expecting to head to the market, she was surprised when they ventured to a different part of town. The streets became cleaner, the people well-dressed. The shops they passed bore elegant signs and large glass windows displaying their wares.

They came to one particular shop and, upon passing the window, Sam sucked in a breath. Glittering strands of jewelry lay across black silk pillows. Diamond necklaces, sapphire tiaras, pearl earrings, and a cluster of delicate brooches all sparkled elegantly in the light. A different brooch came to mind—her mother's. She'd given it to Rhett as a promise he'd return to her. Did it, too, lay at the bottom of the sea?

To Sam's surprise, Kharzul opened the door to the shop and motioned her in, following close behind. She caught a whiff of his sickly sweet musk and was reminded that this gentlemanly facade was only that—a facade.

The jeweler rushed forward to greet them, his gaze moving between Kharzul and Sam. "Welcome back, Lord. Lady."

The titles caught Sam off guard. Did he not know the man before him was a pirate?

The jeweler continued, his words carrying the slight lilt of a Phagean accent. "The piece you commissioned is complete, milord. Shall I fetch it?"

Kharzul dipped his chin in acknowledgment, and the jeweler bowed deeply before vanishing behind a curtain at the back of the room. Moments later, he returned, reverently carrying a sleek black box, which he presented to Kharzul with a flourish. Sam craned her neck as he lifted the lid, curious what a man like Kharzul might have commissioned from a jeweler.

The answer was a stunning mask, its delicate gems catching the light as Kharzul lifted it from its satin bed.

Then Kharzul gestured for her to turn around.

She hesitated, then obeyed, feeling a prickle of both anticipation and uncertainty.

Her breathing hitched as Kharzul settled the mask against her face, securely tying it behind her head. She turned slowly to face him again. His lips turned upward. With a subtle motion, he guided her toward a long mirror propped against the wall. She thought she heard a small sigh of relief from the jeweler as he backed away.

As Sam gazed at her reflection, she found herself entranced.

The exquisite metalwork had been formed to fit comfortably over her eyes and nose, coming to points near her temples. Thin gold leaf accented the glossy, deep green coating. Intricate, swirling designs swept outward from the center of the forehead where a large, flat emerald had been set. Petite pearls and emeralds adorned her cheekbones, the bridge of her nose, and her brows. Most strikingly, they dripped in strands from the bottom of the mask like tears on her cheeks.

Through the mirror, she could see Captain Kharzul's satisfied smile. "I see my taste is impeccable, as always."

Sam's hands instinctively reached for the ribbons, and she gently untied the mask. She felt a strange discomfort, an itch from the thief inside her who knew just how precious this piece was. "I... I can't accept this," she stammered, casting her gaze down.

Kharzul cocked his head. "Why not?"

"It's..." She hesitated, searching for words. "It's remarkably expensive. And what if I lose it?"

Deep down, she knew her reluctance was less about the mask itself and more about what accepting it meant. Accepting the mask felt as if she were binding herself to him, as if she were committing to this life of piracy.

Kharzul let out a soft chuckle. "Consider it a token, poppet. Its worth means little compared to yours." His words were both smooth and unsettling. "Besides, everyone will know the *Golden Krina*'s navigator when they see her in this."

The mask was, she realized, just another piece in the spectacle Kharzul created—a theatrical display of power and presence. A piece intended to be flaunted. Like her.

Sam carefully handed the mask back to the jeweler. Captain Kharzul watched silently. She couldn't read his body language to tell whether or not he was disappointed in her reaction. The jeweler closed the lid once more.

"Have it sent to my ship," Kharzul instructed, then strode to the door. "Come along." He held it open, and they exited onto the cobblestone street. "I have one more matter of business to attend to while we are in this vicinity. It won't take long. We can take a stroll through the market afterwards."

They continued through the town, walking in silence. Sam was content to observe. They passed fewer and fewer shops, replaced by larger and larger residences.

Kharzul glanced at her as they traveled, his gaze lingering. "Your hair," he mused, almost to himself. "It marks you in ways you may not yet fully realize."

Sam brushed off the comment. "I've become accustomed to the attention it brings."

"Hair such as yours *demands* attention," he replied, studying her with a thoughtful intensity. "Red shades were once the mark of a people who held great knowledge and power. You're familiar with Astoenia, I assume?"

Sam looked up, hesitant to reveal what little Sefina had once told her. "Astoenia? I've heard some tales. It was once a nation, wasn't it?"

"The Astoenians were a mighty people. Many were descended from the gods themselves." He closed his eyes for a moment, as if reminiscing.

"They commanded elements and wielded crafts lost to us now. Their hair burned like fire in the sun, as yours does."

Sam recalled that Sefina had said the same.

Kharzul had trinkets and books from distant lands, yet she'd never considered he might hold some expertise on extinct lands too.

"If they were so powerful," she asked, "why doesn't Astoenia exist anymore?"

Kharzul's tone softened, almost wistful. "Power comes with a cost, and those closest to it rarely see the end coming. One day, Astoenia thrived, and the next day... ashes and silence."

She felt a chill. "And you... believe in these old tales?"

"Believe?" he repeated, a half-smile touching his lips. "I've seen enough to know that power, true power, leaves its mark. And some"—he paused, flexing and unflexing his hand as if considering whether to continue—"still search for traces of it."

It took a moment for the words to sink in.

"You're searching for it," Sam said, a question as much as it was a statement.

"Indeed, my life does not lend itself to staying still. Old powers linger, poppet, and there are those who would take them if they could."

"Do the gods not hold all the power?" Sam probed, knowing that Kharzul wielded power of his own.

"They do not. Though they would not hesitate to take what I have." His gaze flickered to her hair again, as if her red curls held some meaning, some answer he searched for.

Sam resisted the urge to touch her hair, feeling inclined to cover it as she once had.

A moment later, Kharzul ascended a handful of steps to rap on a large, paneled door. Sam remained on the street and studied the building. Made from cream-colored bricks, the townhouse boasted no less than ten windows, with lavish stone decoration covering the exterior.

A maid appeared through one of the doors, and, upon seeing Kharzul, promptly invited them in. Sam hesitated, but Kharzul ushered her forward, and she followed him into the house.

She gawked at the high ceilings decorated with carved wooden accents and the portraits filling nearly every wall. Luxurious woven rugs covered polished wood floors, and the hallway tables held expensive crystal vases.

They were led to a parlor with several invitingly plush armchairs. Kharzul sat and gestured for her to claim the chair adjacent to him. Sam promptly melted into the glorious softness of the cushions. She hadn't sat on something this soft since... well, ever.

But the luxury of the house couldn't fully distract her from her conversation with Kharzul.

They would not hesitate to take what I have.

His words echoed in her mind. What extent of power did Kharzul have? And why, if he already had power, was he searching for more? Were the gods also searching for this power? Or were they... were they searching for *him*?

And her hair... What significance could her hair possibly hold in any of this? She could feel Kharzul's gaze again, his eyes tracing over her red curls as though they held the secrets of the world.

She shivered, trying to shake off the unsettling thoughts.

She was still stewing when the man of the house was announced and entered the parlor through a door to their right. Kharzul stood at his arrival, Sam quickly doing the same. Though they were in Phago, the man was stylishly dressed in Ducrian fashion, his lavish coat a vibrant shade of green. His brown hair was graying at his temples and wrinkles formed around his sharp eyes.

"Why, if it isn't my old friend Salik Kharzul." Though he said "friend," his undertone was strained. "It's been some time. You haven't aged a day! Come, join me in my study."

Kharzul addressed Sam. "Wait here, poppet. I'll be back shortly. I suspect you'll behave?"

She nodded, and he followed the man out of the parlor, a footman closing the doors behind them with a soft click.

Sam looked around uncomfortably. The two footmen stationed at each door stood silent and impassive, their gazes fixed straight ahead. Her eyes drifted to the polished handle of the nearest door, a thought tugging insistently at her.

Another chance to escape.

She silently cursed as Kensley's name appeared in her mind.

Besides, even if she managed to evade the footmen here, she recalled additional guards stationed at the front entrance.

Rather than sit, she meandered toward the perimeter of the room, inspecting the wall decor and baubles that lined it. Her hand lingered on a small, carved statue made entirely of blue stone. It depicted a woman with two flowing fish tails instead of legs. A siren.

The thought brought Sefina to mind—Sefina with her hauntingly beautiful voice that could silence even the rowdiest of crews, a voice powerful enough to rival any siren's. But Sefina definitely had two *human* legs. In truth, Sam knew painfully little about Sefina's past. She wished she'd asked more when she had the chance.

A quiet throat clearing snapped Sam out of her thoughts, and she placed the statue back with a touch of guilt, offering the footman a quick, apologetic glance. She walked to the next table, taking care not to touch anything, and admired the pieces. Each represented mythical creatures and beings. She found several depictions of the gods, along with a fang that was at least the length of her arm. Eventually, she sat back in the cloudlike armchair.

When the doors opened again, Kharzul was still speaking with the man.

"I am disappointed that you have not placed greater urgency behind my request. I fear I am no longer in need of your business." The shadows around his feet flickered with his words, and, for a brief moment, they appeared to darken, like oil swirling in water. "We shall take our leave."

Sam stood hastily, catching a fleeting look of panic on the man's face. He bowed low. "My lord, I will not fail you again."

There it was again. That title. Who was Kharzul to these people?

He strode from the room without a backward glance. "No," he said, almost lazily, "you will not."

As they passed a maid carrying a vase of fresh lilies, Sam's heart gave a lurch.

Lilies—she hadn't seen one in a long, *long* time. *It's a coincidence*, she told herself, trying to ignore the dread unfurling in her chest. They were in Phago, after all. The Lily Company had no presence here; the Slaver had merely been an extension of that monstrous enterprise.

But as she glanced toward Kharzul's impassive face, chilling questions snaked into her mind.

Does he know about the Lily Company? Is he involved somehow?

The shadows at his feet, his ties to mysterious powers, his vast knowledge—everything she couldn't make sense of only seemed more ominous.

On the street, they met two men who appeared seemingly from nowhere. Pirates from the *Golden Krina*, Sam realized, recognizing their weathered faces and the cold glint in their eyes. Kharzul made a subtle swirling motion with his hand, and the men darted past, weapons drawn. Her heart hammered as they stormed through the very doors she had just exited.

Screams pierced the air, and she felt herself shrink back, her stomach lurching as darkness spread over the house, shadowing it despite the bright, cloudless sky above.

She took half a step toward the house, gripped by an impulse to turn back, to do *something*, but then she felt a light pressure on her shoulder. Kharzul's jeweled hand rested there, a firm reminder to stay in line. He slipped her arm into his and led her forward, strolling down the street as if nothing unusual had happened.

Sam couldn't bring herself to look at him.

They arrived at the bustling market, the sights and sounds so incongruously cheerful that they only sharpened Sam's disquiet. Kharzul moved between stalls with the ease of a man at home, oblivious, or simply indifferent, to the chaos he'd left behind.

When they reached a flower stand, he paused and selected a bloom from the vendor. He held it out to Sam with a smile, as if it were the most natural gesture in the world. She accepted it without really looking, her mind still lingering on those Kharzul had left screaming.

"Thank you," she whispered meekly. She held the flower to her side, a weight in her hand as she mindlessly twisted the stem between her fingers.

Back aboard the *Golden Krina*, Kharzul thanked her for her company, departing for his cabin without another word. Sam retreated to her quarters. Upon entering the room, she could see that the black box holding the mask had been set on her bed along with several feminine-looking shirts.

Placing the flower next to the box, she paused, finally taking in the bloom that had been gifted to her.

Of all the flowers he could have picked, Kharzul had chosen a *lily*.

THIRTY-ONE

The lily's petals were of the purest white, with pale yellow stamens in the center. A beautiful flower had her image of it not been so tainted.

Sam had seen lilies *twice* today. Could it be coincidence?

Kharzul must *be connected*. And what business had he discussed with that man, business important enough to leave a trail of shadows and blood?

The thought unsettled her deeply, weaving Kharzul's world of darkness with her past in a way that felt almost inevitable.

Desperate for a distraction, she pulled the emerald and pearl mask from its box. It seemed to shimmer with an otherworldly allure as she ran her fingers along one of its delicate strands, marveling at how it could hold so much value.

The entire crew wore masks during raids. She recalled the chill she'd felt seeing them descend upon the *Queen Mary*, their faces obscured, unrecognizable. The fear they'd inspired was undeniable, the very essence of piracy itself. But could this mask—so refined, so beautiful—strike the same terror into others?

A strange thought occurred as she gazed at it. Beauty was a kind of power. Perhaps with this mask, she could be more than just Sam, the cautious, uncertain thief. She didn't have to become someone like Kharzul, but maybe she could be someone fearsome and bold. Someone capable of taking on something bigger than herself.

The Lily Company crept back into her mind. She imagined, if only for a moment, being powerful enough to bring that monstrous network down.

A soft knock interrupted her thoughts. Startled, Sam closed the lid carefully and slipped the box beneath the edge of her mattress. She looked up just as Kensley peeked his head inside.

"I heard you were back. Enjoy your stroll about town?"

Sam averted her gaze, biting her cheek.

Kensley hesitated, then stepped into the cramped space and sat down on the edge of Sefina's old mattress. "That bad, huh?" he asked gently.

A lump rose in her throat. "I think he had someone killed today."

Saying it aloud made it real. Kharzul had ended a life as casually as he'd decided the route to the next port. And she'd just stood by, watching, unable to do anything about it. The reality hit her in waves, chilling her more deeply with each one. She wasn't strong enough to intervene. She could hardly hold her own in a sparring match, let alone challenge someone like Kharzul.

Then Kensley asked, "Is it so out of his character?"

No, and that was the problem, wasn't it?

Sam looked up to meet Kensley's eyes. "How can he talk of 'balance between men' when he doesn't value life? Not even that of his crew."

"What he does, he does *for* that balance." The faint edge of admiration in Kensley's voice made Sam's skin prickle. "He believes that his actions, no matter how brutal, are justified if they bring change to the world."

"What kind of balance can justify so much bloodshed?"

"What if these sacrifices are necessary to prevent worse from happening? He's seen things, Sam—felt things. I may not agree with everything he does, but I know he believes in a cause bigger than himself. Sometimes balance isn't about saving everyone. It's about... choosing the right sacrifices."

Kensley's faith in Kharzul was unsettling, but he wasn't alone; Kharzul's presence commanded fierce loyalty from most of his followers.

"And what if he's wrong?" she asked softly, more to herself than to him. "What if there's a way to reach that balance without... without becoming a monster?"

Kensley's tone was gentle. "Maybe there is, but it's a path I haven't seen yet. Sometimes the only way to survive in this world is to wield power that others can't challenge."

Sam stared at Kensley, unease settling in her chest. He wasn't shaken by Kharzul's ruthlessness, not the way she was. He didn't flinch at the violence, didn't question the blood staining the decks. He wasn't weak, nor was he blindly loyal, but he had *chosen* this life. He had *chosen* Kharzul.

How could he look at Kharzul and see a leader while all she saw was a man capable of unrestrained violence?

And what if, in the end, she wasn't so different from him? What if she stayed too long, made too many compromises, and one day found herself looking at Kharzul not with fear but with the same detached acceptance Kensley had?

That wasn't the person she wanted to become.

And yet... it might be the person she *needed* to become.

She'd made two promises of vengeance, and whether Kharzul was tangled in the Lily Company or not, she didn't have the strength to challenge either him or the Lily Co. Not in her current state.

Determination settled over Sam like one of Kharzul's dark shadows. Maybe she would have to stand by Kharzul, become something ruthless, something powerful. Enough to bring about change. Even if it meant fighting alongside a monster and becoming something close to monstrous herself.

The *Golden Krina* buzzed with activity as it readied to depart, but everyone paused when Kensley hauled a bulging sack of coins up the gangplank. The crew gathered eagerly around him as he set up a table and chair on the deck, calling, "Fall in line!"

Sam sidled to the back of the line, curiosity flickering. "What is this?" she whispered to the man in front of her.

"Earnings," he replied, and her eyes widened.

One by one, each crew member received a share of the profits from the goods they'd sold in Atral—the goods they'd plundered from other ships.

When it was her turn, Kensley handed her a small but weighty sack. She held it, surprised at its heft. "Are you sure this is right?"

He gave her a slight smile. "Navigator receives one share and a half."

It was more money than Sam had ever held at one time. Her mind whirred as she imagined exactly how she'd use it. She considered the sparkling jewelry in the shop window, the delicious scents of food in the market, then landed on something she'd found herself wanting more and more lately.

She wanted a pistol—a cold, reliable weight in her hand. Though she knew they were preparing to sail soon and getting to town wasn't possible, she couldn't shake her determination.

She waited until Kensley finished handing out the shares, watching as the last of the crew dispersed. Only then did she step forward, her gaze dropping to the leather holsters at his hips.

"You're staring," he said.

"I am."

"That's usually when trouble starts."

Sam's lips quirked. "You once told me you only carry two pistols." Her eyes flicked back up to his. "Which means you have more."

Kensley huffed a laugh, hands drifting to rest on his holsters as he studied her. "And?"

"And I want one." Sam lifted the sack of coins between them, letting it sway once.

Kensley didn't even glance at it. Instead, his gaze lingered on her.

"I'm listening," he said, "but I don't want your money."

That wasn't what she'd expected.

She let the coins fall back to her side, brows pulling together. "Then what do you want?"

"A trade."

Sam folded her arms, shifting her weight onto one hip. "Now I'm the one listening."

"I've seen your hands," Kensley said, attention dropping briefly to them. "Light. Quick. Things disappear when you've been around."

Sam didn't deny it.

"You want me to teach you to pickpocket," she said.

Kensley shook his head. "I want you to teach me how you do it without getting caught."

Sam considered the offer. Kensley, eight years a pirate, asking *her* to teach him how to steal better.

"And you'd give up one of your pistols for it?" she asked.

"Aye, but only because you're an excellent teacher."

A smile tugged at her mouth despite herself. "Bold of you to assume I am."

"I've been paying attention."

The words landed softer than the rest. Heat crept into her chest. She knew the look people usually gave her when they realized what she could do—guarded, uneasy, accusatory.

Kensley's gaze held none of that and it threw her off more than she cared to admit.

Clearing her throat, she said, "Throw in some bullets and it's a trade."

Kensley's mouth curved. "So greedy."

He reached down, drawing one of the pistols from his holster. He turned it once in his hands before stepping close. Sam's breath caught as he placed the pistol in her palm. But instead of letting go, his hand lingered over hers. His thumb brushed across her knuckles.

"If you shoot me with it," he said quietly, "I'll be very disappointed."

The warmth of his hand against hers made it difficult to think clearly. She swallowed, forcing her fingers to tighten around the pistol instead of his.

Then she smirked. "You'd be dead."

"Still disappointed."

Sam leaned casually against the rail, tracking the crew with quiet focus. Kensley stepped up beside her, easy as ever, like he had nowhere else to be.

"First rule," Sam said, nodding toward the crew. "Don't look like you're about to steal something."

Kensley glanced down at himself. "I look the same as I always do."

Sam rolled her eyes, and Kensley grinned.

"Watch," she said.

She slipped away from the rail. Kensley stayed where he was, arms loosely folded, eyes following.

Sam picked her mark quickly—O'Toole, half-distracted and laughing with another, had no idea that his coin pouch was loose. Pity, with all those newly earned wages nestled within. She stepped into his space like she belonged there, pretending to tighten a rope. Then she brushed past, fingers moving. Hook, twist, lift. She never broke stride.

Returning to Kensley, she dropped the pouch into his palm.

He glanced down, then back up at her. "You make it look easy."

"It is," she said lightly. "If you're not over-thinking it."

He handed the pouch back, gaze sharpening just a little. "All right. My turn."

Sam shook her head, attaching O'Toole's purse to her belt. "Not yet. You start with me."

Kensley arched a brow. "With you," he repeated.

"Take something off me," she said, spreading her arms.

His smile shifted, a challenge lighting his eyes. "Don't go easy on me, Red."

"I'd never."

She stepped closer. Close enough that he could reach her without trying. Too close, maybe. But neither of them moved away.

"Go on," she breathed.

Then Kensley's hand moved. Not clumsy or slow. Just... not enough. Sam caught his wrist before he got far, fingers wrapping around it easily.

"Too obvious," she said.

"Difficult to blend in with you watching me."

Sam smirked and then turned around, letting her eyes scan the waves. "Try again."

He did, quicker this time, but she anticipated his movements, pivoting so that his hand brushed her side instead of her belt.

"You're enjoying this far too much," Kensley rumbled.

She was.

"Again," she said.

He didn't answer this time, just moved. Sam barely had time to register the shift in his weight before his arm slipped around her waist.

"Kensley!" she yelped, half-laughing as he lifted her just slightly, spinning her a fraction away from the rail.

"That's not pickpocketing," she said, breathless, trying to twist out of his grip. "That's cheating."

"Is it?" Kensley asked, far too pleased with himself.

"You didn't even try—"

"Didn't I?"

He released her just enough for her boots to find the deck again, steadying her with a hand at her back. Then he nodded to her hip. Sam's smile faltered as her gaze dropped too.

O'Toole's coin pouch. Gone.

She blinked, then looked back up at him. "You—"

Kensley held it up between them, grin sharp. "You were saying?"

Sam made a grab for it immediately, but he lifted his arm higher, effortlessly keeping it just out of reach.

"You're insufferable."

She tried again, but he caught her wrist in his free hand, holding it suspended above her head. The mood shifted into something less playful. Kensley's eyes bored into hers. She glanced at his lips involuntarily, the space between them growing smaller.

O'Toole's voice cut across the deck. "Oi, where's my coin?"

Sam snapped her head to him.

O'Toole patted at his belt, confusion melting into irritation as he turned in a slow, suspicious circle.

Kensley's hand dropped from Sam's wrist. The coin purse returned to her palm a moment later. She closed her fingers around it, slipping it up her sleeve as she straightened her posture.

"You owe me another lesson," Kensley said quietly, amusement lacing his tone. "The deal was to teach me to thieve without getting caught."

Sam fought the urge to elbow him in the gut.

THIRTY-TWO

Sam awoke to the creak of a door swinging open. Her mind snapped to alertness as she realized it was *her* door. She bolted upright, barely able to make out a darkened silhouette hovering near the foot of her bed. Before she could react, the figure lunged forward, pinning her down.

Sam thrashed, kicking wildly at him as a scream tore from her lungs.

"Corrigan," came a harsh whisper from the doorway. "Shut her up before someone hears!"

Corrigan grunted as Sam's knee found a weak spot, causing him to falter. "Give me a hand, O'Toole! She won't stop squirmin'."

Sam's fingers fumbled beneath her pillow until they met cold steel. With a surge of desperation, she yanked the dagger free and slashed outward. Corrigan jerked back with a curse and Sam slid out from under him.

She bolted for the door, her bare feet pounding on the wooden floor as she fled into the hall in nothing but her undergarments. The footsteps thundered behind her, closing in fast.

A rough hand seized her arm, yanking her back and twisting it painfully. She gasped as she was slammed face-first against the wall, her cheek pressing into the wood.

Corrigan pressed in close, twisting her arm until her knife dropped free. "You've been gettin' real comfortable, haven't you?" he hissed. "O'Toole's coin pouch gone yesterday. Mine the week before that. And no one says a thing 'cause Captain has Cavenaugh keep you tucked away like some sort of lucky charm."

So that was it.

Not desire. Not drunken stupidity.

She'd been found out.

"You've been takin' from all of us," Corrigan continued, voice tightening with anger. "And walking around this ship like there ain't rules for you."

O'Toole's voice drifted from the hall, bitter and loud. "Captain's pet thief. That's what she is."

Sam ground her teeth and fought to keep her voice steady. "If you don't let go of me this instant, I'll make sure you stop accusing people *permanently.*"

O'Toole chuckled from behind them, his voice dripping with mockery. "Oh, feisty one, aren't we?"

She whipped her head around, shooting him a glare. "Only with spineless cowards like you."

O'Toole whistled in mock surprise. "Hear that, Corrigan? She bites."

Sam drove her foot back, hooking it around Corrigan's knee before yanking it forward. His leg buckled, throwing him off balance as Sam shoved off the wall. They toppled backward, but before they even reached the ground, Sam twisted, rolling clear of his grasp.

She was on her feet in an instant. Corrigan was still scrambling to recover when she wrenched her arm free of his sloppy grip and snatched the cutlass from his hip.

O'Toole lunged, but Sam raised the blade, driving it deep into his flesh.

He gasped, staggering back as blood bloomed across his shirt. His hands flew to his gut, his expression filled with shock.

Sam barely spared him a glance. She was already crouching over Corrigan, pressing the bloodied cutlass to his throat before he could make another move.

Then a shadow shifted in the hall.

Sam glanced up as Kensley stalked forward, his features dimly lit by the soft glow of the lantern on the wall. He stood tall, his frame tense and coiled like a predator about to strike. Several strands of hair hung loose around his face, framing stormy eyes that blazed with barely restrained fury. His jaw was set, muscles taut with anger, and his normally easygoing smile was nowhere to be found; instead, his mouth was a thin, uncompromising line.

Corrigan saw him too. His panic-stricken gaze darted between them before settling on Kensley.

"Cavenaugh," he choked. "Tell her to get off, mate. This is about our coin—our property. She's gone and gutted O'Toole for it."

Kensley's gaze flicked to O'Toole, who was groaning on the floor. His face remained cold. "He probably deserved it."

Corrigan stiffened, his skin taut against the blade Sam still held to his throat.

Sam was breathless, hair a wild mess around her face, her shift damp with sweat. She should have been afraid—her hands were slick with sweat, her breath came fast—but fear didn't feel quite right. Not anymore.

She held the weapon. And Kensley wasn't stopping her.

But she wasn't like these men. Her grip on the cutlass tightened just for a moment before she raised herself and took a step back from Corrigan.

"Pick him up." She gestured at O'Toole, venom lacing her words. "Unless you want to explain to the captain why his crew is short a man."

Corrigan hesitated only a moment before scrambling to obey, hauling O'Toole up with shaking hands.

Sam watched them go before turning back to Kensley. The anger in his expression had shifted to concern. "Did they hurt you?" he asked.

Sam shook her head as she worked the soreness out of her arm.

Kensley nodded, though the tension in his jaw didn't ease. "They won't touch you again."

"Thanks, but I can take care of myself," Sam said, squaring her shoulders. She hated feeling vulnerable, especially in front of him.

His gaze held hers. "That doesn't mean you should have to."

She blinked, momentarily taken aback by his words. "I... I should get back to sleep," she finally said. "I've got to be up at first light to take the helm."

Kensley inclined his head. "Let me walk you back."

They made their way back to her quarters, where Sam gathered the blankets that had been tossed aside during the struggle. Kensley stooped to pick up her compass, which had fallen onto the floor. He examined it for a moment before handing it to her carefully, his touch lingering just slightly on her hand.

"Good night, Sam," he said, his voice barely a whisper as he turned to leave.

Before Sam could second-guess herself, she blurted out, "Will you stay?"

Kensley paused, a hint of surprise flickering in his eyes. Then he nodded. "If that's what you want."

"It is," Sam whispered.

Kensley stepped back into the room without hesitation, closing the door quietly behind him. He moved to the edge of the second bed, as if uncertain where to sit, but Sam's nod reassured him. Without a word, he settled onto the mattress across from her bed, leaning his back against the wall.

Neither of them spoke for a while, the weight of the night lifting bit by bit. Sam, curled under the covers, found herself at peace with him there.

She wasn't sure why she had asked him to stay—perhaps it was the need for reassurance, or the comfort in knowing someone else was watching over her—but for now, she didn't need to analyze it. Kensley was here, and with his steady presence, she quickly drifted to sleep.

Sam squinted down the barrel of her pistol, aligning her aim with a makeshift target of barrels stacked on the open gun deck. She exhaled and squeezed the trigger, but the shot veered to the left, missing her mark. Her shoulders sagged as she lowered the pistol, annoyed at herself. Several men nearby snickered, and Sam felt a burn rising to her cheeks.

"Relax your hand a bit, Atherton," came a familiar voice from behind her. She turned to see Kensley leaning against a nearby crate, his easy grin making her feel a little less self-conscious. Though he'd stayed in her room last night, when she awoke that morning he was already gone. Seeing him now set her mind at ease.

"Mind if I help?" he asked, strolling over.

"Please do. At this rate, I'll end up hitting myself before I hit a target," she muttered.

He chuckled, positioning himself beside her. "First, you're gripping it too tight. Loosen your hand, like this." He reached over, adjusting her fingers so her grip felt secure but relaxed. "And don't lock your elbow. Let your arm absorb the recoil, or you'll tire yourself out and lose accuracy fast."

Sam nodded, resetting her stance as he directed, his hand remaining on her arm to guide her angle. She took a breath and fired again. Closer but still off.

"Better." Kensley nodded approvingly. "Now, don't anticipate the shot. Focus on breathing—slow and steady. Let the shot happen, don't force it."

As Sam lined up her next shot, Kensley moved in closer, his hands slipping over hers to guide her fingers back into place on the pistol grip. His breath warmed her cheek, his presence solid at her back as he steadied her aim.

"Like this," he murmured, his voice low. The sound shivered down her spine, and she found herself hyperaware of how close he was. She held her breath, waiting as he gently nudged her elbow into position.

"Breathe," he reminded her, a distinct note of amusement in his voice.

She considered glaring at him, but if she turned her head, it would bring her face too close to his. She steadied her breathing, and it fell naturally into rhythm with his.

"Ready?" he asked, and she gave a small nod.

When she fired, the shot rang true, splintering into the barrel. Her heart leapt, partly at her success and partly at the simmering heat of his touch.

"That was perfect," he said, his smile holding something more than just encouragement. Their eyes met, and, for a moment, the sound of the ship around them faded. Sam swallowed, the intensity of his gaze stirring something unfamiliar and thrilling.

Kensley cleared his throat. "You're a natural."

It was another moment yet before he pulled away, and she didn't step back. Part of her wanted to stay forever in that small space, with only the ocean waves breaking the stillness.

The following days were laced with the same quiet intensity. Each time he joined her for practice, Kensley would drift close, his hand resting on her arm or grazing hers as he showed her how to reload. Between lessons with the dagger and practice with the pistol, Sam's confidence soared. She started to feel the weapons becoming an extension of herself.

When she fired off three shots in quick succession, all of them striking the mark dead center, she turned to Kensley, beaming. He returned her smile, but his eyes held something deeper, something unsaid. As he lifted his hand to brush a stray lock of hair behind her ear, Sam felt her pulse quicken, and she stood like a statue, unwilling to do anything that might lose his touch.

"Keep at it and soon you'll be a better shot than I am." Kensley winked.

Sam reluctantly holstered her pistol. "I think I'm getting there."

Sam eyed her supper plate with mild disappointment. The fresh produce they'd enjoyed in the weeks after departing from Atral had dwindled, leaving the crew with meals that were functional at best. Tonight's offering was a glob of porridge topped with hunks of salt pork and an egg.

Balancing her plate, Sam joined Kensley on the main deck, where he sat on a crate, his long legs stretched out as he idly carved a piece of wood with his knife. She leaned casually against the rail beside him as she popped a bite of pork into her mouth.

"I must say, you're looking dashing this evening." Kensley's broad grin teased her. "Very... frilly."

Sam stiffened, instinctively glancing down at herself. The shirt wasn't much different from her usual attire except for the delicate frills at the neckline and cuffs. Hardly extravagant, but enough to make her feel exposed. She adjusted the snug vest she wore over it, as if that might somehow lessen the effect.

It was one of three garments she'd found waiting for her upon returning from her outing with Kharzul. She'd avoided them until now, but her other clothes were stiff with salt and stank of days at sea. *It's just fabric,* she told herself. Wearing something Kharzul had provided didn't mean she had to accept everything he stood for.

"It's intentional," she said defensively. "If I'm not going to wear a dress, I may as well wear frills to emphasize my femininity."

"You don't need frills to emphasize that." Kensley's eyes flicked up and down her figure before he gave an audacious wink.

Sam's cheeks burned, and she fought the urge to pull her vest higher over her neckline. Instead, she shoved another bite of food into her mouth, ignoring Kensley's soft, infuriatingly smug laughter.

She opened her mouth to retort.

"Ship on the horizon!" The lookout's voice rang out across the deck.

The call jolted her with a kind of sick thrill. She turned and saw the small dot of a vessel in the distance, silhouetted in the fading light. Orders struck the ship like lightning, sending everyone into motion.

Sam's stomach fluttered, but it wasn't just nerves. She'd been waiting for this moment, itching to prove herself. She glanced at Kensley, and for a brief moment, their eyes met. His subtle nod felt like an acknowledgment of what this meant to her.

Heart pounding, Sam stowed her plate and raced to her cabin. She pulled the sleek black box from its hiding place beneath her mattress and opened it. The mask was even more beautiful than she remembered, its emerald and pearl strands breathtaking. She tied it carefully to her face, feeling it settle like armor, then untied the leather cord binding her hair. Her curls spilled freely, fiery and unrestrained. The effect was startling—she barely recognized herself in the small mirror on the wall. Staring back at her was someone fierce, someone who'd put fear into those who crossed her.

As she gazed at her reflection, she steadied herself, recalling the reasons that fueled her. This wasn't just about surviving or blending in with the crew.

She was going to become something formidable, something capable of challenging both Kharzul and the Lily Company. She couldn't confront him yet, but she would inch closer with every step, every skill she mastered, every layer of her old self she stripped away.

First, she would convince Kharzul that she was on his side.

With a final glance in the mirror, she lifted her chin, feeling the new weight of her purpose. She was ready to be bold, to be more than just Sam. She was becoming someone who could conquer whatever battles lay ahead.

As she returned to the deck, her pistol twirled smoothly in her hand, a fluid reminder of the hours of practice and the intent behind each session. She stepped into the sunlight, prepared to claim her power with a heart blazing as fiercely as her hair.

THIRTY-THREE

Grappling hooks flew, wood slammed against wood, and shouts tore through the air.

Sam jumped with the crew, repelling down the side of the *Golden Krina*, then leaping to the other ship. Her boots barely landed before a sailor rushed her, blade flashing in the sun. She raised her cutlass, and the impact jolted up her arm when her blade met his, pain blooming in her wrist as she staggered back. She shoved him away and fumbled for her pistol. Her arm shook as she raised it, too slow, too uncertain.

The sailor collapsed before she could fire. Sam's eyes snapped up to see William already turning away, his blade slick with blood.

"Get a move on, Red," he called, already striding forward.

Sam shoved the pistol back into her belt and drew her dagger instead.

Another sailor lunged. Sam ducked on instinct, driving her knife into the man's side. She wrenched the blade free and spun away, reeling with nausea.

She had thought she was ready for this. But sparring with Kensley was nothing like fighting to take a life.

Her first thought was to escape, to climb the rigging or retreat to the *Golden Krina*, but if she turned her back, she'd make an easy target. She thought of Kensley's words after her first raid. *You don't value your own life?*

She'd been backing down for years, and if she backed down now, she'd never avenge anyone.

She pulled her pistol and fired, closing her ears to the answering scream. She had to fight. There was no turning back.

After a short, brutal conflict, the noise began to fade. Sailors surrendered. The ship was theirs.

The pirates cheered from the deck of the captured merchant vessel. Its remaining crew, a ragged band of sailors and merchants, were gathered on their knees, hands bound, their faces etched with fear and fatigue. Sam's gaze swept over them, her stomach twisting as she met their pleading eyes. She'd seen this scene unfold before but never with the same blood on her hands.

She waited for Kharzul to pass his sentence, but, instead, his hand fell heavily on her shoulder, his voice low in her ear. "The choice is yours, poppet. Leave them on that islet"—he gestured to a barren strip of land in the distance—"or sink them here." He gave her shoulder a slight squeeze. "Your call."

Was this a test?

Her heart hammered as she took in the desperate faces of the captured men and women. She could also feel the pirate crew's eyes on her, their anticipation thickening the air. She'd thought participating in the raid would be enough to please Kharzul with her loyalty; she'd never imagined a decision like this.

"They'd be stranded," she murmured, glancing toward the distant isle. "It's a death sentence."

"A slow one," Kharzul agreed with a half-smile, eyes glinting. "Better than they'd give you, were the tables turned."

Her gaze flickered to Kensley. She hoped for a hint of guidance in his eyes, but he only looked away, jaw tight. She was alone in this choice.

Drawing a deep breath, she turned to the merchant captain kneeling in front of her. "I won't kill you," she announced, voice steadying, "but I can't save you either." She gestured to Kharzul's men. "Put them in the skiff."

A low murmur ran through the pirates, but they obeyed, dragging the terrified sailors toward the skiff one by one. The merchant captain's voice broke as he stammered his thanks, but Sam's expression remained hard. This was mercy enough, she told herself, watching as the skiff disappeared across the choppy sea, bound for the isle.

Back on the *Golden Krina*, Sam remained by the rail, staring at the empty waters, unable to shake the bitter taste left by her decision.

Kharzul approached, coming to stand beside her. "You showed them mercy," he said. "A gift I rarely give. They'd slit your throat if given the chance."

"Would they?" she asked, unable to hide the doubt in her voice. "They were just merchants. They didn't choose this life, not like you—" She paused. "Not like we did."

Kharzul chuckled, a dark, knowing sound. "Those in power don't spare those who stand in their way. If you intend to become a force on my crew," he continued, eyes sharp, "you'll have to be prepared to make sacrifices like this—cold decisions for a greater end."

Sam clenched her fists, the reality of his words settling heavily over her. What she wanted was bigger than Kharzul imagined, which meant she'd have to be ready to make even darker choices.

Kharzul turned away. "Remember, poppet, the sea has no mercy. And neither should you."

THIRTY-FOUR

Nine months of relentless training passed in a blur. Weapons lessons, practice, and battle-hardened experience all worked to mold Sam into something new. Her weapons now felt like an extension of herself, as familiar as her own hands. And those who had once doubted her? They weren't laughing anymore.

She favored the dagger. It was light, quick, and deadly. Unlike a heavy sword, her dagger could be thrown or concealed with ease. She never left her room without at least one knife tucked securely into her boot and her flame-engraved dagger gleaming openly on her belt.

Moving to the rail, Sam dropped a line to check the ship's speed. They traveled along Eclor's isle, just south of her homeland, intercepting vessels as they cut west to avoid the notorious Eclorian Redpass. Soon, though, they would turn south to avoid the cold of winter.

Kharzul never remained in one place for long. She knew he was looking for something—the power he'd spoken of in Atral. But she found herself increasingly wondering if he was *running* from something as well.

She'd tried to learn more about him and come up blank. No one seemed to know anything about his power beyond witnessing it when his mood darkened. The strange, swirling shadows answered his call in a summoned fog, roiling and churning as if alive. She often wondered how he'd discovered it and what had driven him to harness it so fiercely.

Kharzul's vision of balance shaped everything they did: taking from those who preyed on the poor, the merchants profiting from peasant labor, lords trampling over their servants, and kings growing rich off others' toil.

After every raid, Kharzul insisted on reviewing the spoils himself, an almost obsessive ritual. It was as if he felt personally responsible for each piece of gold and every jeweled trinket. Once tallied, the bounty was meticulously divided, overseen by Kensley. Every crew member received a fair share, a tradition Sam had come to respect. Ruthless though he might be, Kharzul practiced the balance he preached, and his diligence kept the crew united.

For the first time in her life, Sam had coin to spare, but, ironically, precious few chances to spend it. They seldom made port and always in specific, strategic harbors far from naval patrols. The few times she was allowed off of the vessel, she was always accompanied by Kharzul himself.

As navigator, Sam had become familiar with the tells of the Rutane Ocean, down to which currents flowed in which direction and how they changed with the seasons. Sunny days on deck had tanned her face, encouraging her freckles to deepen. Her vibrant red hair grew long, tied in a single plait down her back, save for battle when she donned her emerald mask and let her loose curls run wild in the wind.

By now the entire process of piracy had become as familiar to Sam as picking pockets had been back in Milderre. The thrill that surged through her each time she swung from a rope between vessels sent her pulse racing. When she drew her knives, she couldn't help but dance on her toes, reveling in the moment, fierce and free.

But all too quickly, the raid would end, and she'd retreat to the *Golden Krina* as swiftly as she'd boarded the other ship. While the fight itself left her breathless with excitement, the aftermath—the blood and carnage that followed surrender—still twisted her stomach in unexpected ways. Each time, that lingering discomfort reminded her of the line she walked and the cost of achieving something for the greater good.

After yet another raid, Sam retreated from the small brigantine they'd overtaken, hoisting herself into the *Golden Krina*'s rigging. She'd been distracted during this fight, her thoughts on their next destination: Virona. It had been an eternity since she'd last stepped foot there—and since she'd seen Sefina.

Sam paused, gripping the rigging tighter as her thoughts drifted. She wondered if Sefina would recognize the person she'd become.

Shaking her head, she climbed higher, hoping for a better view of her surroundings so she could set a course. The fog that often accompanied their raids was dissipating, light leaking through the sky in patches. The fog always proved a nuisance whenever it was time to set a new course.

Reaching the top sail, she perched herself on the sturdy wooden beam, swinging her legs over the side to dangle high above the deck.

After months at sea, Sam was eager for solid ground and even more excited to indulge in mouth-watering sweet cakes and fresh meat. Perhaps she'd treat herself to some scented soap as well, since she was determined to retain a touch of femininity aboard a pirate ship.

As she peered out over the water, she was surprised to see a small dinghy filled with a handful of sailors—escapees. Somehow, these men had eluded capture during the raid. Sam pulled out her spyglass, spotting the faint outline of land in the distance. They might make it to shore before dehydration set in.

The sailors rowed frantically, already losing the cover of fog, and would soon be spotted. If Kharzul found out Sam had seen them and done nothing, he would be furious. She'd lose months of hard-won trust.

Still, she hesitated.

They didn't have to die, but only if she could play a convincing part of "doing something."

Thinking fast, Sam scrambled up to the crow's nest, where she knew there were several extra lengths of rope. Swinging a thick coil of rope over one shoulder, she had just stepped out of the nest when a shout erupted from one of the crew below.

"Escapees spotted!"

Dropping onto the beam, she called out, "Mine!"

The crewmen aiming guns at the fleeing sailors laughed but lowered their weapons, calling back in challenge.

"All right, Red, let's see what you've got!"

"Fleeing *you*, are they?"

"Can't hit 'em with your knife from up there!"

Balancing precariously, Sam scurried outward across the top sail with the rope in hand, then tied it securely around the outermost edge of the spar. She glanced downward where, far below, the water lapped against the ship. Falling from this height would hurt.

Don't slip.

She wrapped her wrist several times near the end of the rope and held on tightly. With her other hand, she unholstered one of her pistols, backing toward the mainmast.

Kharzul loved theatrics; why not give him a show?

She considered momentarily that this was not the best idea. Shoving that thought aside, she sprinted forward and leaped off the edge of the sail, diving gracefully into the air.

Sam's stomach rose to her throat as she fell through the air only to be jolted down again when the rope pulled tight. Her arm screamed, muscle and bone threatening to snap at any moment, but the rope held strong. She swung in an arc over the water. Raising her pistol, she fired, emptying the chamber, then shoved it in her belt. As she swung around again, she pulled out her second pistol and emptied it as well.

She heard their screams but knew it was only fear. She'd intentionally shot wide. If Kharzul asked, she'd blame her poor aim on shooting while swinging from a rope.

Her momentum slowed, and she landed gracefully on the railing, still holding the rope and letting the wind blow through her curls as she listened to the cries of the frightened sailors.

"She came from the sky!"

"Hair like a mane of fire!"

"Firemane!"

They'd stopped rowing, paralyzed by the spectacle. And they were still too close.

She wanted to yell at them. Instead, she did what she had to do. Plucking a pistol from the nearest man before he could protest, she aimed it at the dinghy. She knew she couldn't miss again; it would be too suspicious. *I'm sorry.*

She aimed for one of the escapee's shoulders and fired. A scream pierced the air, sending the others into action.

Blowing the smoke from the barrel, Sam lowered the gun. The sailors rowed with renewed desperation, putting distance between themselves and the *Golden Krina*.

She forced a composed smirk onto her face and returned the borrowed pistol. The crew member gave her a hearty clap on the shoulder. "I'd watch that again." He chuckled. "Those poor blighters won't be forgettin' you anytime soon."

Nearby crew members laughed and called taunts after the disappearing boat.

As Sam walked away, still shaking from the adrenaline, Kensley joined her stride.

"So... Firemane, is it?" Kensley crossed his arms with a grin, clearly amused by the nickname the fleeing sailors had shouted. "Does that fierceness carry over to setting a course, or is it just for the theatrics?"

Sam felt the corners of her mouth tug upward, but she hid it by turning back to the sea, her gaze sweeping over the waves, already picturing the route.

"Prepare to turn south by southeast!" she called to the crew, her voice steady and commanding, just as it had been during the raid.

She moved to the rigging, pausing to glance down at Kensley. "Quartermaster, be listening for my next instruction."

He gave a mock salute, his grin widening. "Aye, aye, Firemane."

With a roll of her eyes, Sam climbed, hands wrapping confidently around the ropes as she ascended. From her vantage in the rigging, she could see the path ahead and the crew bustling below, responding to her commands as they worked to adjust the sails. The sight filled her with a surge of satisfaction—and, if she was honest, a touch of pride.

She had come a long way from her days in Milderre, stealing in shadows and relying on the goodwill of the streets. Up here, with the open ocean stretching before her, she was in her element.

She pulled out her spyglass again, tracking the line of land that now lay to her left.

Four days later, the *Golden Krina* approached the inlet that led to the thieves' town of Virona. The thick jungle canopy framed the narrow waterway. The small brigantine they'd captured trailed behind, slowing their progress. It was a sturdy vessel, but it couldn't compete with the larger ship's speed.

As they neared the river's mouth, Kensley stood at the helm, hands wrapped firmly around the wheel. Sam hovered close by, studying his every movement. He navigated the ship through the cramped, twisting bends of the river with a skill that left her in awe as he seemed to anticipate every shift in the current, every potential snag along the shore. She'd never seen anyone handle a vessel so masterfully, especially through such tight quarters.

As they rounded the final bend, the dense foliage parted to reveal Virona. A cascade of makeshift docks sprawled along the shore, brimming with vessels of every shape and size, from rickety fishing boats to sleek pirate schooners. Shacks and colorful market stalls clung to the water's edge, while weathered wooden balconies connected homes that almost stacked on top of one another. The hum of Virona's bustling streets carried over the water, a blend of raucous laughter, shouted haggles, and the occasional outburst of music.

Once they docked, the crew erupted down the gangplank, eager for the promise of fresh food, ale, and entertainment. Sam watched them go, their laughter and shouts filling the air, and couldn't help the tug of jealousy in her chest.

Kensley hung back, leaning against the railing with his arms crossed. He watched her for a moment before speaking.

"Fancy joining me for an evening of fun?" he asked, his tone light yet inviting.

Sam arched a brow. "Kharzul is allowing it?"

Until now, Kharzul had only allowed her off the ship under his watchful eye. The idea of exploring without him—even better, *with* Kensley—sparked a thrill.

Kensley grinned. "Yes, so long as you're with me. Think of it as your tour of the finest mischief Virona has to offer. Might as well get the proper introduction."

Sam didn't hesitate. "Lead the way, Cavenaugh."

Kensley's grin widened, and he gestured with a flick of his head for her to follow.

They moved through the winding streets, passing all manner of shops and taverns. It wasn't long before she began to notice the lingering stares of the townspeople. These stares felt... different. Though she tried to ignore it, she felt the weight of attention with each step. Strangers brushed past her in the crowd, their eyes trailing, some even reaching out to touch the fiery strands cascading down her back.

"You're drawing a lot of attention," Kensley remarked.

"I usually do. But this—" Sam yanked her arm out of reach of an older woman's outstretched hand. "It's a lot more than I'm accustomed to."

Sam purchased the very next scarf she could find and tied it securely over her head. With the red of her hair hidden away, the attention subsided.

Kensley led her into a lively tavern on the edge of the market, filled with laughter and chatter, the sharp scent of ale mingling with the rich aroma of roasting meat. A few heads turned as they entered, though most seemed absorbed in their own revelries.

They found a small table, and Sam sank into the wooden chair, her shoulders relaxing as the hum of the tavern enveloped them. Kensley flagged down a passing barmaid, who brought tankards of ale a moment later. Sam drained hers in one swift gulp.

As the cool ale settled, a boisterous voice rose from directly behind her.

"She's ruthless!" the man said, his tone brimming with a strange mixture of awe and fear. "With a mane of flaming hair, she soars through the skies! You'll never see her face, only an emerald mask, befittin' a goddess. Though if you're close enough to see the detail, it's the last thing you'll ever see." He chuckled. "Wouldn't be the worst way to go, eh? Death by the Firemane."

Sam froze. Kensley radiated delight.

Without thinking, she abruptly stood, knocking over her empty mug in the process. She hastily snatched it and made her way to the counter. There, she ordered another ale, trying to compose herself as the bartender filled her mug. She glanced over her shoulder, catching snippets of conversation from a man and woman standing nearby.

"Hair as red as dawn," the woman whispered, glancing around as if the legend herself might appear. "She's here in this very town, along with the Pirate Lord. Didn't you see the ship dock?"

Sam abandoned her ale and retreated back to the table, sliding onto the bench across from Kensley.

His eyes sparkled with amusement. "It sounds like there's a new pirate in town. She sounds awfully familiar, don't you think?"

Sam narrowed her eyes, feeling her cheeks flush. The name *Firemane* rolled around in her mind, echoing with each whispered conversation that drifted to her ears from around the room. Rumors spread like wildfire; nearly everywhere she turned, someone was talking about "the female pirate with red hair" or "the Firemane."

The more she let it sink in, the more her apprehension faded. This was what she'd wanted, wasn't it? To build a name and presence for herself. This was the culmination of months of effort, and there was something thrilling about hearing her own exploits spoken of with such admiration—and fear.

Sam leaned back in her seat, a faint smile tugging at her lips.

Firemane. The name felt powerful, like armor. She could almost imagine it cloaking her in strength and fearlessness.

Kensley must have noticed the subtle change in her demeanor. "Already embracing it, are we?" he asked.

"Maybe," she replied, tapping her fingers on the edge of the table. "Seems it's about time I had a name for myself."

He raised his mug in a mock toast, his eyes gleaming with approval. "To the Firemane, scourge of the seas. May her legend grow stronger with every raid."

THIRTY-FIVE

Sam scanned the carnage around her, stepping carefully over crimson-stained planks. Only two survivors remained, bound to the mainmast, their terrified whimpers carrying through the air. This raid was the seventh she'd actively taken part in since becoming the "Firemane" months prior, and each time, they seemed to bother her less. She felt a dangerous thrill in the heat of battle, a sharp satisfaction in striking down an enemy.

What still stirred her emotions, however, were the tortured deaths. She took no pleasure in those and always made her own kills swift—or let a few escape when she could.

As she stepped over lifeless bodies, she told herself they'd been rich merchants. Men who'd left their families to reap profit from distant lands, just as willing to kill as her crew was, given the chance. Stopping them was a service to the world, she reminded herself. But this wasn't Kharzul's mission to "balance the world." It was her own journey of vengeance, of taking back control. This was for her.

She moved to the supply crates, lifting the lid of an oak barrel. Sticking in a finger, she felt the familiar grit of gunpowder. She closed the lid and scratched a rough "X" into the side with her knife. As she straightened, the scent of damp musk and leather washed over her. She went rigid as a jeweled hand slipped around her waist.

Kharzul stood beside her, one hand resting possessively on her hip, the other gesturing grandly. "What do you think, my Firemane? Shall we keep it?"

Sam's gaze moved over the small vessel. They rarely kept ships, usually sinking or burning them. Wasteful, she thought.

"It seems sturdy enough," she replied. "Six guns. Little in the way of supplies—they must have been close to returning home."

Cataros was less than two days to the east from where the *Golden Krina* currently sailed the Prestos Ocean. They could sell the ship there, if Kharzul was willing to dock.

Kharzul's hand moved from her waist to toy with her hair, twirling a fiery curl around his finger. "Every ship we spare is a ship we have to deal with twice."

Too late, Sam realized they weren't speaking of ships.

"In recent raids," he said, "men somehow escape with their lives nearly every time."

Her heart raced, though she forced herself to remain calm. Did he suspect she was the one letting men slip away?

She replied as smoothly as she could. "How else would tales of the *Golden Krina* spread?"

"They've spread enough, poppet. Each escape is a future problem while each death brings us closer to evening the balance."

Always "the balance," but never a real explanation of what that meant.

Kensley approached Kharzul, holding a worn piece of parchment, yellowed with age and tattered at the edges, confiscated from the captain's cabin.

Kharzul unfolded it carefully, revealing faint ink markings and a few symbols Sam didn't recognize. A map. She caught only a glimpse, enough to see that it wasn't of Eclor. Whatever it was, it was significant enough to make Kharzul's reserved expression crack open with a spark of greed.

Kharzul snapped his attention to Sam. "Set a course for Dunrith. Immediately."

"Dunrith, Captain?" Sam wasn't sure she'd heard right. Dunrith was a town at the northernmost tip of Ducria, cloaked in cold for most of the year. Few dared to sail those icy waters. Sam had never been that far north.

Kharzul's golden eyes narrowed. His excitement was unmistakable, yet there was something else beneath it—anxiety, perhaps. Whatever they were about to pursue, Kharzul was eager to reach it.

"Did I not make myself clear?" he asked, his voice low.

"It'll take *months* to get there, sir," Sam warned. "We don't have the supplies for such a long journey."

She felt the shadows beneath her deepen, Kharzul's silent, uncanny threat making the hair on the back of her neck prickle.

Quickly, Kensley stepped forward, his tone calm yet commanding enough to draw Kharzul's gaze from Sam. "I recommend we make port in Atral, Captain. They'll have everything we need to complete the journey without delay."

Kharzul watched him, impatience warring with practicality in his eyes. Finally, he inclined his head, though his expression held a trace of irritation. "So be it."

He folded the map with careful precision, sliding it into the inner pocket of his coat before turning on his heel. His velvet frock swished with each step, and the shadows trailed after him, dissipating like mist as he retreated to the *Golden Krina*.

"Do you think that was a key to whatever he's been chasing?" Sam asked quietly.

Kensley nodded, frowning slightly. "Whatever it is, he doesn't want to wait, even if it means risking the entire crew." He leaned in, his voice dropping. "I've seen him obsessed, but this feels different. More... urgent."

"What do you think it is?" Sam asked. "This thing he's been chasing? He hinted that it was some sort of..." She hesitated on the word, then forced it out. "Power."

It sounded fantastical, almost absurd, but Kensley was well aware of the strange abilities Kharzul already possessed.

Kensley's gaze drifted to the horizon. "It's hard to say," he murmured. "But it's more than treasure. It's something he believes will change everything."

Sam let that sink in. If this new pursuit meant that much, there was no telling what he'd do to achieve it. Would he even consider the good of his crew? Or only his own ambitions?

Kensley's expression darkened, his eyes shadowed and brooding. Finally, he said, "Come on. Let's get back to the ship before they leave without us."

Back in her quarters, Sam reached behind her head to untie the ribbon holding her emerald mask in place. She examined it, thinking how each piece she wore held meaning. The mask, a symbol of her ferocity and bravery. A single gold hoop she'd carried from her time aboard the *Queen Mary*, and a few more lining her ears as trophies of her journey since. Her brass-chained compass, and her flame engraved dagger—all reminders of who she was and what she was becoming.

She was only nineteen and had achieved what most only dreamed of—riches, freedom...even love, once. She was the Firemane, feared by men and whispered about across the seas. She felt power in that name. Freedom. And she wouldn't give it up.

This time upon docking in Atral, the mood of the crew was different. Kharzul's foul, anxious temper had rubbed off on the rest of them. They had one purpose—restock the ship as quickly and efficiently as possible.

It wasn't until Sam saw the colorful decorations strung from rooftops and poles that she realized they'd arrived just in time for the Festival of the Gods. Her disappointment at not being able to linger grew.

She worked alongside the crew, securing supplies, but her gaze kept straying to the bustling city, where people moved through the streets in bright costumes, and ribbons fluttered like leaves caught in the wind.

The festive energy in the air was infectious, a stark contrast to the grim determination on the ship.

As the sun began to set and the crew's work slowed, Kensley appeared beside her, hands tucked casually into his belt as he took in the scene. "The ship's stocked and ready, but the tide won't turn until morning," he said, a glint of mischief lighting his eyes. "Which means we're free to celebrate."

Sam glanced toward the captain's cabin, where Kharzul had locked himself away hours ago. Hesitation tugged at her—Kharzul was already in a dark mood, and he'd made it clear he expected everyone to remain vigilant tonight. Wandering off into the city, especially in the heart of a festival, was bound to provoke his anger.

The sound of laughter and music swelled from the streets below. Her gaze drifted back to Kensley, who watched her with that familiar, daring grin, one brow raised as if to say, *Are you coming or not?*

"Let's go," Sam said, a rebellious smile forming on her lips as she slipped her arm through his and walked down the gangplank.

The city buzzed with merriment. Colorful ribbons hung from every street lamp, draped buildings, and decorated sticks twirled by giggling children. Nearly everyone wore costumes representing their favorite god or goddess, whether it be masks, cloaks, headdresses, accessories, or complete costumes. It was a sight to behold!

They moved deeper into the heart of the city, where the market was packed with festival stalls—rows upon rows of tents filled with gleaming trinkets, sumptuous fabrics, and sweet-smelling foods that made Sam's mouth water. She bought a skewer of meat from a nearby grill, savoring the rich flavor as she watched the vendors hawking jewelry and amulets, headdresses adorned with feathers, and cheap masks.

Kensley darted away, returning with a mischievous grin and two impossibly flamboyant cloaks draped over his arm. He held one up, a patchwork of vivid purple, red, green, and gold that shimmered in the lantern light.

Sam gaped at him, half-laughing. "What are those?"

"Our attire for this evening," he replied triumphantly.

"I'm not going around in that," she insisted, holding the patchwork fabric up to examine it better.

"Oh, but you are."

Before she could protest further, he stepped in close, swinging the cloak around her shoulders. His hands moved to fasten it at her collar, fingers brushing lightly against her skin as he worked.

"Hold still," he murmured, far too focused for someone who had been joking moments before.

"You're ridiculous," Sam said, though a smile tugged at her lips.

"And yet—" he finished securing the clasp and stepped back just enough to look at her. "It suits you."

He fastened his own cloak with far less care, then with an exaggerated flourish, extended his arm to her, as though to a fellow deity.

Sam rolled her eyes but took his arm, unable to resist his infectious playfulness. Though she initially felt ridiculous in the cloak, her self-consciousness melted away as they moved through the festival. Under the lights and surrounded by people in costumes far bolder than her own, she began to relax, grinning as they blended into the lively sea of revelers.

There were performers of all kinds, including jugglers and acrobats and musicians. A highly anticipated parade was to pass through later that evening. And six towering statues marked the city center.

There were seven main gods worshiped across the great nations. It was believed the gods' firstborn demi-god offspring divided the land, becoming rulers of the seven great nations: Ducria, Eclor, Phago, Zuhuoriel, Haapa, Lin, and Astoenia.

Sam found herself drawn to a towering statue of Aspos, the Sky God, which rose above the rest and glowed with a radiant light from within. Stars had been intricately carved into the dark metal skin of the god's form, with a torch placed inside to make them shine. As she looked up, it was as if she were gazing into a night sky brimming with stars. She let out a quiet breath of awe, wishing she could stand here all night, watching the stars twinkle through Aspos's frame.

Kensley gave a low whistle. "Quite the sight, eh? They say his torch only goes out on the day of reckoning. Something about reminding us to look up." He gave her a sidelong look, lips quirking. "With the way you love the sky, you could be descended from Aspos himself."

Sam huffed a laugh, but it faded quickly as her gaze lingered on the glowing constellations carved into the god's form. What would it be like to be descended from the gods?

The next statue was of Udrait, the God of War. The statue was as intimidating as it was impressive. Carved from dark stone, it depicted a muscular figure with fierce eyes, gripping a broad shield in one hand and a wicked longsword in the other. The sculptors had emphasized every muscle, every sinew, making the god seem alive, poised to leap into battle at any moment.

Sam raised an eyebrow as she glanced at Kensley. "Look familiar? Though I think he's got you beat on muscle."

Kensley scoffed, flexing his arm with exaggerated pride. "What, this? Udrait would be green with envy. Besides." He cast a playful look at the god's weapon. "I'd sooner take an axe to a fight any day. Easier to throw."

"Yeah, I've noticed." Sam remembered the countless times Kensley had sent an axe sailing through the air with deadly accuracy.

With a cocky grin, Kensley slid an arm around her waist, guiding her toward the next statue. "Course you have," he said with a smirk.

They came to Delmada, Goddess of Light. The artist had crafted her in bronze, with an elaborate headdress that flared around her like the rays of a burning sun. Torches had been strategically placed to catch the reflective edges of the statue, giving the impression that she herself was ablaze, a beacon against the night.

Eflos, the God of Mischief and Thieves was a favorite among pirates. Unlike the others, the statue had a slightly unsettling quality, with an exaggerated, toothy grin that looked unnervingly out of place on an otherwise dignified face.

Larideia's depiction was the most beautiful. Crafted from stone as white as pearl, Larideia seemed as though she were carved from the depths of the ocean itself. Her flowing hair was embedded with seashells, starfish, and beads of glass that glistened like droplets of water. Her gown, painted in rich blues and greens, shimmered with iridescent scales that caught the light, creating the illusion that she was underwater.

Sam felt a pang as she gazed up at Larideia's serene face, her expression calm and powerful. It reminded her of Sefina.

"She's beautiful," Sam whispered, almost to herself.

"Beautiful," Kensley echoed, but his gaze was fixed on Sam, his smile softening.

Realizing his gaze rested on her, Sam cleared her throat, turning to leave the statues behind. They reached a band of musicians playing a lively tune, surrounded by townsfolk dancing hand in hand. Grinning mischievously, Kensley grabbed Sam's hands, pulling her into the crowd of dancers.

She laughed. "I don't know the steps!"

"You don't need to," he replied, his eyes gleaming as he spun her around.

They moved through the square, weaving among masked dancers draped in flame-colored scarves that flickered like firelight. The drums grew louder, and Sam's laughter mixed with the rhythm as they twirled, leapt, and clapped until she found herself face to face with Kensley once more. He leaned in close, his warm hand finding her waist, his voice a low murmur meant only for her ears.

"You've been hiding," he teased. "I didn't know the Firemane could dance."

Sam raised an eyebrow. "The Firemane has a great many talents, thank you."

Kensley chuckled as he guided her in a surprisingly graceful arc. "Well, maybe she'll show me more of them," he replied, his tone almost too sincere, sending a thrill up her spine.

As the music quieted, the crowd dispersed in anticipation of the parade. Kensley kept Sam's hand in his, and she glanced down, noticing the way their fingers fit together. For a fleeting moment, her heart tightened in a way she hadn't felt before.

Her thoughts drifted to the dagger tucked against her skin. It wasn't just the blade itself, but the awareness behind the gesture. How he'd *seen* her.

She wanted to return it with something that showed he wasn't the only one paying attention. Something that said *I see you too.*

Sam slowed her pace, glancing sideways at Kensley. He was watching the crowd, posture deceptively loose, attention drifting—but not far. Never far.

"I need to relieve myself," she blurted. "I can go alone."

"I'd imagine you can."

"I mean—you don't need to accompany me."

One brow lifted, suspicion plain on Kensley's face. He studied her for a long beat before he finally gave a nod. "Meet me back at Perixia's statue before the parade."

The flicker of knowing in his eyes told Sam he knew she was holding something back... yet he had decided to trust her with the distance anyway.

Sam nodded and slipped away. Even as the crowd swallowed her, she could feel his gaze on her back. She moved through the market with purpose, slowing at the first stall that caught her eye—a cluttered spread of trinkets and polished odds and ends. Rings, chains, carved figurines.

Her fingers hovered over a few pieces, turning one over between her thumb and forefinger, but none of them held the weight of the man she was trying to match. She exhaled, leaving the stall empty-handed.

She intended to push forward but as she scanned for the next vendor, her attention caught on the statue of Orrazoth, God of Death and Darkness. Even among the gods, he was rarely celebrated, his legend spoken of in hushed tones. Though Aspos ruled supreme, Orrazoth was the most feared, a name evoking whispers of the Darkbringer he'd sent to walk among mortals, spreading chaos across the lands. Sam remembered the tales her mother had told her as a child, stories that had once made her afraid of the dark, certain the Darkbringer lurked in the shadows to steal her away.

As Sam drifted closer to the statue, she felt a sudden, firm grip on her arm. She turned, her breath catching. A cloaked figure stood close, a mask covering most of their face, except the unmistakable, piercing blue eyes.

THIRTY-SIX

"Sefina?" Sam's voice wavered, caught between shock and relief as she stared at the familiar figure before her. "What—how?"

It had been over a year since she'd last seen Sefina in the chaotic streets of Virona, and she'd long since stopped hoping for a reunion. It felt surreal, like a dream teetering on the edge of becoming a nightmare.

Sefina raised a finger to her lips, glancing over her shoulder with sharp, hawk-like eyes. "Hush," she whispered, her voice nearly drowned out by the raucous sounds of the crowd. "Come with me."

"I—" Sam hesitated, her brow furrowing as she instinctively tugged her arm free. "I can't."

Sefina's eyes narrowed dangerously. "You *can't*?"

"I... don't want to." The words surprised her even as they left her lips. But they were true. She had worked too hard, risked too much, to turn away now. Firemane was finally more than a name.

And then there was Kensley. His face flashed in her mind—the set jaw, the resigned look in his eyes as he faced Kharzul's wrath in her absence. She couldn't do that to him.

Sefina stiffened, her frustration bubbling over in a low growl. "We must speak, Atherton. If only for a moment."

With her heart thudding painfully in her chest, Sam relented, letting herself be led into the shadowed alleyways. The music and lights of the festival faded as they wound through the darkened maze of backstreets. The quiet creak of a rickety staircase greeted them as Sefina guided her into an old building.

On the upper floor, Sefina lit several candles, their flames casting long shadows across the room.

Sam broke first. Letting out a shaky breath, she crossed the distance between them and wrapped her arms tightly around Sefina's waist. The embrace felt like a dam breaking—relief, fear, and longing all spilling out in the simple gesture.

Sefina tensed for a moment, then returned the hug, her hands steady and grounding. When Sam finally pulled back, her lips curved into a small, tentative smile.

"You've changed," Sefina murmured, her sharp gaze taking in Sam's attire—the tailored vest, the frilled shirt, the gleam of jewels at her throat, and the array of weapons strapped to her belt.

"I have," Sam replied, lifting her chin slightly.

Sefina's expression darkened. "Yet I wonder," she said softly, "if it is for the better."

Sam bristled, her hands curling into fists at her sides. "You don't get to put that judgment on me. Not after what we went through on the *Golden Krina*. Not after what happened in Virona. I know we agreed the other should get away, and don't get me wrong, I'm glad you got out. But *I* was the one left—*I* was the one fighting to survive." Sam's voice quieted. "I always hoped you would come back for me. I just didn't realize it would take so long."

Sefina's lips pressed into a thin line, her composure unshaken. "What is it you think I've been doing these months? Not enough, it seems. From what I hear, you are Kharzul's newest pet. Or are you not the Firemane?"

"That's not fair." Sam's voice wavered slightly, but her glare didn't falter. "I'm doing what I have to do to survive. And perhaps I've made something of myself along the way."

"And what is it you think you're doing, Atherton?" Sefina challenged, stepping closer. "A legacy built on blood and fear? A name whispered like a curse?"

Sam's chest tightened, but she refused to back down. "I'm preparing for the future," she said firmly. "The more I learn about Kharzul, the more I understand his actions. Understand how he could be *defeated*. But I'm not ready for that. He's connected to the Lily Company somehow, I know it, and I need to figure out how. In the meantime, I have to keep playing my part. Doing what I must even if the means are... questionable."

"Questionable?" Sefina's voice rose, her brows arching sharply. "You call taking the lives of entire crews *questionable*?" She stepped closer, her presence towering, the anger in her voice palpable.

Sam straightened as well, unwilling to be dwarfed by Sefina's fury. Her stomach churned, but her voice held firm. "I think that, sometimes, sacrifices are necessary to achieve our goals."

They stood face to face, neither one backing down. Eventually, Sam conceded, as she often had when it came to Sefina. Taking a step back, she tucked a loose strand of hair behind her ear.

Sefina's stance relaxed, but her tone remained cold. "If what I believe is true, then Kharzul is not taking part in the Lily Company. He is something much more dangerous. There is a tale I think you should hear."

Sam hesitated, her posture softening as curiosity crept in. Sefina began:

> *"There once was a man who summoned the gods*
> *And asked for their aid, their pow'r over man."*

Sam knew this story. The *Tale of the Darkbringer*—the one her mother used to sing before bed.

> *"This man, he had been through horrors unknown,*
> *And sought for a way to bring change.*
> *The gods did refuse, "There's more to this world."*

And left him alone in his grief.
But the God of the Dark, his interest piqued,
Appeared to the man and offered his service.
A transfer of pow'r in exchange for a debt.
A Darkbringer he would become.
No longer a man, nor is he a god,
With power and vengeance, his sway over darkness.
Eager to change the fate of mankind,
Corrupted right from the start.
He seeks for a balance, but takes what he will.
The Darkbringer prowls through the night."

Sefina ended the tale, her voice lingering in the air like smoke. Sam licked her lips, a single line echoing in her head. *He seeks for a balance.*

"That is just a story," Sam said, throat feeling dry.

"All stories have their origins," Sefina replied coolly. "Have you ever known someone to control the power of darkness as Kharzul does?"

A shiver worked its way up Sam's spine as memories surged to the surface—of the way the darkness bent to Kharzul's will, slithering like living tendrils.

"Magic is not something many possess," Sefina continued. "It is dangerous. And I believe the captain's control of it is much greater than we have seen. I hesitate to draw conclusions with little evidence, but Kharzul... You are not safe with him, Atherton."

Sam stared at her, disbelief mixing with the unease bubbling in her gut. "You think Kharzul is the Darkbringer?" she said, shaking her head. Even as she spoke, her mind raced with the possibility. Had she not thought the very same thing? "No, that's not possible. The Darkbringer is a myth. A tale told to children to keep them in their beds at night. Besides, Kharzul gave me a *lily*, Sefina. He's wrapped up with the Lily Company, I know it."

"There is no other explanation of the dark power that he wields," Sefina countered. "The way he never stays in one place for any amount of time. The Darkbringer brought the wrath of the gods upon himself when he made a deal with the God of Darkness. They are searching, even now, to set the scale of power right again."

"But the Darkbringer is supposed to have *immense* power," Sam argued, though her words came out more like a plea than a rebuttal. "Kharzul's power—it's terrifying, yes, but if he were the Darkbringer, he wouldn't need a crew to plunder ships. He'd use his 'immense power' to accomplish his goals."

"And what *are* his goals?" Sefina asked, her voice cutting through Sam's rationalization like a blade.

"He wants... *balance*," she admitted, hating that the word felt like a betrayal. "For the wealthy to fall from their mighty pedestals." She breathed out, considering. "Is that really so bad?"

"Not all the wealthy are corrupt. And not all the poor are unhappy. There are good and bad in both. Kharzul's intentions may have started out pure, but they have been distorted. Or perhaps they were never pure at all."

Sam's stomach churned at the thought. She opened her mouth to speak but faltered, unsure what to say. The words that tumbled out were half-formed and defensive. "I can change that. I'm not—I'm... I won't become him."

"But what is to stop you from becoming something much worse?" Sefina shot back, her voice cold.

The tension between them was thick. Sam clenched her fists, her mind a tangle of memories, doubts, and loyalties.

The silence that followed was suffocating. Sam turned away, her gaze falling on the flickering candlelight. She hated how much Sefina's words unsettled her, how they planted seeds of doubt in a place she'd thought was untouchable.

"Just... think about what I've said," Sefina urged, her tone softer now but no less firm. "Please, Atherton. Before it's too late."

Sam's thoughts churned. "Even if I believed you," she said slowly, "what could we do about it anyway? The Darkbringer is an immortal being, halfway to a god. I'm not ready to confront something like that."

"We are not," Sefina admitted, her voice steady. "But I have learned much these past months. There is hope—if we are willing to act."

Sam blew out a breath. "All right," she said at last. "I'll think about it." She paused, chewing her lip as an old, unspoken question rose to the surface of her mind. "But only if you tell me something first. Something I never had the chance to ask before."

"What is it you wish to know?"

"Your voice. Is it... magic?"

Sefina sighed, a weight pressing visibly on her shoulders. She paused for a long moment, then said softly, "As you know, my father is Haapari. My mother, however... is not. She is a creature of the depths. *Vanomasa*. A siren."

Sam sucked in a sharp breath. That meant Sefina was half-siren, with a siren's song that could kill. She'd seen it firsthand in those initial days aboard the *Golden Krina*, though at the time, she hadn't fully understood. It made sense now—why Sefina's voice had always seemed to pull at her, to captivate and soothe in ways that defied logic. It wasn't just her voice. It was her blood.

Sam unconsciously took a half step away from the beautiful woman standing before her. She wasn't sure what caused her to do it. This was *Sefina*, her dearest friend.

Sefina's piercing blue eyes followed Sam's retreat, her expression unreadable. "Sam, I would never hurt you."

Sam shifted from one foot to the other. She hated the vulnerability coursing through her. She was afraid, and Sefina could see it.

"I would never hurt you," Sefina repeated, her voice insistent. "Everything I have done—everything—has been to protect you. Yes, I can do things others cannot. But my song is not a gift. It is a curse. I have spent years learning to control it, out of fear that someone I care about might get hurt. Someone I cared for has already been hurt by my doing."

"Like when you lured Joss over the side of the ship," Sam murmured, then raised her eyes to meet Sefina's piercing gaze. "That *was* you, wasn't it?"

Sefina's expression hardened. "I will not defend that man, nor my decision to save your life."

"How does it work?" Sam asked, curiosity and accusation blooming in her words. "If you have so much power in your voice, why didn't you use it when the *Queen Mary* was attacked? Or when you escaped while pirates dragged me back to Kharzul?" Her tone grew sharper. "You blame me for becoming a pirate, but perhaps you should blame yourself."

A flicker of guilt crossed Sefina's face, her lips tightening as though to hold back the weight of her emotions. "I cannot just *sing*," she explained. "I must summon the voice first, and it is... draining. Controlling a single soul takes immense effort. Controlling many? I cannot sustain it. If I had tried, I would have failed. My secret would have been exposed, and if that had happened, I would have been used."

Sefina's voice grew quieter, tinged with a bitterness Sam had rarely heard from her. "Do you understand what that means? They would have seen me as a weapon. Something to control. My freedom would have been forfeit. My choices stripped away."

"Yet, in not using it, *my* choices were stripped away," Sam said coldly.

"By the very man you now seek to defend," Sefina countered, her eyes flashing dangerously.

"I'm not defending him!" Sam snapped. "By remaining at his side, I can understand his goals, his weaknesses. That's the only way I'll ever defeat him."

Silence stretched between them, heavy and fraught, before Sefina let out a long breath. "There is never only one way. You must consider what *thing* you are becoming and decide if you truly believe it is worthy of who I know you are."

Sam looked away. There was truth in Sefina's words, and it stung.

"I need to go," she said finally. "Kensley will be looking for me."

"You are sure?" Sefina asked.

Sam hesitated. She thought of a day when she'd stood on the *Golden Krina's* deck with the chance to leave, watching as Kensley tended to his duties without looking back. Trusting her. She'd chosen him then.

She chose him still.

"We're headed north, for Dunrith," she said, her voice steadying. "Kharzul is searching for something there. If you're truly worried that he's the Darkbringer, I'd suggest finding whatever that something is before he does."

Sefina stepped closer, her hand reaching out to clasp the back of Sam's head. Their foreheads pressed together, the gesture intimate and grounding.

"Watch yourself, Atherton," Sefina murmured. "You are an important piece in this—I only need to figure out what role you are to play. We will meet again. And when we do, it will be to end the reign of the Darkbringer."

Sam swallowed hard, stepping back as the weight of Sefina's words settled in her chest. "Goodbye, Sefina," she said, her voice quieter now.

Sefina nodded but didn't speak again, her eyes lingering on Sam as if memorizing her face.

Turning on her heel, Sam exited the building, weaving her way back through the labyrinth of darkened alleys. The festival's lights and sounds grew louder with every step, but her mind remained clouded with Sefina's warnings and her own tangled emotions. Her pace increased until she was darting through the crowds, rushing to Perixia's statue.

She spotted Kensley from a distance. He stood a head above most of the crowd, his broad frame commanding attention even while wrapped in a silly patchwork cloak.

Sam smiled, her steps slowing as she soaked him in, her gaze catching on the pieces of hair that always escaped their knot at the back of his head. She couldn't help but notice how his confident stance and easy smirk drew more than a few appreciative glances from passersby. His presence balanced confidence with warmth, and there was a life to him that made him stand out more than anyone else around.

When his gaze landed on her, his expression shifted. The tension in his face melted, replaced by relief and maybe a hint of irritation. He closed the distance between them with a few long strides.

"Where were you?" Kensley asked, his voice low enough not to draw attention but firm enough to convey his concern. "Is everything all right?"

Sam's heart clenched. In a single step, she crossed the space between them, wrapping her arms around his middle. Kensley stiffened for half a beat, surprised, before his arms came around her just as firmly, holding her in place.

Sam kept her face pressed against him, breathing him in, letting the world narrow down to something simpler. Something safe.

If Kensley knew Sefina was here, he'd tell Kharzul. The captain would hunt her down without hesitation.

She couldn't risk that.

"Sam." Kensley's voice was tinged with worry. "Talk to me."

She exhaled slowly, still not pulling away.

A thought struck—she'd meant to bring him something. Instead she'd come back with secrets.

"Yes," she said at last, voice muffled against his chest. "Sorry. I was..."

Her mind scrambled for something believable, something quick. When she finally eased back just enough to look up, her gaze caught on the towering statue across the square.

"I got distracted looking at the statue of Eflos," she finished quickly, the words coming out a fraction too fast.

The lie felt thick on her tongue, souring her taste.

His brow arched slightly as he studied her. "The statue of Eflos," he repeated, his tone neutral. He nodded after a moment, though the faint crease in his brow told her he didn't entirely believe her. "You missed the parade."

"I didn't. I watched it from across the square."

"You're hiding something."

"What makes you say that?"

"You've got that look—the one you get when you've done something reckless or stupid. Which is it this time?"

Sam crossed her arms, tilting her chin up in defiance. "I'm neither reckless nor stupid."

"Debatable." Kensley's smirk widened, though there was an edge of genuine concern beneath his teasing. "You can tell me the truth, Sam. Whatever it is, I can handle it."

For a fleeting moment, Sam considered telling him—about Sefina, the Darkbringer, all of it. Her lips parted, but the words refused to come.

She forced a laugh. "It was just the statue, Kensley. I didn't want to admit I got lost admiring the details."

His smirk faded, and he nodded slowly. "If you say so."

As they reached the edge of the square, they stopped to watch a performance of fire dancers. Flames twirled and leaped in mesmerizing arcs, their heat brushing against Sam's skin. But her mind was elsewhere. She couldn't shake Sefina's words, the weight of her friend's warning heavy in her thoughts. Kensley stood close beside her, his presence steady, yet she couldn't stop the gnawing unease.

"I think I'd like to retire for the evening," she said finally, her voice tight.

Kensley turned his head toward her, one brow arching. "You're sure?"

Sam nodded.

Kensley frowned but nodded. "All right. I'll take you back."

As they turned from the bustling square, the glow of the festival faded, replaced by the dim lanterns lining quieter streets. The shadows stretched long across the cobblestones, and a chill settled over Sam's skin that had nothing to do with the night air.

They hadn't gone far when a figure stepped from an alley, blocking their path. Then another. And another.

Sam's hand moved instinctively to the hilt of her dagger as Kensley stepped protectively in front of her, his hand drifting toward his sword.

"Phagaen mercenaries," he murmured, his tone low and sharp.

"Firemane," one of the men sneered, his voice heavily accented and his eyes fixed on Sam. "That scarf cannot hide you."

His companions fanned out, circling them.

"Step aside," Kensley said, his voice laced with steel.

The mercenaries didn't heed the warning. They lunged, but Kensley was already moving, his sword flashing in the lantern light as it deflected the first attack.

Sam drew her dagger just in time to block another assailant. Her muscles burned with the effort as she twisted to avoid a wild swing, countering with a slash that caught her opponent's arm. A blade grazed her side, sharp pain flaring as it cut through fabric and skin, but she ignored it. She drove a kick into another attacker's chest, sending him stumbling back.

She moved to press the advantage, but the leader appeared before her, the cold barrel of his pistol jammed against her chest. Sam bared her teeth, her breath coming in quick, shallow gasps. She could stab him, but not before he pulled the trigger.

The leader's expression darkened. "We have a message for your master," he said, the words slurred by his accent. "Tell the thief of power that the gods are watching. They know he's searching for that which he lost. It's only a matter of time before they catch up."

A cold, commanding voice responded, "He already knows."

Kharzul emerged from the shadows, his presence sweeping in like an ocean storm. His dark coat flowed behind him as he strode forward. He drew both pistols in one smooth motion. Two deafening shots rang out, and the two mercenaries closest to Sam crumpled to the ground, lifeless.

The remaining attackers froze.

Kharzul's gaze swept over them, his dark eyes filled with quiet fury as he stowed his pistols. Shadows gathered around him, trembling at his feet.

"It's him," one of the mercenaries whispered hoarsely. They turned to flee, boots pounding against the cobblestones.

They didn't make it far.

Kharzul lifted his arms, palms open to the sky. Black tendrils poured from him like snakes, swallowing the mercenaries whole. Screams tore free, then silenced as abruptly as they had begun.

When the shadows receded, the street lay still. Fallen bodies littered the ground.

Sam remained rooted, the men's screams still ringing in her ears. Her dagger hung limply in her hand as her mind tried to catch up with what had just happened.

Kharzul turned to her, his expression composed, though there was something behind his eyes—a flicker of worry, buried beneath layers of control. His tan skin seemed a shade paler than before.

"Cavenaugh. Atherton. Return to the ship," Kharzul ordered. "We depart immediately."

"Yes, Captain," Kensley said without hesitation, sheathing his sword.

Sam nodded, the pain in her side now a sharp, persistent throb. She pressed her hand against the wound and winced as her fingers came away sticky with blood.

Kharzul's expression darkened, his lips pressing into a thin line. "See to that wound before it festers, Firemane." His voice was sharper than usual, laced with an edge she couldn't quite place.

Kensley's head snapped toward her. His gaze dropped, scanning, and then his entire posture changed. "You're hurt?" he said, already stepping in closer. "I didn't realize—"

Sam waved him off. "I'll be all right."

She took a step. Then the world tilted.

Pain lanced up her side, and her breath hitched as her footing faltered.

Kensley caught her before she could fall. One arm slipped beneath her knees, the other bracing her back as he lifted her cleanly off her feet.

Sam sucked in a breath, instinctively grabbing hold of him as the world shifted again, her fingers curling into his shirt.

"I can walk," she muttered.

"You don't have to prove anything right now," he said quietly.

Something in his tone drained the fight out of her. She let herself settle against him, the steady rise and fall of his chest grounding.

Kharzul watched them, his gaze sharp and assessing, before striding ahead without another word.

As Kensley carried her back toward the ship, Sam's thoughts returned to the mercenary's words. *The thief of power. The gods.*

A chill ran through her as Sefina's warnings began to feel dangerously close to the truth.

THIRTY-SEVEN

Back on the ship, Kensley's voice rang out with commanding precision. "All hands on deck! Get the oars out, boys. Connor, O'Toole—fetch the rest of the crew. Now!" The urgency in his tone sent a ripple through the men, who scrambled to obey.

Sam ducked into the shadows near the helm, unclasping the flamboyant cloak at her neck. She then untied her scarf, her breath hitching as she pressed it against her side. The cut wasn't deep, but it stung with every movement. Gritting her teeth, she wound the length of the scarf tightly around her waist, tying it off with a secure knot.

She pushed back a stray lock of red hair that clung to her damp forehead and forced herself to focus on the moment. The familiar creak of the oars lowering into place steadied her frayed nerves. Sam moved to the navigation table on the quarter deck, her hands tracing the edges of a worn map as she charted their course north. Numbers, bearings, and constellations offered a strange sort of solace; they didn't lie like people did.

Below her, a shaft of golden light spilled onto the polished deck as the door to the captain's cabin swung open. Kharzul emerged to pace the deck, the light catching the sharp angles of his face and the fine stitching of his coat as it fluttered behind him. He looked like a predator penned in too tight a space.

Sam observed him carefully, her thoughts swirling. What was he thinking?

Kharzul's gaze swept across the dark horizon, his fists clenching and unclenching behind his back.

The steady beat of a drum began as the men rowed in time. The *Golden Krina* cut through the waves with grace, slowly moving from the port. Only when the jagged outline of the harbor dissolved into open sea did Kharzul's shoulders loosen. But the tension never fully left him. Sam could see it in the set of his jaw and the way his eyes flickered toward the stars, as if wary of their gaze.

Kharzul turned, his shadowed eyes meeting hers for a fleeting moment before he disappeared back into his cabin. She couldn't help the feeling that something had shifted. Was he angry she'd heard the mercenary's message?

Worse, did he know about Sefina?

Her gaze lingered on the door he'd vanished behind, worry knotting her stomach.

After the ship was well underway, most of the crew went back to sleep. Sam sat on the ship's deck, her back against the rail. Her side still ached. She pressed her hand lightly against it, wincing, then exhaled, tilting her head back.

Above her, the stars scattered across the velvety sky in a neverending map. Sam's fingers tapped mindlessly on the chart she'd set beside her, its edges weighted down by her compass and a small dagger. She hadn't been able to focus long enough to plot their next course yet.

The faint sound of boots against the deck pulled her from her thoughts. She turned just as Kensley approached, illuminated by the moonlight. The shadows softened the sharp lines of his face, and the concern in his eyes was unmistakable.

"You should be resting," he said.

Sam managed a half-smile. "And yet, a course still needs to be set."

Kensley crouched beside her, setting a flask and a folded cloth down within reach. He nodded toward her side. "May I?"

"You didn't have to come check on me," she said, keeping her tone light, though her pulse had picked up.

"I didn't have to," Kensley replied, his storm-blue eyes locking onto hers, "but I wanted to."

Something in the way he said it made her breath catch.

She nodded, and he reached for her makeshift bandage, untying it with careful precision. As he peeled it away, his fingers skimmed her skin, the touch featherlight but enough to jolt her anyway. She inhaled sharply, forcing herself to stay still.

Kensley tilted his head as he examined the wound. His jaw tensed, a flicker of something unreadable passing through his expression—frustration? Worry? She could see it in the way his lips pressed into a firm line, the way his grip on the cloth tightened.

Moonlight pooled across his face, highlighting the strong cut of his cheekbones, the small silver hoop in his ear. Sam rarely allowed herself to really look at him—it was too easy to get lost in his details, like the way the wind tousled the blonde hair he only half attempted to keep tied back.

It was dangerous.

Kensley pressed the cloth, now soaked in alcohol, to her side, and she gasped at the sting of pain. He rewrapped the bandage with far more skill than Sam had managed earlier.

"This'll do for now," he murmured with a final knot. His hands stilled at her waist before he pulled away, his touch leaving behind an absence of warmth. He grabbed the flask and uncorked it, offering it to her. "Atral's finest ale. It won't heal you, but it might make you forget for a while."

Sam chuckled softly, taking the offered flask and tipping it back for a small sip. It burned down her throat before its warmth spread through her chest, chasing away the chill of the night.

Kensley reached over her, sliding the chart from beneath her makeshift weights. Spreading it across his lap, his fingers traced the parchment, following the inked lines with an absentminded ease. His gaze flickered between the stars above and the course she had started to chart, the faint crease in his brow betraying his concentration.

It *was* dangerous to watch him too closely, because as Sam watched him, something shifted inside her.

For so long, she had been careful and guarded. The walls she had built around herself were made of iron, reinforced by loss, by anger, by survival. But now, here, beneath the vast sprawl of stars, with the scent of the wind and sea weaving between them, those walls felt... unnecessary.

Because Kensley wasn't just the confident, infuriating man who challenged her at every turn. He was also the one who steadied her when everything felt uncertain, the one who saw her as both the Firemane and as Sam. He never flinched from any of her sides.

Kensley glanced up from the chart, catching her gaze. The corners of his mouth quirked up into a lopsided grin. "You're staring."

"Again?" Sam replied, her voice breathier than she intended.

Kensley laughed, the sound rich and unguarded. It was rare to hear him laugh like that. And suddenly, Sam was tired of waiting.

Her heart pounded as she made her decision, closing the space between them before doubt could creep in. She leaned forward, tilting her chin up, and pressed her lips to his.

Kensley stilled, surprised—but only for a moment. Then his hand slid to her cheek, fingers threading into her hair as he deepened the kiss. The heat of him was overwhelming, intoxicating, like a fire catching against dry tinder.

Sam's hand found his chest, her fingers curling into the fabric of his shirt as she leaned into him. The ache in her side was forgotten, replaced by something far more potent.

When they finally broke apart, Kensley's forehead rested against hers, his breathing uneven.

"For the record," he said, his voice rough but laced with amusement. "You're terrible at resting."

Sam grinned. "I think I'll manage," she whispered before tugging him close to kiss once more.

The next day, Kharzul summoned Sam to his cabin. A flicker of apprehension coiled in her chest as she made her way across the deck. Her fingers unconsciously grazed the tender spot on her side. Memories of last night still flitted in her mind—Kensley's touch, the warmth of his breath against her skin, the way her pulse had thundered in a way that had nothing to do with fear. But now, in the sober light of morning, reality pressed back in.

She forced herself to focus. The attack, the mercenaries, the message they'd left—those were the things that mattered now. Not the way Kensley had looked at her or the way she had felt in his arms.

In his cabin, Kharzul stood near the window, his back to her, unmoving except for the slow rise and fall of his shoulders. Beyond the glass, the sea stretched endlessly toward the horizon, indifferent and unyielding.

Sam swallowed, shifting her weight as she waited. Whatever this conversation was about, it would not be idle chatter.

"Firemane," he said without turning. "I trust you are healing?"

"Aye, Captain."

He turned then, his piercing eyes locking onto hers. "I have come to the realization that you have been allowed too much freedom. You are much too valuable to be risking life and limb so recklessly."

Sam frowned, confusion tightening her brow. "But... isn't that what you wanted of me? To raid and plunder like the rest of your crew?"

"To a point," Kharzul replied smoothly, pacing toward her. "And that point has been reached. From now on, you will remain on the *Golden Krina*. Your place is here."

The words landed like cannon fire in her chest.

"No."

The defiance slipped out before she could stop herself. Kharzul's eyes narrowed, and the shadows in the room gathered, thickening in the corners like a stormcloud threatening to break.

Sam straightened her spine. "Captain, I want to fight. You are not the only one who wants to bring change—to bring *balance*—to the world."

Kharzul's expression didn't shift, but his presence felt larger, more suffocating. Silence stretched between them as his golden eyes bored into hers.

When he moved, it was slow, deliberate. His gloved hand rose, and she flinched as he brushed the back of his knuckles against her cheek. He picked up a lock of her hair, eyes glazing over as he stared at it.

Rubbing the strands between his fingers, he murmured, "You are much too valuable to me."

That word again. *Valuable*. Was he planning to sell her to slavers?

Her chin trembled despite herself. "I want to fight," she repeated, her voice quieter but no less firm.

Kharzul blinked, dropping her hair. A faint smirk twisted his lips. "The fighting is temporary, poppet, though your devotion is... cherished." His voice dropped to a quiet, ominous timbre. "Once I have what I seek, there will be no fighting. All will suffer at my hand."

Her breath hitched. "All?" she asked hesitantly, her voice barely audible.

Shadows began to coil about his shoulders, shifting like living things. His voice was a rasp, deep and unearthly. "*All.*"

Sam stumbled back, her hip bumping the edge of a table. Her hand darted out to steady herself, fingers curling around the wood as she tried to process his words. "I... don't understand."

"You don't need to." Kharzul stepped closer, the air between them charged. His lips curved faintly, though it was more predatory than pleased.

Sam stifled a gasp as he caught her braid in his fist, using it to jerk her close.

"What you do need to understand," he said, his tone iron-hard, breath warm and bitter against her face, "is that I've given you an order, *Firemane*. You will remain on this ship. You are of no use to me dead."

Sam clenched her teeth against the pain. "Then how do you intend to use me?" she ground out. "Will you lock me away until it suits you?"

"If I must." His voice dripped with quiet menace as black tendrils coiled around her ankles, pinning her in place.

Sam glared up at him. She wouldn't give him the satisfaction of fear, not outwardly.

Slowly, Kharzul released her, the bruising grip on her head fading as the darkness lifted. She stumbled back, her boots thudding against the floor as she regained her footing. Kharzul turned away from her, his hand moving to the brass key that always hung from his neck. Another mystery Sam had yet to solve.

Minutes stretched into what felt like hours while he toyed with it, the silence broken only by the creak of the ship.

Finally, he waved a hand. "You may take your leave."

Sam didn't need to be told twice. She skittered out of the cabin, and only when the door closed behind her did she allow herself a shuddering breath.

Her head throbbed, but it wasn't the physical pain that bothered her. It was his words, his promise of devastation. *All will suffer.* They settled like a stone in her gut.

The shadows of his cabin seemed to follow her as she retreated, and she couldn't shake the feeling that they were watching, waiting.

She threw herself into mindless tasks, scrubbing the already spotless planks of the helm, sorting through charts, and polishing the brass fittings until her reflection glared back at her. But no amount of work could quiet the storm in her thoughts.

By nightfall, exhaustion anchored her limbs, but she still couldn't bring herself to retreat belowdecks. Instead, she found herself at the bow, legs dangling over the edge. Moonlight shimmered on the water, a silvery path stretching into the distance.

Stray locks of hair had escaped her long plait, whipping against her face in the steady northern breeze. She made no effort to smooth them.

Her mother's voice echoed in her head. *You are destined to do great things, my darling.* A pang of guilt tugged at her heart. Was she? Great things required certainty, and Sam felt anything but certain.

Beneath her carefully constructed facade, she was still that same girl who had recklessly leapt to the sea. The three years since then felt more like a lifetime.

Kensley's voice came from behind. "You look like the weight of the world's about to pull you overboard."

Sam huffed a quiet laugh and shook her head. "I'm not going any-where."

Kharzul had forbidden her to.

"Good," Kensley said, leaning against the railing beside her. His shoulder brushed hers lightly as they stared out at the vast expanse of the ocean.

"You're quiet tonight," he said eventually, his voice softer now. "What's on your mind, Firemane?"

The nickname almost made her smile. But her thoughts were too heavy to banter, and she found herself speaking honestly.

"Kharzul," she said.

Curiosity flickered across Kensley's face. "What about him?"

She took a breath, unsure where to begin. "He said something earlier... about how *all* would suffer at his hand. And I can't stop thinking about it. I thought he wanted to end the suffering. Isn't that what this is all for?"

"That's the story he tells. But Kharzul's goals have always been his own. You know that as well as I do."

Sam turned to face him fully. "What do you think his goals are, Kensley? Really?"

He was thoughtful for a moment before he spoke. "I think he's a man who's lost something. Something he'll do anything to get back. Whatever that is... it's driving him."

Sam swallowed, her voice barely above a whisper. "He's running *from* something just as much as he's running toward it." She looked back at the sea, her brow furrowing. "I think it might be the gods themselves."

Kensley snorted. "The gods don't care about mortals, Sam. They never have."

"You heard the mercenaries. And what about Kharzul's power? You've seen it—whatever he's tapped into, it's not mortal. What if they're after that? What if..." She faltered, the words heavy on her tongue. "What if he's the Darkbringer?"

Kensley's smirk vanished. "The Darkbringer?"

"You haven't heard the tale?"

"I've heard the tale. I just don't see how you reached that conclusion."

Sam hesitated, then decided she owed him the full truth. "Because of Sefina," she admitted, the words a quiet confession.

Kensley blinked. "Sefina?"

Sam looked down, cheeks flushing with guilt. "In Atral."

His tone turned sharper, almost accusatory. "That's where you disappeared to during the festival."

"I couldn't risk her life. I'm sorry."

His gaze bore into her. There was anger, but something else too—hurt, maybe even betrayal. He shook his head, his jaw tight. "Go on."

Sam drew a deep breath, the memory of Sefina's warnings swirling in her mind. "She's convinced that Kharzul is the Darkbringer—said his power, his shadow, is unlike anything she's ever seen."

"And you believe her?" Kensley's jaw tightened further, the muscles in his neck flexing.

Sam searched his face, her own filled with uncertainty. "It makes sense, doesn't it? The way he leaves destruction in his wake. The terror he inspires. The *power*. And in the tale, there is a line: 'He seeks for a balance.'"

She didn't need to explain that connection. Kensley knew it well enough, evident by the way he looked down.

"And if she's right?" he finally ventured. "If he *is* the Darkbringer... What does that mean? For us? For you?"

"I don't know," she admitted, her voice barely above a whisper. "But if he is... then everything he's told us, everything we've fought for—" She closed her eyes, gripping the railing harder. "It's all wrong."

Kensley leaned closer, grabbing her chin so she was staring straight into his stormy blue-gray eyes. "Sam, whatever he is, whatever he's after, you're not bound to his choices."

She opened her mouth to argue, to tell him she wasn't sure she could break free of the shadows curling around her life, but a shout from the crow's nest shattered her thoughts.

"Ship spotted! White sails to the west!"

THIRTY-EIGHT

Sam straightened, tearing her eyes from Kensley as she scanned the horizon, spotting the glint of moonlight against distant sails.

One of the men on deck called out, "Eflos smiles on us tonight!"

Kharzul appeared in the doorway to his cabin. For a moment, he remained silent, fingers flexing at his sides. Then, with a dismissive wave, he ordered, "Stay the course. We don't have time for distractions."

Sam glanced at Kensley. Ignoring a potential raid had never happened before, and it made Kharzul's obsession with reaching Dunrith as quickly as possible all the more frightening.

"Their course is shifting," the watchman called from the rigging. "They're turning straight for us."

A muscle in Kharzul's jaw ticked as he turned sharply back toward the oncoming vessel. The white sails, now fully visible in the moonlight, billowed as the ship cut through the water with clear intent.

"They mean to intercept us," Sam murmured, gripping the hilt of her dagger. The thought unsettled her. A ship deliberately crossing another's path meant one of three things: desperation, deception, or a challenge. Were they in need of aid? Or was this another crew with loot on their minds?

Kharzul's expression darkened, his reluctance giving way to irritation. "They will regret that decision." His hands curled into fists before he stalked to the helm. "Prepare for engagement! Bring us in line to board!"

"Aye, Captain!" Kensley's voice rang across the deck, brimming with authority. "All hands at the ready! Masks on, mates! Tate, back up to the nest. Firemane, take the wheel."

The crew erupted into motion, a chaotic symphony of preparation. Pistols were loaded, cutlasses strapped on, cannons rolled into position. Shouts of praise to Eflos, God of Thieves, rose above the deck as masks were pulled over eager faces.

Sam quickly fetched her own mask. She pulled loose the strip of leather binding her braid, her hair spilling free in a cascade of wild red waves. As she stepped back onto the deck, she was greeted with a strong sea breeze that tugged at her hair until it flew wildly around her like a living flame. *The Firemane.*

The sky churned with unnatural darkness, clouds rolling in with a speed that defied nature. Kharzul's power hung thick in the air, a suffocating presence that seeped into her lungs.

Taking her place at the wheel, she couldn't ignore the nagging unease, the sense that this wasn't just another skirmish—something about this felt wrong.

Kharzul paced beside her, his lavish jewelry jingling with each step, the music of his restlessness. Soon came the fog, curling around the ship in ghostly waves. It rolled across the deck and spilled over the rails, swallowing the waters below. The air felt heavier, colder.

"Hold the course," Kharzul muttered.

Choppy swells began to slap against the hull, growing steadily larger. Then, with a single nod from Kharzul, Kensley bellowed from the gun deck below, "Sails!"

One by one, the sails unfurled, snapping against the wind.

"Drums!"

A steady war beat echoed through the night, each strike vibrating through the planks beneath Sam's boots. Below deck, two dozen men rowed in perfect unison. Through the shifting fog, she glimpsed the rhythmic rise and fall of oars dipping into the water.

The *Golden Krina* surged forward, gaining impeccable speed. Sam balanced her weight against the fast-moving ship, feet planted firmly on the wooden deck, and raised her spyglass to scan the enemy vessel.

Through the gathering fog, she could just make out sailors who pulled ropes and loaded weapons, moving not with panic but with a militaristic precision.

Her breath hitched.

The three masts bore the sigil of the Ducrian king.

A warship.

She stiffened. Ducria's navy, this far south? They were in Eclorian waters. The Royal Navy had no claim here.

A cold unease crept up her spine. Another scan of the ship confirmed her fears. With at least eighty guns, the warship was comparable in size to the *Golden Krina* herself.

And warships didn't sail alone.

Sam turned sharply. "Captain, it's Ducrian," she said, her words coming fast. "A full warship. Armed heavy. If they've let us see one, there are likely three more not far behind."

For a moment, Kharzul said nothing.

The wind howled between them, the ship creaking beneath their feet.

Then, slowly, he turned his head. There was no hesitation in his expression. No doubt.

"If Ducria wishes to engage, then let us engage. They do not dictate where we sail, nor who we choose to face," he said, voice cutting through the gale. "Their mighty king has grown comfortable thinking his kingdom—his seas—are untouchable."

His gaze flicked back to the warship, hand moving to rest on the hilt of his cutlass. A predatory light sparked in his eyes.

"Let us remind him they are not."

The *Golden Krina* didn't slow. If anything, she sailed faster, slicing through the waves like a blade. And then they reached the eye of the storm where the ocean was suddenly calm.

"Hold the oars," Kensley called, his voice cutting through the murk. The drumming ceased.

Sam guided the ship ever closer, her breathing shallow as the fog pressed in. Then, through the swirling mist, the warship's dark hull appeared. Painted in bold, white letters was its name: *The Delight*.

A dry chuckle slipped from Sam's lips. Though they provoked the attack, she was sure they weren't feeling much delight at this moment. The *Golden Krina* was a name that inspired dread on the Rutane. Men whispered of the storm that followed her—unnatural fog, rolling drums, and the masked beasts aboard. Of the ruthless captain who commanded them, and of the crimson-haired Firemane at his side.

Sam watched as the crew moved with disciplined precision, preparing to board. The fog concealed their movements, but it was their silence that made them terrifying.

She adjusted her mask, re-checked the pistols holstered at her hips, and wrapped her fingers around the hilt of her cutlass. Her heart pounded in her ears, adrenaline and anticipation mingling into something sharp.

Then—

"Firemane." Kharzul's cold voice sliced through the tension, freezing her in place. "You will remain at the helm."

Her grip tightened on her weapon as her jaw clenched, eyes flicking between Kharzul and the faint form of *The Delight*.

The Ducrian Royal Navy attacked.

The roar of cannons shattered the stillness. The deck jolted violently beneath her feet, nearly dropping her. Smoke and splinters filled the air as cannonballs tore through the *Golden Krina's* side, a fiery explosion ripping a hole into the main deck.

Sam caught herself against the wheel, twisting it instinctively to the left. The ship groaned in protest, the timbers creaking as it veered. A split second later, the *Golden Krina's* own cannons roared in response, their thunderous blasts sending shockwaves across the water. *The Delight* shuddered as cannonballs struck its hull, wood splintering into jagged shards.

The fog churned as grappling hooks were thrown. They latched onto the enemy vessel with dull thuds, and, one by one, pirates swung across the narrowing gap. Already the sounds of clashing swords echoed through the fog, accompanied by cries of pain and triumph. Kharzul's laughter rose above the din, chilling and otherworldly.

Another blast from *The Delight* sent shrapnel flying, tearing through the stairs leading to the helm. Sam ducked instinctively, shielding her face from the debris. Smoke billowed upward, mingling with the fog, and drawing it away in places. Her stomach twisted as she realized their crew was outnumbered.

Through the haze, she caught sight of Kensley on the enemy ship. He fought with ferocious determination, holding off three attackers at once, but something was wrong—his movements had lost their edge. In one hand, his blade gleamed as he parried and struck. In the other, he swung his axe with brutal precision, but his grip faltered between blows.

A dark smear spread along his sleeve. When he pivoted, Sam saw him favor one side, his breath coming harder than it should. Blood stained the deck around him. Sam prayed that none of it was his but knew with a sinking certainty that some of it was.

Kharzul's order rang in her ears: *You will remain at the helm.*

But Kensley staggered as another blade glanced off his shoulder.

Her control snapped. He was outnumbered. He was hurt. And if she did nothing, he might fall.

Heart pounding, she looped a rope around the wheel, tying it in place. The ship would drift, but it was a risk she had to take.

"Hold steady," she muttered, as if the ship itself could hear her plea.

With a deep breath, she grabbed the nearest rope and leapt, the wind whipping her hair as she soared across the abyss. The fog swallowed her for a moment, the chaotic sounds of battle muffled, and then her boots slammed onto the enemy deck.

Drawing her cutlass, Sam joined the fray, her blade flashing as she cut down the first sailor in her path. The Firemane had arrived.

Everywhere she turned, steel clashed with steel, and desperate cries mingled with the thunder of cannon fire. The Ducrian sailors fought with polished discipline, their movements drilled and measured. But the pirates fought with feral cunning, unorthodox and ruthless. A hooked blade caught one sailor's sword mid-swing, while another pirate hurled chunks of splintered wood into an officer's face before driving a knife into his chest.

Kensley fought near the gun deck, where he held his ground—for now. Farther down the ship, Sam spotted a shadowy figure surrounded by a roiling black mist. *Kharzul.*

Another deafening roar cracked the air behind her. Sam's head snapped around just in time to see the *Golden Krina's* mizzenmast buckle and collapse, the massive timber smashing onto the deck. But she couldn't focus on what was behind.

Sam raised her weapon, engaging another sailor blocking her path to Kensley.

The sailor she fought was strong, but Sam ducked under his swing and drove her hilt into his ribs. He staggered, gasping, and she spun behind him, slashing across his back.

"That's her! That's the Firemane!" someone called out.

Several heads turned toward her, recognition lighting their faces as they peeled away from their opponents to face the Firemane.

Another opponent closed in, and then another.

Sam panted, her chest heavy with the rise and fall of her breathing, but she smiled wickedly. The air was thick with smoke and the tang of blood, and the roar of battle surrounded her. She reveled in every glorious clash of metal on metal, each pop of a pistol, and each thunderous boom of cannons.

Get to Kensley, she reminded herself as she twirled out of reach of the closest opponent.

The soldier she'd spun away from caught back up, slashing viciously. The sharp whistle of steel cutting air warned her, and she narrowly avoided the blade aimed for her chest. Jumping back, she countered with a swipe of her own cutlass, the edge grazing his arm. Before he could recover, she drove her dagger into his gut. He crumpled with a pained grunt, clutching his middle as she turned to assess her path to Kensley.

Sam's gaze swept the chaos of the battlefield—then froze.

Her eyes widened in surprise, mouth falling slightly open. Her feet turned to lead. Her grip slackened.

That was all the opening her enemies needed. All at once, her sword was wrested away, her arms wrenched behind her back as a heavy weight pinned her to the deck. Her mask and cheek scraped against wood and splinters.

"I've got her!" the sailor holding her cried victoriously.

She lifted her head, straining to get another look at the figure who had seized her attention.

The man was devastatingly handsome. He stood tall and command-ing in a pristine navy uniform of deep indigo, its gold accents catching every flicker of light. The uniform clung perfectly to his broad shoulders and lean frame, an emblem of rank glinting proudly on his chest. His movements were calculated, almost graceful, but most of all, they were familiar.

The sweat on his olive-toned skin gleamed faintly, emphasizing the sharp planes of his face. Curly brown hair, cropped shorter than she re-membered, framed a jawline she had once traced with trembling fingers.

"Rhett?" she whispered, her voice barely audible, the name a plea, a question, a fragment of disbelief.

As though he had heard her, his golden-brown eyes turned toward her. Their gazes locked. In that moment, the storm around her stilled. Time stopped.

But the moment shattered as her captor yanked her arms tighter behind her back, slamming her head against the deck. Pain exploded through her skull as splinters tore at her cheek. Her vision blurred, the edges darkening. Through the haze, she thought she saw Rhett take a step forward, his brow furrowing. She tried to hold onto the image, the faintest trace of him moving toward her—but the world tilted... and blackness took over.

ACKNOWLEDGEMENTS

Firemane has been in the works for nearly 20 years—something that still feels surreal to say. Now that it's finally published, I have some very important people to give my thanks to.

Firstly, my husband, Justin. He listened patiently as I talked through plot holes, offered feedback when I asked for help, and watched our children while I attended writing classes, conferences, and meetings. He has been a steady supporter of my desire to do something for myself.

A big shout out to Katie Stone, Liz Lowham, and Allison Mathews. You would not be reading this today without them. These lovely ladies make up my writing critique group, and each has become a dear friend over the years. They have provided feedback and supported me through the very roughest of drafts on this (and other) manuscripts.

A special thank you to Liz—you phenomenal human being! Your detailed, thoughtful, and kind editing has been invaluable, and I could not have asked for a better editor.

Thank you to my family for always believing in my storytelling, praising my talents, and encouraging me to keep growing and sharing them.

To my Meadow Brook Book Club girlies—I love you all! Thank you for your friendship and support, and for encouraging me to submit my manuscript as one of our monthly "books" to read. And though I feel imposter syndrome when you send praise my way, I am forever grateful for it.

Finally, a big thank you to the rest of my beta readers—Kendra and Jake Wright, Dan Cauvain, and Cheryl Lyman Rodgers—for your time, feedback, and support in shaping this story.

And lastly, to my dear friends Tadja Potter, MaKayla Sonnenburg, and Nick Crapo. You may never see this, but if you do, know that it is because of the friendship and adventures we shared as children that this manuscript exists today.

ABOUT THE AUTHOR

Brianna J. Stephens was convinced she'd grow up to be a pirate. Instead, she wrote about them. Bri is a mother of three beautifully wild children, all named after Vikings, with a devoted husband who looks like he could pass for one. Knowing this, it's no surprise that her writing often draws inspiration from the past. When she's not writing, she can be found tending to her (many) plants. And if you can't find her, she's probably camping.